SCREENPLAYS BY C.P. GRAHAM

DESERTERS

Set during the Mexican-American War, a story of people and events which led to the largest mass execution of U.S. soldiers in United States Military history.

GEORGE AND INGER

A romantic and suspenseful story based upon the real lives of an American world-class speed skater and a Norwegian high-fashion model. They fall in love and escape Nazi Germany and Italian fascists.

A FRESNO STORY

A sweeping drama set at the outbreak of World War Two. The story revolves around Armenian brothers. The younger brother loves a Japanese girl who is imprisoned as an enemy alien. This is a tale of love and survival.

OVER SEAS NEVER SAILED

A biography inspired by the life of Alberto Santos-Dumont (1873-1932), the world famous aeronautical pioneer, turn of the century hero and toast of Paris.

THE ARTIFACT

Science fiction. An international team of scientists are challenged to decipher an ancient, metallic object. Could it be evidence of an extra-terrestrial visitation? And can the world handle the truth?

D1441096

This book is a work of fiction. Any resemblance to actual events or persons, living or dead, is entirely coincidental.

"Screenplays by C.P. Graham," by C.P. Graham. ISBN 978-1-62137-185-4.

Manufactured in the United States of America.

DESERTERS

EXT. 1843, IRELAND - DAY

Sheep grazing on rolling green hills overlooking a large, stone-walled estate in the valley below. Twenty-four year old JOHN Riley, his younger brother, SEAN, and young WILLY Kelly are hiding in the bushes near the flock. In the late afternoon, the SHEPHERD is putting out a small camp fire while the SHEPHERD'S SON is starting to drive the sheep down the hill

(Note: a penny whistle underscores the scene with a slow Irish melody. A tabor joins the whistle as the tempo of the music increases during the stalk and chasing of the sheep)

JOHN, armed with bow and arrow, silently indicates where SEAN and WILLY are to position themselves. They disguise themselves with scarves over their nose and mouth, and separate. SEAN and WILLY work their way up the hill to come in behind the flock and JOHN goes down toward the SHEPHERD. Finally SEAN runs from the cover of the bushes and makes several failed attempts to tackle a yearling lamb. The flock becomes alarmed and begins to scamper down the hill

                    SHEPHERD'S SON
          Da, thieves!

The SHEPHERD grabs a rifle and, hurrying up the hill, tamps powder and ball down the barrel and stops to take careful aim at SEAN. Suddenly an arrow whistles in and hits the SHEPHERD in the shoulder. The SHEPHERD fires the weapon wide of his target and falls to the ground. Underscoring out. The SHEPHERD'S SON sprints down the hill to his father

                    SHEPHERD'S SON
          Da! You bastard, you killed my Da!

                    JOHN
          Steady, boy, he's not dead.

JOHN jerks the arrow out of the SHEPHERD'S shoulder. The SHEPHERD groans

                    JOHN
          Put pressure on that to stop the bleeding.

The SHEPHERD'S SON does so. SEAN and WILLY come down the hill dragging a dead lamb

                    SEAN
          Let's run. Someone may have heard that
          shot.

                    WILLY
          Aye.

                              JOHN
                What's in the bag you have there, boy?

                         SHEPHERD'S SON
                Barley. We feed it to the milking ewes.

                         JOHN (taking sack)
                Good. 'Twill make a fine meal for a few
                starving Irish. Let me see your wound, old
                man.

The SHEPHERD'S SON allows JOHN to inspect the wound

                I may have broke a bone but you'll live.

                            SHEPHERD
                That's more than I can say of you when
                his Lordship hears of this.

Suddenly JOHN raises his bow and kills a straggling lamb

                              JOHN
                Tell that British lackey, his lordship, that
                he lost two lambs today. If you would've
                killed this lad, his lordship would've lost
                a shepherd as well. Go on, now, follow
                his sheep.

JOHN, SEAN and WILLY watch the SHEPHERD and his son walk down the hill for a
while. JOHN plucks the arrow out of the dead lamb and puts it on his shoulder to carry

                              JOHN
                Well, let's run.

They run. Underscore in and continues through the transition to the next scene

EXT. DA'S COTTAGE - NIGHT

                         JOHN (knocking on door)
                Da. Da!

                         DA (opening door)
                John. Boys, get in here quick with that now.

INT. INSIDE THE COTTAGE - NIGHT

FIONNA, a lovely sixteen year old girl wearing a lovely red silk scarf, and MAGGIE,
DA'S wife, stand at a table in the larger room

                    DA
Look, Maggie, the boys brought us two
fine English lambs for our party.

                SEAN (crossing to her)
Fionna! What are you doing here?

                FIONNA (taking his hands)
Well, when I found out what you two
were up to, I worried...

                JOHN (hugging MAGGIE)
Hi, Maggie.

                DA (inspecting lambs)
We'll make quick work of them, skin
them and cook the meat. Between the dog
and the rats there will be nothing left for
soldiers to discover.

                SEAN (kissing FIONNA gently)
Fionna, there's no need to worry.

                    DA
You didn't have to do anything desperate, did you, John?

                    JOHN
No, Da.

                MAGGIE (inspecting lambs)
You take this wool, Fionna. My hands hurt
so bad anymore, I don't even try to knit.

                    FIONNA
Give it to me then. I'll make a fine shirt for
Sean to wear for our wedding.

                DA (referring to barely)
And what's in the sack?

                    JOHN
Barley.

                    DA
Look, Maggie, barley. I'll put a wee bit
aside, 'twill make a strong potcheen.

A penny whistle and tabor playing a lively jig is under the rest of the scene as the camera
slowly goes in for a close up of the fire

Come, boys, warm yourselves by the fire
for a good night's work. Well, if not good,
certainly profitable. (chuckles)

EXT. DA'S COTTAGE - NIGHT

Music up. We draw back from the fire. It is a small fire built outside of the cottage.
WILLY is playing the whistle, another young man plays the tabor and a third is dancing a
lively jig to the delight of SEAN and FIONNA. JOHN and three other men are away
from the fire smoking cigarettes. Music ends. Laughter and applause. SEAN drinks from
jug. DA enters from inside of the cottage

>   DA (snatching jug)
>   You're a wee fast and easy with my whiskey,
>   Sean Riley. Don't you know this has got to
>   last us for... let's see, today is Sunday...
>   (pretending to count) This has got to last for
>   at least one more hour or so.

The young people laugh. WILLY plays a soulful tune on the whistle. DA crosses to
JOHN and the other men to pour shots in their tin cups

>   Well, if this isn't the most sour-faced batch
>   of renegades the devil ever blessed...

>   MAN ONE
>   What need we of the devil, we have the
>   British.

>   DA
>   Aye. But the Crown donated the meat for
>   our party. And we're toasting the engaged
>   couple. The least you can do is join us.

>   JOHN
>   Aye, Da, straight away.

DA goes back into the cottage

>   MAN TWO
>   So what are we going to do, there's an-
>   other garrison of soldiers moving up to West-
>   port?

>   JOHN
>   We'll continue to disrupt their supply lines.

>   MAN ONE
>   That's it? That's all?

4

JOHN
What do you propose?

MAN ONE
John, you know British tactics. You know
their weapons. Many of us would follow
you into battle…

JOHN
There is no battle. We don't have the means
to fight a battle. The best we can do is harass
an occupying army.

MAN ONE
We can show the English that we are men!

A beat

JOHN (quietly)
I'll not lead farmers to their certain death, and
make widows of their wives and orphans of
their children. Someday we'll fight, but not now.

The musicians start a lively tune

SEAN (approaching)
John, Fionna will dance for us!

The four men approach the fire. SEAN crosses to those in the cottage

Come, everyone! Fionna will dance!

DA, MAGGIE, FIONNA'S parents and two young girls come out to the fire, one of them
is learning the dances, and soon all are clapping to the rhythm of the drum. FIONNA
starts the dance with the young man who was dancing before. She is teaching him, and
the young girl, as they go. Finally they gain confidence with the dance and the
enthusiasm grows and is shared by all. The camera pans up to follow dust and sparks
rising in the summer's night sky. Music fades to silence as the camera pans back down to
the smaller fire. DA, with jug, and JOHN are seated by the fire. Long silence

JOHN
Da, I put an arrow into a shepherd yesterday. He was aiming at Sean with an English
musket.

DA
Did you kill him?

JOHN
No. An Irishman and his son, working for
wages, trying to kill an Irish boy with an

English weapon- for wages. If our own people... I have no stomach for a fight we cannot win.

                    DA
Aye.

                    JOHN
I've been talking to Sean and Willy about going to America, working and saving our money to buy land there.

                    DA
Aye.

                    JOHN
They say there's land there almost for the taking. And the four of us will be able to work for a while anyway, until Sean knocks Fionna up.

                    DA
Aye, he's a Riley. How will you get there?

EXT. AT SEA ON A LARGE SHIP - DAY

Ship's whistle. Underscoring in- a full orchestration of the lively jig at the party. The ocean slides by the hull of a large ship at sea. Layered on this and other footage depicting the cargo ship at sea, are black and white photographs (very few are posed) which tell the story of JOHN, WILLY, SEAN and FIONNA'S voyage at sea. At first they are optimistic and hopeful but then the drudgery of their ship-board jobs (in the galley and boiler room), bad food and unsanitary conditions take a toll on their spirits. In the deplorable health and living situation on board, more and more people die of disease and are buried at sea. The underscoring will reflect the mood of the narrative.

EXT. ON DECK OF THE SHIP - DAY

Several people are gathered for another burial at sea, among them SEAN (wearing FIONNA's red scarf), JOHN, WILLY and a MINISTER

                    MINISTER
...and so we commit the body of Fionna Riley to the sea with the hope and under- standing which our faith teaches - that we may once more be joined with our dearly departed with the second coming of our Lord and Savior, Jesus Christ in the ever- lasting glory of the Kingdom of God. Amen.

WILLY plays a soulful tune on the penny whistle as they slide the body off of the rail. JOHN holds his crying brother. Music remains through photographs of the 1844 New York City skyline and the boys disembarking is established in photographs as well. Signs read, "Irish Need Not Apply" and "Mick Go Home"

(Note: The high death rate aboard these vessels earned them the nick-name "coffin" ships. Authentic photographs chronicling the many economic and political refugees should be used)

INT. ON THE TRAIN IN DEPOT - DAY

Train whistle. JOHN, SEAN and WILLY are seated next to one another on a bench in the second class car which is still being boarded by other young immigrant recruits. SEAN is seated by the window and looking out at a young couple while holding FIONNA'S silk scarf to his lips

> JOHN
> There isn't anything to soldiering. You just
> do what they tell you to do and keep your
> leather polished.

JOHN is unaware that SEAN is tearing up a little while watching the young couple kiss and finally part

> Seven dollars a month isn't much but if we
> put our money together and save as much
> as we can, we'll have a sizable lump in two
> years. I'll probably get a promotion and
> that will mean more money. You lads will
> likely get a promotion too, most of these
> boys are dumb as posts.

A beat

> They say we're going to fight Mexicans. I
> don't know what the Mexicans did. It's not
> our business to know. Our business is to
> keep our heads down. Seven dollars a month
> is no reason to get killed.

Noticing SEAN

> And you'd better keep that scarf under your
> shirt or some non-commissioned officer will
> take it from you.

Just then, Patrick DALTON a big red-headed Irishman steps into the car

> DALTON (to JOHN)
> That's my seat you're in.

7

JOHN
The Sergeant told us to sit anywhere.

DALTON
Well, he was wrong then, wasn't he? Now
get up and move before I'm forced to move
you.

SEAN (standing)
These seats were unassigned, you lout!

DALTON takes a menacing step toward SEAN and JOHN quickly stands between them

JOHN
Now, Sean, this fellow was addressing me.
Mind your manners. (to DALTON) Please
forgive my brother. He spoke out of turn.
What he should have said was, "These seats
are unassigned, you pig fucking son of a
bastard!"

SERGEANT (entering car)
Keep moving there!

DALTON (to JOHN)
We'll settle this later.

SERGEANT
Keep moving!

EXT. U.S. ARMY DIVISION ENCAMPMENT, SOUTH TEXAS - NIGHT

In a gully by a steam bordering the Division's camp in dusk. A close up of the bruised
and bloodied face of JOHN. He is punched again and falls straight back and face down
into the steam. DALTON is putting his shirt on and being congratulated by his friends.
JOHN crawls out of the stream

JOHN (to DALTON)
Where are you going? I'm just getting
warmed up.

JOHN puts his fists up and DALTON hands his shirt back to one of his friends. They
circle one another as other soldiers watching shout encouragements and instructions.
JOHN and DALTON trade several hard punches but finally DALTON gets the better of
JOHN again, landing head and body blows and finishing with a kick to the head. SEAN
kneels down to address his bloody brother

SEAN (whispering)
Don't get up.

                              JOHN (whispering)
         Shh. I've got him right where I want him.
         He thinks I'm licked.

JOHN struggles to his feet and puts his fists up again to the amazement of all

                              SEAN
         No, John!

DALTON is putting his shirt on again

                              JOHN
         Are you finished then?

                              DALTON (chuckles)
         Yes. I'm tired of hurting my hands on that
         hard skull of yours.

                              JOHN (approaching DALTON)
         Do you concede then?

                              DALTON (incredulously)
         Do I what?

JOHN throws a quick right hand that knocks DALTON down and bloodies his nose.
DALTON leaps to his feet and, once again, the two men exchange damaging punches.
Finally DALTON begins to pummel JOHN, finishing with an uppercut that lifts JOHN
up and he comes down hard on the ground. Three shots are fired close by and the circle
of men watching the fight gives way to the approaching Captain HAMMONS. SEAN
helps JOHN to his feet

                              HAMMONS
         You men are in the U.S. Army now. The
         U.S. Army does not tolerate after hours
         brawling like this. You'll get your chance
         to fight soon enough. In the meantime, any
         man not in his sack in ten minutes will be
         thrown into the stockade. Is that clear?
         (to DALTON and JOHN) You two come
         to attention!

All other men disperse

         Who started this?

                              JOHN
         I did.

DALTON shoots JOHN a look of surprise

                    HAMMONS
          Well, it appears that all of the marching we
          did today wasn't enough exercise for you
          two men. Follow me to the corral.

INT. NON-COMMISSIONED OFFICERS' TENT - NIGHT

Sergeant WEAVER and junior officers are enjoying cigars and whiskey in the large tent.
Rain is coming down hard and making those in the tent speak up to be heard

                    AN OFFICER
          "All the potatoes turned black and putrid,"
          he said, "so we started to eat the grass like
          his Lordship's cattle." He went on to say
          that you could tell an Irish commoner by
          the green color of his mouth. (chuckling)

                    WEAVER
          That explains why all of the Irish are over
          here and as stupid as cows.

                    AN OFFICER
          You don't have to be smart to be a soldier.

                    WEAVER
          I don't trust them to fight.

                    AN OFFICER
          Oh, they'll fight all right. They just won't
          bathe.

Laughter

EXT. ON THE PERIMETER OF THE CORRAL - NIGHT

A CORPORAL is wearing a duster with the hood up in the pouring rain, watching
DALTON and JOHN run the length of two torches staked to the ground about a hundred
yards apart. They are running toward the CORPORAL with their arms extended forward,
each holding a rifle

                    CORPORAL
          That's only five. Keep going.

When the men reach the torch at one end, they turn and run to the other

INT. NON-COMMISSIONED OFFICERS' TENT - NIGHT

Captain HAMMONS enters the tent. All come to attention

                    WEAVER
             Captain?

                    HAMMONS
At ease, gentlemen.

                    AN OFFICER
We were just, uh… wrapping this up,
Captain.

                    HAMMONS
A good idea, Lieutenant, we have an early
start tomorrow. Colonel Taylor should be
joining us in a few days. You'll see to his
accommodations.

                    AN OFFICER
Yes, Sir. Good night, Sir.

Several of the junior officers file out

                    HAMMONS (confidentially)
Sergeant, a word?

                    WEAVER
Yes, Sir?

                    HAMMONS
We'll be marching south in about three days.
We've already had several desertions. Once
we get into Mexico I'll want nothing but
native born soldiers assigned to guard duty.
The immigrant recruits will dig latrines and
fortifications. Understand?

                    WEAVER
Yes, Captain.

EXT. THE CORRAL - NIGHT

Still raining hard. DALTON and JOHN are running toward the CORPORAL

                    CORPORAL
And that makes fifty. Lower your weapons.

The CORPORAL takes a step toward JOHN

            I'd wash those cuts out before I hit the
            sack, Private. The two of you are dismissed.

JOHN crumples to his knees and then falls face first into the mud

            What's the matter with him?

                    DALTON
          I beat the crap out of him just before our…
          exercise.

The CORPORAL rolls JOHN onto his back

                    CORPORAL
          Do you think he's dying?

                    DALTON
          No.

                    CORPORAL
          How do you know?

                    DALTON
          Because he won't quit, even when he should.
          I'll take care of him, Corporal. Come on,
          John.

DALTON puts JOHN'S arm around his neck and helps him to his feet

          And try not to take a poke at me this time.

DALTON and JOHN walk off into the night

EXT. A RANCH IN NORTHERN MEXICO - DAY

The Division has been marching all morning on a hot, dusty trail toward a large ranch on
a hill. A scream is heard. The Division stops at the well below the ranch house to water
horses and fill canteens. Two armed Texas Rangers are guarding several tied and beaten
Mexican civilians while several other Rangers are up at the house shouting at an old
Mexican man with a noose around his neck. A young, Mexican woman is being
restrained by another Ranger off to the side. JOHN, SEAN, and WILLY are standing side
by side in formation. It is apparent that many of the soldiers in formation are disturbed by
what the Texas Rangers are doing and are muttering in rank

                    WILLY (to WEAVER)
          What are they doing, Sergeant?Those are
          civilians!

                    WEAVER
          Quiet back there!

                    JOHN (whispering)
          Shut up, Willy, this is none of our business.

Suddenly the old man is hoisted off his feet by a couple of Rangers who tie off the rope
to a rail

WILLY

Sergeant!

The young woman screams, breaks away from the Ranger who was holding her, and tries to lift the old man who is strangling. A LARGE RANGER pulls the young woman away from the old man by her hair

LARGE RANGER

I'll interrogate this one myself.

The LARGE RANGER starts to drag the young woman into the house. WILLY and three other immigrant soldiers break rank and run up the hill to stop the Rangers. Fights ensue. Gun shots are fired and Captain HAMMONS and two junior officers ride in to stop the melee

EXT. THE U.S. DIVISION ENCAMPMENT - DAY

The four U.S. soldiers involved in the fight with the Texas Rangers are "bucked and gagged". That is; in a seated position the victim's hands are tied in front of their knees. A large, wooden pole is then inserted under their knees and over their arms. They sit in this agonizing position for hours. A close up of each soldier shows their suffering. WILLY, the last of the four, is sobbing bitterly

EXT. THE U.S. DIVISION ENCAMPMENT - NIGHT

SEAN, Michael O'CONNEL and a dozen or more Irish soldiers are sitting around a small fire. DALTON approaches

SEAN

How's Willy and the others.

DALTON

They couldn't walk. But they have to march
at dawn.

O'CONNEL (producing paper)

Aye, they would as soon shoot them as leave
them behind. Listen, men, this is the paper
many of you have seen. It says, (reading)
"Are Catholic Irishmen to be the destroyers
of Catholic churches and murderers of Cath-
olic priests? Your armies have come to
Mexico to take our lands and ravage this
pious nation. Come over to us. You will be
received under our laws…

SEAMUS, a young Irishman, watches JOHN approach the group carrying his shoes and wet socks

SEAMUS

Aye, boyo!

SEAN
It's all right. It's my brother.

JOHN sits and starts to dry his socks on a twig over the fire

O'CONNEL (reading)
"You will be received under our laws of
Christian hospitality and good faith which
Irish guests are entitled to expect and ob-
tain from a Catholic nation. May Mexicans
and Irishmen, united by the sacred tie of
religion and benevolence, form only one
people!" It is signed, "By the order of General Pedro de la Ampudia"

Silence for a while. In the small gathering, the men start to quietly share their thoughts
with the man next to him

SEAMUS
When they say, "Come over to us", do they
mean fight for the Mexicans? I've only
been in the army for a month now but that's
got to be a wee more serious than just
sneaking away, isn't it?

Several men chuckle at SEAMUS who wasn't trying to be funny

FIRST IRISH SOLDIER
Who is the enemy? No Mexican has ever done
anything to me. But that young spit and polish
Lieutenant "no-cock" broke my jaw with his
saber a week after I joined.

SECOND IRISH SOLDIER
Aye. We are punished severely for trivial
offences. The native-born soldier does the
same thing and he is barely reprimanded.

O'CONNEL
I'm sick of being treated like an animal. I'm
sick of watching brutalities like we saw today.
How many of us felt like doing what only
four of us had the courage to do? And they
are punished for it. Is that justice?

JOHN (quietly)
No. But that paper calls for your desertion.

Murmurs of agreement and more conversation as JOHN continues to dry his socks.
Finally…

                    DALTON
          What do you think, John?

                    JOHN (slowly)
          I think... (a deep breath) Like most of you
          men, we came to America in hopes of get-
          ting land and a new start. We're trying to
          make a new home here. There were no jobs
          so we joined the army. When we... when
          we all enlisted, we swore an oath of alle-
          giance to our new country. I don't know
          exactly what that means. I guess every man
          has to decide for himself.

Long silence, then murmurs as the group disperses to their tents

                    DALTON (to O'CONNEL)
          Here, you don't want this to be found on
          you by an officer.

DALTON takes the paper from O'CONNEL and throws it into the fire

EXT. A DESERT PLAIN, MEXICO – DAY

On a mountain overlooking the plain, a Mexican soldier is peering through a field glass at
the U.S. Division's artillery exercises. Six pound cannons are being fired at stationary
targets. The soldier is clearly impressed. Now, from a closer P.O.V., we see the cannons
fired, moved quickly, and fired again by several battery crews

INT. THE U.S. DIVISION ENCAMPMENT - NIGHT

Early evening. Colonel TAYLOR, his ADJUTANT, and Captain HAMMONS are seated
at a table reviewing maps under a canopy adjacent to TAYLOR'S tent. Sergeant
WEAVER is talking to an armed Corporal a few feet away from the table. JOHN
approaches the group and comes to attention

                    TAYLOR
          Who is this man?

                    ADJUTANT
          The battery commander you wished to com-
          mend, Colonel.

                    TAYLOR
          Oh, yes.

JOHN salutes TAYLOR who remains seated but returns the salute

          Congratulations. The pace of fire and your
          accuracy was impressive. Where did you
          learn to handle artillery like that?

JOHN
From the English, Sir.

TAYLOR
You were in the British army?

JOHN (hesitates)
Not exactly.

TAYLOR (chuckles)
What's your name, soldier?

JOHN
Private John Riley, Sir.

TAYLOR (to WEAVER)
Sergeant, I saw this man giving instruction to
several soldiers of superior rank. Why haven't
you recommended a field promotion for him?

WEAVER (hesitates)
He's a… he's Irish, Sir.

TAYLOR
What has that to do with his mastery of the
six pound cannon?

HAMMONS (confidentially)
Colonel, we've had several incidents of desertion, most notably from Irish recruits.

TAYLOR
I see.

Silence

JOHN
Colonel, if I may say, there are many of us
Irish who are hoping to prove ourselves in
battle.

TAYLOR
Well, if they all shoot as well as you, they'll
acquit themselves admirably. Congratulations.
That's all, Private.

JOHN hesitates

HAMMONS (tersely)
Dismissed, Riley.

JOHN salutes. HAMMONS half-heartedly returns the salute. JOHN turns on his heals to leave, slumps a little and walks away

EXT. THE U.S. DIVISION ENCAMPMENT – NIGHT

A small gathering of soldiers sit around a campfire talking softly. Among them are SEAN, DALTON and WILLY playing a slow melody on the penny whistle. WILLY finally finishes his tune

>   A SOLDIER
>   Hey, Willy, why don't you play something
>   cheerful?

>   WILLY
>   I could sing something cheerful but you
>   won't like it.

>   A SOLDIER
>   Why not?

>   WILLY
>   You've never heard me sing, have you.

>   A SOLDIER
>   No.

>   WILLY
>   Well, if you did, you would know why I
>   play the whistle.

Chuckles. A distant gun shot. Then several more and a shout from a hundred yards away. JOHN comes running to the campfire

>   JOHN
>   Muster up, men, we're being attacked!

>   SEAN
>   What? Now?

>   JOHN
>   Get your rifles!

A bugle confirms with a "call to arms" and shots ring out much closer

>   Sounds like horses.

A surprise night raid by a regiment of Mexican cavalry charging through camp panics the Division. The skillful "hit and run" attack lasts several minutes. JOHN kills a couple of Mexicans defending his comrades. The fight ends as suddenly as it began, leaving smoke and the cries of wounded men

EXT. THE U.S. DIVISION ENCAMPMENT - NIGHT

An hour later. HAMMONS approaches Sergeant WEAVER and a few officers

                    HAMMONS
            Report, Lieutenant.

                    PEACOCK
            We have twelve dead and several wounded,
            Captain. The surgeon is tending to them now.
            We've gathered the Mexican dead and wound-
            ed over there, as you ordered, Sir.

HAMMONS looks toward the Mexicans guarded by two armed soldiers. WILLY is
giving water to the wounded Mexicans

                    HAMMONS
            What's that man doing?

HAMMONS walks briskly over to the guarded enemy soldiers followed by WEAVER

            I gave orders that no one was to go near these
            Mexicans!

                    A GUARD
            Yes, Sir…

                    WILLY (at attention)
            I was only giving water to these wounded,
            Sir.

                    HAMMONS
            Sergeant, put these two men on report. As
            for you, Private, if you love these Mexicans so
            much you can sit with them all night.
            Buck and gag him!

                    WILLY
            But, Sir, I was only…

HAMMONS hits WILLY in the mouth with the flat of his sword breaking several teeth.
A slow melody on the penny whistle underscores the transition and into the next scene

EXT. THE U.S. DIVISION ENCAMPMENT – NIGHT

WILLY sits "bucked and gagged" bleeding through his gag and weeping bitterly as the
Mexicans look on pitifully

EXT. THE U.S. DIVISION ON THE MARCH - DAY

A close up of WILLY. One side of his face is badly bruised and his mouth is swollen. But he has a detached look in his eyes. A bugle calls for the Division to stop. The men are exhausted. From the high desert plain they can look down to the river valley below. HAMMONS is peering through a field glass as TAYLOR rides up to join him

> HAMMONS
> It looks like they are massing on the other side of the river, Colonel, and digging in.

> TAYLOR
> Where is their artillery?

> HAMMONS
> I only see four sixteen pounders, Colonel, but those guns seem to be too far to their rear to hit us with any accuracy. It appears that they want to fight us on their side of the river. We'll have a tactical advantage if we hit them now, Sir.

PEACOCK rides up to HAMMONS and TAYLOR

> TAYLOR
> No. We'll be ready to do that when Scott's Division gets here in a few days.

> PEACOCK
> There's a bridge about a half mile up river. It's study enough to take horses, Sir.

> TAYLOR
> Excellent. We'll camp there and dig a fortification in case they try anything. We'll defend that bridge, Captain. The men will sleep in shifts tonight.

> HAMMONS
> Yes, Sir.

EXT. THE U.S. DIVISION ENCAMPMENT – NIGHT

Early evening. JOHN, DALTON and several other artillery crews are preparing the cannons. SEAN enters, walks briskly over to JOHN

> SEAN (confidentially)
> John, I overheard Willy and several others talking about swimming the river. They are going to surrender to the Mexicans or make a break for the mountains tonight.

JOHN
What should I do about it?

SEAN
They're posting guards up and down the river
with orders to shoot deserters. John, Willy
can't even swim.

DALTON
Boyo, "no-cock" is coming.

PEACOCK rides up

PEACOCK
I've called no break. You men get back to
work.

JOHN (to SEAN)
I'll talk to Willy at mess tonight.

SEAN hurries off to the fortifications

EXT. THE U.S. DIVISION ENCAMPMENT - NIGHT

Soldiers are filing by a table where ladles of beans and squares of "hard tack" bread are
slopped into tin plates. JOHN is standing in line with DALTON. SEAN walks briskly up
to JOHN

SEAN (confidentially)
I can't find him.

JOHN
Who?

SEAN
Willy! I've looked everywhere.

A shot is heard coming from the river. Then two more shots are fired. SEAN, JOHN and
others run

EXT. THE U.S. DIVISION ENCAMPMENT - NIGHT

At the river, guards, with men holding torches, are firing at men swimming the river to
the other side. SEAN runs to the bank of the river

SEAN
Willy! There he is, John! Willy!

A bullet strikes WILLY

No! He'll drown!

SEAN dives in and tries to swim to WILLY

                              JOHN
                   No, Sean, come back!

WEAVER runs up, and scurries down to the bank to help shoot at deserters with his
pistol. WEAVER fires just over SEAN's head. Pulls the hammer back and is aiming
again

                         JOHN (running at WEAVER)
                   No!

JOHN tackles WEAVER just as he fires. A slow rendition of the jig played on penny
whistle at DA's cottage underscores from WEAVER's second shot through the next
scene

EXT. THE RIVER BANK ON THE MEXICAN SIDE - NIGHT

SEAN pulls himself partially out of the black water. He has been hit by WEAVER's
second shot and bleeding badly. SEAN sees a small campfire and has a vision of
FIONNA dancing at their engagement party. She bends down to kiss SEAN and all goes
black

EXT. THE U.S. DIVISION ENCAMPMENT - DAY

It is morning. JOHN is tied to a tree by the river with his shirt off. WEAVER, junior
officers, DALTON, and several other enlisted men are in attendance

                              WEAVER
                   The penalty for striking a superior is fifty
                   lashes.

Officers look at one another and among the mutterings by enlisted men are, "fifty!" and
"that will kill him"

                              WEAVER
                   Commence, mule skinner.

The mule skinner lays on with a raw-hide whip designed to rip skin with every lash.
WEAVER begins the count. JOHN manages to be brave through the first few. At lash
number twelve, PEACOCK rides up. The whipping continues but WEAVER does not
count at least three lashes as he is addressed

                              PEACOCK
                   Sergeant, we have recovered six bodies from
                   the river. Captain Hammons has ordered that
                   they be displayed before burial as a warning
                   to any man considering desertion.

                              WEAVER
                   Very well, Lieutenant.

WEAVER turns his attention back to the whipping but counts the seventeenth lash as "thirteen"

                         DALTON
          That's not right.

                         WEAVER
          What did you say, Private?

                         DALTON (hesitates)
          Nothing.

                         WEAVER
          Very well... fourteen.

JOHN looks out upon the river and sees FIONNA's red silk scarf floating by and knows that SEAN is dead. JOHN weeps bitterly as the whipping continues

INT. TAYLOR'S TENT - DAY

ADJUTANT, HAMMONS, and PEACOCK are in attendance of TAYLOR

                         TAYLOR
          These desertions are a distraction and are
          having a demoralizing effect on our troops.
          You've seen Ampudia's propaganda. We
          are not at war with the Catholic Church,
          Captain. You would have done well to
          recruit a Catholic priest to serve as Cha-
          plain to these Irishmen instead of trying to
          beat loyalty into them.

                         HAMMONS
          I don't care about their souls, Colonel, I
          need them to fight.

                         TAYLOR
          A man whose spirit is broken makes for a
          poor soldier. (to ADJUTANT) Is the
          Mexican priest you've found ready to
          provide services tomorrow?

                         ADJUTANT
          Yes, Colonel. We'll accommodate him with
          whatever he needs just off our right flank
          fortification.

                         TAYLOR
          Very well. (to HAMMONS) You will pass
          the word that Catholics wishing to attend
          church services may do so starting early
          tomorrow. Are my orders clear?

                              HAMMONS
                         Yes, Sir.

INT. JOHN'S SMALL TENT - NIGHT

DALTON enters the tent carrying a tin cup

                               DALTON
                         John, take some water.

JOHN drinks, DALTON produces a small bottle

                         I got a little iodine from the Doctor. We'll
                         put some on these deeper cuts to keep them
                         from getting infected.

DALTON puts iodine on his back and JOHN grimaces with pain

                         Oh, I forgot to warn you that this stuff stings
                         a little.

                          JOHN (sarcastically)
                         A little, yes.

A beat

                               DALTON
                         John, tomorrow is Sunday. Colonel Taylor
                         has approved some of the Irish recruits going
                         to Mass. Can you imagine? We're going un-
                         der armed escort but we're going. How
                         about you? Are you up for it?

                                JOHN
                         Yes.

                               DALTON
                         Good. Sleep now. You'll need it.

EXT. A LARGE TENT - DAY

Early morning. A company of about fifteen Irish soldiers are being marched to the large
tent. JOHN is unsteady on his feet and being attended to by DALTON and O'CONNEL.
They are guarded by eight armed soldiers, commanded by WEAVER. PEACOCK, on
horseback, and six more armed soldiers are already at the tent. WEAVER salutes
PEACOCK

                              PEACOCK
                         Is this all?

WEAVER
It's the last of them, Sir. We're ordered to
strike the tent afterwards.

The Irishmen begin to file into the tent. Four of PEACOCK's armed soldiers go into the
tent and stand in the back

PEACOCK
There's no need for that. My detail can handle
these few. You and your men can grab some
breakfast, Sergeant.

WEAVER
Thank you, Sir.

In the tent, O'CONNEL kneels next to DALTON as the Mass begins

O'CONNEL
Weaver's men are gone. The Lord is with us,
Patrick.

DALTON
And with your spirit.

EXT. ON THE U.S. RIGHT FLANK FORIFICATION - DAY

Two guards on post. GUARD ONE looks toward the tent

GUARD ONE
Well, there's "no…" um, there's the Lieutenant
and several guards. I guess everything is squared
away.

GUARD TWO (with field glass)
Those Papists aren't near as interesting as those
women washing clothes on the other bank.

GUARD ONE (takes glass)
Really? Where?

GUARD TWO (pointing)
There.

INT. IN THE LARGE TENT - DAY

The Mass is almost over. Several Irishmen have worked their way to the back,
complaining to the guards of their knees. Two others excused themselves to urinate and
are now standing in the back with the guards. The priest gives his benediction in Spanish
and exits. DALTON stands

> DALTON
> In the name of the Father, the Son, and the
> Holy Ghost. Amen.

When DALTON says, "Amen", the guards standing in the back of the tent are quickly and quietly disarmed, subdued, bucked and gagged with a tent pole. O'CONNEL sticks his head out of the tent and addresses a guard

> O'CONNEL
> Pardon me but one of the guards just fainted
> away and, b'Jesus, he's heavier than sin.
> Could you lend a hand?

The guard steps inside the tent and is instantly subdued, bucked and gagged. After a minute

> PEACOCK
> What the hell is going on?

PEACOCK dismounts and walks into the tent followed by the guard who sees what's going on and tries to step out of the tent but is jerked back inside. Before long seven men are sitting bucked and gagged on the same pole

> DALTON
> O'Connel, take the Lieutenant's hat and coat
> and get on that horse Look like him for a few
> minutes.

> O'CONNEL
> Do I have to cut my dick off or can I just act
> more important than I am?

> DALTON (grins)
> Get out there. Two of you grab rifles and be
> his detail for a few minutes.

The three exit

> Pay attention, Peacock.

DALTON addresses company

> I know this is a surprise to several of you men.
> We are deserting. You may decide to come
> with us. But you only have a minute to make
> up your minds.

A beat. Murmurs of men speaking confidentially

> (to JOHN) How about you? Are you coming?

JOHN (hesitates)
I can't serve in this army anymore. But, no, I
won't go. I'll only slow you down.

DALTON
I have a plan for that.

IRISH SOLDIER
Patrick, there are two of us who won't go
with you. We have families in Michigan.
If we follow you, we may never see them
again.

DALTON
I understand. Gag and tie these two. I'll not
give the army reason to beat them. Hear that,
Peacock?

AN IRISHMAN
I'm running out of rope.

DALTON walks over to PEACOCK and knocks him out

DALTON
Here, take his ropes. Some of you grab those
rifles. Now listen to me, men. There's a gully
behind this tent. Run in the gully. It will take
you right to the river.

DALTON cuts a vertical hole in the tent with a bayonet

If you will go, then go now! Go quickly and
quietly!

The tent empties, leaving only JOHN, DALTON and nine bucked and gagged men

After you.

The two men step through the hole in the tent, DALTON whistles and O'CONNEL (on
horse) and his two guards join them

JOHN
When did you hatch this plan?

DALTON
While you were convalescing. Some of us
have to work, you know.

O'CONNEL dismounts, DALTON mounts the horse and O'CONNEL helps JOHN to
mount the horse behind DALTON

All right, run boys. We'll see you on the
other side.

The horse gallops and the men run

INT. THE MEXICAN ENCAMPMENT - DAY

A small, dark tent serves as a stockade. JOHN, DALTON, O'CONNEL, SEAMUS and
the rest of the deserters sit on a hard dirt floor

> O'CONNEL
> If this is Mexican hospitality, I'd hate to be
> their enemy. Oh, wait a minute, they think I
> am their enemy.

Just then the flap of the tent is opened

> MEXICAN GUARD
> Vaminos.

> O'CONNEL
> What did you have in mind; thumb screws,
> hanging us by our heels? I warn you, we've
> been tortured by the best.

> MEXICAN GUARD
> Vaminos a todos!

> O'CONNEL
> Well, all right, don't have a conniption.

The deserters start to file out

EXT. THE MEXICAN ENCAMPMENT - DAY

Early evening. The deserters are herded in front of a table and chair with a canopy
overhead. General AMPUDIA makes an entrance from his tent to sit at the table. The
General's ADJUTANT steps forward

> ADJUTANT
> You are in the presence of General Pedro de
> la Ampudia.

> O'CONNEL (whispers)
> Should we genuflect?

> AMPUDIA
> Who is your leader? Who speaks for you?

> DALTON (whispers to JOHN)
> Let's both step forward. Odds are they'll
> only kill one of us.

JOHN and DALTON step forward

AMPUDIA

Two men?

DALTON

We can't make up our minds.

AMPUDIA

Are you here to fight for Mexico?

DALTON

What's your offer?

AMPUDIA

Ah, mercenaries. Verdad. Are not all men,
to some degree, mercenary? If you fight,
we offer you freedom, Mexican citizenship,
and pesos. If you fight well, we offer you
three hundred acres of good Mexican land.
If you are here to spy, we offer you death.
Which is it to be?

DALTON defers to JOHN

JOHN

May I confer with my men before giving you
an answer?

AMPUDIA

Of course.

The deserters walk to a private place in the camp

SEAMUS

I say we head for an ocean and then for
South America. Anywhere where there
isn't a war going on.

FIRST DESERTER

I don't trust them. I think they will shoot us
just in case we're spies. So, we're hung if the
U.S. Army catches us and shot if we stay
with the Mexicans.

SECOND DESERTER

Here's something else to think about. We
haven't been gone for a full day yet. Any man
here can say that he was captured or forced to
be Absent With Out Leave. We're not deserters yet.

FIRST DESERTER
Aye. But I'm not going back.

DALTON
What do you think, John?

A beat

JOHN
This is an old fight, one I've been running
from for years. I've thought it wasn't the right
time to fight, or that it wasn't my business.
But this is an old fight that the Irish know
well. It's a fight against the powerful who
take advantage of the weak. I don't know
who will win. Maybe it doesn't matter. I
can't run anymore. I'll fight for the Mexicans. All of you will do what you must.

Pause

SECOND DESERTER (standing)
I'll fight with you, John!

FIRST DESERTER (standing)
Aye!

SEAMUS (standing)
Me too!

DALTON (seated)
I've got nothing better to do.

O'CONNEL
Who's there? Who's behind that rock?

MARTA, a Mexican woman in her late twenties, starts to run and is caught by
O'CONNEL

JOHN
What are you doing here?

O'CONNEL
You know what they do to spies in this man's
army. Does that apply to women too?

MARTA
No. Yes. There is death for all of you on both
sides of the river. I wanted to see what kind
of men you are. (looks at JOHN) Now I know.

INT. AMPUDIA'S TENT - NIGHT

Late at night. Several Mexican officers, AMPUDIA, and JOHN are standing around a table with maps on it

                         JOHN
          I'm telling you, General, in about thirty six
          hours General Scott and another full Divi-
          sion will be in the field. You will be out-
          manned, out-gunned and fighting on two or
          three fronts. Once Taylor crosses the river,
          the crossfire will be murderous. You will
          not be able to hold your position.

                         AMPUDIA
          What you tell us confirms our information.
          I can get most of the infantry out under cover
          of darkness. And the cavalry will follow in
          the early morning. But I will need a delay-
          ing action. We cannot move quickly fighting
          a force on our heels.

                         JOHN
          Aye. You need a head start. Do you have any
          dynamite and light artillery?

                         AMPUDIA
          Si. Why?

                         JOHN
          I have an idea.

EXT. AMPUDIA'S TENT - NIGHT

A few minutes later. JOHN is exiting the tent

                         MARTA
          Señor, you are bleeding on your back. You
          are wounded. You have been hit, yes?

                         JOHN
          No. Yes. I have been hit fifty times or so.
          I'll be all right.

                         MARTA
          No, señor. I'm medico on the General's staff.
          I will help. Come to my tent. I will bandage.

                         JOHN (hesitates)
          Lead on.

INT. MARTA'S TENT - NIGHT

JOHN takes his jacket off and yelps with pain. MARTA pours something in a small glass

> MARTA
> Your shirt has dried onto your wounds. I will
> use water. But drink this tequila first.

> JOHN
> No, I really don't...

> MARTA
> Drink! It is necessary.

JOHN drinks. She pours one more shot

> MARTA
> And one more.

> JOHN
> No, I...

> MARTA
> Drink!

JOHN drinks. MARTA pours water on his back

> This is going to hurt a little.

> JOHN
> Where have I heard that...

She rips the shirt off quickly and JOHN yelps again

> You're not going to put iodine on, are you?

> MARTA
> No, lie on your stomach.

JOHN lies on a mat

> I have a salve and oils that will heal you from
> the inside out.

> JOHN
> That would be a trick.

> MARTA
> Que?

                         JOHN
            Nothing.

MARTA begins to apply the medicine

                         MARTA
            You will have bad scars, señor.

                         JOHN
            Well, you know what they say, what doesn't
            kill you... hurts like hell. My name is John.
            What's yours'?

                         MARTA
            Marta.

                         JOHN (getting sleepy)
            Marta. I like that.

A pause as she continues to apply the medicine

                         MARTA
            I heard what you said to your men, Juan.

                         JOHN
            What? Oh, they're not my men.

                         MARTA
            You spoke to them from your heart. They
            listen to you.

                         JOHN
            Maybe.

                         MARTA
            They love you. They need you.

                         JOHN
            Marta, I... Marta...

JOHN sleeps, MARTA continues her work

EXT. THE MEXICAN ENCAMPMENT - DAY

Dawn. A close-up of DALTON peering through a field glass at the U.S. camp. DALTON
is standing behind the four sixteen pound cannons which have been moved closer to the
river. A U.S. bugler sounds a "call to arms"

DALTON (to himself)
Well, come on, John, give us the signal. We
don't have to worry about waking them up
anymore. Come on, John, wave that flag!

JOHN and others have placed three six pound cannons about fifty yards directly in front
of the bridge. They have just completed the placement of heavy barricades between the
artillery pieces for protection from light arms fire. JOHN turns toward DALTON and
waves the Mexican flag

INT. COLONEL TAYLOR'S TENT - DAY

Dawn. TAYLOR is putting on his boots

TAYLOR
What do you mean, everyone is gone?

ADJUTANT
There is no one in their camp, or very few.
And those sixteen pound guns are a lot
closer to us.

TAYLOR
Impossible. It's a full days' work to dig those
heavy cannons out and move them down that
ridge.

Just then the bombardment from the heavy Mexican cannons begins. TAYLOR and his
ADJUTANT run out of the tent. TAYLOR is shouting now to be heard over the
explosions all around him

TAYLOR
Get the battery crews returning fire! Find
Captain Hammons!

HAMMONS (arriving)
I'm right here, Sir!

TAYLOR
Assemble your cavalry, Captain! Cross them
over the bridge and stop those cannons before
they make rubble of this whole camp!

HAMMONS (exiting)
Yes, Sir!

EXT. THE MEXICAN ENCAMPMENT - DAY

DALTON rides to a MEXICAN SERGEANT and another man holding six horses

DALTON
When that bridge blows, get these horses
down to Riley and the others. Comprende?

MEXICAN SERGEANT
Sí. Yes.

DALTON rides toward the river

EXT. ON THE MEXICAN SIDE OF THE BRIDGE – DAY

U.S. infantry charges across the bridge have been shattered by "grape shot" (small pieces
of metal) from the six pound cannons. But now the U.S. cavalry is mounting charges and
JOHN knows he cannot hold his position for long. JOHN waves the Mexican flag

EXT. ON THE MEXICAN SIDE OF THE RIVER - DAY

DALTON is hiding about eighty yards up river from the bridge and sees JOHN'S signal

DALTON (to himself)
That's the signal, light the fuse... Come on,
light the damn fuse!

DALTON focuses his field glass and sees a dead Mexican soldier draped over an under-
structure timber. He sees the bundle of dynamite tied under the bridge

Oh, crap.

On foot, DALTON works his way toward the bridge

EXT. ON THE MEXICAN SIDE OF THE BRIDGE - DAY

JOHN and others continue to fire their artillery but are taking a lot of fire and even
engaging in hand to hand combat. JOHN waves the flag again. They are running out of
time

EXT. ON THE MEXICAN SIDE OF THE RIVER - DAY

DALTON is only about forty yards from the bridge. His back to a tree, he loads a round
into the breach of the rifle, steps away from the tree and fires at the dynamite. He misses,
takes fire and ducks behind the tree again. He loads another round and takes a deep
breath

DALTON
Hail Mary, full of grace... Oh, hell, just hit
the damn thing.

He steps away from the tree again and fires. A huge explosion throws timber, horses and
men into the water. What remains of the bridge is in flames. A minute later, the
MEXICAN SERGEANT with his string of horses and DALTON, on horseback, arrive at

JOHN'S position and all ride toward the mountains. A dozen U.S. cavalrymen have swam the river and ride in pursuit a few hundred yards behind

EXT. A HILL NEXT TO THE MOUNTAIN TRAIL – DAY

O'CONNEL and JOSE, a Mexican Private and other Mexicans are concealed, waiting to ambush the U.S. cavalry. JOHN, DALTON and the others ride by

> JOSE
>
> Ahora? Now?

> O'CONNEL
>
> Not yet. So, who are the women I have seen in your camp?

> JOSE
>
> They are nurses and cooks and officers' mistres-
> ses and...

> O'CONNEL
>
> Wait. The officers bring their mistresses to a
> war?

> JOSE
>
> Sí, they would not put their wives in danger.

> O'CONNEL (hesitates)
>
> I guess that makes sense

> JOSE
>
> Sí. Now?

> O'CONNEL
>
> Yes, now.

O'CONNEL, JOSE and others stand and fire at the U.S. cavalry, wounding a few and discouraging the rest

EXT. THE U.S. DIVISION ENCAMPMENT - DAY

Under a canopy adjacent to TAYLOR'S tent. There is a map on a table. Around it, TAYLOR, his ADJUTANT, several officers, and a Texas RANGER speaking softly. HAMMONS and PEACOCK are in the foreground

> PEACOCK (bleeding)
>
> I recognized the U.S. soldier directing their
> artillery fire at the bridge, Sir. It was John
> Riley. (almost in tears) He was cutting us to
> pieces.

HAMMONS
Go get that shoulder taken care of, Lieutenant.

PEACOCK (exiting)
Yes, Sir.

HAMMONS stares hatefully across the river

RANGER
Ampudia is desperate, Colonel. He's going
over the mountains. It's a direct route to
Monterrey but the trail is treacherous. It
will take him sixteen to eighteen days. He's
traveling light. They'll be eating their horses
in a week. It's cold up there. He'll be lucky
to make Monterrey with two-thirds of his men.

TAYLOR (refers to map)
How about this route just east of the mountains?

RANGER
It's two hundred miles out of your way. But
if you can make twenty-five miles a day, you
might beat him there.

EXT. THE MEXICAN ENCAMPMENT IN THE MOUNTAINS - DAY

Early evening. In a small valley off the mountain trail, a village of sheep, goat and llama
ranchers are hosting AMPUDIA'S force. A YOUNG MEXICAN SOLDIER on a hill
with a view of the trail starts to shout

YOUNG MEXICAN SOLDIER
Están aquí! Están aquí! Los San Patricios
están aquí!

Many, in their enthusiasm, run down to meet the Irish and Mexican soldiers walking their
horses up the trail. MARTA meets JOHN at the valley entrance. As they turn into the
valley, they are cheered by AMPUDIA'S army with chants of "San Patricios!"

JOHN
San…what?

MARTA
San Patricio. Saint Patrick. Is he not the
patron Saint of the Irish?

JOHN
I guess so.

MARTA
Tonight, you and your men are our heroes.

They honor you with the name of your
Saint Patrick.

                    JOHN
How did news travel so fast?

                    MARTA
These mountains are full of eyes and ears
for the General.

AMPUDIA makes his entrance from his tent. More cheers go up and more chants of "San
Patricios!" AMPUDIA walks down to greet JOHN with a big hug and slaps on the back
which JOHN endures, wincing a little. AMPUDIA addresses the gathering.

                    AMPUDIA
Nuestras horaciones han sido contestadas por
medino de estos valientes guerreros. Empiesa
nuestra dificultosa jornada a Monterrey, pero
está noche celebramos nuestra liberacion
del enemigo y les brindamos la bienvenida a
nuestros hermanos quien lo hicieron possible.
Que sea grabado que se otorgo una comicion
de campo al Mayor Riley. Los San Patricios,
estos valientes hombres a quienes se les
a otorgado esté nombre, me honoraran está
noche con su presencia en mi mesa. Vivan
los San Patricios! (more cheers)

                    JOHN
What did he say?

                    MARTA
He is happy to see you. Congratulations on
your promotion, Major. And we are dining
with the General tonight.

EXT. THE U.S. ENCAMPMENT - DAY

Early evening. Under the canopy adjacent to TAYLOR'S tent, General SCOTT,
TAYLOR, HAMMONS and other officers are standing around a table with maps on it

                    SCOTT
Worth landed right here. He has two of the
Fifth Army's seven Divisions. Twiggs and
Smith landed here and here, each with a
Division apiece. Worth will approach the
capital from the east. Twiggs and Smith will
come up from the south-east. We will smash
Ampudia here at Monterrey and march to the
north of Mexico City. It has been proposed
by some of our detractors, politicians, that

this war will end in a protracted siege of the
city. I do not subscribe to this idea. Many of
our military leaders believe, as I do, that once
U.S. forces are in sight of the capital, the Mexican government will capitulate. I think Santa
Anna knows this to be true. He will move
his forces south and try to engage us one at a
time. He will not succeed. We will skirt Mexico City and attack him from behind. This war
will not end diplomatically, but with an un-
conditional surrender. Gentlemen, we have
the better soldier who has the best equipment,
fighting under officers who are single-minded.

SCOTT raises his glass of whiskey. All do the same

To meeting and defeating the enemy. (they
drink) I hear that the top Mexican brass likes
to bicker with one another like old women.
(laughter) Let's shake those old bitches by
their tails. We break camp at dawn. Good luck.

Salutes given and returned. Soon TAYLOR and SCOTT are
alone. Pause

You are wondering why I didn't can you after
the Mexicans caught you with your pants down.

TAYLOR
It's a fair question, General.

SCOTT
You almost sound disappointed that I didn't
can you.

TAYLOR
It feels like I've been soldiering all my life,
Sir. But I think I'm a farmer at heart.

SCOTT
Well, you'll not retire to a farm just yet,
Zachary. I need you down here. Your men
like you. They trust you. It must be that
grandfatherly charm. (TAYLOR chuckles)
In my not-so-humble opinion, I am the best
field commander in the army. Therefore I
will command. You will continue to handle
the enlisted men. Together we will achieve
our goals.

TAYLOR (standing)
Yes, Sir. If there is nothing else this evening,
I'll retire...to sleep, that is. Good night, Sir.

SCOTT studies TAYLOR as he walks away

EXT. ON THE MOUNTAIN TRAIL - DAY

Horses laden with rifles and ammunition, AMPUDIA'S expedition climbs the steep trail
with difficulty

EXT. ON THE MOUNTAIN TRAIL - DAY

Early evening. A narrow trail against a sheer rock face has everyone moving slowly for
safety. Snow dusts their shoulders

EXT. ON THE MOUNTAIN TRAIL - NIGHT

Everyone is bedding down on a safer part of the trail. Campfires dot the mountainside.
AMPUDIA is visiting campsites with an escort of torch bearers and soldiers carrying
extra blankets. JOHN and MARTA each have a blanket and are sitting silently by a small
fire, bracing themselves against the cold

JOHN
Come and sit closer to me. We'll share body
heat and be warmer.

They do so and take turns adjusting the end of their blanket around the other. She sits
staring into the fire. He puts his blanket over her head and puts an arm around her
shoulder. He wants to kiss her but refrains and then stares into the fire. She finally looks
up at him, takes his free hand and holds it in her hands, perhaps wanting to kiss him as
well. Finally, tentatively, they look at one another at the same time. Slowly, silently,
romantically they kiss

MARTA
Good night, Juan.

EXT. ON THE MOUNTAIN TRAIL - NIGHT

A few minutes later. JOHN and MARTA are still seated together. She is sleeping, her
head upon his shoulder. AMPUDIA and his entourage stop in front of their small fire and
AMPUDIA sees the sleeping MARTA

AMPUDIA
Good night, Major.

JOHN
Good night, Sir.

EXT. ON THE MOUNTAIN TRAIL - DAY

Morning. A woman ('Lupe') is climbing a steep part of the trail, pulling herself up by a rope that has been strung against the sheer rock face. She slips and before she can secure her hold on the rope, she falls, screaming. JOHN and MARTA move as quickly as they can to the place on the trail where she fell

MARTA

Lupe! Lupe!

Two soldiers lower a third man tied to a rope to look for Lupe

Lupe! Is she alive?

The third man on the rope shakes his head 'no' to confirm that Lupe is dead. MARTA turns to JOHN and sobs in his arms. AMPUDIA has made his way back to the site of the tragedy

AMPUDIA

Vaminos.

JOHN

May we stop for a minute, Sir?

AMPUDIA

No.

JOHN

May we stop to say one prayer?

AMPUDIA

No!... I knew Lupe. If we do not make Monterrey before the enemy, her death will be meaningless. I will not have that. Vaminos! It is an order, Major.

JOHN (quietly)

Yes, Sir.

EXT. ON THE MOUNTAIN TRAIL - DAY

Afternoon. They are on the downhill stretch of the trail, within sight of the walls of Monterrey, at a place where an old lava flow meets the valley. Soon the church bells start to ring. The huge wrought iron gates open and Mexican soldiers and civilians come out to give the exhausted army food and drink

EXT. THE WALL/FORTIFICATIONS OF MONTERREY - DAY

Morning. JOHN is supervising the placement of artillery

O'CONNEL (approaches)

John, there are over forty U.S. soldiers in town. They are all deserters from other units.

And many of them are Irish. They want to
fight for the Mexicans too.

JOHN
Where are they?

O'CONNEL
Looking for weapons, I think.

JOHN
Tell them to roll that twenty-four pound
cannon to the gate. Tell them to be careful, it
weighs a ton.

O'CONNEL
Yes, Sir.

AMPUDIA enters with his ADJUTANT

AMPUDIA
No. If civilians want to fight then give them
uniforms. I'll not have the enemy targeting
civilians unnecessarily.

ADJUTANT (exiting)
Sí, General.

AMPUDIA (to JOHN)
How is this coming?

JOHN
Good. I've put our lightest artillery on heavy,
iron-yoked swivels. We can pepper them
with 'grape shot' on both sides of the gates.

A woman with a wooden box approaches AMPUDIA

AMPUDIA
Excellent. Will you join me for a cup of
coffee, Major?

The woman pours two tin cups and leaves. A beat

Marta and Lupe were close. Is Marta still
angry with me?

JOHN
No, Sir. She understands.

AMPUDIA
A woman can understand but still be angry.

You have been spending some time with Marta.

                        JOHN
Yes, Sir.

                        AMPUDIA
What do you think of her?

                        JOHN
Well, she's smart. She's tough. She's…

                        AMPUDIA
Beautiful?

                        JOHN
Yes.

                        AMPUDIA
You love her?

                        JOHN
We've only known each other for a short time…

                        AMPUDIA
A man knows if he loves a woman.

A beat

                        JOHN
Yes, I do love her.

                        AMPUDIA
Ah, then I must tell you, she is a strong-
willed, strong-minded woman who will
cause you much distress. I tried to
discourage her from serving on my staff
but she would not listen. She is stubborn
like her mother.

                        JOHN (shocked)
Wait. Are you…? Is she your daughter?

                        AMPUDIA
Sí.

                        JOHN
She never told me.

                        AMPUDIA
No, she would not. She is stubborn, I warn
you. And believe me, I speak from experience.

If you marry such a woman, you will fight with
her night and day. And you will not win these
fights. You will be angry with her. But you
will cherish her all the more for being your
friend and lover. Her mother was such a woman.

A beat. AN OFFICER approaches

> AN OFFICER
> Excuse me, General, you wanted to inspect
> these rooftop arms placements.

> AMPUDIA
> Yes. Show me.

AMPUDIA and AN OFFICER walk off. JOHN is in thought

INT. MONTERREY HOSPITAL - DAY

JOHN enters and watches MARTA working on a soldier with a wounded arm. She
finally notices him

> MARTA
> Juan…

JOHN joins her and produces something from a cloth bag

> JOHN
> I brought you something to eat.

> MARTA
> Thank you.

> JOHN
> And I wanted to ask you something.

> MARTA
> Well…?

> JOHN
> Not here. Can I see you later?

> MARTA
> Yes, of course.

DALTON enters

> DALTON
> Scott and Taylor have been seen not more
> than three hours from here.

JOHN looks at MARTA and leaves quickly with DALTON

EXT. ON THE WALL/FORTIFICATION – DAY

Late afternoon. DALTON and JOHN (with a field glass), are looking over the busy U.S. troops establishing their camp in the foothills

                    JOHN
          There is so much dust that I can't find their
          artillery.

                    DALTON
          We'll find them soon enough.

                    SEAMUS
          Major?... John?

                    JOHN
          Yes?

                    SEAMUS
          I was explaining to some nuns here in Monter-
          rey that we were in need of our own standard.

He produces a flag

                    And this is what they came up with. Do you
                    like it?

It is a green banner with an Irish Harp and the words, 'Erin Go Bragh' and, on the other side, a picture of Saint Patrick with 'San Patricio' under the picture

                    JOHN (to DALTON)
          What do you think?

                    DALTON
          I think it's beautiful. Tie it to that pole up
          there and see what the other men think of it.

SEAMUS does so. At first there is only a smattering of cheers. But as more and more notice the flag, the cheers are sustained. These cheers are interrupted by artillery fire from the U.S. forces

                    JOHN
          Maybe they're just trying to find their range.

JOHN looks through field glass

                    JOHN
          No, they are getting ready for an assault,
          damn. Better go tell the General.

44

SEAMUS scampers down the wall. JOHN peers through the glass

>There they are, up against that hill. Get
>down there and handle that pig of a cannon,
>Patrick. We've got to try to knock out their
>sixteen pounders.

EXT. THE IRON GATES OF MONTERREY - DAY

The large U.S. cannons continue to fire, some shots taking out sections of the wall. It takes eight men to swing the nose of the twenty-four pound cannon to the right. DALTON looks to JOHN for the range signal, then lifts the nose of the cannon with a block and fulcrum. JOHN gives the signal to fire. The cannon fires and lobs a shell well over the large U.S. cannons. JOHN signals down to DALTON and they move the nose of the cannon to the right and JOHN signals to raise the nose of the cannon again

                    SECOND IRISH SOLDIER
          We over-shot the first time. Why are we
          trying to shoot even farther?

                    DALTON
          I think I know what he's doing. Half a foot
          up, men!

The signal to fire is given. An explosion high up on the hill starts a rock slide that knocks one of the big U.S. cannons off of the yoke. Spontaneous cheers erupt among the Mexican on the wall but simultaneous fire from a dozen U.S. artillery pieces quell the cheers

EXT. MONTERREY - NIGHT

U.S. troops surge through holes blasted in the walls and fighting continues within the city. SCOTT advances on horseback to a forward position

                    SCOTT
          Report, Captain.

                    HAMMONS
          We've breached the wall in several spots,
          General, but they're stopping us with roof-
          top snipers. If we wait until morning, we'll
          be able to see them and take them out.

                    SCOTT
          I don't have the time for this. Bring mortars
          into range and start lobbing incendiary rounds.

                    HAMMONS (exiting)
          Yes, Sir.

Small arms and light artillery fire continues to be exchanged as the short-barreled mortars are brought forward and start to lob fire-starting shells. Colonel TAYLOR joins SCOTT

> TAYLOR
> Is it true, General, are you going to burn this town?

> SCOTT
> I'm going to burn it to the ground.

> TAYLOR
> General, there are hundreds of civilian lives at risk.

> SCOTT
> I didn't choose the battleground, Ampudia did. Let me explain something to you, Colonel...

Just then a bullet grazes SCOTT's head. He is knocked off his horse, alive but unconscious

INT. MONTERREY HOSPITAL - NIGHT

JOHN runs into the hospital to find MARTA hard at work

> JOHN
> Marta, the General is pulling men off the wall to fight the fires. It's only a matter of time before he has to surrender. The other men will be safe under a white flag but I may not be so lucky...

> DALTON (entering)
> Come on, John, we've got to go!

> JOHN (to MARTA)
> I want you to come with me.

> MARTA
> No, I cannot leave so many wounded here.

> JOHN (hesitates)
> Then I will stay with you.

> DALTON
> No, John! We've got to go now!

> MARTA
> He is right, Juan. Go. The General will retreat to Mexico City. I will meet you there.

JOHN

Promise me.

MARTA

With my life, mi amore.

JOHN kisses her hands. MARTA kisses him quickly, passionately

Go now.

DALTON and JOHN run

INT. MONTERREY HOSPITAL - DAY

Thirty-six hours later. SCOTT is alert, sitting up in bed with a bandage on his head. He is surrounded by officers and his ADJUTANT. TAYLOR walks in

TAYLOR

General, it's good to see you with us again.
Have you received any reports?

SCOTT (ominously)

Yes, I have. Gentlemen, I'll ask all of you,
except my Adjutant and Colonel Taylor, to
clear the room.

Officers leave without making eye contact with TAYLOR

SCOTT

Is it true, Colonel, that when Ampudia waved
a white flag of surrender, you sued for a
truce and, in fact, helped him put out the
fires in Monterrey?

TAYLOR

Yes, Sir. Ampudia was more interested,
at that point, in saving civilian lives than
winning a battle and I gave him dynamite
to stop the spread of the fire. I thought it
was the right thing to do.

SCOTT

And then you let his army march out of
here with their weapons?

TAYLOR

That's not entirely accurate, Sir. I con-
fiscated their artillary, ammunition, black
powder and military issued weapons. I
allowed Ampudia's officers to keep their
side arms and other men to keep their non-
military issued weapons.

SCOTT
Did it occur to you that we may have to fight
Ampudia's army later in this campaign and that
this stunt of yours may cost American lives?

TAYLOR
Yes, Sir, the thought did occur to me. I did
not see a viable alternative course of action.
Our mission requires us to remain mobile
and it would be untenable for us to maintain
hundreds of prisoners…

SCOTT
I make the decision about what is untenable!

TAYLOR
Yes, Sir.

SCOTT
And then you just let the deserters go?

TAYLOR
Once again, Sir, I did not see a viable
alternative course of action…

SCOTT
I would have hung the bastards from the gate!

TAYLOR (deliberately)
Sir, even in time of war there is due process.
Soldiers must face a court martial before
hanging…

SCOTT
That's enough! (To ADJUTANT) Clear the
room, Lieutenant!

ADJUTANT exits

I find you to be incompetent, Colonel. Frankly,
I don't think you have the balls to be a field
commander.

TAYLOR (calmly)
That may be, Sir, despite my record to the
contrary. In my defense, I thought I was
doing the proper thing.

SCOTT
Save the platitudes for your court martial. As
of now, you are relieved. You will take a

small detail and withdraw to the north. Is that clear?

                    TAYLOR
Yes, Sir.

TAYLOR holds a salute until it is half-heartedly returned and then turns to leave. He hesitates, then turns back

                    General, as long as we are being frank with
                    one another, I don't think you'll make good
                    on your threat to court martial me. It would
                    not be to your advantage for your detractors
                    to hear a Colonel testify as to the brutality
                    and barbarism with which this war has been
                    prosecuted. Nor would you want them to hear
                    about the cruel treatment of Mexican civilians
                    and our own troops by U.S. Army officers.

                    SCOTT (furiously)
Get out! Get out of here!

                    TAYLOR (calmly exiting)
Yes, Sir.

EXT. CHURUBUSCO - NIGHT

Early evening. A large stone building on top of a steep hill. Fires dot the hillside. JOHN and DALTON approach JOSE, a Mexican private, who points a pistol at them

                    JOSE
Alto!

JOHN and DALTON stop and put their hands up

                    JOHN
Estoy Juan de Los San Patricios.

                    JOSE
Ah, sí, I know you.

                    JOHN
Where is the General?

                    JOSE
El General está aquí. I take you to him. Come.

As they walk to the stone building, a guitar played by a Mexican soldier strums an anthem about the San Patricio Battalion

INT. CHURUBUSCO - NIGHT

A large dining hall. A gathering of AMPUDIA's officers, JOHN and DALTON

> AMPUDIA
> Come in, gentlemen. This place was a mon-
> astery. The monks here have a large basement
> where General Santa Anna has locked away
> weapons and ammunition for his armies, thank
> God. But thank God, too, for the cases of wine
> he left behind. We do not drink in celebration
> but as comrades before a battle. Es mi honor
> a servite en la posición de su General con la
> poder de Dío triunfaremos. Drink, my friends!

Officers start to pour wine and make toasts

> JOHN
> Is Marta not with you, General?

> AMPUDIA
> No, Marta is in Monterrey. She cares for your
> General Scott who was shot. She will join us in
> Mexico City.

> JOHN
> What forces do you face?

> AMPUDIA
> There has been a regiment of cavalry trailing
> us ever since we left Monterrey. I am sure
> they will be joined by others. (confidentially)
> The war goes badly for us, Juan. Santa Anna is
> besieged in the south. U.S. armies are, even
> now, close to the capital.

> JOHN
> You can count on us to fight, Sir.

> AMPUDIA
> Thank you.

> JOHN
> May I take a few bottles to my battalion,
> General?

> AMPUDIA
> Of course.

DALTON grabs a few bottles and they exit

EXT. CHURUBUSCO - NIGHT

JOHN and DALTON walk up on O'CONNEL, SEAMUS and others sitting quietly around a fire

                              JOHN
             Well, if this isn't the most sour-faced batch
             of renegades the devil ever blessed...

                              SEAMUS
             It's John and Patrick. Hey, everybody, it's
             John and Patrick!

Cheers. Irishmen from nearby campsites join them. O'CONNEL shakes hands with the two

                              O'CONNEL
             It's good to see you. We thought you were
             dead.

                              JOHN
             It was easy to get out of Monterrey. But we
             were almost shot coming to Chero... Churo...

                              O'CONNEL
             Churubusco. It means 'place of the war God'.

                              DALTON
             Well, we brought offerings to the war God but
             I expect you Irish will drink this wine instead.
             (cheers)

                              FIRST IRISH SOLDIER
             Thank heavens, something to wash the taste
             of jack rabbit and cactus out of my mouth.

The bottles start to be passed around and the guitar starts the anthem again

EXT. CHURUBUSCO - NIGHT

An hour later. JOHN, DALTON, O'CONNEL, SEAMUS and others are seated by the fire, the guitar strumming softly in the distance

                              O'CONNEL
             Some U.S. soldiers wanted to kill us. Colonel
             Taylor saved our lives. You two would have
             been shot for sure.

                              SEAMUS
             John, do you remember Tim and Oliver Duffy?

JOHN

No.

SEAMUS

Sean knew them. We were friends. From
County Cork, they were. As we marched
out of Monterrey, Tim kept following me
and screaming at me, "You killed Oli,"
he said, "You killed my brother!" I never
felt so bad. We were like kin and yet there
was such hatred in his eyes. I felt like I
had … deserted them.

Pause

JOHN

If you start walking west, in about a week
you'll come upon a big inlet sea. And you
can fish there for the rest of your life and
no man here will blame you for doing so.

A beat

SEAMUS

No, you fellows are my brothers now. I'll
not be a deserter again.

SECOND IRISH SOLDIER

Aye.

DALTON

Aye. And on that note I'll get my beauty rest.
It's a big day tomorrow and I'll not want to
disappoint the war God.

JOHN

Good night, Patrick.

All men disperse to their blankets and sleeping bags except JOHN and SEAMUS. Pause

SEAMUS

We're going to lose tomorrow, aren't we.

JOHN

I don't know.

SEAMUS

If I felt like I did what I should have, then I could
be all right with whatever happens tomorrow. Did
we… did we do the right thing, John?

A beat

                         JOHN
            I don't know, Seamus. I don't know. I think
            we did what we had to do.

A beat

                         SEAMUS
            Thank you. Good night.

SEAMUS stands and goes to bed down. JOHN is staring into the fire as the glow on him
fades to black

EXT. CHURUBUSCO - DAY

Early morning. DALTON approaches a tree and starts to urinate. He is barely awake. He
finally opens his eyes and sees clouds of dust and artillery rolling on their caissons

                         DALTON (buttoning up)
            Oh, crap. Muster up, men, we have com-
            pany!

JOHN joins him at the tree and looks at the gathering force through a field glass

                         JOHN
            That's not just cavalry, that's both divi-
            sions. Damn.

EXT. CHURUBUSCO - DAY

Midmorning. The U.S. artillery has been pounding the monastery for an hour. The
Mexican force and light artillery, manned by the San Patricios, remain relatively safe
behind the thick walls. A soldier on the roof signals the advance of the U.S. infantry.
Mexican soldiers open the heavy, wooden gates of the courtyard and the San Patricio
Battalion wheel their cannons out to wait for the enemy to come into range. They are
taking heavy fire and several men are shot. The U.S. infantry reaches the base of the hill
and start to run up hill. The cannons are fired and kill many soldiers but many more
soldiers are coming behind them and JOHN signals to the soldier on the roof. Waves of
Mexican soldiers descend upon the U.S. infantry and there is much hand to hand fighting.
Through the smoke and dust, Sergeant WEAVER makes his way to the Mexican cannons
and finds JOHN fighting with a rifle and bayonet. WEAVER aims his side arm carefully
and fires, hitting JOHN in the shoulder, knocking him down. WEAVER walks over to
kill JOHN with a second shot but is, himself, shot in the shoulder. WEAVER goes down
to one knee. JOHN grabs his rifle with one arm and runs WEAVER through the chest
with the bayonet. WEAVER discharges his weapon into the ground and dies. A Mexican
bugle sounds retreat and a white flag of surrender is hoisted onto the roof

INT. CHURUBUSCO - DAY

Two days later. Forty or more of the surviving San Patricio Battalion are in the chapel, serving as a stockade. They are guarded by U.S. soldiers. JOHN's arm is in a sling. He sits in the first pew of the chapel with DALTON and SEAMUS

                    DALTON (to JOHN)
          You mean to tell me that you don't remem-
          ber me shooting Sergeant Weaver just be-
          fore he was about to put a bullet between
          your eyes?

                    JOHN
          Not really, no.

                    DALTON
          What do you think he was doing, then, when
          he grabbed his arm and went down to one knee?

                    JOHN
          I don't know- having a heart attack?

                    DALTON
          That does it! That's the last time I save your
          life. From now on, you're on your own.

                    JOHN
          Fine.

Pause

                    DALTON
          You know, the only thing that bothers me
          about this whole thing is being hung like
          a common criminal. As an officer, you'll
          be shot by a firing squad. At least that's
          respectable.

                    JOHN
          I never thought being shot by a firing
          squad was so respectable.

                    DALTON
          It beats hanging like a criminal! I've never
          done anything criminal, if you don't count
          killing a few soldiers, even your own.

A beat

                    SEAMUS
          I'll bet hanging hurts like hell.

JOHN and DALTON share a look

54

                              JOHN
                No, it will kill you. It won't hurt like hell.

                              SEAMUS
                Oh… good.

EXT. CHURUBUSCO - DAY

AMPUDIA waits at the open gates of the courtyard as MARTA, a Mexican officer and
six U.S. soldiers arrive on horseback. MARTA quickly dismounts

                        MARTA (anxiously)
                Did you see General Scott?

                              AMPUDIA
                Yes.

                              MARTA
                And what did he say?

                              AMPUDIA
                The man is implacable. They are to face a
                court martial. But he will not, he chooses
                not to show leniency.

                              MARTA
                Did you beg for Juan's life?

                              AMPUDIA
                I did everything in my power.

                              MARTA
                Then I will beg.

MARTA turns quickly to enter the building. Two armed guards move to impede her
access. AMPUDIA takes her arm

                              AMPUDIA
                Come. We only have a few minutes before
                our escort must leave.

                              MARTA
                Then I must go to him.

                              AMPUDIA
                Marta, Juan and others will die. But they do
                not know this yet. Don't take their hope, it's
                all they have left.

MARTA studies her father for a moment and turns to go to the chapel

INT. CHAPEL – DAY

JOHN, DALTON and SEAMUS are seated in the front pew apart from the rest of the prisoners and guards

                        MARTA (entering)
Juan.

                        JOHN (standing)
Marta.

                        MARTA (approaching him)
You are hurt?

                        JOHN
It's nothing. The surgeon has taken care of
me.

                        MARTA
Your wound has been dressed properly?

                        JOHN
Yes. I'm fine now that you are here.

                        DALTON (standing)
I've got some tobacco, Seamus. Let's go to
the back and roll a cigarette.

                        SEAMUS
I don't want one.

                        DALTON (deliberately)
Walk with me anyway.

SEAMUS finally understands that he is to give MARTA and JOHN a little privacy and walks to the back of the chapel with DALTON

                        JOHN (holding her hands)
What have you heard?

                        MARTA
Nothing. There is to be a court martial.

                        JOHN (lying for her sake)
Yes. Half of these fellows will go free by
claiming they were drunk and kidnapped.
(chuckles) When this is over, we'll meet
in Mexico City, just as we planned.

                        MARTA
Yes.

JOHN
Marta, do you remember the day of the battle
at Monterrey when I came to see you in the
hospital?

MARTA
Yes.

JOHN
I brought you lunch… And I was going to
ask you to marry me.

MARTA
Yes!

Sobbing, she throws herself into his arms, or rather, arm

I will marry you! I will!

A moment passes

JOHN
Well, that wasn't so hard. Now if we only
had a priest, a white dress for you and a
shave and a bath for me. (chuckles)

MARTA
We don't need these things.

JOHN
We don't?

MARTA
No. Marriage vows are sworn between two
people in the sight of God.

JOHN
That's true.

MARTA
So, if I vow to love you and you vow to love
me, then God is here.

They both look at the stained glass above the alter

JOHN (taking her hands)
Then I vow to love you forever. I vow to love
you more than my life, with all of my heart
and soul.

MARTA
And I vow to love you, my husband, forever.

No matter where you are, I will love you with
my every thought, with all of my heart and soul.

They kiss almost reverently and hold one another as if holding a precious gift

                    A SERGEANT (enters)
I'm sorry, Miss, we must go now.

                    MARTA (crying)
I cannot leave you!

                    JOHN
No, go. I'll see you, Marta. And when we
meet, we'll never be parted again.

                    MARTA
I know that to be true.

                    A SERGEANT
Miss?

                    MARTA (crying, exiting)
Yes. Goodbye, my husband. Goodbye, my life.

EXT. A LARGE WHITE WALL - DAY

In front of the wall is scaffolding designed to hang several men at the same time. In front
of that is a shoulder-high post. JOHN's hands are tied behind the post. He is looking at
his firing squad. Behind the firing squad, are his men destined to be hung after watching
JOHN die. HAMMONS, on horseback, is watching the proceedings. PEACOCK
tentatively offers JOHN a blindfold. JOHN quietly refuses. Suddenly SEAMUS starts to
shout

                    SEAMUS
Viva San Patricios!

He shouts this over and over again until he is hit by a guard. It doesn't stop him from
shouting and soon many of the prisoners are shouting the same thing. They are hit in the
face with the butt of rifles but they get up bleeding and shouting. They finally stop when
they see DALTON holding a salute to JOHN. They all stand quietly holding the salute.
HAMMONS is quite moved by the devotion of the prisoners

                    HAMMONS
Lieutenant!

                    PEACOCK (crossing to him)
Yes, Sir.

                    HAMMONS
Untie his ropes.

                                PEACOCK
Sir?

                                HAMMONS
Untie his ropes so he can return the salute.

                                PEACOCK
Are you sure, Captain? General Scott will be
hopping mad if he finds out about this.

                                HAMMONS
Then he'll be hopping mad! Carry out my
order, Lieutenant!

                                PEACOCK
Yes, Sir.

PEACOCK unties JOHN and JOHN holds a salute while looking at every one of his
comrades. JOHN drops his hand

                                HAMMONS
Let's get this over with.

                                PEACOCK
Should I tie his hands again, Sir?

                                HAMMONS
Does he look like he's going to run?

                                PEACOCK
No, I guess not, Sir.

                                HAMMONS
Get on with it.

We watch the faces of the San Patricios until shots are fired. Underscoring of a slow
ballad on penny whistle through to the end

                                PEACOCK
Detail, attention!... Present arms... Detail
aim!...Fire!

A sepia photograph of the hanged men is shown on the upper half of the frame. This
photo slowly turns into a high definition picture of the hung men while the following
paragraphs roll up on the lower half of the frame

                This hanging remains the largest
                mass execution of U.S. soldiers
                in United States Military History

                Forty years later, charges of
                desertion for all U.S. soldiers

engaged in the Mexican-American
War were officially dropped by
an act of Congress

The San Patricio Battalion is
commemorated both in Mexico and
Ireland

General Winfield Scott wanted to
be President of the United States.
He ran for the office but was
defeated by Franklin Pierce, one
of his former subordinate officers

Colonel Zachery Taylor wanted to
retire to farming. Instead, he was
pressed into political service and
become the twelfth President of the
United States

GEORGE AND INGER

EXT. OCONOMOWAC, WISCONSIN - DAY

February, 1939- the ice skating stadium. A large crowd is on hand to witness the final fifteen hundred meter men's race. The tall, twenty-two year old bespectacled GEORGE Wallace is one of a dozen or so competitors gathering around the starting line. There are two racers wearing Dartmouth sweaters, GEORGE and his friend, EDDIE Schroeder. GEORGE'S pink racing slacks make him stand out against the black or grey slacks worn by the other racers. GEORGE'S MOTHER is standing by the rail

> MOTHER (waving)
> Georgey!

GEORGE skates over to her

> GEORGE
> Hello, Mother.

> MOTHER
> I just talked to Mister Grieves from the
> Examiner and he tells me that your
> Father will be able to read all about your
> races in tonight's paper.

> GEORGE
> That's nice, Mother. Why did you buy me
> pink pants?

> MOTHER
> They were the only ones I could find,
> Georgey, the only ones in your size. Don't
> worry, dear, you look fine.

> GEORGE (sadly)
> No I don't. I look like a ballet dancer.

> MOTHER
> I'm sorry, Georgey.

> GEORGE
> It's all right, Mother. It's not your fault I
> forgot my racing slacks. It's just that, I'd
> better do well.

Someone in the crowd "wolf" whistles loudly at GEORGE and several college-aged boys laugh as GEORGE looks toward the whistler

On second thought, I'd better win.

PUBLIC ADDRESS
Last call for the men's fifteen hundred meter
race. Last call.

GEORGE
I've got to go, Mother.

MOTHER
Good luck, Georgey.

GEORGE returns to the starting line and to EDDIE to shake his hand

GEORGE
Good luck, Eddie.

EDDIE (smiling)
You too, George. And, Georgey, nice pants.

GEORGE acknowledges the remark with a sickly smile

STARTER
Skaters to your mark!

The skaters ready themselves. The STARTER'S gun fires and the crowd cheers as the men try to sprint to the lead to gain the advantage of the inside track. GEORGE gets jostled a bit and, coming out of the first turn, a skater in front of GEORGE gets tangled up with another and goes down, tripping up GEORGE and one other man. All three skaters scramble to their feet and try to catch the pack. By the fourth turn GEORGE has caught the pack, swings wide in the turn and stays well away from the other skaters. GEORGE is extending his stride in an attempt to catch the leader, EDDIE, who has almost twenty yards on him. By the bell lap GEORGE is close to EDDIE and, coming out of the last turn, the two men sprint furiously for the finish line to the roar of the crowd. Their hands on their knees now, both men are breathing heavily as their momentum takes them down the track

GEORGE
I think I got you, Eddie.

EDDIE
I don't know, George. Good race.

A PHOTOGRAPHER runs out on the track

PHOTOGRAPHER
How about a picture for the papers, boys?

GEORGE and EDDIE stand up for the PHOTOGRAPHER, their arms around each other's shoulders with big smiles. The photo flash transitions to the still black and white newspaper photo, under which is the headline, "California Mystery Man Mops Up Olympic Trials"

EXT. OSLO, NORWAY - DAY

April, 1939. Overview of downtown Oslo drenched in sunlight with snow covered mountains in the distance

INT. ANDERSON'S CLOTHING STORE, OSLO - DAY

Anderson's is a large, two-story building with display rooms, storage and offices upstairs. Downstairs, OLGA, an older, stern-faced woman is ordering young, female employees about in preparation for a fashion show catering to wealthy wives of dignitaries and the Norwegian royal family. Among the employees is INGER Dahlberg, a plainly dressed eighteen year old girl with reading glasses and clipboard. Her hair is tied in a bun

OLGA
Has Celeste arrived yet?

INGER
No, ma 'me.

OLGA
Have you called?

INGER
Yes, ma 'me. There was no answer.

OLGA
Well, then, we'll just have to proceed
without her. Double check the racks for
the other girls and make sure accessories
are clearly marked and on the right racks.
And see to it that Helga serves coffee and
pastries as soon as our guests arrive.

                              INGER

Yes, ma 'me.

                              OLGA

I'll be right back.

OLGA goes upstairs and walks into MARCELLA Anderson's office. MARCELLA, in
her fifties, is at her desk

                           MARCELLA

Is Celeste here?

                              OLGA

No. We'll just go on without her.

                           MARCELLA

That's a shame. The best of the line was fitted
for Celeste.

                              OLGA

I can't think of anyone in her dress size who
could substitute.

                           MARCELLA

What about your dresser, Inger?

                              OLGA

No, that would be a mistake. She has the
bearing of a timid maid.

                           MARCELLA

But the clothes will fit her. Let me talk to her.

                              OLGA

Very well.

OLGA turns on her heels, descends the staircase and crosses to an elegantly dressed
middle-aged woman with two teen-aged girls

                              OLGA

Good afternoon, Countess. Thank you for
your attendance. We'll be ready to show
you our recent acquisitions from London
in a few moments. Until then, please enjoy

the shop. Helga, you will attend to the
Countess.

The Countess wanders off with her daughters and Helga

Inger, Mrs. Anderson wants to see you in
her office immediately.

OLGA takes the clipboard from INGER

                    INGER
But...what...

                    OLGA
Now!

INGER moves to the staircase and up as if to the gallows. She crosses to the open door of
MARCELLA's office

                    INGER
You wanted to see me, Mrs. Anderson?

                    MARCELLA
Yes, come in, Inger. What's the matter,
dear?

                    INGER
Well, I assumed that I have done something
wrong.

                    MARCELLA
No, no. On the contrary, you can be a big help
today. Let me see you without those glasses.

INGER removes the eye glasses as MARCELLA sizes her up

                    MARCELLA
Yes, you will do nicely. You will be a sub-
stitute model today and wear the dresses on
Celeste's rack.

                    INGER (panicking)
But I have no experience.

MARCELLA

Nonsense, you have helped the models with
their hair and makeup, have you not?

INGER

Well, yes...

MARCELLA

And you've seen how they move to feature
clothing?

INGER

Yes, but...

MARCELLA (finally)

Yes?

INGER

I'm afraid.

MARCELLA crosses to her and takes her hands

MARCELLA

There is a secret to modeling and I'm going
to share it with you now. You must say three
things to yourself over and over again until
you believe them. They are: I am beautiful
in these clothes. I enjoy wearing them. And,
lastly and most importantly, I belong in them.
Will you repeat those three things for me?

INGER (tentatively)

I am beautiful in these clothes. I enjoy wearing them. And I...

MARCELLA

belong...

INGER

And I belong in them.

MARCELLA

Once again.

INGER

I am beautiful in these clothes. I enjoy wearing them. I belong in them.

MARCELLA

Good. Go now. Apply your make up. Brush
out your hair. And, as you dress, repeat
those three things over and over until you
believe. Do you understand?

INGER

Yes, ma 'me.

Glassy-eyed, INGER turns to leave, mumbling her new mantra. MARCELLA quietly
closes the door to her office and looks up prayerfully

MARCELLA

God help us.

INT. ANDERSON'S CLOTHING STORE, OSLO- DAY

A small, elevated stage is surrounded by couches and comfortable chairs. Recorded
orchestral music is softly playing as the dozen or so clients watch the first model
demonstrate a full length, burgundy gown. The second model enters as the first leaves.
The second model is also wearing evening clothes, a jacket and matching skirt with a fur
wrap. She exits as INGER enters wearing a three-quarters length, formal gown with a
lace overlay on the bodice. By contrast to the other two models who seemed bored or
distracted, INGER is glowing with a lovely presence, modestly smiling and making eye
contact with her audience who are clearly charmed by her. MARCELLA and OLGA are
in shock. INGER retires backstage as the first model enters wearing a Nile green dress
that is a little too tight. The second model rotates in wearing a dress that is a little too
dramatic or perhaps she is a little too serious. And finally INGER reenters wearing a very
simple satin, full-length gown which is off the shoulders. There are audible reactions to
INGER and the Countess's daughters spontaneously walk on to the stage to touch the
gown and ask questions of the charming INGER

OLGA (to MARCELLA)

Well, this seems to be going well.

MARCELLA

Yes. You'll need to train another dresser.
I'm taking Inger with the other girls to
London next trip.

INT. LIMOUSINE TRAVELING IN SAN FRANCISCO - DAY

German General Consul Hauptman "Fritz" WEIDEMANN is in the back seat
accompanied by Herb CAEN, journalist

                    WEIDEMANN
          Germany lost its best and brightest young
          men in the Great War. The land was left
          desolate and its people were bitter and hu-
          miliated. I was a Captain and Private Hitler
          was in my command. That was over twen-
          ty years ago. Now I may only serve my
          country in this exile.

                    CAEN
          You had a falling out with Hitler?

                    WEIDEMANN
          No. We rarely had a disagreement about
          policy and never in public. I only question-
          ed his methods occasionally. He had no
          patience for the delicate business of di-
          plomacy. And I questioned blaming any
          group or race of people for our internal
          problems.

                    CAEN
          It sounds to me like you had too many
          questions.

                    WEIDEMANN
          You'll know better than to print that,
          won't you.

                    CAEN
          Of course.

                    WEIDEMANN
          Herb Caen, do you love your country?

                    CAEN
          Yes, I suppose so.

WEIDEMANN

I don't suppose, I know I love my country.
It pains me to be abroad when I could be
making a difference at home.

CAEN

Well, I can think of worse places to be
exiled. And, if your hobnobbing with the
social elite of this town at the finest restaurants in San Francisco is any indication,
you seem to concur.

WEIDEMANN (chuckles)

Hobnobbing- it's a funny word. But as
Consul General it is my business to be in
touch with the politically influential. Your
articles referring to me seem to hint of
drunken debaucheries.

CAEN

Yes, hint only. I don't cross the line and
accuse. You see, my readers prefer juicy
rumor to dry fact. In my own twisted way,
I think I'm depicting you sympathetically.
San Franciscans identify with, and even
cheer, a little debauchery.

WEIDEMANN

I'll agree with you about two things: San
Francisco is a beautiful city and you are
twisted.

CAEN chuckles. WEIDEMANN sees GEORGE walking on the sidewalk and addresses
the driver

Hans, pull over for a minute.

The limousine comes to a stop and WEIDEMANN steps out to get GEORGE'S attention

WEIDEMANN

Georg! Gehst Du in den Club? (subtitle)
George! Are you going to the club?

GEORGE

Ja, Herr Weidemann. (subtitle) Yes, Mr.
Weidemann

WEIDEMANN

Kann ich Dir helfen? Ich kann sehen, Du
hast dein Deutsch doch geuebt. (subtitle)
Let me give you a lift. You have been
practicing your German.

GEORGE

Ja, mit dem Norwegisch braucht ich noch
Hilfe.(sutitle) Yes, but my Norwegian needs
work.

WEIDEMANN

Oh?

WEIDEMANN follows GEORGE into the back of the limousine and the vehicle pulls
away

George, this is Herb Caen of the San Francisco Chronicle. Mr. Caen, this is the young
speed skater, George Wallace.

CAEN

I've heard of you. Curley Grieves called you
the fastest man west of the Mississippi. I
didn't know there were any ice skaters west
of the Mississippi. I'm strictly a baseball,
football, basketball man myself.

WEIDEMANN

In Europe speed skaters are worshipped
athletes. This is the fellow you should be
writing about, not me.

CAEN

Let's explore that possibility. Have you been
scandalous in any way, George?

GEORGE

I don't think so.

                    CAEN
Then I'm not interested. What are you doing
in the city?

                    GEORGE
Weight training. Even if the Olympic Games
are called off next year, the Norwegians have
invited me to join them again for several
world cup races in Norway, Latvia and
Austria.

                    WEIDEMANN
Really?

The vehicle comes to a stop

Well, here we are. Are you sure you won't
join us, Mr. Caen?

                    CAEN (as GEORGE gets out)
No, no. I break into a sweat at the thought
of exercise.

                    WEIDEMANN
Fine. Just tell Hans where to drop you.

WEIDEMANN closes the car door and it pulls away

Wait up, George! Tell me about your travel
plans.

                    GEORGE
The Norwegians have made all of the arrangements.

                    WEIDEMANN
George, if the Olympic Games are cancelled
and America gets into this war... Well, an
American moving about in Germany...
it could be complicated.

                    GEORGE
But I'm a speed skater. I have nothing to
do with politics.

                              WEIDEMANN
              You're an American first. Nothing else will
              matter.

                              GEORGE (finally)
              Athletes have only a short time. I'm in my
              prime. I must skate now.

                              WEIDEMANN (finally)
              I'll write a letter to the German Consulate
              in Oslo. Carry a copy of it with you, it
              might help.

They go into the Olympic Club

INT. A COMMERCIAL AEROPLANE IN FLIGHT - DAY

INGER and MARCELLA are seated together in front of the two other models. All are
wearing heavy coats as the plane is not heated effectively or pressurized. INGER is air sick

                              MARCELLA
              Well, I think it's wonderful that you host
              poor, inner-city German children in the
              spring. Give them a chance to get out of
              the cramped, smoky neighborhoods,
              breathe fresh air and run and play. And,
              most importantly, eat healthy food. Food
              harvested from the earth is what makes
              kids strong, not that green, globby stuff
              you get out of a can. My God, I can barely
              recognize what it is supposed to be. Oh,
              dear, you don't look well. (looking in her
              handbag) Perhaps if you chewed a chocolate
              it would equalize the pressure in your ears.

Declining the chocolate, INGER seems to be turning green. She looks to the back only to
find the restroom occupied

              Oh, dear, there's someone in the restroom.
              Perhaps we can find a paper bag.

In desperation, INGER finds the first container she can get her hands on (MARCELLA'S
hat box) and throws up in it

Or my hat box will do.

EXT. THE ANNE CURIES SANITARIUM, OSLO - DAY

Exhausted, GEORGE steps up onto the large, snow covered deck of the sanitarium, a three storied building. He drops his heavy duffle bag and suitcase. GEORGE looks back over the steep steps below and shakes his head, breathing heavily. He finally picks up his bag and suitcase and steps inside

INT. THE SANITARIUM - DAY

A big sweeping staircase empties into a den/living room where two older men are playing cards next to a window. To the right is a dining room area. The plump, middle-aged Mrs. BJORN enters from the kitchen and puts something behind the counter in the dining room and exits without noticing GEORGE. UTE, a woman in her mid-thirties descends the staircase and immediately notices GEORGE. She is attractive but strangely exotic in her heavy eye makeup and evening wear. She approaches GEORGE dramatically

                    UTE
          Are you a guest here?

                    GEORGE
          I may be a tenant. Is there a manager or
          someone who could show me a room?

                    UTE (meaningfully)
          You have to see Mrs. Bjorn.

Mrs. BJORN enters again, sees GEORGE with UTE, assumes an expression of concern, and crosses quickly to them

                    BJORN
          Good morning. I am Mrs. Bjorn. May I
          help you?

                    GEORGE
          Yes, I may rent a room, if one is available.

                    BJORN
          Surely. You can put your things behind
          the counter there and follow me upstairs.
          Ute, would you be a dear and sort the mail.
          Thomas left it out front on the reception
          desk.

GEORGE (depositing bag)
This isn't the front?

BJORN
No. Oh, dear, you didn't walk up the back trail, did you?

GEORGE
Yes.

BJORN
It's too steep in the snow, how did you manage?

GEORGE
With difficulty.

UTE is standing there checking GEORGE out

BJORN
Ute, the mail...?

UTE smiles and exits

This way, Mr...?

GEORGE
Wallace. George Wallace.

Mrs. BJORN leads GEORGE upstairs

BJORN
Where is your home?

GEORGE
America.

BJORN
I thought so. Texas?

GEORGE
No. California.

                        BJORN

Good. There are several third floor rooms
to choose from. A silly superstition has it
that the third floor is haunted.

                        GEORGE

Really?

                        BJORN

Yes, isn't that foolish. The service elevator
at the end of the hall creaks and groans,
someone falls out of a window... Well, it's
enough to fuel imaginations about ghosts.
(unlocking a door) Here we are. This has a
spectacular view of the fjord as you can see.
And at night the lights of the city are at your
feet. I'll charge you a very competitive price
but I'll need a substantial deposit, identifi-
cation, and a copy of your visa.

                        GEORGE

Very well, thank you. Mrs. Bjorn, I assumed
that this sanitarium was a, sort of, health resort.

                        MRS BJORN

Yes, it was, sort of. But now there are no
other services offered but the room and two
meals a day; a continental breakfast and
supper. I'll have Thomas bring up your
luggage right away.

She exits closing the door behind her. A moment later there is a knock at the door.
GEORGE answers and UTE enters past him carrying linen

                        UTE

I've brought the bedding.

She proceeds to make the bed

                        GEORGE

There's no need for that. I'll make my own
bed.

UTE

As you wish. My name is Ute.

GEORGE

George.

UTE (crossing to door)

George, will you be joining us for the evening meal?

GEORGE (smiling vacantly)

I guess so.

UTE (meaningfully)

Good. We'll talk then.

UTE closes the door slowly. A terse, whispered argument ensues on the other side of
GEORGE'S door, then silence. A moment later, a loud knock

GEORGE

Come in.

THOMAS, a large, bald man in his late thirties enters and abruptly drops GEORGE'S
luggage on the floor

THOMAS (challenging)

I'm Thomas. Ute is my girl.

GEORGE (vacant smile)

You make a lovely couple.

THOMAS scowls and stomps out, slamming the door behind him. GEORGE sinks to
sitting on his bed

INT. ANDERSON'S CLOTHING STORE, OSLO- DAY

MARCELLA'S office, late afternoon. INGER enters

MARCELLA (at desk)

Are we locked up?

INGER

Yes.

                    MARCELLA
Do you have a moment to sit?

                    INGER (sitting by desk)
Certainly.

                    MARCELLA (getting wine)
Don't tell your father that I offered you wine.

                    INGER (smiling)
Of course not, Mrs. Anderson.

                    MARCELLA (pouring)
Dear, if we are going to drink wine together,
please call me Marcella.

                    INGER
Thank you, Marcella.

                    MARCELLA
I wanted to thank you for all of your hard
work and companionship this past week.

                    INGER
I quite enjoyed myself, except for the flight
back to Stockholm.

They giggle and sip

                    MARCELLA
I'll never wear that hat without thinking of
you.

They laugh, sip, a beat

                    INGER
How are your travel plans to Italy pro-
gressing?

                    MARCELLA
Not well. What with Herr Hitler panzering
around Europe and those street thugs
posing as police in Italy, I'm afraid travel
has become not only expensive but dangerous.

INGER

Oh. I read only a little of a newspaper in
London but I didn't realize...

MARCELLA

Yes, the war seems to be expanding. Maybe
Germany and Italy will team up to become
Europe's problem children. (drinks) I'm
afraid for my family in Florence. God, I
miss the last war. The victorious were restrained and the vanquished were treated
with respect. At least, it seemed that way.
In those days the war never bothered my
husband, Curt. He had many friends and
they had many friends both in Germany
and France. "We'll sell cotton and canvas
to whoever wins this damn thing," he
would say. And we did too. I miss his
strength. (drinks) Now if war comes, I
don't know what will happen.

INGER

Why would the Germans make trouble for
you? You have many important clients.
Surely the Royal Family would intervene
on your behalf.

MARCELLA

If war comes to Norway, the Royal Family
will have its hands full protecting the government from dissolution. The Germans will
take what they need from private industry.

INGER

Papa says that they would leave civilians
alone.

MARCELLA

In so far as it suits them. But they will
maintain garrisons of soldiers here. They
will bleed us of our labor and goods. They
will bleed us of our profit and our spirit.

The worried expression on INGER'S face transitions to:

INT. THE TRAM RIDE HOME - DAY

The worried expression remains on INGER'S face as she sits in the front of the tram. The tram makes another scheduled stop and GEORGE steps onto the tram at the back door, sits. He is in sweats with an equipment bag and skates over a shoulder. The tram is crowded. An old woman gets on at the next stop and stands, holding on to an overhead strap. GEORGE offers the old woman his seat and, standing, notices INGER in the front, still deep in thought. GEORGE is fascinated by the beautiful but sad young woman. Several stops later, more people are getting off than on as the tram leaves downtown and into residential areas. A seat empties next to INGER. GEORGE is determined to strike up a conversation with her. He catches sight of his reflection in the glass and starts to comb his hair with his fingers and tuck in his tee shirt. The tram stops again and GEORGE loses his balance a little and the skates and bag fall from his shoulder. He scrambles to get the bag and skates. The tram starts again and he almost loses his balance again. Suddenly he is aware that the beautiful girl is no longer on the tram. He searches for her through the windows, forces open the back door and jumps off the moving tram. He lands on wet tram tracks, slips and comes down hard on bricks, cutting his cheek on a skate blade. The tram comes to a stop and the OPERATOR gets off of the tram and approaches GEORGE. Two concerned PEDESTRIANS help the dazed GEORGE to his feet

                    OPERATOR
          Look here, are you all right?

                    GEORGE
          I think so.

                    PEDESTRIAN ONE
          You don't look all right to me, your cheek
          is bleeding.

GEORGE dabs his cheek with his sleeve and is looking for INGER

                    OPERATOR
          You frightened me jumping off the tram
          like that. You're supposed to wait until it
          comes to a complete stop. You can get
          seriously hurt doing what you did.

                    PEDESTRIAN TWO
          I thought he cracked his gourd.

                    GEORGE (looking around)
          I'm sorry, I missed my stop. Did anyone see
          the girl who got off just before me?

                                    PEDESTRIAN ONE
What?

                                    OPERATOR (returning to tram)
Be more careful next time.

                                    GOERGE
Did you see a beautiful girl?

                                    PEDESTRIAN ONE
Girl? No.

PEDESTRIAN ONE and TWO walk off together

                                    PEDESTRIAN TWO
Maybe he did crack his gourd.

                                    PEDESTRIAN ONE
He certainly took a thumping.

GEORGE continues to look around and just misses INGER as she descends down
concrete steps

INT. THE SANITARIUM - DAY

GEORGE is writing at his small table under the window. A bang on the door startles
GEORGE

                                    GEORGE
                  Come in.

THOMAS walks in without acknowledging GEORGE and drops fresh linen and towels
on the bed. THOMAS turns on his heels and starts to walk out

                                    GEORGE
                  Thomas, do you have a minute?

THOMAS stops without looking at GEORGE

                  I think you are under the impression that
                  I am your rival with regard to Ute. And
                  that is simply not the case.

A beat

THOMAS

Good.

THOMAS starts to leave again

GEORGE

Wait a minute. You said that she was your
girl. But for a week now, I have rarely seen
the two of you together. At supper you
barely even talk to her.

THOMAS

So?

GEORGE

So you two don't act like a couple. Does
she know she's your girl?

THOMAS

What do you mean?

GEORGE

Well, I could be way off here. You might
be a real romantic guy when you are alone
with her...

THOMAS (quickly)

That's none of your business.

GEORGE

Of course, I only suspect that you have
deep feelings for Ute. Am I right?

THOMAS

So?

GEORGE

Do you tell her as much?

THOMAS

She knows.

GEORGE

Yes, but women like to be told in differ-

ent ways. They like romance. You've got
to be romantic.

                    THOMAS
What are you, an expert?

                    GEORGE
No, but it's not hard to tell that women like
things like flowers and chocolate?

                    THOMAS
Ute doesn't like chocolate.

                    GEORGE (incredulously)
What's wrong with her?

                    THOMAS
Nothing is wrong. She's different, special.

                    GEORGE
There, that's perfect. Just say that. She
would love to hear that she is special to you.

                    THOMAS
That's stupid, like play acting. She'd laugh.

                    GEORGE
Well, you don't have to try to sound like
Ronald Coleman. Look, we're getting off
the track here. Let me start again. Do you
think she's pretty?

                    THOMAS
She's beautiful.

                    GEORGE
Do you ever tell her that?

THOMAS is silent

Bring her flowers and tell her that she is
beautiful.

THOMAS (hesitating)

She'd laugh.

GEORGE

She might not. Don't rehearse anything.
Just be yourself and let her know how
wonderful she is.

THOMAS (moving to door)

Flowers, huh?

GEORGE

Tell her how you feel.

THOMAS (opening door)

She better not laugh.

GEORGE

She won't.

THOMAS closes the door behind him. GEORGE goes back to his little table. Through the window he sees UTE walking up the road with a covered wicker basket. GEORGE sees THOMAS enter the garden and pick a small handful of blossoms. THOMAS waits for her

GEORGE (to himself)

Don't laugh, he'll kill me.

THOMAS says something and hands her the blossoms. Her reaction is one of surprise. She then kisses THOMAS lightly on each cheek and they walk to the front of the building, arm in arm, with smiles. GEORGE turns back into the room with a sigh of relief. Then he wonders if there isn't a lesson in this for him with regard to the beautiful woman on the tram

EXT. FROGNER STADIUM, OSLO - DAY

The drinking song from Verdi's "La Traviata" blares from stadium speakers as skates crack down rhythmically on the ice. GEORGE absentmindedly skates the track. OLIE Hagen, the Norwegian coach is standing by with MISHA, his plump female assistant. OLIE is shaking his head in disappointment. A blank expression on GEORGE'S face transitions to:

INT. ON THE TRAM - DAY

The music continues as GEORGE is daydreaming of his encounter with INGER. She is seated in the front of the tram. She looks back at GEORGE and gives him a coquettish smile. GEORGE moves to her confidently and sits next to her. It is difficult for her to hide her adoration. She touches his skates delicately. The tram stops. INGER very slowly rises and moves to the front door. She steps down, turns to GEORGE and blows him a sensual kiss. She is gone. GEORGE stands and runs, crashing through the back door in a head first dive. This transitions to:

EXT. FROGNER STADIUM, OSLO - DAY

Music out. GEORGE has fallen on the track. OLIE, with MISHA, skates to GEORGE and helps him to his feet

                         OLIE
          Are you all right?

                         GEORGE
          Yes, Olie. I don't know how I fell.

                         OLIE
          Where do I begin? In the first place, you're
          chopping at the ice like an American sprinter.
          Knock it off! Extend those strokes. Lengthen
          them, don't speed them up, just yet. And stay
          on the out-side edge of your skates. You're
          skating like a knock-kneed hockey player.
          The inside edges are for pushing off. And
          your balance is way too high. Bend your
          back and spread out on the ice a little. Keep
          your head down and your mind (slaps
          GEORGE on the forehead) on your skating!
          Any questions?

                         GEORGE
          No.

                         OLIE
          Good. Give me eight laps. And concentrate!

GEORGE skates off

                         MISHA
          Lots of talent.

OLIE
And no technique.

INT. ON THE TRAM, OSLO - DAY

GEORGE is seated in the back of the tram, skates and gym bag on his lap when he notices INGER seated up front. GEORGE musters his courage and goes to sit across from her

GEORGE
Hello, my name is George.

She nods curtly to him and looks back in the direction of travel

Perhaps you recognize me from the other day
on tram. Actually it's more likely that you
would remember me getting off the tram.
(chuckling) I fell on my head and caused
quite a stir. I'm fine, though. I fall on my
head all of the time. (chuckling)

INGER stands to get off as the tram pulls to a stop. GEORGE stands

Oh, I'm getting off here as well. Perhaps
we could walk together for a while?

She is not happy about his proposal. They get off the tram

INGER
Do you live around here, Sir?

GEORGE
Uh, George. No, I rent up there at the sanitarium.

INGER
I see. And you fall on your head frequently.

GEORGE
I'm a skater...

INGER
You should have gotten off the tram two
stops ago.

                    GEORGE
I enjoy walking…

                    INGER (challenging)
Are you following me, Sir?

                    GEORGE
No, not like that...

                    INGER (firmly)
I do not wish to be escorted.

                    GEORGE
Fine. I wasn't making any assumptions,
Miss. Where I come from a gentleman may
speak to an interesting woman until she
refuses his attentions. You have made
yourself clear. As I am annoying you, I'll
not bother you again..

                    INGER
Thank you, Sir

                    GEORGE (softly)
Uh, George.

GEORGE turns to leave and takes a few steps

                    INGER
        George.

GEORGE turns to her

        Perhaps I've been less than gracious. My
        name is Inger.

                    GEORGE
It's a nice name.

                    INGER
If you would like to walk with me for a
while, you may.

GEORGE
May I also buy you a cup of tea at the shop
over there.

INGER
Coffee for me, and I'll buy my own.

He smiles at her and they walk

EXT. FROGNER STADIUM - DAY

The "La Traviata" music again. Several skaters are working out on the track. GEORGE is
skating with a determined look on his face. His strides are long and smooth which seems
to be pleasing OLIE and MISHA, who are timing him with watches. GEORGE makes his
final turn and sprints to the finish. He coasts, hands on knees, breathing heavily

MISHA
Did you get what I got?

OLIE and his MISHA compare the times on their stop watches

OLIE
Close enough. One month to go before the
Riga and Vienna meets. If he keeps this up,
he'll have a shot at a world record.

INT. THE FRONT ROOM, DAHLBERG HOUSE - NIGHT

GEORGE is seated across from BERGIN, INGER'S father and her older brother,
CLAUS and brother in law, HENRIK, both drinking beer. GEORGE is waiting in silence
for INGER. He is dressed in formal attire

GEORGE (finally)
You have a nice home here.

Silence

CLAUS
All Americans are rich. Are you rich?

GEORGE
No. I mean, my family owns some land but
I don't think we're rich.

                    BERGIN
          Are they farmers?

                    GEORGE
          Well, they grow grapes for wine and have
          some horses so I don't know if you can
          call them farmers or not.

                    BERGIN
          You don't know if they are farmers or you
          don't know what farming is?

ERICA, INGER'S older sister, wife to HENRIK enters from the hall with her very young
daughter, SONYA by her side

                    ERICA
          She'll be down in a minute. Henrik, you
          didn't offer Mr. Wallace a refreshment?

                    HENRIK
          He refused.

                    GEORGE (quickly)
          I only meant that I wanted to wait for the
          champagne at the restaurant.

                    BERGIN
          My daughter doesn't drink.

                    GEORGE
          Well, then we'll have soda or something
          else with supper.

Silence

                    ERICA
          How nice.

INT. THE BALLROOM OF THE HOTEL BISLETT, OSLO - NIGHT

A mirror ball and bright wall sconces light a crowded dance floor. GEORGE and INGER
are dancing to a slow ballad played by a small orchestra on stage. INGER is giggling

                    INGER
A fish that is like a cat?

                    GEORGE (smiling)
No, not really. But catfish do have whiskers.

                    INGER
Now you're telling traveler's tales to a
gullible girl.

                    GEORGE
I am completely serious. My grandmother
is the queen of catfish catchers.

                    INGER
They sound too cute to eat.

                    GEORGE
Her secret was rancid chicken livers.

                    INGER
Lovely.

                    GEORGE
And they smelled even worse. But to catfish,
the aroma was like...

                    INGER
Chocolate cake?

                    GEORGE
Thank you, like chocolate cake. They go
into a large wash tub of water for two days
and add a little corn meal. The catfish would
eat the corn meal and this would clean them
out of all bad tasting things like algae and...

                    INGER
Hair balls.

                    GEORGE (grinning)
And hair balls. And soon they were ready
to cook. But one day my younger sister
tried to pet them.

                    INGER
Did they purr?

                   GEORGE
Apparently so because by the time she was
finished they all had names. And everyone
knows you can't eat something that you
name. So my grandmother and my sister
took the catfish back down to the river and
let them go.

                    INGER
How sweet.

                   GEORGE
That's my grandma. You'll love her. Someday you'll meet her. But don't pet the catfish.

INGER chuckles, they continue to dance

EXT. THE WALK HOME - NIGHT

There is much snow and ice on the ground for the middle of March. Both GEORGE and
INGER have heavy over coats, gloves and rubber over shoes or boots. GEORGE is
straddling the pipe rail of a set of descending concrete steps. He slides down the rail on
his belly, hanging on to the pipe. He hits the landing area and falls on his rear. INGER
laughs. She is a little intoxicated and holding on to an almost empty bottle of champagne

                    INGER
Here I come. Wait, I can't do both.

She drains the little bit of champagne in the bottle and puts it down

                   GEORGE
Your Father said you didn't drink.

                    INGER
I don't. I sip like a Lady.

                   GEORGE
Just don't fall off that rail and crack your
skull like a Lady.

                              INGER
See here, Mister, I was raised in this ice
and snow, skiing and skating since I was
that high. You are just a pretender, raised
in a desert.

                              GEORGE
..not exactly a desert.

                              INGER
So shut up and prepare to catch me.

She slides down the rail and GEORGE catches her. She is laughing. GEORGE is helping
her off the rail and on to her feet. He holds her, her hands on his chest

Now see here, Mister, I've heard all about
men like you preying on unsuspecting
young women.

                              GEORGE
You are certainly a young woman but hardly
unsuspecting. Why don't you tell me all
about men like me. Wait. Check this out.

GEORGE crosses down to the next flight of steps that is longer

We would have to be fools to slide down that.
We could get hurt.

                              INGER
I agree.

                              GEORGE
Responsible adults would resist the temptation.

                              INGER
I'm resisting.

                              GEORGE
Mature people do not take unnecessary risks.

GEORGE jumps on the rail

But I can't help myself!

And down the rail he goes, landing at the bottom with a thud. He is motionless on his back

                    INGER
          George!

She scurries down the steps and kneels at his side

          George?

GEORGE opens one eye

                    GEORGE
          It's not good. I'm going to need mouth to
          mouth resuscitation.

                    INGER (relaxing)
          Thank God you've only fallen on your head
          again.

                    GEORGE (points at his chest)
          Here's where it really hurts. You've stolen
          my heart.

                    INGER
          I have one of my own. What would I want
          with yours'?

                    GEORGE
          Then give it back, you fiend!

They wrestle playfully for a moment

          Oh, no.

                    INGER
          What is it?

                    GEORGE
          I've ripped my pants.

INT. THE FRONT ROOM, DAHLBERG HOUSE - NIGHT

GEORGE is seated with a quilt over his legs. INGER is just finishing sewing the back seat of his trousers. BERGIN is standing by

                              INGER
          Here you are.

INGER turns her back on GEORGE as he puts his pants on under the watchful eye of BERGIN

                         BERGIN (retiring)
          It's late.

                              INGER
          I'll just see George out, Papa.

INGER throws the quilt over her shoulders. GEORGE crosses to the mud room to put on his over coat and boots. INGER is smiling

                              GEORGE
          What's so funny?

                              INGER
          The look on Papa's face.

They chuckle

                              GEORGE
          When can I see you again?

                              INGER
          I'm hosting my first batch of German child-
          ren starting next week. Would you like to
          go cross country skiing with us?

                              GEORGE
          Yes.

GEORGE gives her a quick little kiss on each cheek and then a little longer kiss on the mouth

          I'll see you soon.

He leaves with a smile on his face. She turns back into the mud room, charmed by him

EXT. CLEARING IN THE FOREST NEAR OSLO - DAY

GEORGE waits in the snowy clearing as a hay wagon comes up the wet road. HENRIK is at the reins of a large horse. Next to him sits ERICA who waves at GEORGE as they approach. INGER is in the back of the wagon with four children. Three are inner-city German children; JAN (pronounced "yawn"), a thirteen year old, rather stoic boy, his ten year old brother, MAX and their seven year old sister, EFFIE who sits holding hands with SONYA. HENRIK brakes the wagon and GEORGE walks to the back

                         INGER
            Hello, George. Boys, this is my friend who
            will be coming with us. This is Jan and his
            brother, Max. Effie will be staying with
            Erica and Sonya.

                         EFFIE
            Hurray!

                         INGER
            They have become good friends.

                         SONYA
            Effie is my best friend!

                         INGER
            Excuse me, they have become best friends.

                         HENRIK (to GEORGE)
            Let's get the sleigh off-loaded. Weather is
            coming in pretty fast.

                         ERICA
            I'm worried, Inger. Maybe we all should
            turn back.

                         INGER
            If the weather gets bad, we'll stay in the
            cabin until it clears.

                         GEORGE
            My God, this sleigh is heavy! What's on
            it?

                         HENRIK
            Skiing gear, sleeping bags, firewood, food
            and white gas- all the comforts of home.

GEORGE ties a short rope to the sleigh and loops it around himself to pull it

> INGER
> The cabin is two miles up the trail. Are you
> boys ready?

> JAN
> Of course we are.

> INGER
> Then let's go.

INGER hugs ERICA and the four hikers depart

EXT. ON THE STEEP TRAIL - DAY

The snow is coming down heavily

> INGER (to GEORGE)
> I've never seen a heavier storm this late in
> March. Little Max is having difficulty. His
> feet are sinking too deep.

> GEORGE
> If you can help me with the sleigh, I'll carry
> Max.

> INGER
> Yes. Jan, stay close to the sleigh.

EXT. ON THE STEEP TRAIL - DAY

The wind is whipping up the falling snow into a "white out" condition. The hikers are
having to shout to one another

> INGER
> I can't see! It's getting too dangerous to
> go on!

> GEORGE
> Let's take cover in that stand of trees!

They move to the trees

This may not let up before dark! Take
these small lower limbs down and we'll
make a shelter!

EXT. UNDER THE TREES - NIGHT

They have fashioned a simple "lean to" over a big bed of tree limbs at the base of a large
tree. GEORGE has built a fire and the boys are tucked into their sleeping bags around the
fire. GEORGE is seated with his back against the tree trunk, his legs in his sleeping bag.
He is tending the small fire. INGER is just settling into her sleeping bag

                    INGER
        I gave them cookies. They'll sleep now. The
        weather looks like it's breaking. We should
        be safe here tonight.

                    GEORGE
        Thanks for being so brave.

                    INGER
        It's not my first snow storm.

                    GEORGE
        Still, I know a lot of debutantes in San
        Francisco who would go hysterical in a
        situation like that.

                    INGER
        You know a lot of them, do you? I think
        you are a regular Casanova.

                    GEORGE (arm around her)
        You are wrong.

                    INGER
        I don't think so. Look how casually you
        just put your arm around me. I think that
        takes practice.

                    GEORGE
        Maybe I'm just comfortable around you.

                    INGER (smiling)
        Shut up, you smooth operator.

96

GEORGE chuckles, INGER gets a little more comfortable with her head on his chest and gazes into the fire

EXT. UNDER THE TREES - NIGHT

The fire has burned down to flickering light on their faces in an indication of a passage of thirty minutes or so

> GEORGE
> My Father was an only son. He always had
> a passion for traveling. He talked about the
> places he wanted to go. But he could never
> get away. The property kept him busy. He
> married and helped raise the three of us.
> But the drudgery of the ranch made him
> grow old quickly. And I watched the pas-
> sion die. He wasn't depressed. He just
> became a regular guy. And then he became
> a regular old man. And someday he'll die,
> never having achieved his dream. Who will
> remember him other than his kids?

> INGER
> Are you afraid of being a regular guy?

> GEORGE
> No. I'm pursuing my dream. In the next few
> weeks I'll have a chance to set a new world's
> mark in the fifteen hundred meter race.
> If I do that, then my name will always be in
> the record book. Even when my record is
> someday broken, I will always be in the book.
> It's a kind of immortality. That's silly, I guess.

> INGER (hand on his cheek)
> No, no it's not. And maybe your Father just
> traded one dream for another. As long as
> you love him, he may look into his child-
> ren's eyes and see a bit of his own immortality.

A beat when GEORGE appreciates what she has said

> GEORGE
> Thank you.

A romantic kiss

                            INGER
              Good night.

INGER rolls over and zips up her sleeping bag. There is just enough light from the fire to
watch GEORGE realize that he is in love with her

INT. KITCHEN, DAHLBERG HOUSE - DAY

INGER is at the sink washing dishes. She is also searching through the window for the
Postman. JAN and MAX are seated on one side of the kitchen table and EFFIE and
SONYA are seated on the other. They are finishing their lunch of sandwiches, milk and
cookies

                            EFFIE
              May I have a cookie?

                            INGER
              I'm sorry, honey, there are none left. I'll
              make more this afternoon.

                            JAN (admonishing EFFIE)
              You've already had a cookie.

                            SONYA
              I'll share my cookie with you, Effie.
              (breaking the cookie) Here, you take the
              biggest half.

                            EFFIE
              Thank you, Sonya.

EFFIE looks at her disapproving oldest brother and is a little intimidated by him. INGER
sees the Postman while this is happening and scurries outside to get the mail. Through the
window we see them exchange pleasantries. INGER is excited to find a letter from
GEORGE. She comes up the front steps, into the mud room and opens the letter

EXT. ICE SKATING STADIUM, RIGA - DAY

This is a silent scene. GEORGE'S VOICE OVER reading of his letter to INGER from
the previous scene will be heard throughout this Riga scene.

GEORGE is racing the clock with one other man on the track in the one thousand meter race. OLIE and MISHA are checking their stop watches and shouting (silently, of course) at GEORGE as he passes by. GEORGE looks determined and checks the stadium clock on his final lap. GEORGE is clearly ahead of the other man on the track but, as he is racing the clock, GEORGE sprints at the end. His time is good enough to win first place. As he celebrates with OLIE, his joy is mitigated by the fact that it was not a world record performance. During all of this:

> GEORGE'S V.O.
> Dear Inger- I have won two races at the
> Riga meet. The team captain is planning
> a big celebration in town tonight. Then in
> the morning we take trains all the way
> down to Vienna. I wish we could fly but
> the Nazis are not allowing many commer-
> cial flights over Germany these days. Oh,
> well. By now, Mother has sent those letters
> I asked for to the U.S. State Department.
> Now, getting your visa to America should
> be a mere formality. But take care of the
> paper work right away. If this war gets any
> worse, it could mess up our plans for your
> visit to the States. The Vienna meet is
> scheduled for April ninth, my birthday.
> Olie says that the indoor ice there will be
> my best opportunity for a world's record.
> Wouldn't it be something to set the mark
> on my birthday? I'm not sure when we'll
> get into Vienna. I'm told they stop and
> search the trains often and that the food
> at the stations are terrible. We will be liv-
> ing on bundles of food we brought from
> home. I'm munching on one of your
> cookies as I write this. I miss you very
> much. If all goes well, I'll see you in a
> little more than ten days. Love, George

INT. A BAR IN RIGA - NIGHT

Long tables in a crowded bar/restaurant. A lively string ensemble with percussion has the Norwegian team dancing with local girls. The song ends with a big finish and the team and others join GEORGE, OLIE and other skaters at a long table. Another tray of pints is delivered and distributed with cheers from the celebrating skaters

                    TEAM CAPTAIN (toasting)
To our generous, and in some cases, quite
beautiful Latvian hosts (girls giggle).
To our coach, Olie Hagen, an evil but
wise task master. (cheers and laughter)
To our adopted Yank and new one thousand and fifteen hundred meter champion,
George Wallace. (cheers) To my team,
to everyone skating today in a fine world
cup event, congratulations all!

Big cheers and drinking. DORIS sits next to GEORGE and OLIE. She is older than
GEORGE but very sexy

                    DORIS
So you're the new champion,
huh?

                    OLIE (leaving)
I'm going to find Misha.

                    DORIS (offering her hand)
My name is Doris.

                    GEORGE (shaking hands)
George.

                    DORIS
I just love skaters. They have such stamina.

                    GEORGE
Well, if it's stamina you want, talk to the
ten thousand meter guys..

                    DORIS
No, I like you.

DORIS drinks deeply from her pint and licks her lips lasciviously. GEORGE swallows
hard and sips his pint

So what are you doing this evening?

                    GEORGE (sipping again)
Celebrating.

DORIS

No, I mean after. Would you like to come
to my flat for a little rest?

GEORGE

I'm sorry, the dialect here is a little different
from the Norwegian. I'm not sure I understand you.

Under the table DORIS squeezes the inside of GEORGE'S thigh

DORIS

I think we understand each other just fine.

MISHA appears on the opposite side of the table

MISHA (angrily)

So I leave you alone for five minutes to
check on the kids and you try to get
lucky with one of the locals?

DORIS (to MISHA)

Sorry. I didn't know.

MISHA

Well, you do now!

DORIS (leaving)

You should have told me, George.

MISHA casually walks around the table and sits next to GEORGE

GEORGE

The kids?

MISHA

You looked like you were trying to do the
right thing. I just thought I'd help.

GEORGE (smiling)

Here, help me with this too.

GEORGE slides his pint in front of her. She smiles and drinks

INT. ON THE TRAM, OSLO - DAY

April 9, 1940. INGER is riding home after work when everyone on the tram hears a loud explosion in the distance. The tram is slowly coming to a scheduled stop when another explosion is heard

                              YOUNG MAN ON TRAM
                         That's coming from the airport!

Two more explosions are heard, then a third. The tram stops and many get off with INGER. They look up and see a formation of bombers overhead. Many are crying and running. INGER runs to the concrete steps and down, headed for home

INT. ICE SKATING ARENA, VIENNA - DAY

April 9, 1940. Under huge flood lamps, GEORGE and another skater in his own lane ready themselves for the start of the thousand meter race. OLIE and MISHA, with stop watches, anxiously wait for the start as the Norwegian team shouts encouragements to GEORGE. The starter's pistol fires

EXT. FRONT OF THE DAHLBERG HOUSE. OSLO - DAY

Still running, INGER sees BERGIN at the top of the house stairs. He comes down to meet her

                              BERGIN
                    The Germans are bombing the airport. The
                    invasion has begun.

BERGIN holds his weeping daughter as HENRIK, ERICA and little SONYA pull up in an old pick-up

                              ERICA (running to BERGIN)
                    Papa, the Germans are coming up the fjord
                    in a big warship!

                              BERGIN
                    Yes, they will be moving quickly now.

INT. ICE SKATING ARENA, VIENNA - DAY

GEORGE is making a turn. He is well ahead of the other skater

                    MISHA (checking her watch)
He's got a chance!

                         OLIE
Yes, it's a very good time.

The Norwegian team is cheering as is most of the crowded arena

EXT. FRONT OF THE DAHLBERG HOUSE, OSLO - DAY

BERGIN is holding his two tearful daughters when, over his shoulder, INGER is startled
by the appearance of JAN, MAX and EFFIE dressed in uniforms of the Hitler Youth;
khaki pants or skirt, collared white shirt, red scarf with a swastika on a white field.
SONYA is happy to see EFFIE and moves to her

                         SONYA
Effie!

                    EFFIE (like-wise moving)
Sonya!

                    JAN (ordering)
Effie! Max, take her hand.

                    ERICA (quietly)
Sonya, come here.

The little girls obey but don't understand. They are very hurt that they have been pulled
away from one another

                    JAN (announcing)
We are proud children of the Hitler Youth.
We are to report to your judicial building to
receive a new billet and further instructions.
You are ordered to accommodate us. We
require transportation.

A long pause

                    HENRIK (to BERGIN)
I suppose I could give them a ride.

                         BERGIN
Good. Get them out of my house.

INT. ICE SKATING ARENA, VIENNA - DAY

The crowd is cheering madly as GEORGE makes the last turn

> MISHA (holding watch)
> He's got it, Olie! He's got it!

Suddenly, inexplicably, GEORGE falls. The crowd groans in their disappointment/sympathy. GEORGE scrambles to his skates to finish the race but his hopes of a world record in the last race of the season are dashed. In despair, he puts his hands on his knees and coasts, head down

EXT. FRONT OF THE DAHLBERG HOUSE - DAY

The German children are loaded into the pick-up. SONYA and EFFIE are crying. As the pick-up pulls away, EFFIE sadly waves goodbye to her dear friend

INT. AMERICAN CONSULATE, VIENNA - DAY

The American CONSUL and his younger CLERK are packing cardboard boxes. GEORGE looks very anxious

> GEORGE
> But can't you even make an inquiry?

> CONSUL
> Yes, we can file an inquiry. And the
> German High Command might even get
> around to it in three weeks. Please get
> out of the way.

GEORGE moves out of the way and the CONSUL carries a large box to the door and returns with an empty box and starts to pack more books and papers

> GEORGE
> May I at least place a telephone call to her?

> CONSUL (packing)
> You haven't been listening to me, Mr.
> Wallace. This is no longer a working office.
> We have been ordered to withdraw. We
> don't have telephones. This place will pro-
> bably have swastikas hanging on the walls
> within the week.

104

                           GEORGE
Then I have no choice but to travel back up
with the team to get her. I should be able to
send a telegram to her from any of the larger
hotels, right?

                           CONSUL
Wait a minute. You think going back up
through Germany is a good idea, Mr. Wal-
lace? Let me tell you that it is plain stupid.
In fact, as I am American Consul until five
PM today, I order you not to travel into
Germany. (to CLERK) Make a note of that
order. When does our ship sail?

                           CLERK
In ten days, sir.

                      CONSUL (to GEORGE)
In ten days the passenger liner USS Man-
hattan will be sailing for New York out of
Genova. She may be the last one out of the
Mediterranean for some time. I suggest you
book passage. Please get out of the way.

CONSUL exits past GEORGE with another full box

                           CLERK
He's right. The U.S. could be in this fighting war soon. American citizens should
maintain low profiles now in Europe and
should not be traveling in Germany.

                           GEORGE
If I just knew she was safe. If I could just
talk to her.

                           CLERK
Banks and the German Military Headquarters
here in Vienna are sure to have working
international telephone lines.

                      GEORGE (exiting)
Thanks.

CLERK (calling after him)
I hope you're going to a bank. Because
going to the German Military Headquarters isn't exactly low profile!

INT. GERMAN MILITARY HEADQUARTERS, VIENNA - DAY

A large, impressive office. GEORGE is standing in front of the desk. Major WENZEL is
seated, reading a letter, then looks up at GEORGE

WENZEL
Consul Wiedemann suggests that we assist
you in any way we can. You are an American skater?

GEORGE
Yes. Norway was kind enough to host my
stay here in Europe. We have ended our
tour of competitions here in Vienna and
have learned only today that Germany has
invaded Norway. I guess that is none of my
business except that my fiancé is a Norwegian girl in Oslo. We understand that
there was bombing in Oslo. I would like
to know, first, if she is safe. And then if I
could bring my bride home to America.
We would need to travel back down
through Germany and sail home out of
Genova.

WENZEL
Does she have her visa to America?

GEORGE
She should have her visa by now.

WENZEL
Currently America is still a neutral country.
Your visa papers allowing you to travel
in Germany are in order. (he hands letter
and papers back to GEORGE) But your
fiancé is a citizen of an enemy country.
This could be a problem. But if she has her
American visa and she was traveling with

106

her American husband, a twenty-four hour
travel visa through Germany might be ar-
ranged.

>   GEORGE
> Thank you. May I telephone her to give her
> this information?

>   WENZEL
> Do you have the numbers?

>   GEORGE (producing paper)
> Yes.

>   WENZEL (on the telephone)
> Corporal, place a call as instructed by Mr.
> Wallace and patch it into this telephone.
> (he hangs up) Give your paper to the man
> at the switch board. You'll take your call
> in here.

GEORGE exits. WENZEL lights a cigarette. George re-enters

>   GEORGE
> Thank you, Major.

>   WENZEL
> Don't thank me yet. A lot can go wrong.
> Telephone lines could be down.

A minute later the telephone on the desk rings. WENZEL picks it up

> Yes?...For Major Wenzel. Thank you, I'll
> hold...Be quick, we cannot have this line
> for long.

WENZEL hands the telephone to GEORGE

INT. SPLIT SCREEN: GEORGE/INGER AT HOME - DAY

>   GEORGE
> Hello?

                    INGER

Hello, George?

                    GEORGE

Inger! Are you all right?

                    INGER

Yes.

                    GEORGE

Thank God. I was so afraid.

                    INGER

I'm fine. How was your world cup meet?

                    GEORGE

That doesn't matter. Listen to me, we don't
have much time. The USS Manhattan sails
for America in ten days out of Genova.
I've booked passage. Do you have your
visa yet?

                    INGER

Yes, but I didn't think we we're going for
another month.

                    GEORGE

Listen to me, darling, I know we were talking about a visit to meet my family but...
this morning when I thought you could be
hurt or even killed, I realized how much
you mean to me. I love you very much,
Inger. (she is crying)

INT. GERMAN MILITARY HEADQUARTERS, VIENNA - DAY

WENZEL has opened his office door to see the soldier at the switch board chuckling as
he eavesdrops on GEORGE'S call. WENZEL crosses to him

                    WENZEL

Go get some coffee, soldier.

The soldier raises his coffee cup and takes a sip and remains seated

Take a break, Corporal!

The soldier takes off his headset and walks away

INT. SPLIT SCREEN: GEORGE/INGER - DAY

> GEORGE
> The truth is, I don't want to take the chance
> of losing you again. The truth is, I don't
> want you to visit my home to meet my
> folks. I want them to meet my wife. (she
> is crying) So, I'm coming back to Norway
> with the team. We could marry in Oslo or,
> if we were pressed for time, we could
> marry on the trip down or we could marry
> on the ship. Ship Captains can do that,
> can't they? I mean, it's legal and every-
> thing, isn't it?

> INGER (still crying)
> George, shut up. The answer is yes.

> GEORGE
> Well, I'd say you made me the happiest man
> in the world but you're still over a thousand
> miles away.

> INGER (holding her heart)
> No. You're right here with me.

The line goes dead

INT. GERMAN MILITARY HEADQUARTERS, VIENNA- DAY

> GEORGE
> We were disconnected.

> WENZEN
> I warned you to be quick.

> GEORGE
> Thank you, Major Wenzel.

WENZEL
Be careful, Mr. Wallace.

INT. ANDERSON'S CLOTHING STORE, OSLO - DAY

In MARCELLA'S office. MASRCELLA is on the telephone, INGER is seated reading a
letter

MARCELLA (on telephone)
Everyone's check will be ready on schedule.
But there is just no point in keeping the store
open with no one on the street. Let's see
what happens over the next few weeks... No,
Olga, it's a time to be with your family.
We'll worry about the business later... Yes,
I am... Be safe, my friend. (she hangs up)

INGER
I understand some of this but this Italian is
so different.

MARCELLA
Yes, the southern dialect is different and my
Father's hand writing is atrocious.

INGER
There was something about a new land tax
being levied.

MARCELLA
Yes. The federal thieves are requiring large
ransoms for property that has been in families for generations. If the tax is paid, fine.
If properties are forfeited, even better.

INGER
Can you help them?

MARCELLA
I have the money but it may not be safely
sent or even wired, for that matter. The
fascists run the banks and all public services.
I have sent word to old friends of the family.
They will help. I only hope their help comes

in time. The foxes are in charge of the hen
house and they are hungry.

INGER carefully considers what she is about to say

> INGER
> George and I will be in Genova by the middle
> of the month. Florence is only a few hundred
> miles south. Maybe I can take the money to
> your family.

> MARCELLA
> No, absolutely not. It would be too dangerous.
> It would have to be cash and too difficult to
> hide. If the Germans don't find it, the Italian
> police will.

> INGER
> Please, it's the least I can do for you.

> MARCELLA
> No, I will not ask you to endanger yourself.
> You have your whole life ahead of you. I will
> trust in old family friends. They will help us.

> INGER
> Marcella, you are my dear friend, as close
> as my own family. You say you will not
> ask me to put myself in danger but we are
> all in danger. And all we can do is help
> one another. Maybe you cannot ask me
> but I can make the offer. Please, before it
> is too late, don't refuse me.

Pause, they hug one another

INT. ANDERSON'S CLOTHING STORE, OSLO - DAY

INGER is walking around MARCELLA'S office in a beautiful gown, rich in color and
texture. High boots, a full length coat and a fur hat complete the ensemble

> MARCELLA
> How does it feel?

                    INGER

A bit like walking around with a pillow between my legs. How does it look?

                    MARCELLA

If you mean, does it look like you're smuggling thousands of lira, I would have to say no.

                    INGER

Well, then?

                    MARCELLA

Well, then.

INT. ON THE TRAIN, BERLIN- DAY

GEORGE, OLIE, MISHA, the Norwegian team and German civilians are stopped at a
station in Berlin. Soldiers are checking passengers' travel papers and searching luggage.
A German CAPTAIN is looking at GEORGE'S papers

                    CAPTAIN

You are American?

                    GEORGE

Yes.

                    CAPTAIN

You are traveling alone?

                    GEORGE

No, my visa says that I am with the Norwegian skating team.

                    CAPTAIN

I am looking at your passport. Just answer
my questions. Why do you travel with these
people?

                    GEORGE

My visa... I am a skater too. I am their guest.
We are returning to Norway.

                    CAPTAIN

Your second time through Germany?

                              GEORGE
Yes.

                              CAPTAIN
And yet your passport has been stamped
only once.

GEORGE has no answer

                               OLIE
He was admitted as a member of our team.

                              CAPTAIN
You lied for him?

                               OLIE
No.

                              CAPTAIN
So, Mr. Wallace, you must have lied.

                              GEORGE
No. It wasn't an issue.

                              CAPTAIN
Is this your camera?

                              GEORGE
Yes.

                              CAPTAIN
And what do you take photographs of?

GEORGE'S patience is wearing thin

                              GEORGE
Skating events.

                              CAPTAIN
I'll need to confiscate it. Stay where you
are. Do not get off of the train. (confidentially to GEORGE) I know you're
a spy.

The CAPTAIN leaves. There is much hushed conversation among the passengers

> GEORGE (wondering aloud)
> Why would he accuse me of being a spy?

> OLD MAN (finally)
> You are an American. You travel back into
> Germany when you could have left. There
> is no business in Germany. There is no plea-
> sure, only spying.

Suddenly, an SS LIEUTENANT appears with two army regulars in helmets, carrying
bayoneted rifles

> LIEUTENANT
> Mr. Wallace?

> GEORGE
> Yes.

> LIEUTENTANT
> I'm afraid your papers are not in order. This
> may only be an administrative oversight.
> But it will take us several days to authentic-
> ate documents and verify your activities.
> Meanwhile, you will be treated as our guest.
> Please come with us.

> GEORGE
> This is absurd. What about my letter from
> Wiedemann?

> LIEUTENANT
> Yes, all of your materials will be returned to
> you after our questions have been answered
> satisfactorily. Please gather your things.

GEORGE does so. The TEAM CAPTAIN steps toward the LIEUTENANT

> TEAM CAPTAIN
> You can't do this!

One of the soldiers lowers his bayonet

                              OLIE
No!

                    LIEUTENANT (calmly)
I can't? No, I'm sure I can. And if you try
to prevent me from doing my duty, I can
arrest you. And you will not be treated as
a guest.

The TEAM CAPTAIN sits. The SS LIEUTENANT, soldiers and GEORGE start to leave

                            GEORGE
Olie, tell Inger what happened. Tell her it
will only be a few days. Tell her!

                              OLIE
    Yes, George.

The train whistle blows and they have taken GEORGE away

Note: The next nine scenes are a montage, edited in the order indicated. All scenes can be
as long as twenty seconds, silent, and underscored by the "preludio" from Verdi's "La
Traviata". It is played by a string quartet or by a single instrument such as a violin, piano,
or oboe

EXT. HISTORICAL BLACK AND WHITE FOOTAGE OF NAZI ARMORED
VEHICLES RACING ACROSS AN OPEN FIELD - DAY

INT. FRONT ROOM, DAHLBERG HOUSE, OSLO - DAY

MISHA and OLIE are explaining what happened to GEORGE on the train in Berlin.
INGER is in shock

INT. SS INTERIGATION ROOM, BERLIN - NIGHT

An exasperated GEORGE is pacing the small room, telling his story, once again to two
men, one in civilian clothes and one SS Officer

EXT. HISTORICAL BLACK AND WHITE FOOTAGE OF NAZI SOLDIERS FIRING
FIELD ARTILLARY - DAY

INT. FRONT ROOM, DAHLBERG HOUSE, OSLO - DAY

INGER is crying on MISHA'S shoulder as OLIE stands by

INT. SS INTERROGATION ROOM, BERLIN - NIGHT

GEORGE is seated at a table listening to the SS Officer and the civilian. GEORGE is responding to them with yes or no answers

EXT. HISTORICAL FOOTAGE OF HITLER RIDING IN AN OPEN CAR, WAVING TO CROWDS - DAY

INT. KITCHEN, DAHLBERG HOUSE, OSLO - DAY

INGER is staring out the window. She is making her decision to go to Berlin

INT. SS INTERROGATION ROOM, BERLIN - DAY

GEORGE is staring out a high window at a grey sky. He is contemplating his situation

EXT. THE TRAIN STATION, OSLO - DAY

INGER'S family and MARCELLA are there to see her off. INGER is dressed plainly but formally as is CLAUS, who will travel as far as Stockholm with her

> MARCELLA (hugging INGER)
> Thank you, Inger. Here, I want you to take
> this as well. (she produces cash) This is to
> pay for your brother's return trip and for
> you to stay in the best hotels. In Italy they are
> the safest.

> INGER
> Thank you, Marcella. I will write to you when
> I have met your family.

Next to hug and kiss INGER is her sister, ERICA. Both girls are in tears. INGER then gives little SONYA kisses on both cheeks. INGER'S brother HENRIK hugs and kisses his sister goodbye and then shakes CLAUS'S hand. Finally INGER'S Father, BERGIN steps forward. He is silent for a moment. He reaches into his pocket and produces a small gold medallion with gold chain

> BERGIN
> Here, take this.

> INGER
> No, papa. That was your gift to mama. You
> should keep it.

BERGIN

Listen to me. It was your mama's dream to
see you get married. Wear it on your wedding day and we'll both be there.

INGER takes it, cries and hugs her Father. The train whistle blows. CLAUS gently pulls
INGER away from BERGIN. They board the train. A teary INGER waves goodbye
through the window as the train pulls away

INT. ON THE TRAIN, HAMBURG - DAY

Pulling into the Hamburg station. INGER is wearing the traveling ensemble that she
modeled for MARCELLA and she is smuggling cash. INGER is seated in the back of the
car filled with civilians. As the train slows to a stop, a rumor seems to be spreading from
the front of the car to the back. She hears the word, "strip". She turns to a WOMAN she
is seated close to

INGER

What are they saying?

WOMAN

They are strip searching foreigners at the
station.

INGER is now in a panic. The train is stopped and she is not gathering her belongings
like everyone else is doing. She looks out the window and a German officer is screening
passengers. As most have German identifications, they are being directed into the station.
Foreigners are being directed to a long table attended by the German military, both male
and female. Behind the table are changing rooms marked "male" and "female". INGER
starts her mantra under her breath, gathering her two suitcases. She is last in line to exit
the train

INGER (softly)

I am beautiful in these clothes. I enjoy
wearing them. I belong in them. I am beautiful in these clothes. I enjoy wearing them.
I belong in them.

WOMAN (turning to INGER)

Did you say something?

INGER

No.

INGER pulls a large denomination bill out of her shoulder bag and gives it to the porter by the exit

> Would you be so good as to carry these suit-
> cases for me?

As the porter has just been handed a huge tip, he is delighted to carry her two suitcases. INGER stands at the exit, closes her eyes and whispers her mantra

> I am beautiful in these clothes. I enjoy
> wearing them. I belong in them.

EXT. THE TRAIN STATION, HAMBURG - DAY

INGER steps down the stairs of the train, the porter following her with the suitcases. She is beaming with a lovely smile. She is quite transformed from the frightened woman to a vision of beauty and grace. She offers her passport to the Officer. He doffs his cap before taking the document. He politely directs her to the foreigners' line in front of the long table. She is transcending the experience. She is drawing attention to herself. By comparison, everyone else is seriously focused and depressed. She approaches the table. The porter puts the suitcases on the table, wishes her a good day and leaves

> INGER (to military)
> Excuse me, but is all this (referring to the
> dressing rooms) really necessary?

The ranking OFFICER at the table is clearly impressed by her obvious wealth and stature and defers to her

> OFFICER
> We'll only need to search the Lady's lug-
> gage.

> INGER
> Thank you.

She gets the attention of a STATION PORTER who, with others, was watching her already. He approaches. She hands him a large denomination bill

> Would you please take these cases when
> these ladies and gentlemen are finished and
> find me in the station. I'll be traveling on to
> Berlin.

STATION PORTER

Yes, madam.

And she walks grandly into the station

INT. GERMAN MILITARY HEADQUARTERS, BERLIN - DAY

A small, basement room. INGER, in a black skirt and jacket, stands before a uniformed, LARGE WOMAN seated at a desk. She is reviewing INGER'S papers

LARGE WOMAN (checking clock)

You have only thirteen hours left on your
travel visa.

INGER

Yes. That is why it is imperative that I see
my husband right away.

LARGE WOMAN

Your husband?

INGER

Is he under arrest?

LARGE WOMAN

No. They are only questioning him.

INGER (patiently)

May I see him?

LARGE WOMAN (finally)

Wait here.

LARGE WOMAN exits down a hall. Minutes pass torturously for INGER. At last the SS LIEUTENANT who took GEORGE off the train enters

LIEUTENANT

You are Inger Dahlberg?

INGER

Yes.

LIEUTENANT

Are you married to Mr. Wallace or not? He
says, no. You say, yes.

119

                    INGER
We are engaged.

                  LIEUTENANT
More ambiguity. Mr. Wallace has made an
illegal entry into this country. Are you aware
of that?

                    INGER
No.

                  LIEUTENANT
Mr. Wallace's visa says that he skates in
Europe "unattached". And yet the Norwegians list him as a team member. Do
you know what "unattached" means?

                    INGER
His own country did not sanction his com-
peting here.

                  LIEUTENANT
Why is that?

                    INGER
I don't know. But he has done nothing
wrong.

                  LIEUTENANT
We will determine the nature of his activi-
ties. At this time, he is not charged with
any crime. But you can see the difficulties
we are facing here. When half-truths are
brought to light, we wonder about the
veracity of all that we are being told. You
may see Mr. Wallace now. Your five
minute visit will be supervised. Do you
understand?

INGER nods yes

Come with me.

He leads her down the dimly lit hall and opens a door. GEORGE jumps to his feet when he sees INGER and they run into each other's arms

                    GEORGE (finally)
How did you get here?

                    INGER
You booked my ticket on the USS Manhattan in my name. That and my American visa was enough. Four days, George. We only have four days before the ship sails.

                    GEORGE
Yes, I know, don't worry, I'll be there. Wait for me on board. (he looks to the SS LIEUTENANT) If something should happen, sell those tickets and wait for me in Milan. We'll be all right.

                    INGER
George, I don't understand. What did you do?

                    GEORGE
Nothing. I took photographs from inside the train. It was just rural farmland but they have issues with it.

                    INGER
Oh, George.

                    GEORGE
Don't worry, darling. They allowed me to write to my Mother. I'll be getting help.

                    INGER (teary)
George, I'm so afraid!

                    GEORGE
Don't be. Please, darling, you'll have to be strong. I'm no spy, you know that. Soon they will have no choice but to let me go.

                    LIEUTENANT (grabs her elbow)
All right, that's enough. Let's go, Miss.

                    INGER
But you said five minutes.

                    LIEUTENANT (pulling her out)
That will be enough.

                    GEORGE
Wait for me. I'll be there. You believe me,
don't you?

                    INGER
Oh, George!

                    GEORGE
Wait for me!

                    INGER
Yes!

The SS LIEUTENANT slams the door behind him and walks her out to the small room

            You didn't post George's letter to his
            Mother, did you. George is not a spy,
            you know that don't you.

                    LIEUTENANT
            There are no spies. There are only bus-
            inessmen and tourists, teachers, artists
            and, perhaps, athletes who pass on or sell
            information to the enemy. Good day, Miss.

He leaves her. She walks out of the building under grey skies and cries

INT. TRAIN STATION, GERMAN-ITALIAN BOARDER - DAY

INGER is wearing her travel ensemble. She has cleared customs and is in line to board
another train. Across the big, tiled lobby in one of the telephone booths against the wall,
ANTONIO, a handsome, well-dressed Italian man, places a call

                    ANTONIO (on telephone)
            Mr. Cagliari, please.. Mr. Cagliari, I found
            her. I heard the ticket agent call her Dahlberg.

She's coming down to Milan, just as you
guessed... Very good, Sir, I'll keep an eye
on her.

EXT. TRAIN STATION, MILAN - DAY

As INGER'S suitcases are being loaded into the trunk of a taxi, she notices a lovely, two
toned coupe across the street. ANTONIO gets in to drive. In route to the Hotel de la
Luce, she notices the coupe following her taxi. In front of the Hotel, the coupe parks
three car lengths back of her taxi. A bell man runs out to get her luggage. She is attracting
much attention, not only for her elegant attire but for her blondish hair which is in
contrast to the mostly dark haired people of Milan. Again, she notices the coupe and the
man driving who appears to be reading something.

INT. HOTEL DE LA LUCE - DAY

INGER is registering at the Hotel Lobby desk. In the mirror behind the desk, she sees
ANTONIO looking at her over his newspaper. When she looks around, he pretends to
read. The AUDITOR hands her key to the bell man

                    AUDITOR
          Room two twelve. Thank you, Madame.

                    INGER
          Thank you. One thing more, I am expecting
          no one and I am not to be disturbed this
          evening.

                    AUDITOR
          Yes, Madame.

INGER follows the bell man up the stairs. She stops behind a pillar at the top of the stairs
and then peers around it. ANTONIO is conversing with the AUDITOR. He makes a note,
hands the AUDITOR cash and thanks him before leaving. A look of concern crosses
INGER'S face

EXT. OUTDOOR CAFÉ, MILAN - DAY

The next day at an outdoor café across from the Hotel de la Luce, EMILIO Cagliari, a
distinguished Italian man in his sixties and his fifty-ish wife, MARIA, sit sipping
espressos at a table. INGER, in a light blouse and skirt, crosses the street to the café

                    EMILIO
          Be patient. Let's get a little of her trust first.

Here she comes. Ask her to take our picture.

INGER gets a few "wolf" whistles from young men on the street. She approaches the tables of the café

                    MARIA (to INGER)
        Excuse me, young lady, would you mind
        taking our photograph?

                    INGER
        Not at all.

                    MARIA (handing her camera)
        Just look through that thing and push the button.

                    INGER
        Yes.

INGER takes the picture and hands the camera back

                    MARIA
        Thank you. My name is Maria and this is
        my husband, Emilio.

                    INGER
        Nice to have met you. I'm Inger.

                    MARIA
        From Norway?

                    INGER
        Why, yes.

                    MARIA
        I thought so, such a lovely accent. Would
        you care to join us for coffee?

                    INGER
        Thank you.

EMILIO gets the waiter's attention who crosses to the table

                    EMILIO
        Another coffee, sweet rolls and fruit. (waiter

exits) You must forgive those young dogs
on the street. It may be true what they say
about Italian men but Italian gentlemen, at
least, have manners.

INGER
They are young boys who will grow to be
gentlemen, I'm sure.

MARIA (to EMILIO)
As gracious as she is lovely.

INGER
Thank you.

The waiter brings the order

MARIA
Where do you plan to travel in our country,
Inger?

INGER
I'm going to Florence today.

MARIA
What a coincidence, we are too. Have you
ever been to Florence?

INGER
No.

MARIA
You must see the art museums. Florence is
the most beautiful city in Northern Italy.
(confidentially) I have to make that distinc-
tion or Emilio will protest. Sicilians think
their home is the most beautiful place in
the world.

EMILIO (smiling)
It is.

MARIA
There, you see? Emilio, might we offer

Inger a ride to Florence? (to INGER) We
are driving down in our automobile.

                    INGER
No, I couldn't impose.

                    MARIA
But it's not an imposition, is it, Emilio?

                    EMILIO
Of course not.

                    INGER
Well, if you are sure.

                    MARIA
It would be our pleasure. Here is our car
now.

The two toned coupe pulls up on the street and ANTONIO gets out and crosses to their
table

                    EMILIO
Inger, this is Antonio. He is like a son to me.

Unaware that INGER has "made" him, ANTONIO smiles and offers his hand. INGER
smiles faintly and shakes his hand

                    EMILIO
When shall we depart?

                    MARIA
If we are finished with breakfast, that is really
up to Inger.

                    INGER (nervously)
I need to shop at the pharmacy and back to
my room to pack. Shall we say, an hour?

                    MARIA
Fine. We'll pick you up at the Hotel.

As casually as she can, INGER withdraws, crosses the street and enters the pharmacy
next to the Hotel. Through the window she watches the three of them in discussion. They

get in the car and leave. She exits the pharmacy, goes into the Hotel and crosses to the lobby desk.

                    INGER (to AUDITOR)
          I'll be checking out right away. Please send
          a man up for my things and call a taxi for
          me. I'll be going to the train station.

INT. TRAIN STATION, MILAN - DAY

INGER sits in a corner of the station, suitcases by her feet. She looks up at the clock on the wall. Suddenly she sees ANTONIO enter the station. She grabs her cases and hides behind a support pillar. She spots an exit door a few feet away and exits the station. She crosses a parking lot, a street, into an alley which empties into a neighborhood. She sees a little restaurant and ducks into it. It is a small place with only a few tables. An older couple are near the back. She sits, suitcases by her feet. An old man, the PROPRIETOR, approaches her

                    PROPRIETOR
          Just got off the train, huh? What can I get
          for you, Miss?

                    INGER
          A menu?

                    PROPRIETOR (gives menu)
          The scallops are very good.

The PROPRIETOR withdraws behind a counter. Three policemen walk in. POLICEMAN THREE stands at the front door as POLICEMAN ONE and POLICEMAN TWO sit at INGER'S table

                    POLICEMAN ONE
          Excuse us. We saw you coming out of the
          station. You had the look of someone who
          had just stolen something. I'm never wrong
          about these things.

                    INGER
          I've stolen nothing.

                    POLICEMAN TWO
          Are these your bags?

                    INGER (afraid)
Of course.

                    POLICEMAN TWO
Mind if we have a look?

                    INGER
I have done nothing wrong.

POLICEMAN TWO puts one of her suitcases on a table behind her. The older couple
gets up and leaves. POLICEMAN THREE locks the front door behind them and turns the
open sign around to read closed from the outside

                    POLICEMAN THREE
Go wash your dishes, old man.

The PROPRITOR reluctantly leaves the dining room. POLICEMAN TWO pulls a slip
out of the suitcase, sniffs it and smiles. POLICEMAN THREE grins at this

                    POLICEMAN ONE
What is it, then? Something was wrong. I
always know.

                    INGER (hesitates)
I was hiding from someone.

                    POLICEMAN ONE
Ah, I knew it. Who were you hiding from,
a husband, a boyfriend?

POLICEMAN TWO has continued to smell her clothes

                    POLICEMAN TWO
I think we should take her into the back
room and search her.

POLICEMAN THREE grins at his suggestion. Suddenly EMILIO enters from the back
of the restaurant with a big smile on his face. A very serious ANTONIO follows EMILIO
in

                    ELILIO (animated)
There you are! Your Aunt has been crazy
with worry. You shouldn't wander about a
city that you don't know. Thank God these

fine policemen were here to protect you.
(shaking POLICEMAN ONE'S hand) I
am Emilio Cagliari and I want to thank
each of you personally.

At the mention of the name CAGLIARI, the policemen get very serious and focused

                    POLICWEMAN ONE
You are Emilio Cagliari?

                    EMILIO (smiling)
Yes.

POLICEMAN TWO closes INGER'S suitcase

                    POLICEMAN ONE
We had no idea she was related.

                    POLICEMAN THREE (to ANTONIO)
Cagliari?

ANTONIO nods solemnly

                    POLICEMAN ONE
We hope there has been no misunderstandings,
Miss.

                    EMILIO (smiling)
I'm sure there won't be. Once again, thank
you.

The policemen almost stumble over one another going out the front entrance. EMILIO
calmly seats himself

Did those criminals hurt you in any way?

                    INGER
No. Who are you people?

                    EMILIO
This was a conversation I was saving for the
trip down to Florence but we may have
gained your trust and now you may believe that we have a mutual friend, Marcella

Luciano. No, she married that textile merchant. Anderson is her name now. But to answer your question, the Cagliaris are one of a few families in Southern Italy who have adhered to and (choosing his words) maintained certain traditions. Governments come and go. But loyalty to family and friends are sacred virtues that have sustained us for hundreds of years. That is why I come to the aid of the Lucianos and why I come to protect you and the money you bring them.

INGER
Thank you. But this money is a ransom. The government will be stealing the money I bring.

EMILIO
Yes. But soon the crimes will be brought to light and reparations will be made. For now, the ransom may prevent bloodshed.

INGER
Couldn't Marcella's family borrow the money from someone like you?

EMILIO
A proud Italian family like the Lucianos would borrow money only as a last resort. It was Marcella's place to help her family if she could. Her cable said she trusted you implicitly. I can see that her trust was well placed. But, tell me, why did you run from us?

INGER
It was Antonio. I was frightened.

EMILIO
Antonio? He's harmless. (standing) I'm confused but it's all right. You can explain on our trip down to Florence.

INGER

Should I go? I mean, can't you take the money to them.

EMILIO

Absolutely not. You honor the family and
Marcella by personally delivering the money.
You will be making life-long friends.

INGER

I see. I must be in Genova by Saturday.

EMILIO

I'll see to it. By the way, where is the money,
in your suitcases?

INGER (sheepishly)

No, I'll explain on our trip down to Florence.

INGER leads the exit out of the restaurant. EMILIO and ANTONIO share a look of
confusion and then follow her

EXT. THE USS MANHATTAN DOCKED AT GENOVA, ITALY - DAY

The large passenger liner is minutes from letting go her lines and departing for the United
States. The ship is carrying three times the number of passengers she is designed to carry.
There is a lot of movement and shouting with last minute preparations. Passengers pack
the gang plank, bands are playing and there are confetti streamers everywhere. In contrast
to all this happiness, an anxious and fearful INGER searches in vain for GEORGE. The
ship's big horns announce their eminent departure and the ship's public address confirms.
INGER has no choice but to go ashore and sell the tickets as GEORGE had instructed.
She pulls the tickets out of her shoulder bag just to be sure she has them and starts down
the gang plank. There is much pushing and shoving. About half way down she gets
pushed into a man. She looks up. It is GEORGE. INGER squeals with joy and throws her
arms around him. The tickets envelope she was holding goes flying out of her hand and
flutters into the water below the gang plank

INGER

George, the tickets!

GEORGE hands her his eye glasses and dives into the water. He is under water for a
while. He finally comes up gasping for air. For a moment it appears that he has failed but
then he thrusts his arm through the surface of the water, the tickets envelope firmly in his
grasp. The crowd on the gang plank cheers

EXT. ON BOARD THE USS MANHATTAN - DAY

The ship is in route. Hundreds of passengers are gathered on and around the fan tail, quietly listening to an Italian radio broadcast. GEORGE (wrapped in blanket) and INGER are among them

                    INGER
What are they saying?

                    GEORGE
They are expecting Mussolini to make a de-
claration of war any time now. If he does before we reach the strait of Gibraltar, the ship
will have to turn back to Genova.

                    INGER
What will happen to us?

                    GEORGE
Probably nothing. But some of these people
are refugees running for good reason. If we
turn back, they are caught.

                    PUBLIC ANNOUNCEMENT
Your attention, please. This is Captain
Chandler. Maritime law requires that the
USS Manhattan remain in Italian juris-
diction until we reach inter-national waters.
That's almost ten miles past Gibraltar there
in the distance or about forty minutes. I
advise you to use this time to secure your
accommodations. Because of the over-book-
ing, many cabins will be doubled up and
some public areas will become sleeping
quarters. Please avail yourselves of the
lockers for private property and see the
Purser to secure valuable items. That is all.

                    GEORGE (to INGER)
I think he is trying to make the waiting less
torturous.

The Italian radio broadcast continues with musical selections. We listen to something like jazz as we watch young Italian men smoke cigarettes and joke with one another. We listen to traditional folk music as we watch an old woman praying the rosary. We listen to a big band selection as we watch children playing around their parents. We hear Doris Day singing a popular song as we watch young lovers staring out to sea. We hear more Italian news when we go back to GEORGE and INGER. She is trying to sleep on a lounge chair. He is eating an apple

INT. BRIDGE, USS MANHATTAN - DAY

Captain CHANDLER, JOHN, his Executive Officer, BILLY, a steward, a radioman and helm (man at the wheel) are on the Bridge

> JOHN (pulling off a headset)
> Skipper, that was navigation. They think we
> are past the I.W. buoy, forty minutes, right
> on the nose.

A small grin crosses CHANDLER'S face

> BILLY
> Captain, can I make the announcement and
> play my Kate Smith?

> CHANDLER
> Just play the song, they'll know what it means.

EXT. ON BOARD THE USS MANHATTAN - DAY

The Italian broadcast is interrupted. A scratchy record plays. It is Kate Smith's moving rendition of, "America, the Beautiful". It isn't long before there are shouts of joy and people congratulating one another all over the ship

> GEORGE (to INGER)
> You know what that means?

> INGER
> We made it?

> GEORGE
> It means Grandma's catfish. We're going
> home.

After what GEORGE has been though this past week, it is impossible for him not to be emotional. And, with others, GEORGE sings full voice with Kate Smith

INT. BRIDGE, USS MANHATTAN - DAY

The next morning, a very serious GEORGE slides the door open on the bridge and steps in

                         GEORGE
          Captain Chandler, do you have a minute?

                         CHANDLER
          No.

                         GEORGE
          Please, sir, it's urgent.

                         CHANDLER
          Billy, go get those kids off of that hatch
          lock. Find their parents (follows BILLY
          out) and keep them off the safety rails!
          And find a hand to square up those tarps!

CHANDLER walks back into the bridge past GEORGE

          What is it, young man?

                         GEORGE
          Well, sir, it's the accommodation. My
          fiancé and I have an eight by twelve foot
          cabin with only one bed.

                         CHANDLER
          It's a perfect accommodation for a young
          couple. You're lucky to have a cabin at all.
          Many men are sleeping in the gym.

                         GEORGE
          It's not really the accommodation, sir.
          We're not married yet. She's a very tra-
          ditional young lady. And I'm trying to
          be a gentleman but it's going to become
          impossible for me to guarantee my success
          in that little room.

CHANDLER sees INGER leaning over the rail just off of the bridge

CHANDLER

Is that her?

GEORGE

Yes, sir.

CHANDLER

I see what you mean.

GEORGE

I'm not getting any sleep, Captain. All I
can think about... All I want to do is get...
the few minutes of your time that it will
take to marry us.

CHANDLER

No. Get off of my bridge, can't you see
that I'm busy? Billy, go get the X.O. and
take this. (hands Billy a cup) Tell Cookie
that I want something close to coffee.

GEORGE

Please, Captain, it's a health and welfare
issue. It's about my sanity. We can skip
the ceremony, I just need the legality. It's
very important to the lady.

CHANDLER picks up a hand held microphone and flips a few switches for Public
Announcement

CHANDLER ON P.A.

Your attention, please. This is the Captain.
Would the parents of the children playing
on the safety rails in the bow, please come
and supervise their safe removal.

JOHN walks on to the bridge

JOHN

What's up, skipper?

CHANDLER

This guy needs to get married. It's an emergency.

                    JOHN

Well, that's not too difficult. I'll need to log
you in. You'll need to provide your passport
and your passage paper work. Do you have a
wife in mind?

                    GEORGE

Yes, she's just outside.

                    JOHN

Excellent choice. We'll need her paper work
too.

INT. BRIDGE, USS MANHATTAN - DAY

CHANDLER, JOHN, Radioman, Helm, GEORGE and INGER. BILLY comes running
in with coffee and a book

                    BILLY

Is this it, Captain?

                    CHANDLER (opens book)

Yes. Let's take a look. Burials at sea,
christenings, hangings, I haven't had to
use that one yet. Here we are, weddings.
Civil service good enough?

                    GEORGE

Fine.

                    CHANDLER

Do you, George Wallace...

                    INGER

Wait!

She goes into a pocket and produces the medallion her Father gave to her

George, would you put this on me?

GEORGE puts the necklace on and clasps it in the back. When she turns to him, he sees
his lovely bride in his mind's eye, complete with a white veil. She sees her handsome
husband to be in a tuxedo. They both hear organ music and the soothing voice of a
MINISTER (VOICE OVER) as well as CHANDLER'S voice

136

MINISTER V.O.	CHANDLER
Do you, George Wallace	Do you, George Wallace
take this woman to be	take this woman to be
your lawfully wedded wife	your lawfully wedded wife
to have and to hold, from	What the hell? (he picks
this day forward, for bet-	a com line) Engine room,
ter or worse, for richer	what happened?... Fine,
or poorer, in sickness	keep me posted. (to JOHN)
and in health until death	A pressure line broke.
do you part.	Well, do you?

GEORGE

I do.

MINISTER V.O.	CHANDLER
And do you, Inger	And do you, Inger
Dahlberg, take this man	Dahlberg, take this man
to be your lawfully wed-	to be your lawfully wed-
ded husband. To have and	ded husband... (sips his
to hold, from this day	coffee, spits it out)
forward, for better or	This stinks! Here, stand
worse, for richer or	there while he makes more.
poorer, in sickness and	Make damn sure he doesn't
in health until death	use dish water. Well, yes
do you part?	or no?

INGER

I do.

MINISTER V.O.	CHANDLER
I now pronounce you	You are legally married.
man and wife.	Get off of my bridge.

GEORGE and INGER walk outside and the organ music swells. We draw back to include
a beautiful view of the ocean as they kiss passionately and romantically.
Finally, this appears on screen:

> George never skated competitively again.
> But he distinguished himself it the field of
> photography. He worked with Edward
> Weston and Ansell Adams. He invented
> and patented photographic instruments and
> processes.

Inger modeled for a while in the U.S. The couple became accomplished ballroom dancers.

Eventually, they settled on the Central Coast of California where their marriage flourished with over sixty children, grandchildren and great-grandchildren. And still counting...

A FRESNO STORY

EXT. FRESNO, THE BUSY FARMER'S MARKET ON SATURDAY - DAY

Spring, 1927. FATHER is carrying his son, four year old ARAM Basanian, on his shoulders. He is holding ARAM'S hands so he doesn't fall backwards. MOTHER is walking next to him. She is pushing a stroller in which the infant MICHAEL is wrapped in a blanket. There is a trio of musicians (stringed instruments) playing a lively Armenian folk tune and FATHER is dancing a little to make the "ride" fun for his son. MOTHER is smiling as do all who see Father and son dancing. ARAM is having the time of his life bouncing on FATHER'S shoulders. ARAM looks up at the swirling sky of clouds and is very happy

EXT. A NEIGHBORHOOD BOARDERING RURAL FRESNO - DAY

Spring, 1935. Eleven year old ARAM, straddling his bicycle, is looking up at the clouds in an afternoon sky. He puts two fingers in his mouth and whistles loudly. Seconds later TOBY peers over his backyard fence

> TOBY
> Hey, Aram!

> ARAM
> Toby, go get Jake and Chui and tell them to
> bring their gunny sacks.

> TOBY
> OK.

TOBY runs off. ARAM'S little brother, eight year old MICHAEL approaches ARAM from behind

> MICHAEL
> Where are you guys going, Aram?

> ARAM
> None of your beeswax.

> MICHAEL
> Can I come too?

> ARAM
> No.

Eleven year old VARTAN rides up on his bicycle

> VARTAN
> I don't know, Aram, them apricots don't look
> too ripe.

139

ARAM
They're ripe enough.

MICHAEL
You guys going to steal apricots? Let me
come too, Aram, I can be your look-out!

ARAM
No! And you better keep your mouth
shut too.

TOBY and two other boys on bicycles join the small group

Let's go.

The boys ride off. MICHAEL runs after them

ARAM (over his shoulder)
Go home, Michael!

MICHAEL continues to run even though he can't keep up with them. In the distance he
sees the boys turn right on a rural road and MICHAEL cuts across an empty field to try to
catch up

EXT. A DIRT ROAD NEXT TO THE OACHARD - DAY

ARAM
Let's get our bikes out of sight.

The boys walk their bikes in to the shade of a tree

EXT. RURAL HOUSE IN FRONT OF THE ORCHARD - DAY

MICHAEL stops running in front of the house. He doesn't see ARAM or the other boys
but notices KIYOTO, an eight year old Japanese girl sitting on the porch. They look at
one another for a moment, then she points toward the orchard. MICHAEL smiles at her
and runs into the orchard

INT. RURAL HOUSE IN FRONT OF THE ORCHARD – DAY

Buddy, a large dog, hears the boys in the orchard and is scratching the door of the
screened porch to get out. ITO Imada, a middle aged Japanese man and his slightly
younger Japanese wife, KIYO, walk out onto the porch

KIYO
What is it, Buddy? What's wrong, boy?

ITO
Sounds like kids. They're pretty young, too.
(chuckles) They sound like they're having a
good time. Well, they'll only take a few.

140

KIYO

Now, Ito, those little thieves will grow
up to be big thieves. Take the dog.

ITO (leashing Buddy)

Come on, Buddy.

As soon as the screened door is opened, Buddy bolts at a dead run into the orchard,
breaking the leash

Buddy!

EXT. THE ORCHARD - DAY

The boys are up in tree with gunny sacks. MICHAEL is several yards away and sees
Buddy charging toward them

MICHAEL

Aram, the dog!

The boys shout and drop out of the tree to run out of the orchard. ARAM, who was
highest in the tree, drops down to a limb which breaks. ARAM falls head first onto an
exposed root. He is unconscious with a bloody gash on his head. MICHAEL has stayed
to run with his brother and tries to help ARAM up while the dog is closing the distance to
them quickly. MICHAEL'S impulse to run is as strong as his instinct to protect his
helpless brother. He looks around quickly and picks up a pathetic, little stick to use as a
weapon and cries in his fear as the large, dangerous dog bears down on them

ITO

Buddy!

Buddy whines and breaks his run

Buddy, come here!

Buddy dutifully retreats and ITO secures him on his leash

MICHAEL (crying)

Mister, my brother's hurt!

ITO crosses to look at the unconscious ARAM

ITO

He's breathing. What's your name, son?

MICHAEL

Michael.

ITO

Michael, go to the house and get my wife.

MICHAEL runs. ITO leans down to ARAM and opens an eyelid. ARAM has a vision of his great uncle, MELIK

                                    MELIK
                          Stop crying, Aram. You must be strong for
                          your Mother. You are the man of the house
                          now. Stop it, you must be a man now.

INT. THE IMADA HOUSE - DAY

In a darkened living room, the unconscious ARAM is lying on the couch with a bandage on his forehead. KIYO is putting an ice bag on his head. MICHAEL is sniffling at the foot of the couch. KIYOTO, KIYO and ITO's daughter, crosses to touch MICHAEL on the shoulder

                                    KIYOTO
                          Don't worry. My momma will make him
                          all better.

MICHAEL looks gratefully into KIYOTO's eyes. ARAM gains consciousness and tries to sit up

                                    KIYO
                          Wait, don't try to move just yet. My hus-
                          band has gone to get a doctor…

                                    ARAM
                          No!

                                    KIYO
                          Why not?

                                    ARAM (hesitates)
                          Mom will be mad.

                                    KIYO
                          Why?

                                    ARAM (hesitates)
                          Because we were in the orchard… we
                          were taking apricots.

                                    KIYO
                          You were stealing.

ARAM nods 'yes'

                          And your Mother will be angry with you
                          because you were stealing. Good. How
                          does your head feel?

                  ARAM

It hurts.

                  KIYO

You may need a few stitches but I think
you are going to be all right.

                  KIYOTO

See, I told you my momma will make
him all better.

MICHAEL looks hopefully at a glum ARAM

EXT. THE IMADA FRONT PORCH – DAY

KIYO and MOTHER (late thirties, mother of MICHAEL and ARAM) are seated at a
small, shaded wicker table having iced tea. KIYOTO and MICHAEL enter from inside
the house

                  KIYOTO

Momma, can I show Michael my paints?

                  KIYO

"May I show Michael" Yes, you may
but don't make a mess.

The kids run back inside

        Ito and I met rather late in our lives and
        Kiyoto was a bit of a surprise but a wel-
        comed one, as you can imagine. She has
        been a blessing to us in many ways. When
        we first came here the law would not
        permit us to own land. But Kiyoto was
        born in Fresno, a naturalized citizen. And
        Ito was able to purchase this property in
        Kiyoto's name.

                MOTHER

Thank God.

                  KIYO

Yes, we have been very fortunate. And
Kiyoto will always have a home.

                MOTHER

She's a very sweet child. Michael has been
a little shy with children his own age. But
they seem to get along nicely. Aram, on the
other hand, isn't shy at all. But he can be a
trial. I punished him for stealing the apricots

by not allowing him to play with his friends for a while. But he sometimes sneaks out of the house. He doesn't lie to me directly but I seem to have little control of him.

                    KIYO
The scar on his forehead may be a punishment for some time. It must be difficult to raise boys without a husband. You've done well.

                    MOTHER
They're good kids. But Aram is growing up so fast. I'm afraid for him.

                    KIYO
You've given them a good start.

                    MOTHER
We've done our best, my mother-in-law and I. Takoohi has been a big help in raising the boys and she's been a good friend to me. Although most people find her a bit eccentric.

INT. THE BASANIAN KITCHEN - DAY

TAKOOHI (in her seventies, sister to MELIK, and mother to the dead FATHER of ARAM and MICHAEL) pours milk for eight year old MICHAEL and KIYOTO seated at the table with a plate of cookies between them. The children have been listening attentively to her story

                    KIYOTO
Thank you.

                    TAKOOHI
Where was I?

                    MICHAEL
Your second husband, Grandma.

                    TAKOOHI
Oh, yes, a shorter story. Victor, my second husband, died gallantly defending our home and our people. He was young and brave. But our fighters were no match for the Turks who came up from the desert with their armored machines. Thirty years ago our people fled before their enemy. They fled north into lands held by their Slavic neighbors and still farther north into Russia where they had to eat rotting roots and potatoes to survive.

They fled west into Europe where they weren't wanted and finally they fled to America. But one man refused to flee before the Turks. And do you know who that man was? (the children shake their heads 'no') It was Krikor Basanian- freedom fighter and Scourge of the Turks. He was a tall, rugged looking man with a dashing mustache, fierce in the battlefield and fierce in his love for his people and a woman. And do you know who that woman was? (the children shake their heads 'no') Here, have another cookie. (they do) War is certainly no time to foster romance but Krikor was hopelessly in love with me even though I was no longer a young woman. One day he rode into our village and told my father and brothers of his devotion and of his intention to marry me. No one dared to object. I took pity on him. He swept me into his arms and off to his camp in the mountains. A day later, between battles, we were married with his captains as witnesses. For a few days… for a few glorious days it seemed to us that there was no war, only warm days and moonlit nights. We talked about what our lives might be like without this war. It was like a beautiful dream. But then soon after a nightmare came true. Krikor was ambushed in the valley and he was mortally wounded. His men brought him back to camp and there, lying in my arms with my name last upon his lips, I kissed him. Krikor Basanian, Scourge of the Turks, my third and last husband, your Grandfather and greatest love of my life, was dead. Part of me also died that day but ultimately his spirit gave me the courage to go on. And so today I live in America. But I shall never forget the man who fought for our home and loved me with his last breath.

TAKOOHI finishes with the aplomb of an experienced story teller. The children are quietly impressed

EXT. EXPANSIVE VIEW OF RURAL FRESNO COUNTY - DAY

Traditional Armenian folk music (stringed instruments) underscores views of vineyards, citrus groves, cotton and alfalfa fields. This transitions to view of a brand new 1937 Oldsmobile convertible (top up) traveling on a narrow county road

INT. IN THE CAR - DAY

Uncle TAJ (driving- 27 year old younger brother of MOTHER), MOTHER (seated in front), TAKOOHI, ARAM and MICHAEL. Underscoring is muted for this interior scene

                              ARAM
                    How fast will it go, Uncle Taj?

                              TAJ
                    I don't know for sure.

TAJ notices the stern look from his sister

                              But I don't think we'll find
                              out today.

                              MOTHER
                    Sit back, Aram. How are you doing with the
                    cake, 'Koohi?

                              TAKOOHI
                    It's starting to melt on my lap. And I'm feel-
                    ing a little nauseous. I hope I haven't soiled
                    myself. Is there a paper bag I could throw up
                    in?

                              MOTHER
                    You're kidding.

                              TAKOOHI
                    Sort of.

                              MOTHER
                    Well, we're almost there now.

EXT. BACK TO OVERHEAD FIEW OF THE CAR - DAY

Underscoring transitions back to original volume

EXT. MELIK'S RURAL HOUSE SURROUNDED BY VINEYARDS - DAY

Music continues. In the shaded backyard musicians are playing the underscoring from the previous scene. It is 'grandpa' MELIK's birthday party. MELIK is really a great uncle to ARAM and MICHAEL. The large gathering consists mostly of Armenian relatives but there is a nice sprinkling of Mexican and Italian friends and neighbors. Children are playing, others are dancing and drinking

EXT. WEST SIDE OF MELIC'S HOUSE - DAY

The Oldsmobile is parked. TAJ and ARAM are watching colorful balloons float and bounce over the tops of the vineyard. Back by the car, MOTHER and TAKOOHI are still being greeted and hugged. Finally young girls with balloons tied to their wrists emerge from the vineyard carrying baskets of tender grape leaves. Among the girls is CLAUDETTE, a lovely sixteen year old in a mid-calf, white cotton dress. Both TAJ and ARAM are transfixed by her. MELIC has approached TAJ from behind

                         MELIK
              My great niece, Claudette- a beauty, is
              she not?

                         ARAM
              Happy Birthday, Grandpa!

                         MELIK (a little hug)
              Thank you, my boy. Go and help your
              cousins now, they are making ice cream.

ARAM runs off

                         TAJ (shaking MELIC's hand)
              Happy Birthday, Grandpa.

                         MELIK
              Now don't you start calling me that, I'm
              feeling old enough.

They chuckle

                         TAJ
              So that was Claudette? The last time I saw
              her she was just a young girl.

                         MELIK
              And now she's a young woman and quite a
              prize for some lucky fellow. She'll graduate
              from high school in a year or so. You should
              declare yourself to her before it is too late.

                         TAJ
              She's too young for me.

                         MELIK
              Nonsense. Besides, we've always wanted
              a rich banker in the family.

                         TAJ (chuckling)
              I'm afraid I'd disappoint you there.

                         MELIK
              These days, any man with a good job is rich
              enough. Come, we'll discuss your courtship
              of my great niece over a glass of wine.

TAJ smiles and they walk off

EXT. IN THE BACKYARD OF MELIK'S HOUSE - DAY

Late afternoon. ARAM is eating a bowl of ice cream and watching CLAUDETTE play a hand clapping game with the other girls. CLAUDETTE finally notices him watching. ARAM is so enamored that he can only manage a weak smile. She smiles back and continues the game

EXT. EAST SIDE OF MELIK'S HOUSE - DAY

Late afternoon. Fifteen year old BARLOW has gathered a mostly younger group of boys and is "teaching" them sword fighting. As he talks he trusts and parries with a stick sword

>   BARLOW
>   Any coward can shoot a gun. There ain't
>   nothing to it. All you do is pull the trigger.
>   Or if you're a Nazi or a Red, you can even
>   shoot a guy in the back. But I prefer the
>   sword for fighting all of my duels. You got
>   to look your opponent in the eye. It's a test
>   of courage. The ancient and honorable
>   sword is a tradition that goes back thousands
>   of years to Shakespeare's time. Here, I'm
>   going to need some help to demonstrate.

BARLOW picks out a ten year old boy, gives him a second stick sword and directs him. MICHAEL is among the group of boys

>   OK now, come straight down on me like
>   you're going to split my head like a ripe
>   watermelon.

The boy does so, BARLOW deftly parries the blow and slaps the younger boy on the ribs with his stick

>   Now, you see there? I blocked my op-
>   ponent's attack and delivered a blow
>   myself. A blow which could have been
>   much worse if this was mortal combat.

The boy rubs his ribs

>   Now I know that didn't hurt. Come on,
>   I want you to try to stab me in the gut.
>   Go on. Well, come on.

Hesitantly, the boy lunges with his sword. BARLOW parries the thrust and hits the boy again, this time on his shoulder

There, you see, once again…

Impulsively, the boy thrusts again, this time hitting BARLOW in the stomach, knocking the wind out of BARLOW. MICHAEL and the other boys laugh until they see BARLOW's anger. The young boy drops his stick sword and scurries into the backyard. BARLOW picks up the second sword and crosses to MICHAEL

Take the sword, I'm not through with the demonstration yet.

MICHAEL shakes his head 'no'

BARLOW
Take it!

MICHAEL feebly takes the sword

EXT. IN THE BACKYARD OF MELIK'S HOUSE - DAY

ARAM is engaged in a hand clapping game with CLAUDETTE with others watching. The sequence and variation of how the hands are clapped remains the same but the speed steadily increases until one of the two players makes a mistake and the game is over. The faster the game goes, the more enjoyable it is to watch and play. ARAM is doing very well but finally makes a mistake and everyone laughs and applauds his effort. ARAM steps aside to allow another young person to play the game with CLAUDETTE. As he watches the game, ARAM notices a young boy (the young boy who ran from BARLOW) run into the backyard and then peer around the corner of the house to the east side. ARAM is curious as to why the boy seems frightened

EXT. EAST SIDE OF MELIC'S HOUSE - DAY

BARLOW
The last demonstration will be about respect. On guard!

BARLOW assumes a fighting position. MICHAEL does not know what to do

That means put your sword tip up.

MICHAEL does so

Sword fighting is no laughing matter. For
instance, what do you do if your opponent
does this?

BARLOW lightly slaps MICHAEL on the side of the head with his stick sword

You're supposed to block it. So block it
this time. Ready?

MICHAEL is ready to block the blow but BARLOW faints the slap on one side of MICHAEL's head and hits him on the other, scratching him under his eye. BARLOW leaves the sword tip inches from MICHAEL's nose

                          BARLOW
             And that's what happens when your oppon-
             ent has superior speed and skill. Why aren't
             you laughing now?

A trickle of blood drops from MICHAEL's nose and his eyes well up with tears. Suddenly ARAM's hand grabs the end of BARLOW's sword. BARLOW tries to pull his sword back but ARAM jerks it away and throws it down. BARLOW steps toward ARAM but ARAM is clearly not afraid of the older, slightly larger boy. Unsure of himself, BARLOW attempts to deflect/defuse the situation

             What's everybody so serious about? (fake
             laugh and exiting) I'm going to get some ice
             cream.

Several boys try to congratulate ARAM but he is embarrassed by the incident and gives MICHAEL a stern look as he walks away

INT. ARAM AND MICHAEL'S BEDROOM - NIGHT

Late at night, the boys are in bed. They are whispering

                          MICHAEL
             Where are you going, Aram?

                          ARAM (calmly)
             None of your beeswax.

                          MICHAEL
             Mom will be mad if she finds out.

                          ARAM
             Well, she won't know unless you rat me out.

                          MICHAEL (hurt)
             I'd never rat you out.

                          ARAM (sarcastically)
             Sure.

A beat

                          MICHAEL
             What are you going to do?

                          ARAM
             I don't know. Just drive around, I guess.

                    MICHAEL
Are you going to the river?

                    ARAM
No. What's at the river?

                    MICHAEL
Just some high school kids drinking and
smooching and stuff.

                    ARAM
Is that right. What do you know about
smooching and stuff?

                    MICHAEL (embarrassed)
Nothing.

ARAM chuckles

                    ARAM
No, I don't cruise with those jocks and
socialites.

                    MICHAEL
What's socialites?

                    ARAM
It's bullshit and rich daddies.

MICHAEL doesn't understand

                    MICHAEL (being 'cool')
I won't cruise with them either. Bullshit and
rich daddies. We don't even have a daddy.

                    ARAM
We did have one. And he could kick the
crap out of all their daddies. Until he got
sick… he just got sick, that's all.

                    MICHAEL
I know.

                    ARAM
Don't ever say we never had a father. He
just got sick and died, that's all.

                    MICHAEL
OK.

ARAM turns the clock toward the moonlit window

                              ARAM
                    If you rat me out I'll clobber you.

                              MICHAEL
                    I ain't going to rat you out. But what if
                    Mom finds out? Why do you want to
                    make her mad?

                              ARAM
                    I'm not... I just got to get out sometimes.
                    She doesn't understand. You don't either,
                    probably.

A beat. ARAM gets out of bed. He has a shirt on. He quickly puts on a pair of pants and
shoes. He silently opens the window for his escape

                    All right, Michael, keep your mouth shut
                    and I'll take you with me someday.

                              MICHAEL
                    OK!

MICHAEL silently closes the window behind his brother

EXT. THE FRESNO COUNTY FAIRGROUNDS - DAY

Summer, 1938. The sights and sounds of the crowded midway: calliope music of the
Ferris wheel, the squeals of children on the rides, food and game booths with the barkers,
Mariachis on a bandstand in the distance

EXT. THE FRESNO COUNTY FAIRGROUNDS - DAY

MICHAEL and KIYOTO are sharing a candied apple. They are taking turns biting the
apple and are laughing as they are getting it all over their hands and face. MOTHER
approaches

                              MOTHER
                    Oh, look at the mess you kids are making.
                    Kiyoto, your mother would kill me.

MOTHER is giving paper napkins to the kids. TAKOOHI shouts at them from across the
midway at a tented attraction

                              TAKOOHI (eating popcorn)
                    Ella, kids, come here!

They cross to her

                    We're going inside to see this flying whatever.

MOTHER

'Koohi, you didn't pay money for it?

TAKOOHI

I did. I spent thirty cents like there was no tomorrow. Michael, why is your face like that?

MOTHER

You bought them a candied apple.

TAKOOHI

Good. Here are your ticket stubs, kids. Go inside, it might be educational.

MICHAEL and KIYOTO take their stubs and walk inside the tent

Here's your stub, sourpuss.

MOTHER takes her stub, rolls her eyes and steps inside the tent followed by TAKOOHI

EXT. THE FRESNO COUNTY FAIRGROUNDS - NIGHT

Uncle TAJ is escorting CLAUDETTE down the midway. He is in a cream colored suit, she is in a chiffon dress- a floral pattern. They are not as casually dressed as most of the crowd. She is eating a bowl of ice cream

TAJ

Would you like to go inside to see any of the displays?

CLAUDETTE

I think I'd like to stay outside.

TAJ

How about the car show? They have the latest models.

CLAUDETTE

We can go see them, if you want to.

TAJ

Well, no, I only wanted to... I was hoping that you might, uh...Never mind. Let me get you some napkins for that ice cream. I'll be right back.

TAJ leaves. CLAUDETTE notices two young couples, teenagers like herself, having a great time. They are tossing baseballs at metal bottles in one of the game booths. They are laughing and enjoying themselves and CLAUDETTE wishes she was playing as well.

Suddenly she recognizes one of the young men. It is ARAM. He has just won a stuffed animal. ARAM notices CLAUDETTE about the same time. CLAUDETTE looks away

                        ARAM (to VARTAN)
              Hey, that's Claudette.

                        VARTAN
              You know her? She's pretty.

                        ARAM
              Yes, she's my cousin. Or my second cousin,
              I'm not sure. I'll be right back.

ARAM starts his cross to CLAUDETTE. The YOUNG LADY escorted by ARAM shouts after him

                        YOUNG LADY
              Don't be long, Aram!

                        ARAM
              Hi, Claudette.

                        CLAUDETTE
              Oh, hello.

                        ARAM
              Aram.

                        CLAUDETTE
              Yes, of course, Aram. How are you?

                        ARAM
              Good. I keep beating all these games they
              have here. Would you like to throw some
              baseballs with us?

                        CLAUDETTE
              No, thank you.

                        ARAM
              Oh, yes, that dress might get in the way.
              Maybe we can toss ping pong balls into
              goldfish bowls?

                        CLAUDETTE
              No, I'm going to the car show with your
              uncle.

                        ARAM
              Oh, that's, uh… (offering stuffed toy)
              Would you like a Teddy Bear?

CLAUDETTE

No, thank you. Why don't you give it to
your young girlfriend there?

ARAM

She's not... Yes, maybe I'll do that.

CLAUDETTE (abruptly)

Well, goodbye.

CLAUDETTE turns and walks in the direction that TAJ left. ARAM glares after her

INT. EXHIBIT TENT, FRESNO COUNTY FAIRGROUNDS - DAY

MICHAEL and KIYOTO are fascinated and horrified by strange and exotic "specimens"
in large, glass bottles, suspended in a clear, viscous fluid. MOTHER is appalled at the
obvious fraud and TAKOOHI is amused as the final curtain is pulled and a recording
begins: African drums under a VOICE OVER

VOICE OVER

Do not be alarmed, ladies and gentlemen!
The Flying Iguana of Borneo is now available for your inspection but do not get too
close. Although this specimen is harmless,
when alive, the Flying Iguana of Borneo is
a savage creature with an appetite for hu man
blood. The government has denied the existence
of the legendary half-reptile, half-bird but
the local natives know and fear the poisonous
bite of the Flying Iguana of Borneo as it
feasts on domestic animals and can kill a
small child in minutes. Do not be alarmed,
ladies and gentlemen! The Flying Iguana of
Borneo is available for your inspection...

The recording repeats

TAKOOHI

It's a flying whatever or a lizard with turkey
feathers stuck in it. What do you think?

MOTHER

It's a waste of time and money.

TAKOOHI

What do you think, kids? Do you want some
popcorn?

As the children look at the 'specimen', the thought of eating popcorn nauseates them

EXT. TAJ'S SPEEDING CAR, CONVERTIBLE TOP DOWN - DAY

Car radio is blaring some popular music of the day. TAJ is driving on a rural, county road. ARAM sits in the front enjoying the speed. MICHAEL is in the back looking straight up at a pair of soaring birds

EXT. FROM A DISTANCE, THE SPEEDING CAR - DAY

Music continues. The shimmering horizon is evidence of the mid-day heat

EXT. IN THE CAR - DAY

TAJ turns the radio down a bit

> TAJ
> It's coming right up. There's not much around the property but it already has a house on it. And I can get all forty acres for four bits on the dollar in a no cost loan. It's a good investment. And who knows, in a few years I might settle down and raise a family out here. That would sure shock your Mother, wouldn't it?

> ARAM
> How is Claudette?

> TAJ
> Fine, I guess. I haven't seen her in a while.

> ARAM
> I thought you were dating her.

> TAJ
> I was. She doesn't know what she wants.

AMAM barely masks his appreciation of this news, TAJ slows the car

> This is it. See the house?

> ARAM
> That's a house?

> TAJ
> Well, it could use a little work. Let's take a look.

TAJ pulls to a stop, steps out and walks to the porch. He takes a step up and the step breaks

> Look out for the, uh…

TAJ climbs to a second step and into the house. The boys follow. TAJ sees a lizard move in the corner and then scurry out the back

Wow! What was that?

                    ARAM
It's just a horny toad.

                    TAJ
Well, we'll just have to evict the current re-
sidents and get to work. I'll bet I could fix
this place up pretty nice.

TAJ walks to the back porch followed by the boys

            I'll own about half way to the foot of those
            hills. All I need is water. And we're stand-
            ing on it. Dig down a ways, pump it up and
            you can grow anything; figs, dates, persimmons
            and pomegranates. It could be a garden.

INT. THE BASANIAN KITCHEN - DAY

MOTHER is finishing cleaning the kitchen. She sits and folds her hands on the table,
staring at her wedding photograph. She steps over to a cabinet to get a bottle of wine and
glass and sits back down at the table. She pours a glass of wine and weeps. TAKOOHI
enters and puts a paper bag on the counter by the sink

                    TAKOOHI
You're drinking alone?

                    MOTHER
Yes.

                    TAKOOHI
It's my wine.

                    MOTHER
So?

                    TAKOOHI
Where is my glass?

                    MOTHER (extending glass)
Here, I haven't had a sip.

                    TAKOOHI
Thank you.

TAKOOHI sips and puts the glass on the table

            I think I'll pour you some.

TAKOOHI gets another glass, pours MOTHER wine and sits

You may drink as much of my wine as you
want but I must drink with you. Especially
if you are going to get drunk and cry in the
middle of the day. I want to get good and
kinov and we'll bawl our eyes out.

They chuckle, a beat

                    MOTHER
It's my anniversary.

                    TAKOOHI
Really, of what? Oh, that anniversary! (she
crosses to the counter to retrieve the bag)
Maybe that's why I got this white cake with
the coconut frosting like you like.

TAKOOHI produces the cake and puts it on the table. MOTHER stands and hugs and
cries with her mother-in-law

Well, we got the crying part down. Let's get
the drinking part started. (she sits) Bottoms up!

TAKOOHI takes a big gulp

EXT. THE SCHOOL TRACK - DAY

MICHAEL and eight other twelve year old boys are lining up for the two hundred and
twenty yard race. They take one knee, with their hands just behind the chalked line
waiting for the starter's pistol to fire. KIYOTO and a mixed crowd are on hand to watch.
The gun fires and the crowd cheers nine boys running as hard as they can. MICHAEL
and a tall, blond boy next to him start to pull away from the rest. They are running evenly
with neither boy clearly beating the other through the finish line and big cheers from the
crowd

INT. THE BASANIAN KITCHEN - DAY

Late afternoon. MOTHER and TAKOOHI have finished one bottle and are on another. A
couple of pieces of cake have been eaten. TAKOOHI, elbow on the table, is propping her
head up with one hand. A beat

                    MOTHER
No, he wasn't much of a drinker. (she starts
to giggle) He'd get green at the smell of alcohol. Sometimes he'd get so embarrassed
about it. (she starts to laugh) You remember
our wedding toast? Everyone was drinking
their wine in one gulp. He hesitated. But then

MOTHER is roaring with laughter. TAKOOHI is enjoying this

158

he thought, "What the hell, it's my wedding."
So, being a good sport, he took one big gulp.
(laughing again) It was as if he had been shot.
I thought we were going to have to carry him
out of the place. But no, he gathered himself
and walked out quickly just in case he had to
throw up... God bless him, he was a good man.

MOTHER starts to cry a little again. TAKOOHI takes her hand across the table

Thank you, 'Koohi.

TAKOOHI gestures with a wave of her hand as if to say, 'don't mention it'. MOTHER
hears the front door open and close. She takes the wine off of the table

                          TAKOOHI
                   What is it, the cops?

ARAM walks into the kitchen and sees that MOTHER has been crying

                           ARAM
              What's the matter? Where's Michael?

                          MOTHER
                 He's eating supper with Kiyoto and her
                 parents.

                           ARAM
                     Who's cake?

                          MOTHER
                    It's mine. Want some?

                           ARAM
                 Sure.

ARAM cuts himself a bite size piece, eats it, goes to the refrigerator and takes out a bottle
of milk

                          MOTHER
                  Get a glass.

ARAM crosses to the cupboard, gets a glass, pours milk, returns the bottle to the
refrigerator, takes a drink of milk

                           ARAM
                What are you and Grandma doing?

                          MOTHER
                 Today is my anniversary.

ARAM

Oh.

ARAM finishes the milk, puts the empty glass on the sink and starts to walk away

MOTHER

Aram, we never talk about your father.

ARAM does not respond

TAKOOHI (standing)

I'm going outside for a smoke.

MOTHER

You don't smoke.

TAKOOHI (exiting)

I'm going to start.

A beat

MOTHER

Michael doesn't remember him much. He was
too young when your father died, but you…

ARAM

I remember him.

MOTHER

He loved you very much.

ARAM (hesitates)

I don't know what you want me to say.

MOTHER

You don't have to say a thing. But it's OK
if you did. Do you understand?

ARAM nods 'yes' and MOTHER gives her son a hug

Wash your hands and help me with supper.

MOTHER walks out to the laundry room/pantry and sees TAKOOHI smoking a cigar
and coughing on the back porch. MOTHER joins her

MOTHER

Where did you get that?

TAKOOHI

From Melik. I'm drinking during the day, why
not smoke. I'm thinking of taking up gambling too.

                            MOTHER
              Give me a puff.

                         TAKOOHI (dryly)
              Maybe we should get tattoos.

MOTHER puffs and coughs

INT. THE IMADA DINING ROOM - NIGHT

MICHAEL, KIYOTO, ITO, and KIYO are finishing their evening meal. KIYO is holding
MICHAEL's second place ribbon

                             KIYO
              You have done very well. Look, Ito, look
              how pretty. Very nice.

ITO looks at the ribbon and nods

                         MICHAEL (darkly)
              I should have won.

                             KIYO
              Next time you will run even faster.

                           MICHAEL
              No, I won this time. I didn't get first place
              because the coach doesn't like Armenians.

ITO stops eating and studies MICHAEL

              Kiyoto was there, she saw.

                           KIYOTO
              I thought you won but I was too far away
              to see for sure. I'm sorry, Michael.

                           MICHAEL
              Well, anyway, I won.

Note: it is ITO's habit to speak only when he is sure that the other person is finished and
has nothing to add

                             ITO
              You have won a ribbon. Are you angry?

                           MICHAEL
              Yes. I can beat that kid. They just don't
              want me to because I'm Armenian.

                              ITO
              You have won today, Michael. You have com-
              peted honorably. You were awarded second
              place. Be patient. Next time you may be
              awarded first place.

                            MICHAEL
              But I won this time.

                              ITO
              Yes, you have won more than a race. People
              like your coach are getting fewer and fewer.
              And people like your Mother and the two of
              you are getting more and more. Things are
              getting better, I've seen it. Congratulations,
              Michael.

MICHAEL turns to KIYOTO and returns her smile

                            MICHAEL
              Thank you, Mr. Imada.

EXT. MELIK'S VINEYARDS – DAY

It is midday and very hot. A crew of about twenty men (mixed races) are 'turning trays'.
That is, turning wooden framed boxes with mesh wire on the tops and bottoms. They are
filled with grapes and are turned so the grapes dry evenly for raisins. Seventeen year old
ARAM is stacking dried trays onto a flatbed trailer, hitched to a field tractor. An older
Mexican man speaks to him briefly, calls lunch break and the men move to shade of a
large oak tree

                         ARAM (to older man)
              Voy por agua.

ARAM unhitches the trailer from the tractor and drives to the house. He off-loads a five
gallon, galvanized can and takes it to the faucet and hose in the backyard. He starts to
hand water Grandma's vegetable garden. CLAUDETTE has been watching him from
inside the screened porch/laundry room. She has volunteered for house work while
Grandma and Grandpa are gone. She can't help but notice that ARAM, the shy, thirteen
year old boy with a crush on her has, in four years, turned into a strong, beautiful young
man. She is three years older than ARAM and would not consider having an affair with
him. She is, however, flattered by his attentions. She steps down out of the enclosed
porch with a laundry basket in hand

                          CLAUDETTE
              Hello, Aram! I thought I heard someone out here.
              Grandpa said you were supervising the harvest.

                            ARAM
              No, these men don't need supervision. They
              just need someone to pay them at the end of

162

the day. I was wondering who had hung
those sheets.

                    CLAUDETTE
          I promised I'd help.

CLAUDETTE moves to the clothes line. ARAM turns off the water and follows her over

                    CLAUDETTE
          By the way, they're not coming home to-
          morrow.

                    ARAM
          What's wrong? Is everybody all right?

She is taking sheets off the line

                    CLAUDETTE
          Yes. Only Grandpa got a little sick in Visalia.
          The doctor thinks it was just a little heat
          stroke but they want to keep him for another
          day just to be sure.

                    ARAM
          That old man pushes himself.

                    CLAUDETTE (smiling)
          Try to tell him.

Her smile completely disarms ARAM. He suddenly feels that he has been staring at her
and blurts out something that he hopes is conversational

                    ARAM
          Don't bother watering her garden if she
          asked you to because I can do it. It's really
          easy for me. I come here two or three
          times a day for water. Or the roses for that
          matter.

                    CLAUDETTE (finishing)
          OK, thanks. Well, I guess I'll see you
          around the place.

                    ARAM
          Yes, I'm here a lot.

CLAUDETTE crosses to the porch and in. ARAM hates his shyness around her and
angrily turns on the faucet to fill the can. In the laundry room, CLAUDETTE is standing
in front of the washing machine on its' spin cycle. She is watching ARAM swear to
himself. He douses his head and shoulders with water, turns it off, grabs the can with one
hand and shakes water off like a dog on his walk back to the tractor. CLAUDETTE has

been watching ARAM while the spin cycle winds down and, thus distracted, gets her right hand caught by some linen in the machine and twisted violently. She screams, ARAM drops the can and runs into the laundry room. She is still trying to unwrap her hand

                         ARAM (crosses to her)
              Here, let me help. You could have broken
              it.

                         CLAUDETTE (crying)
              I feel so stupid.

                         ARAM (holding her arm)
              It was just an accident. Can you bend your
              elbow? (she does so) Can you turn your
              palm up? (she does so)

ARAM is still cradling her arm and then touches her on the shoulder

              Well, then I…guess…you're…beautiful.

He kisses her impulsively but tenderly on the cheek. She kisses him back gently. Their passion grows quickly and profoundly. Suddenly, before any disrobing, she pushes him away

                         CLAUDETTE
              I can't! I'm sorry, I can't! I'm sorry.

                         ARAM (moves to her)
              What?

                         CLAUDETTE (pushes him again)
              No! I'm sorry, Aram. It's my fault, I'm
              sorry.

Silence

                         ARAM
              I'm not sorry.

He moves to the door

              I'm not sorry at all.

He leaves. A teary CLAUDETTE watches ARAM load the water can and drive the tractor into the vineyard

EXT. DOWNTOWN FRESNO - NIGHT

ARAM is walking in a neighborhood just south-east of the hotel bars in the early evening. There are several prostitutes soliciting and he approaches one, NOELA, a young Mexican woman. She is not particularly pretty but she is sexy

                    ARAM
          What's your name?

                    NOELA
          Noela.

                    ARAM
          What do you know, Noela?

                    NOELA
          Sí, we'll talk about that. Follow me.

NOELA leads ARAM to an alley and ducks into the shadows with him

          So, what are you looking for, boy? You
          ain't policía? You're not a cop, are you?

                    ARAM
          No.

                    NOELA (fondling him)
          Well, you're a nice looking boy. How
          much money you got?

                    ARAM
          Not much.

                    NOELA
          Well I'm worth ten bucks at least. How
          much you got?

                    ARAM
          Five.

                    NOELA (still fondling)
          Well, you are pretty. Follow me.

NOELA leads ARAM up a stairwell off the alley to the second floor of an older building, once a hotel

          Let's do some business first. Where's
          your money?

ARAM hands her the five dollar bill. NOELA unlocks a resident's door and a baby cries in a bedroom

          Come in.

They shuffle past a scantily clad woman and a middle-aged man kissing on the couch and into the bedroom with the crying toddler in an enclosed crib

Give me a minute.

She crosses to the crib scolding the child in Spanish. She takes off the soiled diaper and throws a blanket on the crying child. She finishes the chore by spanking the child to shut it up. After a few blows it understands that it is to be quiet. NOELA turns back to ARAM, folding him and backing him to a wall. Only ARAM's face can be seen as he listens to the child gasping for air as it tries to cry quietly. NOELA goes to her knees in front of ARAM and out of sight. Only ARAM's face can be seen in the dark room as he reacts to the oral sex and the gasping of the child. Finally he can abide the experience no more and pushes her away

                              NOELA
               What's the matter? You ain't getting your
               money back.

ARAM fishes in his pocket for another couple of dollars and throw them on the floor

                              ARAM
               Here, take care of your baby.

ARAM leaves quickly

EXT. THE WALK HOME FROM SCHOOL - DAY

Now fourteen, MICHAEL and KIYOTO are walking in silence on a cool, early November afternoon

                         KIYOTO (finally)
               Are you going to the Christmas Ball?

                            MICHAEL
               I don't know.

                            KIYOTO
               Have you asked a girl to go yet?

                            MICHAEL
               No.

                            KIYOTO
               Well, that's the first step, you pin head.
               You know Augusta Parsejian?

                            MICHAEL
               Who?

                            KIYOTO
               Augusta Parsejian.

MICHAEL
You mean Auggie?

KIYOTO
I don't think she likes that name anymore.
Anyway, she wouldn't mind if you asked her.

MICHAEL
How do you know?

KIYOTO
Her friend, Bethanie, told me. And you better
ask her fast too because girls need some time
to get their dresses and things together.

MICHAEL
Oh. Are you going?

KIYOTO
No, I think we're going out to Dinuba that
weekend, to my Aunt's.

A beat

MICHAEL
What's the guy supposed to do?

KIYOTO
You are such a pin head. Well, first you show
up at her house wearing a tuxedo. And you
have to have a corsage for her too. And she
wears a really nice dress and you take pic-
tures and things.

A beat

MICHAEL
That's too bad you can't go. I would have
liked to have seen you in a really nice
dress.

KIYOTO
Yes, well, you should ask Augusta. She
might be sweet on you.

They walk in silence and arrive in front of her house

I lied. We're not really going to Dinuba.
I only said that because no one has asked
me. And I didn't want you feeling sorry
for me. I don't really need to go anyway.

MICHAEL

I don't either. Hey, if you don't need to
go and I don't need to go, why don't we
go together?

KIYOTO

You mean that? Because I really want to go.

MICHAEL

Sure. We could have fun.

KIYOTO (excited)

I think so too. Let's see, I'll have to go
downtown and look at some material and
make my hair and nail appointments.
You'll need a haircut. And we'll coordinate colors before you order flowers.

MICHAEL

Coordinate colors?

KIYOTO

Don't worry. Leave everything to me.
See you tomorrow.

She scurries inside. MICHAEL starts his walk home

MICHAEL

What have I done?

INT. SHERIFF MICHELL'S OFFICE - DAY

The SHERIFF is looking over some paperwork in a file. MOTHER is seated in a small
chair by his desk. She has been crying, handkerchief still in hand

SHERIFF

Your son, Aaron, gave his birthday as
February eighth.

MOTHER

Aram.

SHERIFF

Excuse me?

MOTHER

Aram is his name.

SHERIFF

Yes. He'll be eighteen in less than three
months. Is that correct?

MOTHER

Yes.

SHERIFF

You're a single parent?

MOTHER

Yes.

SHERIFF

This is the second time your son has been picked up in a stolen vehicle. But this time he was driving. That's a bit more serious. He was with another young man, Vartan Yassarian. Do you know this fellow?

MOTHER

They've been friends since they were little. His parents go to my church, Saint Paul's.

SHERIFF

I see. The car your son was driving came out of a chop shop off of Jensen Avenue. That means the car was stolen before they got their hands on it. I could give them a break but they are not cooperating with police as to how they came into possession of the vehicle. And that is very serious. Normally I'd recommend six months detention in a juvenile correctional facility.

MOTHER

Please, Sheriff, he's not a mean spirited boy. He's just restless.

SHERIFF

A restless teenager is trouble waiting to happen. He needs a strong hand.

MOTHER (crying)

Please, Sheriff, can you give us a second chance?

SHERIFF

You mean a third chance. I see him here again and I'll charge him as an adult.

MOTHER weeps. The SHERIFF allows her anguish to go on. Finally

Mrs. Basanian, it's not uncommon for a judge to order induction into military ser-

vice rather than send a young, first time
offender to the state pen. He'll be eligible
to join the Army in three months. If he'll
promise to consider this option, I'll release him to your recognizance.

                    MOTHER (teary)
Oh, thank you, Sheriff!

                    SHERIFF
I'm not sure I'm doing you any favors.
Your restless boy looks like an angry man
to me.

INT. THE IMADA LIVING ROOM - NIGHT

December 5, 1941. ITO is working on a ledger on the table of the adjoining dining room.
The doorbell rings. KIYO enters through the dining room to answer the door. MICHAEL
is dressed in a tuxedo

                    KIYO
Hello, Michael! My, you look handsome.

                    MICHAEL
Thank you, Mrs. Imada.

                    KIYO
Look, Ito, how handsome Michael looks.

                    ITO (barely looking)
Yes.

                    KIYO
And look, Ito, a fancy taxi cab to take
them to the dance.

                    MICHAEL
Where is Kiyoto?

                    KIYO
She is just finishing up. The dress has
taken more time than she thought. I'm
quite surprised. She's a lovely girl, of
course, but this is a transformation.

Just then KIYOTO walks into the living room. She is stunningly beautiful in a simple but
elegant, rather form fitting formal dress. Her hair and make-up is perfect. MICHAEL
cannot take his eyes off of her

                    Oh, my goodness! Look, Ito, how
                    beautiful Kiyoto has made herself.

                ITO (crosses to her)
You are wrong, Kiyo. Our daughter has
always been this beautiful.

KIYOTO gives her Father a big hug

                KIYO
What a lovely couple you two make.

                KIYOTO (gentle warning)
Mother…

She turns to MICHAEL who is speechless

                Well, where's the corsage?

                MICHAEL
Oh, it's in the back of the cab.

KIYOTO pushes MICHAEL to the door

                KIYOTO
Good night, Momma. I'll be back by eleven.

KIYOTO follows MICHAEL to the cab

                KIYO (shouting after them)
Don't forget our photographs! Have a
good time!

MICHAEL opens the back door of the cab for KIYOTO. She gently shoves him in first,
gets in and closes her own door

INT. HIGH SCHOOL GYMNASIUM - NIGHT

The gym is decorated for the Christmas Ball (mirror ball, crepe paper, balloons, big
Christmas tree). The 'transformed' KIYOTO is getting a lot of attention from everyone.
MICHAEL is vying for her attention as the DJ is announcing the next song with
dedications

                MICHAEL
I thought maybe we could dance again.

                KIYOTO
I think I promised this next one to Keith
what's-his-name.

                MICHAEL
The quarterback?

                         KIYOTO
          Is he the quarterback? (MICHAEL nods
          'yes') Isn't he going steady with Karen
          Oates?

                         MICHAEL
          I thought so.

                         KIYOTO
          Here he comes. Follow me.

KIYOTO takes MICHAEL's hand and leads him toward the dance floor. As she passes
KEITH

          I'm sorry, Keith, but I forgot I promised
          this dance to Michael.

KEITH is surprise that he is being spurned in favor of MICHAEL who smiles a little as
he passes KEITH. They begin to slow dance on a crowded floor. A beat

                         MICHAEL
          You really do look great.

                         KIYOTO
          Thanks. You do too. Dressing up is fun. I'm
          glad we came. But it's a little sad too. On
          Monday I'll go back to my school clothes
          and back to not being noticed.

                         MICHAEL
          I don't think so.

                         KIYOTO
          I feel like Cinderella in the fairy tale. She
          had one night to shine. After midnight
          she had to go back to being just herself.

                         MICHAEL
          There will be no going back. Your Father
          was right. He said you've always been
          this beautiful.

They smile at one another and continue to dance

EXT NEWSREEL IMAGES OF PEARL HARBOR BURNING

                         VOICE OVER
          Honolulu, December seventh. War broke
          with lightning suddenness in the Pacific
          today when waves of Japanese bombers
          attacked Hawaii this morning and the

172

United States Fleet struck back with a
thunder of big naval guns. Japanese
bombers, including four engine dive
bombers and torpedo-carrying planes
blasted at Pearl Harbor, the great United
States naval base, the city of Honolulu
and several outlying American military
bases on the island of Oahu. There were
casualties of unstated number.

EXT. SCHOOL YARD - DAY

Note: the newsreel VOICE OVER will 'cross-fade' in volume with this school yard
scene. That is, the VOICE OVER will fade out as the sounds of the schoolyard fade up

MICHAEL is fighting with KEITH and not doing well. MICHAEL keeps getting
knocked down but keeps getting up. There are shouting boys encircling the combatants

                    VOICE OVER
          The United States battleship Oklahoma
          was set afire by the Japanese attackers,
          according to a National Broadcasting
          Company observer, who also reported
          that two other ships in Pearl Harbor were
          attacked. The Japanese news agency,
          Domei, reported that the battleship Okla-
          homa had been sunk at Pearl Harbor,
          according to a United Press dispatch
          from Shanghai.

KIYOTO runs into the circle

                    KIYOTO
          Stop it! Stop it!

KEITH knocks MICHAEL down again and starts kicking him. KIYOTO jumps on
KEITH's back. KEITH knocks her off and throws her to the ground. MICHAEL sees this
and rushes KEITH, hitting him hard in the face several times. A teacher, Mr.
WILLIAMS, steps in between the boys

                    WILLIAMS (shouting)
          Stop this right now! How did this happen?
          Who started this?

                    BOY IN THE CROWD
          He called him a Jap lover.

                    WILLIAMS
          Listen to me. There are no Japs or Wops or
          anything of the kind on this campus. Do
          you understand? On these grounds we are

all students. Now go home. Classes are
over. You two will report to me tomorrow
for detention. Go home, all of you!

EXT. THE WALK HOME FROM SCHOOL - DAY

MICHAEL is walking with KIYOTO. She is crying

                    MICHAEL
            You can't quit school because of one idiot.

                    KIYOTO
            It's not just him, Michael. They all look
            at me like I just crawled out from under
            a rock.

                    MICHAEL
            But you heard what Mr. Williams said.

                    KIYOTO
            You don't understand, Michael, it's everyone.
            People who have been buying produce from
            my Father for years aren't even speaking to
            him. I overheard him tell Momma that we
            could lose the orchard.

EXT. THE CEMETERY - DAY

Early January, 1942. MELIK'S funeral. A large gathering of family and friends under
umbrellas as it is a cold, rainy day. MICHAEL is attending MOTHER and TAKOOHI.
ARAM is off to the side avoiding CLAUDETTE who is escorted by TAJ

                    PRIEST
            ...and forgive us our trespasses as we for-
            give those who trespass against us. And
            lead us not into temptation but deliver us
            from evil. Amen. Lord, your servant, Melik,
            stands before you. His loving family and
            friends intercede on his behalf with their
            prayers and devotions and implore You to
            bless and take him into the bosom of Your
            eternal grace. His work is done. His race
            is won. He has fought the good fight. On
            this inclement day when we pray for our
            dearly departed, let us also pray for the liv-
            ing. As clouds of war are gathering in the
            Pacific, let us pray for the strength and
            courage to endure the trying times ahead.
            We ask this in Jesus' holy name. Amen.
            I'll ask the family now to make their
            offerings.

Two older men help Grandma approach the grave. She mutters something and places a red rose on the casket. And then, one by one, TAKOOHI, a middle-aged nephew, MOTHER and CLAUDETTE follow, placing their red rose on the casket. ARAM puts his red rose in his jacket pocket and backs away from the grave site unnoticed by all except MICHAEL. ARAM walks behind a large tree and lights a cigarette. He smokes thoughtfully for a moment. MICHAEL appears

                    MICHAEL
          Aram, we're getting ready to go.

                     ARAM
          Tell Mom I'll find my own way home.

                    MICHAEL
          OK. Where you going?

                ARAM (playfully)
          None of your beeswax.

                    MICHAEL
          Can I come too.

A beat. ARAM smiles

                     ARAM
          Sure.

                    MICHAEL
          I'll be right back.

EXT. THE GRAVE SITE - DAY

It is raining hard. All have left. The boys run up as the vault lid is being lowered with a back hoe. ARAM throws his red rose into the grave. The boys watch as the lid is placed

                    MICHAEL
          We're getting soaked.

                ARAM (smiling)
          Yes, we will be.

INT. A BAR/RESTAURANT - DAY

VARTAN is seated at a table away from the bar itself. He is reading a flier. ARAM and MICHAEL walk in drenched, cross to VARTAN and sit

                    VARTAN
          Man, you look like you swam here. And
          with little brother in tow. Hey, Michael.

MICHAEL

Hey, Vartan.

ARAM

We walked from the cemetery off of Olive.

VARTAN

Yes. How was the service?

ARAM

Short. Nice.

NICK, the bartender, has crossed to the table

NICK

What are you boys having?

ARAM

Three cokes, Nick.

Nick retreats back to the bar

ARAM

What did you find out?

VARTAN

This sheet has all the dope. First we go to
Pendleton or Fort Ord for basic training.
Six months later we could be in Togo's
front yard.

ARAM

Six months.

MICHAEL

You guys joining the army?

VARTAN

The Marine Corps, if I got anything to say
about it. I say we go in now. It was a surprise attack, the bastards.

NICK (delivers cokes)

That'll be a buck fifty.

ARAM digs in his wet pocket for money

And keep anything else you brought under
the table or you'll be back out in the rain.

ARAM (hands him a five)

Thanks, Nick. Keep the change.

NICK retreats to the bar

MICHAEL (shocked)

Did you just give him five dollars?

VARYAN

Yes, extravagant, ain't he?

VARTAN tops off the cokes with something from a hidden flask

ARAM

Six months, huh? I already know how to
shoot a gun. What can they teach us?

VARTAN

How to follow orders. How to wear them
uniforms that all the girls are crazy about.
You're not just some guy anymore, you're
a soldier. (toasting) Here's to plugging a
few Japs.

MICHAEL finds the toast disturbing but sips his drink quietly, wincing at the alcohol in
it

EXT. THE WALK HOME FROM THE BAR - DAY

MICHAEL and ARAM are walking in a pouring rain. Only now they are very drunk.
They are amusing one another by walking calmly as if were a beautiful day. ARAM
ducks behind a bush and telephone pole to urinate. MICHAEL is playfully pointing
ARAM out to passing cars and people scurrying to get out of the rain. The boys are
laughing and enjoying themselves

EXT. THE WALK HOME FROM THE BAR - DAY

The rain has stopped and the boys are walking quietly

ARAM (finally)

Better me than you. You're just not the
soldier type. I am, on the other hand, a
lean, mean war machine. Shoot, I might
win this thing all by myself.

MICHAEL does not laugh at his joke

Mom needs you here. But me, maybe I'm
somebody who is supposed to do this kind
of thing, I don't know. I'm OK with it.
Maybe I can do some good, who knows.

INT. THE IMADA LIVING ROOM - NIGHT

ITO, KIYO, MOTHER and TAJ are seated

> ITO
> The Sheriff might be right. If the govern-
> ment can detain us indefinitely without
> charge, why wouldn't they be able to take
> our land? If it went to auction, at least it
> might be sold quickly.

> TAJ
> I'm sure it might, but you would not re-
> ceive a fair market price. In fact, it
> wouldn't even be close. You have only
> six days?

> ITO
> Yes. Better to get something than nothing.

TAK looks at MOTHER and then back at ITO and KIYO

> TAJ
> What about a simple Title Transfer? If you
> could avoid escrow, that would be a quick
> and relatively inexpensive way to legally
> dispose of the property.

> ITO
> I don't understand.

> TAJ
> The idea is to sell your property to some-
> one for a token amount with the stipulation
> that they would turn the deed back over to
> you if…when this is all over. Sell it to
> Michael for a dollar. And leave enough
> money in an account to pay for taxes and
> water. Your home will be here for you
> when you return.

ITO and KIYO look to one another and take each other's hand. Ito turns back to TAJ

> ITO
> This country has broken my heart. But you
> have been my good friends. Thank you.

INT. THE IMADA LIVING ROOM - DAY

MOTHER is helping KIYO finish packing. KIYO is holding a small porcelain rabbit.
KIYOTO enters through the front door

KIYOTO

Hurry, Momma. We're supposed to be in
Pinedale by noon.

KIYOTO picks up a suitcase and angrily stomps out

KIYO

"Only what we can carry", the order said.
I shouldn't take this but it was my mother's.
I've had it so long it's a wonder it hasn't
broken. I'll keep it even so.

EXT. IN THE ORCHARD - DAY

ITO and MICHAEL are walking in the orchard

ITO

The notes I've given you include Mr. Sher-
man's name at the Ag and Hardware Supply
on Blackstone. Just describe the condition
of the trees and any insects you see. He'll
make his recommendations. He's always
been honest and good to us.

MICHAEL

Yes, Mr. Imada, it's in the notes.

ITO

And irrigate from the back. There's a slight
slope from the back and it will help save
water.

MICHAEL

That's in the notes too.

ITO

I think I wrote that they should be pruned
in the fall but use your own judgment
about that. Those apricot trees will be fine
for a long while but these almonds can be
damaged (he grabs a lower limb of a tree)
if you let them get too heavy.

His back to MICHAEL, ITO is suddenly overcome with emotion as he holds the lower
limb. It feels to ITO like he is saying goodbye to friends he has nourished for years. He
clutches his heart with one hand. A beat

MICHAEL

Are you OK, Mr. Imada?

                              ITO
                    Yes. I'm ready to go now, Michael. And
                    thank you.

EXT. THE IMADA ORCHARD - DAY

A week later, late morning. MICHAEL is just finishing irrigating. He walks to the small
back porch as SHERIFF Michell comes around the corner of the house

                           SHERIFF
                    Hello. You must be Michael Basanian.

                           MICHAEL
                    Yes.

                           SHERIFF
                    I'm Sheriff Michell. I've met your
                    mother and your brother, Aaron.

                           MICHAEL
                    Aram.

                           SHERIFF
                    Yes. Is he a war hero yet?

                           MICHAEL
                    No, I'm sure he's just trying to come home
                    in one piece.

                           SHERIFF
                    Yes, I guess that's good enough. Well, how
                    are you? Folks tell me that your family owns
                    this place now.

                           MICHAEL
                    I guess so. But we're really just taking care
                    of it until the Imadas get back.

                           SHERIFF
                    Are you folks business partners with Mr.
                    Imada?

                           MICHAEL
                    I don't think so. What do you mean?

                           SHERIFF
                    Well, this war has created a terrible sit-
                    uation. It seems that the government
                    doesn't have a plan for all of the relo-
                    cated Japs once the war is over. I wouldn't
                    be so sure that Imada is coming back.

What do you know about orchards,
Michael?

                    MICHAEL
I just have some notes that Mr. Imada
left for me.

                    SHERIFF
That's good. Good luck with it. Well, I
must be going. Just thought I'd drop by
and see how things are getting along.
You know, the way Fresno is growing,
it won't be long before businesses and
homes spring up even all the way out here.
Why, just the other day I heard talk
about rezoning land not too far from
here for residential and commercial de-
velopers. This house and trees won't
bring too much but the property will
still be worth something. If you folks
ever decide to sell, let me know.

                    MICHAEL
This is the Imadas' home. They'll be
back.

                    SHERIFF
Yes, well, let's hope so. I'll let you get
back to your work. Give my compli-
ments to your Mother for me, will you,
Michael? And good luck.

The SHERIFF shakes MICHAEL's hand and walks to the front of the house and his car.
MICHAEL stares after him as he leaves

EXT. ASSEMBLY CENTER, PINEDALE - DAY

Twenty-five or thirty U.S. soldiers with bayoneted rifles are supervising the loading of
Japanese families and their belongings on to buses which will take them to their
relocation camp. Non-Japanese friends who have brought supplies/gifts are standing in a
roped off section well away from the buses. The Imadas are standing in line with the rest
of the prisoners. They are anxiously waiting for the Basanians

EXT. ASSEMBLY CENTER, PINEDALE - DAY

On the non-loading side of the buses, MR. KITANO, an old Japanese man
absentmindedly picks wild flowers

EXT. ASSEMBLY CERTER, PINEDALE - DAY

On the loading side of the buses, MRS. KITANO, an old, Japanese woman starts to call for her husband

                              MRS. KITANO
                    Takeo! Takeo! Have you seen my husband?
                    Takeo! Takeo!

A CORPORAL approaches her

                              CORPORAL
                    What is it, ma 'me?

                              MRS. KITANO
                    My husband is gone.

                              CORPORAL
                    Did he go back to the barracks?

                              MRS. KITANO
                    No, there would be no reason.

                              CORPORAL (to soldiers)
                    The four of you do a quick re-con of the
                    immediate area. We're looking for an old
                    man. (the soldiers disperse) Are you sure he
                    didn't go back to the barracks for something?

                              MRS. KITANO
                    No, I packed our things. He depends on me.

                              A SOLDIER (shouting)
                    I got him, Corporal. He's on the other side
                    of the bus. What's his name?

                              MRS. KITANO
                    Takeo. But he's almost deaf.

                              CORPORAL
                    Go get him, Private.

TAJ drives up and parks quickly. MICHAEL jumps out of the back with a duffel bag and runs to the roped off area

                              KIYOTO
                    It's him! They made it!

KIYOTO runs toward MICHAEL

                              A SOLDIER (to MICHAEL)
                    Stay well back of this rope, sir. Is the bag
                    for this woman?

182

                    MICHAEL
Yes.

                    A SOLDIER
I'll need to inspect it.

                    MICHAEL
It's just extra clothing and blankets.

The bag is searched

                    KIYOTO
They are looking for the metal file you
baked in the cake.

                    MICHAEL
Do you know where they are taking you
yet?

TAJ and MOTHER have reached the roped off area about the time that KIYO and ITO
get there

                    KIYOTO
I think we're staying in California, that's
all we've heard.

                    MICHAEL
That's good. Maybe I can visit.

                    MOTHER (to KIYO)
I've brought you sweets for the trip.

MOTHER produces a tin can which is intercepted by A SOLDIER. He inspects and
passes it to KIYO. The duffel bag is tied back up and given to KIYOTO. MICHAEL
produces a paper bag

                    MICHAEL
These are the real good cookies. Grandma made them.

A SOLDIER inspects the bag and gives it to KIYOTO. She takes a cookies, bites and
cries. MICHAEL tries to take her hand but is gently pushed back by A SOLDIER

        Be brave, Kiyoto.

KIYOTO stops crying

                    KIYOTO
You're right, Michael. Tell Grandma that I
will think of her with every cookie.

MOTHER
The blossoms are beautiful, Ito. Michael
has been very conscientious. I'm proud
of him.

BULL HORN ANNOUNCMENT
Barracks twenty-seven through thirty
are loading now. Barracks twenty-seven
through thirty, loading now.

KIYOTO (moving)
That's us.

MICHAEL
You'll have to write to me so that I can
write you back.

KIYOTO (moving)
I will. Goodbye, Michael!

KIYOTO waves goodbye to MICHAEL as she gets back in line with her parents to board
the bus. MICHAEL and MOTHER wave goodbye as the IMADAS are the last to board

INT. ON THE BUS - DAY

KIYOTO is waving through the door window at MICHAEL who is still sadly waving
back. The driver starts the bus. Suddenly, KIYOTO starts yelling as if she were injured

KIYOTO
Open the door! Open the door!

In the confusion the driver opens the door. KIYOTO hits the ground at a run. From inside
the bus, we see MICHAEL duck under the rope and they run into each other's arms,
hugging with the urgency of, perhaps, never seeing each other again. Soldiers are alarmed
and move toward the couple. There is a spontaneous little applause on the bus. Soldiers
separate the couple and escort KIYOTO to the bus. Before KIYOTO gets on the bus,
KIYO turns to ITO

KIYO (quietly)
Yippee!

ITO smiles fondly at her and takes her hands

EXT. THE RELOCATION CAMP - DAY

KIYO is digging a flower bed in front of their barracks. KIYOTO is watching without
interest

KIYO
No matter where I am, I must have flowers
to look at. I know you love flowers too.

KIYOTO

By all means, make our cage prettier.

In the distance KIYOTO notices MR. KITANO looking for wild flowers to take to his wife. But he is dangerously close to the fence

Momma, I'm going to get Mr. Kitano
before he gets in trouble.

She starts walking toward him

EXT. THE RELOCATION CAMP - DAY

In the guard tower, Privates GOLIC and STEWART are watching MR. KITANO at the fence

STEWART

Look at this old coot. We better back him
off. (through bullhorn) Attention! Please
back away from the perimeter.

KIYOTO hears this and starts jogging toward MR. KITANO

KIYOTO

He can't hear you! He can't hear you!

GOLIC

He's ignoring you.

STEWART

The son of a bitch. (through bullhorn) You
are ordered to back away from the fence
or we are authorized to use deadly force.

Now KIYOTO is sprinting toward MR. KITANO

KIYOTO

Stop! Stop! He can't hear you!

STEWART

Fire a couple of rounds across his bow.
See if that gets his attention.

GOLIC pulls the lever on the machine gun, aims several yards in front of MR. KITANO but fires four shots instead of two, the weapon jerking out of his hand. MR. KITANO is struck by a bullet

What the hell did you do?

GOLIC

It got away from me. Oh, my God.

Stewart picks up the intercom

                              STEWART
                    Tower Four to HQ. Do you copy?

GOLIC pulls up the trap door and crawls down the ladder

                    Golic, get back up here! (a garbled re-
                    sponse on the intercom) Yes, Sergeant,
                    a weapon has been discharged from
                    Tower Four. Better get the doctor and
                    a company out here quick.

GOLIC crosses to MR. KITANO. KIYOTO is kneeling at his side

                              KIYOTO (screaming)
                    He's deaf! He's dead! He's deaf!

Many in camp heard the gunfire and are gathering as a five ton personnel truck pulls up
and soldiers get out. A corpsman and the CAPTAIN (a doctor) run to attend to MR.
KITANO. The COLONEL pulls up in his jeep. The corpsman reaches down to pull
KIYOTO out of the CAPTAIN's way and she jerks her arm back

                              KIYOTO
                    Get your hands off me!

                              COLONEL
                    Golic.

GOLIC is blubbering with remorse

                    Private Golic!

                              GOLIC
                    Yes, Sir.

                              COLONEL
                    Get in the truck. Now!

GOLIC complies. By now STEWART has come down out of the tower

                    What happened here, Private?

                              STEWART
                    It was an accident, Sir.

                              KIYOTO
                    An accident? You have guns pointed at us.
                    How can this be an accident?

Some grumbling and agreement from the Japanese on hand

186

COLONEL
Get back up in the tower, Private.

STEWART complies. The COLONEL crosses to MR. KITANO

Report, Captain.

CAPTAIN
A pretty clean shoulder wound, Sir. He'll
live. He's stable enough to move, Sir.

COLONEL
Do it.

They carry MR. KITANO and put him in the truck, to some grumbling by the crowd

COLONEL
Sergeant, disperse these people. Use tear
gas if you have to. Let's lock it down with
an early curfew.

The COLONEL steps into his jeep, starts it, slumps a little

God dammit.

He drives away

INT. THE RELOCATION CAMP - DAY

The COLONEL's office. The COLONEL is standing, staring out of a window. There is a
knock at the door

COLONEL
Yes?

The COPORAL walks in with ITO and KIYOTO

COPORAL
The detainees you asked for, Sir.

COLONEL
Thank you, Corporal. Please wait outside.
(looking at a list) Ito Imada and your
daughter, Kiyoto. Is that right?

ITO nods 'yes'

Thank you for seeing me today.

KIYOTO (tersely)
I didn't think detainees had a choice.

                    COLONEL
If there is a more urgent matter you'd
rather attend to in camp, please do so.
We can have this conversation a little
later.

                    ITO
No, we'll stay.

The COLONEL seats himself at his desk

                    COLONEL
Please be seated. (they do) I'm going to
get right to the point. We have a stressful
situation here in camp.

                    KIYOTO (correcting him)
Prison.

                    COLONEL
Very well. I am charged with maintaining
order in this prison. No one wants to be
here, soldiers or Japanese. Two days ago,
a soldier under my command, inadver-
tently shot and wounded a detainee. I take
responsibility and will do every thing I
can to see that this does not hap pen again.

                    KIYOTO
Please, Colonel, I am not stupid. The
machine guns in the towers are pointed
at us. That is not your order?

                    COLONEL (firmly)
It is my standing order that warning shots
be fired before firing to put a target down.
I was there shortly after the shooting. I saw
a volatile situation developing and, frankly,
Miss, you weren't helping.

                    KIYOTO (yelling)
We are imprisoned unjustly! Our only
crime is that we are Japanese! Should I
not be outraged?

The CORPORAL steps through the door

                    COLONEL
It's all right, Corporal. That will be all.

The CORPORAL leaves

188

KIYOTO (tersely)
I will not be your happy little camper.

COLONEL
Please hear me out. I'm not going to pun-
ish you. And I'm certainly not asking you
to be happy. But we all have to get through
this somehow. It will help if we can dis-
cuss the things we need. To that end, I am
encouraging detainees to create commit-
tees from all of the barracks. These com-
mittees will meet on a regular basis. Griev-
ances will be discussed as well as sugges-
tions on how to make our lives more toler-
able here. Mr. Imada, I understand that
you are organizing baseball games.

ITO
Yes.

COLONEL
Good. Maybe I can purchase baseball
equipment for you. Anything we do to nor-
malize our lives here will relieve the stress
and help me to maintain order. And make
no mistake about it, order will be maintained. I guess that's all I had to say. Is
there anything else? (Silence) Corporal?

The CORPORAL walks in

Our meeting has concluded.

KIYOTO and ITO stand to leave with the CORPORAL, the COLONEL goes back to the
window

By the way, Miss, you said that your only
crime was that you were Japanese. I'm
aware of racial and ethnic persecutions
happening in the world. My last name is
Schneider. It sounds German but my family is really from Austria. We're Jewish.
I understand that in Germany now Jews
are being rounded up and shot in the street.
When we look back on this war, the treatment of Japanese in this country may compare favorably to the treatment of my people elsewhere. I don't offer this as an explanation or a mitigation of anything. But
maybe… let's help each other if we can.
That's all.

The door closes. The COLONEL goes back to staring out the window

EXT.THE IMADA HOUSE - DAY

The morning after the fire that burns ITO's house to the ground. MICHAEL is talking to the firemen who are watering the smoldering ashes. TAJ has his arm around MOTHER who is sniffling into a handkerchief. There are concerned friends and family on hand

INT. THE BASANIAN HOUSE - DAY

In a darkened bedroom, TAKOOHI lies in bed, presumably sleeping. MOTHER stands at the foot of the bed with MICHAEL

> MICHAEL (whispers)
> What did the Doctor say?

> MOTHER (whispers)
> It's a very dangerous flu. He's given her an antibiotic. I think her fever is breaking but she's a little disoriented and weak as a kitten.

> TAKOOHI (mumbling)
> Michael…Michael…

> MICHAEL (moves to her side)
> What is it, Grandma? I'm here.

> TAKOOHI (dramatically)
> I'm glad you've come to see me before I go. It's good to have your family around you… at the end.

> MICHAEL
> Don't say that, Grandma. You'll get better.

> TAKOOHI
> No, you heard your Mother. It's a very dangerous flu. I'm weak as a kitten.

> MICHAEL
> You heard that?

> TAKOOHI
> I'm dying, not deaf. Open those curtains, Ella. I want to see my grandchild… once more. (MOTHER does so) What's wrong, Michael, you look like hell?

> MICHAEL
> The Imadas' house burned down two nights ago.

190

TAKOOHI
I heard. What was it; a broken gas line,
electrical?

MICHAEL
The firemen thought it was arson.

TAKOOHI (suddenly alert)
What?

MICHAEL
They said the way the front window glass
was busted in instead of out, they thought
it might have been done on purpose but
they can't prove anything.

TAKOOHI
What are you going to do about it?

MICHAEL
I don't know that there is anything I can do.

TAKOOHI
Come here, Michael.

MICHAEL moves closer to her

Closer.

MICHAEL moves even closer. TAKOOHI slaps him hard

MICHAEL
Ouch!

TAKOOHI (sitting up)
An enemy burns your friend's house to the
ground and you do nothing?

MICHAEL (rubbing his cheek)
But what can I do?

TAKOOHI (animated)
You face your enemies, that's what you do!
Have you inherited no courage from your
Grandfather? If Krikor was here, he'd show
you what to do!

MOTHER (moving to her)
'Koohi, maybe you should lie back down
and rest.

                    TAKOOHI
        While the fox is in the hen house? Now that
        I think of it, we don't need Krikor! I'll
        show you what to do! Where are my shoes?

TAKOOHI is trying to get out of bed. MOTHER is trying to restrain her

                    MOTHER
        Michael, why don't you step outside, you're
        agitating her.

MICHAEL walks out into the hall, closing the door behind him

                         TAKOOHI (though door)
        Michael, the Basanians will not take this
        lying down! Do you hear me? Let go of
        me. Where are my shoes?

EXT. THE BURNED DOWN IMADA HOUSE - DAY

MICHAEL is sitting on the back porch concrete steps trying to write a letter. He's
looking at the desolation around him and starts to write again. After a minute, he
crumples the paper and tosses it in the ashes behind him. He looks up at the blackened
trees that are closest to the house and stares sadly. Suddenly he notices a bit of color on a
blackened branch. He approaches the tree to inspect. It is a bud- a sign that the tree has
not only survived but will bear fruit. He is cheered. He quickly inspects a few of the other
blackened trees and they too are flowering. Excited now, he is running from tree to tree

EXT. THE RELOCATION CAMP - DAY

The baseball diamond. ITO is seated on a bench behind home plate watching the
Japanese players conclude their practice. KIYOTO approaches ITO

                    KIYOTO
        Father, Momma is waiting for you.

                    ITO
        Yes.

KIYOTO sits with ITO for a moment, indifferent to the activity on the field

                    KIYOTO
        Why do you watch this?

                    ITO
        I used to play baseball in my youth. And,
        like me, many of these young men grew
        up playing the game.

                    KIYOTO
        It seems silly to play in here.

DANIEL Ishikawa, a nice looking young baseball player, approaches ITO and KIYOTO

> DANIEL
> Good practice, Mr. Imada?

> ITO
> Good practice. Daniel, this is my
> daughter, Kiyoto.

> DANIEL
> I'm very pleased to meet you, Kiyoto.

She nods curtly

> I hope you will join us on Saturday
> to watch us play.

> KIYOTO
> I think not.

DANIEL gives a quick look to ITO in an attempt to understand KIYOTO's attitude

> DANIEL
> Do you not approve of the game?

> KIYOTO
> Games are played in celebration. What
> have we to celebrate?

> DANIEL
> It helps us to tolerate our lives here.

> KIYOTO
> Then the Colonel was right. He said that
> it would help to normalize our lives. Per-
> haps what he meant was that it would
> numb us to the indignity of our lives.
> Go and play your game, Sir. Maybe it
> amuses the guards.

DANIEL looks to ITO who refuses to enter into the fray of the conversation

> DANIEL (calmly)
> We play to amuse ourselves. And we play
> with pride. The guards have yet to assemble
> a team that can beat us.

KIYOTO refuses to respond, finally

> I guess the real reason I play baseball is
> because it reminds me of home. My fam-

ily owns a farm in southern California. We
work hard, take care of our families and
play baseball when we can. This place,
all of this will end soon and we'll all be
going home. Baseball reminds me of that.
I'll see you on Saturday, Mr. Imada. I've
looked forward to meeting you, Kiyoto.
I hope we can be friends. Good night.

KIYOTO nods to DANIEL again, this time a little more cordially

EXT. THE RELOCATION CAMP - DAY

The baseball diamond. The Japanese team is at bat in the bottom of the ninth inning
trailing the guards' team by one run. KIYOTO sits quietly with her Father amid the
enthusiastic crowd. There is a man on first base. The tall pitcher winds up and delivers a
blazing fastball which the batter swings through for the third strike and out number one.
The 'clean up' hitter comes to the plate and DANIEL comes out to the 'on deck' circle as
the following hitter. The 'clean up' hitter takes the first pitch on the outside corner of the
plate for strike number one. He swings at the next pitch and drives it deep into the left
field corner. It is caught but the man on first tags up and runs to second, sliding in safe.
The guards argue that he is out but to no avail. DANIEL comes to the plate. The first
pitch is a high, inside fastball that makes DANIEL dive to the ground to avoid being
struck by the pitch. He gets up, dusts himself off and steps to the plate again. The pitcher
fires a fastball again and DANIEL lines it deep into the center/left gap. The center fielder
cannot cut the ball off and has to run the ball down. The man on base scores and
DANIEL approaches and rounds second headed for third. The shortstop baubles the relay
throw and DANIEL sprints for the plate. He slides in safe just ahead of the throw for the
winning run. He is mobbed by his teammates. He looks into the cheering crowd and finds
KIYOTO. She grins and applauds him demurely. He flashes her a big, charming smile

EXT.THE RELOCATION CAMP - DAY

The baseball diamond. ITO is sitting on a bench watching the sunset. KIYOTO
approaches him tentatively, holding a letter she has read

KIYOTO

Father, Michael has sent a letter.

ITO

What does he have to say?

KIYOTO

It is addressed to you.

ITO

Oh? I don't have my glasses. Would
you read?

As she reads, the light and life in ITO's eyes seem to fade into despair

194

KIYOTO

Dear Mr. Imada, I should have written this
letter a couple of weeks ago. But I couldn't.
Your house was lost in a fire three Sundays
ago. The firemen suspected arson but can't
prove it. Trees were damaged by the fire but
most survived and, in fact, are starting to flower. I expect there will be a big harvest this
summer and fall. I have talked to my uncle
Taj and he will help me with a loan to
rebuild. The harvest money will repay
most of the loan and by late fall I'll be
able to borrow against the existing structure to finish the house. It won't replace
your beautiful Victorian home but at least
you'll have a house on the property. I'm
sorry I wasn't there to protect your house,
Mr. Imada. I'll try to make up for it by
building you the nicest house I can. I guess
that's all for now. Mom and Grandma
send you their love. I'll do my best, I
promise. Yours' truly, Michael

KIYOTO sees the effect that the news has had on ITO and tries to cheer him

KIYOTO

Did you hear, Father? Michael will rebuild
our home.

ITO (more to himself)

Home? Home is where you feel safe. Home
is where you are wanted, where you belong.
Home? Where?

KIYOTO puts her head on her Father's shoulder and cries quietly

INT. THE RELOCATION CAMP - DAY

In the Imada quarters, KIYOTO is seated at a small table trying to write a letter. KIYO is
sitting on her bed, staring vacantly at the distant mountains. KIYOTO starts to write

KIYOTO VOICE OVER

Dear Michael, I've just gotten back from my
daily walk with Mr. Kitano. I chatter away
as he looks for flowers. I know he cannot
hear me but he graciously pretends to listen.
It's a nice little arrangement. We have been
hearing for months now that the war is going
well and that we may be going home soon.
The Commanding Officer has confirmed
these rumors but cannot give us any infor-

mation in detail. Mother doesn't seem to
understand. Ever since Father's death, she
seems to just drift through her days.
Momma needs me more and more.

EXT. SAINT PAUL'S CHURCH BAZAAR - DAY

A big banner announcing the bazaar has been strung between trees in the shaded park
next to the church. Young and old are out selling and buying at folding tables and
children are running and playing games provided for them. TAKOOHI and MOTHER
are selling baked goods, TAJ and CLAUDETTE are shopping while pushing a stroller.
There is a small combination of musicians playing traditional Armenian music

Note: All sounds of the bazaar are muted so we can hear KIYOTO's letter to MICHAEL

> KIYOTO VOICE OVER
> There are mostly women in camp now. Most
> of the working-aged men, including Daniel,
> have been furloughed out for weeks at a time,
> helping with the harvests in the south. They
> are very happy to do it. They have a future to
> work and save money for now. It makes me
> happy now to see mothers watching their
> children at play. They know that they have a
> future too. It seems so long ago when we
> first came here. Perhaps it's just that I've
> changed so much. I was so angry that I
> couldn't see some of the good people
> around me. And your letters have been
> very important to me, Michael. They have
> been a lifeline to the outside world and a
> dear friend.

At the bazaar, MICHAEL is talking to the lovely AUGGIE Parsejian. They are smiling a
lot and modestly flirting with one another

> I never thought I'd have wonderful news to
> report from this place but I do. Daniel and
> I have grown very close. He has asked me
> to marry him when we get out of here. I
> love him very much. He is kind and generous.
> Above all, he is hopeful. He has taught me
> to be hopeful again. I don't feel like a prisoner
> anymore, I feel like a survivor. Already I
> seem to be looking back on this place, oddly
> enough, with some nostalgia. I'll not miss
> it, of course. But the people I've met and
> lost and our endurance of this tragic place
> will be lasting memories. I sound like a
> philosopher. But this place does give
> you time to think. For a long time I wished

196

I could get out and live a normal life. But
I don't know what that is anymore. What
I know is, when you can lose everything,
everything becomes precious; your life,
the people you love… And so you live and
love with urgency because you never know…

INT. THE RELOCATION CAMP - DAY

In the Imada quarters, KIYOTO is still writing her letter but she is interrupted by a
garbled public address announcement

                    Well, I don't know where that deep thought
                    was going. I'll post this now so you'll get it
                    within the week. Give my love to your
                    Mother and tell Grandma that her cookies
                    continue to make me the most popular wo-
                    man in my barracks. Love always, Kiyoto

EXT. THE NEW IMADA HOUSE - DAY

MICHAEL and two other men are mixing and applying stucco to the outside walls of the
nearly completed new house. TAJ drives up and parks in the driveway

                    MICHAEL (approaching car)
                    Uncle Taj, I thought you were kidding with
                    your offer to help.

                    TAJ
                    Nope. I've got nothing else to do, I haven't
                    processed a loan in weeks. You are the only
                    one I know building anything. What's up?

                    MICHAEL
                    Mudding- more fun than a root canal.

                    TAJ
                    Let's get to it. You only have me for about
                    four hours. I got to take mother and baby
                    to the doctor this afternoon.

                    MICHAEL
                    How are they?

                    TAJ
                    Fine. Claudette is still as big as the sofa. Oh,
                    I almost forgot. (he retrieves a letter from his
                    coat) I'm delivering mail today too. This
                    looks like it's from Kiyoto.

                              MICHAEL
                    Oh, thanks.

MICHAEL takes his gloves off to take the letter and walks to the front of the house to
read while TAJ joins the other two men. It is KIYOTO's letter from the previous scene.
We watch MICHAEL read. He sits on the front porch and continues to read. At the heart
of his reaction to the letter are his dashed hopes of a romantic relationship with KIYOTO.
MICHAEL finishes the letter and sits thoughtfully for a moment. TAJ appears around the
corner of the house

                              TAJ
                    Hey, are we mudding this house today or
                    what?

MICHAEL looks at him, his mind a few hundred miles away

                    Are you all right, Michael? Is Kiyoto all
                    right?

                              MICHAEL (standing)
                    Yes. Yes, she's fine. Let's get some stucco
                    on these walls.

EXT. THE NEW IMADA NOUSE - DAY

Months later. MICHAEL is seated on the porch. He is wearing nice, casual clothes. An
older sedan pulls up in front of the house. MICHAEL stands. DANIEL is driving.
KIYOTO is beside him with KIYO in the back. KIYOTO gets out first

                              MICHAEL (approaches her)
                    Welcome home!

                              KIYOTO (hugging him)
                    Hello, Michael.

                              MICHAEL
                    Is that your Mother back there? Hello, Mrs.
                    Imada.

KIYO does not acknowledge MICHAEL

                              KIYOTO (quietly)
                    She may not know you, Michael. She hasn't
                    spoken much since Father's death. I doubt she
                    recognizes the place.

                              MICHAEL
                    I'm sorry to hear that.

DANIEL has gotten out and is walking around the front of the car

And this must be the baseball player.

>   KIYOTO
> Yes, Michael, this is my fiancé, Daniel
> Ishikawa.

>   MICHAEL
> Congratulations.

>   DANIEL
> Thank you.

>   MICHAEL
> Why don't we all go inside and see the
> new house?

>   DANIEL (to KIYOTO)
> Go ahead. I'll stay with your Mother.

MICHAEL leads KIYOTO into the house

>   MICHAEL
> I still need to get an electrician out here
> to inspect the wiring and hook up the water
> heater. The living room and dining room
> are about the same size but I enlarged the
> master bedroom and added two more bed-
> rooms. And come and see your new laundry
> and pantry. It's huge. You can even use part
> of it as a green house.

>   KIYOTO (interrupting)
> Michael, Momma and I are not coming back
> here.

>   MICHAEL
> Oh?

>   KIYOTO
> We've had to finalize our decisions quickly.
> I should have written to you. Daniel wants
> Momma and I to live with him and his fam-
> ily in the Imperial Valley. They have a farm
> there.

>   MICHAEL
> But this house is yours'. I paid for it with
> money from the orchard. It's my wedding
> gift to you.

                    KIYOTO
Thank you, Michael. But Momma and I will
be starting our new life somewhere else. I
suppose we could try to sell the property…

                    MICHAEL
No. No, don't do that. I've come to love this
orchard as your Father did. I'll buy it.

                    KIYOTO
Well, technically, you already own it.

                    MICHAEL
Yes. Then I should pay you a lot more than
a dollar for it.

KIYOTO crosses to MICHAEL to take his hands

                    KIYOTO
I was hoping you would see it that way. The
money will allow us to make plans.

                    MICHAEL
I'll ask Uncle Taj to draw up the papers and
arrange a new loan. When you get settled,
write to me and I'll wire the money to you.

                    KIYOTO (hugging him)
Thank you, Michael. And thank you for
being my dear friend.

                    MICHAEL
You love Daniel, don't you.

                    KIYOTO
I love him very much.

                    MICHAEL
Then he's OK with me.

MICHAEL wipes away a tear

I only wish your Father could see his orchard.
He would have been proud.

                    KIYOTO
He was proud of us both.

EXT. THE NEW HOUSE - DAY

From inside the house, a view of MICHAEL saying goodbye and congratulating KIYOTO and DANIEL again. They drive off. MICHAEL watches after them for a long while

INT. BASANIAN KITCHEN - DAY

MICHAEL opens a letter from ARAM and begins to read

> ARAM VOICE OVER
> Dear Michael, We're still here on this damned island. I've been detailed with some other guys in my outfit to deliver wounded to the hospital ship. So I've got a chance to write this before the launch takes us back.

EXT. JUNGLE BATTLEFIELD - DAY

Note: jungle battlefield scene is silent

ARAM and VARTAN are pinned down behind a log by enemy fire

> ARAM VOICE OVER
> We can't believe how tough these Japanese are. We can't budge them. We've even tried burning them out of their bunkers and still they fight. Tell Mom that I'm keeping my head down. I can't believe these young jarheads. I swear some of these guys don't give a thought to charging a nest of automatic   weapons fire.

VARTAN sees his Sergeant signaling him to flank the enemy position

> I thought I knew what bravery was. I'm not sure anymore. I'm not sure of a lot of things. I've killed people. There was nothing heroic about it. I was just trying to protect myself and the young men who were dying all around me. Dying looks easy. Maybe the real heroes are guys like you, Michael, who don't get medals for looking after the people they love and keeping their families together. Living may be the harder thing to do.

VARTAN takes off running. ARAM sees him get shot. VARTAN is still alive. ARAM must now save his friend or not

> I hope everybody is all right. I never thought I'd miss home but I do. The next time you see me we'll get good and drunk. Remember the day when Grandpa died and we walked

home in the rain? I can't wait to see you and
that God awful hot town.

ARAM runs to VARTAN. ARAM is dragging VARTAN back to the log

> Dammit, there's the whistle for the launch.
> Give my love to Mom and Grandma. Take
> care of yourself, Aram

We hear the shot that hits ARAM and he falls

EXT. JUNGLE BATTLEFIELD - DAY

Armenian folk music from the very first scene fades in. ARAM is being carried on a
litter. He is seeing a swirling, cloudy sky overhead. ARAM is having a vision. The four
year old ARAM is bouncing on FATHER's shoulders on that Saturday at the farmer's
market and they danced to the music

EXT. ARAM'S GRAVE - DAY

It has been a couple of weeks since ARAM was interred. MICHAEL and AUGGIE are
attending to MOTHER who has a small bouquet to place at the grave. A few paces away,
TAJ is holding his toddler and CLAUDETTE is in sunglasses

> MICHAEL
> Can I place those for you, Mom?

> MOTHER
> No, I'll do it.

MICHAEL and AUGGIE help MOTHER kneel at the side of the grave stone. She places
the flowers in the holder

> MOTHER (quietly)
> He had only just turned five. He couldn't
> understand why his Father was taken away
> from him. He got very angry. But it was
> no one's fault. There was no one to blame,
> no one to punish. I could not help him…
> My boy…

MOTHER touches the grave stone and weeps. A beat

> I pray that he's found some peace at last.

MICHAEL and AUGGIE help MOTHER stand and they start their walk back to the car.
MICHAEL hands MOTHER off to CLAUDETTE and then turns back to the grave. He
has a memory/vision of ARAM on the day they got drunk and walked in the rain. ARAM
is laughing in his vision

INT. MICHAEL'S HOUSE IN THE ORCHARD - NIGHT

Fall, 1953. It is TAKOOHI's birthday party. MICHAEL, his wife, AUGGIE and their two children, six year old ARAM and his younger sister, SASHA along with TAJ, CLAUDETTE and their eight year old son, THOMAS, and MOTHER are singing the birthday song to TAKOOHI. TAKOOHI, with the help of ARAM and THOMAS, blow out the candles to laughter and cheers

INT. MICHAEL'S HOUSE IN THE ORCHARD - NIGHT

Same night. TAKOOHI is smoking a cigar in the laundry/pantry room. She is looking east as the sun is lighting only the tops of the Sierra mountains. Finally MOTHER walks in

> MOTHER
> What are you doing with that?

> TAKOOHI
> I'm trying to stunt my growth.

> MOTHER
> Your Doctor will kill you.

> TAKOOHI
> I've been saying that for years.

MOTHER gives her a wry smile and leans against the washing machine. Finally

> Ninety-one years ago this whole thing
> started. It doesn't seem like "only yester-
> day", it seems like a hell of a long time
> ago, many lifetimes ago. So many people,
> some of their names are gone but somehow
> I remember... What did you say?

> MOTHER
> Nothing.

A beat

> TAKOOHI
> So, say something.

> MOTHER
> Do you want to play cards with us, birth-
> day girl?

> TAKOOHI
> No.

> MOTHER
> Then come in and watch the kids while we
> set up the table.

MOTHER helps TAKOOHI to her walker

INT. MICHAEL'S HOUSE IN THE ORCHARD - NIGHT

MOTHER is putting a record on the phonograph in the living room. It is traditional Armenian folk music.

In the kitchen, TAKOOHI is in the middle of a story she is telling to young THOMAS, ARAM and SASHA seated at a candle-lit table

> TAKOOHI
> Our people fled before the Turks. Some fled
> north into Russia where they had to eat rot-
> ting potatoes to survive. Some fled to Europe
> where they weren't wanted. Eventually, my
> brothers and I came to America because they
> were still taking refugees. But one man re-
> fused to flee before the Turks. And do you
> know who that man was? (the children shake
> their heads 'no') It was Krikor Basanian-
> freedom fighter, Scourge of the Turks, and
> your great grandfather. He was handsome
> with a dashing mustache, fierce in battle and
> fierce in his love for his people and a woman.
> And do you know who that woman was?
> (the children shake their heads 'no')
> Here, have another little piece of cake.

The phonograph music swells as we watch the disappearing light in the west over Fresno

OVER SEAS NEVER SAILED

EXT. SAO PAULO, BRAZIL, 1883 - DAY

Ten-year-old ALBERTO Santos-Dumont and his younger sister, SOPHIA, are flying a box kite from the veranda of the impressive family home

                              SOPHIA
                Let me hold it, Alberto. Let me!

                              ALBERTO
                All right but you must keep it fast against
                the wind.

SOPHIA squeals with glee as she holds the kite string but soon the kite drifts and dives down to the top of a tree

                              SOPHIA
                Oh, no. Fix it, Alberto, please.

ALBERTO scampers across a meadow towards the tree flapping his arms like a bird to his sister's delight. He climbs the tree and while he is trying to free the kite, he hears his older brothers' approach, FRANCIOS (oldest), and HENRIQUE, along with two of their friends. The four boys have been kicking a soccer ball

                              FRANCIOS
                'Berto! Well, I don't know where the loco is.
                Let's go.

ALBERTO is enjoying hiding from them

                              HENRIQUE
                Better not. Papa wants us to take him with us.

                              FRANCIOS
                Alberto is too small to play foot-ball. Let's go.
                He'll be all right.

The four boys run off, kicking the ball as they go. ALBERTO sits in the tree, considering what he has overheard. He begins to tug at the kite. The string breaks and the wind takes the kite high into the air. He watches intently as the kite goes up and back toward the mountains. His imagination takes him soaring like the kite; catching the up-drafts above cliffs towering over rolling hills and swooping into the valley below over orchards and winding streams. He teeters on the tree branch and falls, hitting another branch on the way down. It is a nasty fall. He rolls to his back, touches the blood from his nose and begins to cry. He sits up, decides that he is too old to cry and cleans himself up with his handkerchief. He starts to walk back to the house, turns to look into the afternoon sun and reflect on his daydream of flying

EXT. COFFEE PLANTATION, BRAZIL - DAY

HENRIQUE and other men are loading the last few cars of a train. The fourteen-year-old ALBERTO is chaining down irrigation pipe onto flat cars. FATHER, FRANCIOS, and FOREMAN are on horseback supervising the work. Train whistle blows and the ENGINEER in the locomotive waves to ALBERTO

                         ALBERTO
          Father, the engineer said I could operate the
          train for a few miles! With your permission.

                         FATHER
          Very well, Alberto. Finish dressing that chain.

                         ALBERTO
          Yes, Sir!

ALBERTO quickly ties up the excess chain from the chain jack and runs to the front of the train

                         FATHER (to FOREMAN)
          Do you need any more help today?

                         FOREMAN
          No. We'll work one more hour and I'll let them
          go for the weekend.

                         FRANCIOS (riding up)
          We're ready, Father.

                         FATHER
          Signal them.

FRANCOIS fires a shot from his pistol. ALBERTO leans out of the locomotive and waves. FATHER smiles and waves back

INT. LOCOMOTIVE - DAY

                         ENGINEER
          All right, kid, throttle forward.

ALBERTO pushes the throttle forward until the locomotive wheels throw sparks.

                         ENGINEER
          Throttle back until you get more traction.

As the train gains speed, the chain on the car with the irrigation pipe has fallen to the track. Sparks fly as the wheel shears off pieces of chain. Back at the loading site, FOREMAN and FATHER see sparks from the fallen chain

                         FOREMAN
          What is that?

FATHER
He's going to lose the load!

FATHER and FRANCOIS spur their horses to catch the train, yelling at the ENGINEER to stop. The wheel of the car rolls over the chain and breaks the chain jack off, spilling the pipe onto FATHER who was riding beside the car. FRANCOIS fires three shots in the air

INT. LOCOMOTIVE - DAY

ENGINEER
Stop the train.

ALBERTO
What?

ENGINEER (braking)
Something is wrong, stop the train!

As the irrigation pipe hits FATHER, he is thrown by his horse and hits his head on a rock. The horse is gored and finally impaled by one of the pipes as the train finally comes to a stop. ALBERTO leaps from the locomotive and runs back to his FATHER. The horse screams as HENRIQUE and shouting men run to lend assistance. FRANCOIS helps FATHER to his feet

FATHER
I'm all right. Francois, give me your pistol.

With great difficulty, FATHER shoots his horse and then collapses

HENRIQUE
Father!

FOREMAN
Get him into my wagon!

ALBERTO
What happened?

FRANCOIS
The chain was loose.

ALBERTO
No.

HENRIQUE
Come, let's get father to a physician.

INT. RECORDING STUDIO, 1935 – DAY

Close up of an OLD MAN taking oxygen. He is seated in a comfortable armchair. We can see the microphone on a table in front of him

                    OLD MAN (finally)
          Are you ready?

                    OFF CAMERA VOICE
          Yes.

                    OLD MAN
          Where do we start?

                    OFF CAMERA VOICE
          Tell us about yourself first.

                    OLD MAN
          Well, I was a newspaper reporter for the Paris
          Herald from 1900 to 1904. I saw the turn of the
          century, "La Belle Époque". It was a miracle
          of times. France led the world in the sciences
          and arts; in literature and new technologies, in
          music and painting and fashion. Paris was a
          beacon of inspiration. If you couldn't find
          something to write about you were an idiot.
          Alberto Santos-Dumont came to Paris with his
          parents in '91, his father was seeking medical
          treatment. His mother was scared to death.
          She feared that Paris was such a dangerous
          place for a young man. She was right.
          Alberto and Paris were made for one an-
          other. Alberto was a 'technophile'- a person
          who is in love with all things scientific,
          futuristic and magical.

EXT. GARE D'ORLEANS TRAIN DEPOT, PARIS, 1891 - DAY

The train is slowing to a stop in the depot, the young, dapperly dressed ALBERTO is seated on the train. There are many beautiful people and the city is glowing with excitement. He is giddy but trying to appear calm. Suddenly the Eiffel Tower appears in the distance. He is mesmerized. He gets off the train and starts to walk towards the tower. He takes a horse-drawn taxi, barely taking his eyes off of the tower. Before long he is staring straight up at it from the base. Venders are selling everything from pastries to small Eiffel Tower replicas. He happily gets on the newly invented electric elevators and rides them up and down like a child. Finally he sees a hydrogen balloon in the distance. He quickly goes down to street level to purchase field glasses and back up again to look at the balloon in more detail. The balloon is tethered at about 500 feet. He sees a man in a wicker basket suspended from the balloon. The man is looking down at a woman who is playing the violin. She is seated on an apparatus suspended from the basket. ALBERTO stares in amazement. Two lovely young women, LURLINE and MINA, stand off to his side to view the balloon

MINA

I hope she is wearing her Sunday best.

LURLINE

She is rather exposed up there. Perhaps she is
wearing a pair of pants.

MINA (giggling)

Oh, no. Which is worse, displaying yourself
like that or wearing pants?

ALBERTO (finally)

With your permission, may I say a gentleman
would not take advantage of a lady's exposure.
Especially if the lady was as brave as the woman dangling from the balloon. I imagine
that any gust of wind might precipitate a tragic
fall.

MINA

My parents would not approve of such a vulgar
demonstration.

ALBERTO (to LURLINE)

And what about your parents, would they
approve?

LURLINE

My parents are satisfied that I make my own
decisions as to what is or is not vulgar.

ALBERTO

Bravo. I applaud you- the modern woman.

LURLINE

Not too modern.

ALBERTO

May I guess from your speech you are from
the United States of North America.

LURLINE

Correct.

ALBERTO

Then we are from adjoining continents. I am
Alberto, your neighbor from Brazil. Alberto
Santos-Dumont, at your service, Mademoiselle.

ALBERTO offers his hand. LURLINE offers her hand as if to shake hands but
ALBERTO kisses her hand

LURLINE

Lurline Spreckles, San Diego, California. And this is Mina. She lives here.

ALBERTO kisses MINA'S hand

ALBERTO

Perhaps someday I will make your beautiful city my home as well.

RICHARD (approaching them)

Come, ladies, we must leave for the Bois.

LURLINE

Thank you. Alberto, this is Richard, Mina's brother. Richard, Alberto.

ALBERTO

My pleasure. You are fortunate to escort such lovely young ladies.

RICHARD

Yes.

LURLINE

Well, Alberto, I hope we will meet again.

ALBERTO

There is no doubt we will. Perhaps I shall see you here. I intend to frequent Eiffel's tower.

LURLINE

Very well. Until then, good day, Sir.

ALBERTO watches the three of them get into the elevator. They wave to him, he turns and smiles at the spectacular view of Paris and then trains his field glasses on the balloon again

INT. A HALL LEADING TO FATHER'S BEDROOM - NIGHT

ALBERTO is walking to the bedroom with his MOTHER

ALBERTO

But they are fine doctors with the most advanced methods.

MOTHER

Nevertheless he grows impatient.

ALBERTO (knocks on door)

Father?

FATHER (becoming alert)

Yes? Yes, Alberto, come in.

ALBERTO

It's late. I won't keep you from rest.

FATHER

Nonsense, I wanted to speak with you. Did
you attend to your studies today?

ALBERTO

Yes. Well, most of them. I like mechanical
engineering and some sciences. But I prefer
to read other topics on my own. And the
city itself is the best education- the museums
and architecture. Father, do you remember
that petroleum fueled internal combustion
machine that we saw at the Exposition?

FATHER

I remember I couldn't pull you away from it.

ALBERTO

Well, I saw a bigger one today. It was pow-
ering a carriage mounted on four pneumatic
wheels. The Peugeot brothers had two of
them for sale. I would have purchased one
if it were not such an extravagance.

FATHER

How much were they asking?

ALBERTO

I'm not sure. Perhaps my entire allowance
for the summer.

FATHER

You may afford to purchase one yet.

ALBERTO

What?

FATHER

You have done well here, Alberto. You have
not spent your money frivolously. I think it's
time to trust you with your inheritance.

ALBERTO
You have been generous with me, Father. I
didn't mean to complain.

FATHER
No. But you will need to be self-sufficient
soon. Your mother and I will be sailing back
to Brazil this Fall and you, of course, will
stay. You have thrived in Paris. You should
stay. You may live with our cousins or hire
living quarters for yourself, the money will
be more than adequate. I must go home and
consult with my Brazilian doctors. Their
science may not be as advanced but they
have better manners than the French.

ALBERTO
Please, Father, don't give up on them…

FATHER
I've made up my mind. Going home is the
best medicine for me now.

ALBERTO
I hadn't considered living here without you
and mother. Would I be able to visit you in
Brazil now and then?

FATHER
Your mother will never forgive you if you
do not.

ALBERTO (tearing up)
I wish I could have been a better son to you.

FATHER
You haven't disappointed me. You never
wanted to be a coffee farmer like your
brothers. I finally understood that. And
now you've grown into a fine, intelligent
young man. You've shown good judgment.
Follow your heart. It's all any of us can do.

ALBERTO
Thank you, Father.

EXT. PARC D'AEROSTATION, VAUGIRARD - DAY

Early morning. ALBERTO is seated on a stump next to the workshop/storage shed. A
large grassy field adjoins the shed. LACHOMBRE and MACHURON (large, imposing
man) are rounding the corner of the shed and do not see ALBERTO

212

MACHURON
Why did you agree to such an early flight?

LACHOMBRE
I don't recall agreeing. It was just settled
somehow.

ALBERTO (standing)
Good morning, Lachombre. I hope I didn't
startle you gentlemen.

LACHOMBRE
Well, you're early I see.

ALBERTO
Yes, I wanted to observe the preparation, if
that's all right. I'd like to help, if I can.

LACHOMBRE
Very well. This is Alexis Machuron. He is
the most experienced balloonist in France.
He will be your pilot today.

ALBERTO
That will be an honor, Messier.

MACHURON
That will be 300 francs, Messier.

ALBERTO (paying them)
Yes, of course. I assume the fee includes
any damages incurred?

MACHURON (firmly)
There will be no damages.

ALBERTO
I see. And how long will we be aloft?

MACHURON
Until the gas or ballast is exhausted, an hour
or more perhaps.

LACHOMBRE
Shall we begin? While the hydrogen gas is
produced, we must lay out the envelope.

LACHOMBRE and ALBERTO carry and unfold the balloon. MACHURON uncovers a
phonograph, puts a record on the turntable, winds the machine and applies the needle to
the record- a chanteuse singing popular ballads. He dons gloves and sorts steel trays. He

starts to shovel heavy iron filings into the trays. LACHOMBRE and ALBERTO load the large wicker basket onto a dolly. LACHOMBRE wheels it out to the envelope

                          ALBERTO (to MACHURON)
          May I call you Alexis?

                          MACHURON
          If you wish.

                          ALBERTO
          Henri says that it shall take several hours to
          fill the envelope with gas.

                          MACHURON (shoveling)
          Yes.

                          ALBERTO
          Why is that so?

                          MACHURON (shoveling)
          Because hydrogen gas is the product of a
          chemical reaction when sulfuric acid is mixed
          with the iron. It then has to be pumped into
          the balloon with some consideration of its'
          flammable nature. All this takes time.

                          ALBERTO
          Oh.

MACHURON shovels more

          Could you not make the gas faster with larger
          containers?

                          MACHURON (shoveling)
          I suppose so.

                          ALBERTO
          And then, of course, it could be pumped faster.

                          MACHURON
          Are you going into the hydrogen supply bus-
          iness, Messier?

                          ALBERTO
          Uh, no. I was just thinking that the process
          could be more efficient.

                          MACHURON
          You're right. Bigger vats and bigger fans
          would make and move more gas faster.

214

But I can barely lift these small trays as it
is. And then there's the problem of pump-
ing the gas so quickly that the heat damages
the envelope.

                    ALBERTO
          I see. Perhaps icing the tubes would cool
          the gas sufficiently?

                    MACHURON
          Messier, you said you wanted to help?

                    ALBERTO
          Of course.

MACHURON hands the shovel to ALBERTO. ALBERTO puts the shovel down,
removes his bowler and jacket. He rolls up his sleeves and shovels while MACHURON
turns up the music. LACHOMBRE chuckles

EXT. PARC D'AEROSTATION, VAUGIRARD - DAY

Late morning. The balloon is inflated and staked to the ground. MACHURON is in the
basket loading ballast (bags of sand). ALBERTO is writing in his notebook

                    LACHOMBRE (to ALBERTO)
          This is the finest basket I've ever owned- big
          enough to carry three men and strong enough
          to take a beating. We've made several hun-
          dred ascents in this basket.

                    ALBERTO (still writing)
          It looks heavy.

LACHOMBRE is exasperated, MACHURON chuckles

                    LACHOMBRE (to MACHURON)
          Well, are you ready?

                    MACHURON
          I have everything but the client.

ALBERTO puts a large valise in the basket and climbs in

                    MACHURON (lifting valise)
          What's this?

                    ALBERTO
          Essential supplies.

                    MACHURON (kissing medallion)
          Let go all lines!

LACHOMBRE releases staked lines and up they go

EXT. IN THE BASKET OF THE BALLOON - DAY

ALBERTO is wide-eyed with fear as the balloon climbs quickly. MACHURON chuckles watching ALBERTO clutching one of the lines suspending the basket. One of the chanteuse's ballads underscores much of this scene

                    ALBERTO VOICE OVER
          "Let go all lines!" At this cry, the wind sud-
          denly became calm. All was stillness. In-
          finitely gentle was the illusion of the forward
          and upward progress. It seemed that we did
           not move but that the earth sank down and
          away from us. We rose fast. At about 4500
          feet I looked down into an abyss of space.
          The earth was like a concave saucer beneath
          me, the horizon seemed to lift up to a rim
          that melted into a hazy sky. Villages and
          woods, meadows and chateaux, filed before
          us like pictures on a wheel, out of which the
          whistling of locomotives throws sharp notes.
          These faint, piercing sounds, together with
          the yelping and barking of dogs, are the
          only sounds which I could hear through
          the depths of the upper air. I checked my
          barograph.

                    ALBERTO
          This instrument tells me that we should be
          at about seven thousand feet.

                    MACHURON
          Six thousand.

                    ALBERTO
          How can you tell?

                    MACHURON
          The shape of the balloon. At about seven or
          eight thousand feet the gas starts to expand
          noticeably. Heat from the sun will also ex-
          pand the gas. Then we must vent gas or the
          envelope will explode.

                    ALBERTO
          Explode?

                    MACHURON (enjoying his joke)
          Yes. I didn't bring a parachute. Did you?

216

ALBERTO shakes his head 'no'

Then we shall vent gas when we must.

Through the clouds, they hear church bells. ALBERTO checks his pocket watch

> ALBERTO
> It's time for our noon meal.

> MACHURON (incredulously)
> You want to make a descent for lunch?

> ALBERTO
> No, no. I brought enough for us both.

ALBERTO finds linen napkins in his valise, offers one to MACHURON and they tuck the napkins into their shirt collars

> ALBERTO
> Boiled egg?

They each shell an egg and proceed to eat

> ALBERTO
> Champagne?

With a broad grin, MACHURON accepts a paper cup from ALBERTO who then uncorks the champagne that bursts from the bottle

> MACHURON
> It's the thin air.

> ALBERTO
> Yes, I should have known. Well, let's see,
> I have cold roast beef, chicken and cheese.

ALBERTO produces an ornate box from which the men enjoy their finger food, throwing chicken bones and cheese rinds over the side of the basket

> Fruit and cake?

> MACHURON
> Yes, please.

ALBERTO produces another container and they leisurely continue their meal

> ALBERTO
> Chartreuse?

> MACHURON
> This is better than I get at home.

ALBERTO produces glasses and pours the liquor

                    ALBERTO VOICE OVER
          No dining room could be so marvelous in its'
          decoration. The sun sets the clouds in ebullition,
          making them throw up rainbow jets of frozen
          vapor like great sheaves of fireworks all around
          the basket. Lovely white spangles of the most
          delicate ice formations appear, moment by
          moment, out of nothingness, beneath our very
          eyes in our drinking glasses.

The chanteuse's music swells and for a little while we enjoy the beauty with them.
ALBERTO has transformed from frightened explorer to enthusiastic adventurer- the little
boy who is living his dream of flight. Suddenly the balloon drops into the clouds, the
envelope wrinkles and they descend rapidly. ALBERTO is alarmed but MACHURON is
calm as always

                    ALBERTO
          What's happening?

                    MACHURON
          Ice on top of the balloon has made us heavy.
          These clouds are cooling and condensing
          our gas. Better get rid of some ballast; two,
          no, three bags, I think.

The balloon drops below cloud cover at about 3,000 feet. The wind is blowing hard and
the balloon is plunging rapidly

          Now would be a good time to drop that sand.

ALBERTO drops three bags of sand that slows their descent but they are still moving
rapidly with the wind. MACHURON drops the guide rope over the side to hang off of the
basket

          This heavy rope is one hundred feet long.
          The more of the rope that is touching the
          ground, the lighter we become and the
          slower we descend. Also, the friction of
          dragging the rope will slow our horizontal
          speed. Let's drop down further to read road signs.

MACHURON vents gas and consults his map

          Let's see, I think we've been traveling east,
          southeast. We must be approaching the Forest
          of Fontainebleau. Quickly, throw out a half a
          bag to hop over that stand of trees.

                              ALBERTO
What?

                              MACHURON
Never mind, it's too late.

The guide rope hits the top of a tree, wraps around a branch jerking the basket to a stop.
Both men are knocked off their feet

                         ALBERTO (standing)
What do we do?

                              MACHURON
I don't want to land here. Let's drop most
of our ballast first.

They do. The balloon is freed but climbs with great speed. MACHURON vents gas to
bring them back down.

                              MACHURON
There, that open field. Let's land there.

Still venting gas, the balloon drops down dragging the guide rope. The basket nears the
ground at a walking pace. With a dramatic gesture, MACHURON pulls the emergency
gas release cord. The basket hits the ground, tips over gently spilling ALBERTO onto the
field. But MACHURON steps out of the basket as it tips over and, without breaking
stride, walks over to a farmer sitting in a buck wagon watching all this. ALBERTO
stands, a little dazed, and starts to coil the guide rope and rigging. Finally MACHURON
walks back to ALBERTO

                    I told the farmer that you would be pleased to
                    pay him for transporting us and our equip-
                    ment to the train station.

INT. MOVING PASSENGER TRAIN - DAY

Benches are facing one another. MACHURON is stretched out on one trying to sleep.
ALBERTO is seated on the other sketching and making notes

                              MACHURON
What are you doing?

                              ALBERTO
Drafting my balloon. You and Henri are going
to build it, with my help, of course.

                              MACHURON
No, I don't think so. We're busy.

                              ALBERTO
What is that medallion around your neck?

                    MACHURON (giving it to him)
          Here, you read it.

                    ALBERTO
          It's a Paris Exposition Medal. "Master of the
           Balloon." Impressive.

                    MACHURON (hat over his eyes)
          Of course.

ALBERTO chuckles, we can see MACHURON'S grin

EXT. PARC D' AEROSTATION, VAUGIRARD - DAY

Late afternoon. ALBERTO, LACHOMBRE and MACHURON are talking outside of the
shed

                    LACHOMBRE (looking at draft)
          The envelope is much too small. You'll not
          get the lift you need.

                    ALBERTO
          The basket I'm designing will weigh a third
          as much as yours. It will carry one man-
          myself. And I weigh half as much as Alexis.

MACHURON doesn't quite know how to take the comment

                    LACHOMBRE
          It's not heavy enough to be stable.

                    ALBERTO
          The longer suspension cords will stabilize
          it. Look, just build it and let me worry
          about the practicality. (paying them) Here
          is a substantial advance for materials and
          your fees. I'll see you gentlemen tomor-
          row and we'll discuss the details.

ALBERTO leaves

                    MACHURON
          We've created a monster.

                    LACHOMBRE
          Yes, but the monster has money.

MACHURON nods in agreement

EXT. PARC D' AEROSTATION, VAUGIRARD - DAY

Weeks later. ALBERTO (now sporting a mustache) is supervising the inflation of the balloon. He and two others are icing down the supply tubes

                          ALBERTO
              More ice closer to the vat, gentlemen.

ALBERTO walks over to the enlarging envelope where LACHOMBRE stands. MACHURON arrives and inspects the iced tubes. ALBERTO approaches him

                          MACHURON
              Larger fans?

                          ALBERTO
              Yes.

                          MACHURON
              And?

                          ALBERTO
              It seems to be working.

                          MACHURON (sincerely)
              Congratulations.

A big smile crosses ALBERTO'S face

EXT. SIDEWALK TABLES AT MAXIM'S CAFÉ - DAY

Late afternoon. PIERRE (waiter) is serving George GOURSAT a cocktail. They hear the engine of ALBERTO'S balloon and look up to see him

                          PIERRE
              What is that?

                          GOURSAT
              The balloon?

                          PIERRE
              No, that thing in front of the gondola.

                          GOURSAT
              That is a propeller, Pierre. It propels the air
              ship forward.

                          PIERRE
              Noisy.

Emmanuel AIME and DEUTSCH de la Muerthe step out of the café to see the balloon

                          AIME
              It's Santos-Dumont again.

                    DEUTSCH
          Oh, yes, the Brazilian. I find him a little
          brash. Where are all of our good French
          aeronauts?

DEUTSCH de la Muerthe exits back into the café

                    AIME
          Indeed, where?

                    PIERRE
          It's too noisy. It will scare the horses.

                    GOURSAT
          Perhaps someday we will all be puttering
          around up there, with no horses on the
          ground to frighten.

                    PIERRE (exiting)
          That will be the day.

George GOURSAT and Emmanuel AIME share a smile

EXT. IN THE BASKET OF THE BALLOON - DAY

The engine is running soundly and the air ship is handling well. ALBERTO relaxes a
little in the basket to enjoy the sunset over Paris, perhaps not unlike the sunset he enjoyed
in Brazil as a ten year old child

NEWSREEL FOOTAGE

Ragtime music over images of many of the more outrageous attempts of man to fly

INT. RECORDING STUDIO, 1935 - DAY

                    OLD MAN
          By the end of 1898 Alberto had piloted several
          hundred balloon flights, many of them powered
          by propellers on gasoline engines - dirigibles of
          his own design. He wasn't the first to achieve
          powered, controlled flight. There were a few
          who had had limited success but many had died
          in the attempt. The Wright brothers were
          still five years away from their experiments
          at Kitty Hawk. Count Zeppelin was drafting
          plans for huge, ridged airships, soon to be
          seen in the skies over Europe…

EXT. PARC D' AEROSTATION, VAUGIRARD, 1898 - DAY

ALBERTO is speeding on his motor-tricycle

OLD MAN VOICE OVER
And then there was this Frenchified Brazilian,
'Le Petite Santos', as he was called in the
press. This 'plucky aeronaut' was dashing
around to the finest restaurants of Paris in his
motor-tricycle or his electric car. Brave, well-
mannered and well-moneyed. Slight in
stature but charismatic and good looking.
He knew he was definitely a 'swell'. (chuckles)

ALBERTO slows to a stop at a crowd of spectators and newspaper reporters. He turns off
his engine, puts on his Panama hat and acknowledges the applause

FIRST REPORTER
Messier Santos, will you fly today?

ALBERTO (feigning concern)
I don't know. The winds seem a bit treacherous.
I'll consult with my staff.

FIRST REPORTER
But will you be making an attempt to win the
Deutsch Prize soon?

ALBERTO
What news service do you represent?

FIRST REPORTER
The Paris Herald.

ALBERTO
Are there any more reporters here this morning?

Two other reporters identify themselves

ALBERTO
Good. I want to be on record when I say
that I am not interested in Messier Deutsch
de la Meurthe's 100,000f. As an aeronautical scientist, I shall continue to methodi-
cally pursue my series of experiments, a
pursuit which will, undoubtedly, end with
my life. If in the course of my experiments,
I successfully navigate the Eiffel Tower
and back to the park to satisfy the conditions
of the contest, I shall give half of the money
to the poor of Paris who have demonstrated
their support of me from the start. Now I
ask you to excuse me. And, please, for
your safety and my own, stay back from
the air ship.

ALBERTO walks to the dirigible tethered by LACHOMBRE and MACHURON

MACHURON
You're not going up today?

ALBERTO
Of course I'm going. Who is this?

Aida d' ACOSTA, a beautiful, well-dressed woman approaches ALBERTO

MACHURON
Cuban and rich. That's all I know.

ACOSTA
Excuse me, Messier Santos. I must introduce
myself. I am Aida d' Acosta.

ALBERTO
A pleasure. Perhaps we could speak to one
another after the flight?

ACOSTA
Forgive me, Messier, but I may not be here
upon your return. I would like to consult
with you about the possibility of flying
myself.

ALBERTO
I'm sorry, Mademoiselle. As you can see,
there is no room for another person.

ACOSTA
You misunderstand. I want to pilot the balloon
and freely navigate the air as you do. I assure
you that I am quite prepared to pay you well
for your instruction.

ALBERTO
I see. Are you aware of the risks you would
be taking, not only with your life but with
my balloon?

ACOSTA
I will indemnify you against all loss, despite
the outcome.

ALBERTO
Let me be direct- you could die.

ACOSTA
And so could you, Messier. And yet you take

the risk. I want to know why you take the risk.
I suspect I know why. But I want to experience
it for myself.

                    ALBERTO
Meet me here on Monday at dawn.

                    ACOSTA
Thank you, Messier.

Aida d' ACOSTA withdraws, MACHURON chuckles as ALBERTO climbs into the basket. ALBERTO addresses LACHOMBRE and MACHURON loud enough for the crowd to hear

                    ALBERTO
No, I will not disappoint these good people!
(starts the engine) Let go all lines!

The crowd cheers. He ascends, clears the park and levels off at about six hundred feet

EXT. DIRT ROAD ADJACENT TO THE PARK - DAY

A young BOY and his GRANDPA are taking their vegetables to market in a horse drawn wagon

                    BOY (looking up)
Look, grandpa, Messier Santos!

                    GRANDPA
Yes.

                    BOY
Does he fly by magic, grandpa?

                    GRANDPA
Yes.

                    BOY
Is it a bad magic, grandpa?

                    GRANDPA
I don't know.

                    BOY
He must be very powerful.

EXT. IN THE BASKET OF THE BALLOON - DAY

ALBERTO can see the Eiffel Tower in the distance, he checks his pocket watch and opens up the engine to full speed, constantly checking his rigging and rudder. He hears a drum coming from a party of people on a roof below. They are waving to him. He doffs his Panama hat to them and a cheer goes up

EXT. SIDEWALK TABLES, MAXIM'S CAFÉ - DAY

Two DEBUTANTES are seated at a sidewalk table

                    DEBUTANTE TWO (pointing)
          Look, there he goes!

                    DEBUTANTE ONE
          Yes. He is handsome even from this distance.

The girls giggle. George GOURSAT, DEUTSCH de la Muerthe, and Emmanuel AIME step out of the café to see ALBERTO fly toward the tower

                    GOURSAT
          Is Alberto making an attempt at your prize,
          Messier Deutsch?

                    DEUTSCH
          He is obliged to notify the commission twenty-
          four hours in advance of an attempt. An official
          delegation must be present to time the trial.
          Has he notified us, Emmanuel?

                    AIME
          No, Messier.

                    DEUTSCH
          There is your answer, George. And a good thing
          too. It appears that at his present speed, Messier
          Santos would fail to make the 30 minute
          round trip requirement. But it seems that failure
          is what endears him to Parisians. Does it not?

                    GOURSAT
          His failures are frighteningly spectacular. But
          I must disagree, Messier. It is not failure which
          captures the imagination of Parisians. It is the
          repeated attempt despite failure.

GOURSAT and AIME exit into the café, leaving DEUTSCH to grumble outside

EXT. IN THE BASKET OF THE BALLOON - DAY

As ALBERTO closes on the Eiffel Tower he throttles back the engine to round the tower safely and doffs his hat to the crowd cheering him from the observation level of the tower. He makes his turn, straightens out, and the heavy cord that controls the rudder breaks, flutters in the wind and wraps around the propeller. He shuts off the engine and drops ballast to be sure that he does not drift into the tower. A strong head wind is pushing him across the river. He sees an open field behind an orchard and starts to vent gas for his descent. The venting valve breaks open. He is going down fast and is dumping all of his ballast but it is too late. He crashes into a tree at the edge of the orchard, the basket wedging into a branch. ALBERTO is unharmed but hears the balloon silk ripping as it settles into the tree. A GROUNDS KEEPER and a young man approach.

GROUNDS KEEPER
Are you injured, Messier?

ALBERTO
No. Is this your tree?

GROUNDS KEEPER
No. You are on the estate of Edmond de Rothschild.
Can I be of assistance to you?

ALBERTO
Do you have tall ladders?

GROUNDS KEEPER
Yes, Messier, I'll get them. Come, my boy. The
Master approaches now, Messier.

ALBERTO hears more silk ripping and winces

ROTHSCHILD
Well, I'll be. You must be that Santos-Dumont
fellow. Alberto, isn't it? Are you quite all right?

ALBERTO
Yes.

ROTHSCHILD
Good. I'm your host, Edmond Rothschild.
Excellent, here come the ladders. We'll get
you down straight away.

ALBERTO
Actually, if I may employ your man, I should
like to stay up here to help salvage the balloon.
(to the GROUNDS KEEPER) Put that ladder
on the other side, would you?

ROTHSCHILD
Can I get you anything? Something to drink perhaps?

ALBERTO
You're very accommodating considering that
I've damaged your chestnut tree.

ROTHSCHILD

Think nothing of it. I have a whole orchard of
them. (calling the boy) Fredrick! Tell Madame
Reaux to give you chilled champagne and two,
no, four glasses.

Princess Isabel, COMTESSE d'Eu and Gustav EIFFEL approach the tree

COMTESSE

You've abandoned your guests again, Edmond,
but I forgive you for I know it must be an urgent
matter.

ROTHSCHILD

Indeed. And what a coincidence. Comtesse, this
is Alberto Santos-Dumont, your fellow country-
man.

COMTESSE

I know. And up a tree for the moment.

ROTHSCHILD

Messier, this is Princess Isabel, Comtesse d'Eu,
daughter of the last Emperor of Brazil.

COMTESSE

My goodness, Edmond, I'm old but you make
me sound positively deceased.

ALBERTO

It is my honor, Comtesse. I only wish that I
was in a position to show you a courtesy.

COMTESSE

Never mind, I can see that you are busy. Be-
sides, it is my honor to meet you. I have
followed your career with great interest. But
we must continue our conversation on terra
firma. My neck will get a kink looking up
as I am.

ALBERTO

Of course, Madame.

The boy arrives with the champagne and ROTHSCHILD pours. More silk rips.

ALBERTO (to GROUNDSKEEPER)

Forget the silk. Save the rudder, if you can.

                    ROTHSCHILD
Forgive me, Gustav. Messier, this is Gustav
Eiffel.

                    ALBERTO
Of the tower?

The boy climbs the ladder to give ALBERTO his glass

                    EIFFEL
The same. I recognize you. You're the one
circling around up there. They sell ginger
bread likenesses of you on the observation
deck. Our local politicians wish they were
as popular as you.

A chuckle from the three on the ground. They all have champagne

                    ROTHSCHILD
Comtesse, would you do the honors?

                    COMTESSE (toasting)
Well, then… To fairer winds?

They chuckle and sip

EXT. PARC D'AEROSTATION, VAUGIRARD - DAY

Aida d' ACOSTA is standing in the gondola under a tree without the balloon. The
controls and rigging have been mocked up for instructional purposes

                    ALBERTO
All right let's go over everything once again.
What are these?

                    ACOSTA
They are pitch ballasts. They control ascent
and descent.

                    ALBERTO
How? Show me.

                    ACOSTA (demonstrates)
As I pull the front ballast to me, the center
of gravity is changed and the nose of the air
ship points up. As I pull the rear ballast to
me, the nose points down.

                    ALBERTO
And what do these handles control?

                         ACOSTA
They control the rudder.

                         ALBERTO
Show me.

ACOSTA tries to demonstrate but has difficulty

          No, you must put tension on both lines, re-
          member?

                         ACOSTA
          Oh, yes. Pulling the left line forward makes
          you go left and the right one makes you go
          right.

                         ALBERTO
          And the overhead line?

                         ACOSTA
          It releases gas and decreases the lift.

                         ALBERTO
          And the spigot there?

                         ACOSTA
          It releases water and the lift is increased.

                         ALBERTO
          No, the lift remains constant. You are lighten-
          ing the air ship by releasing the water/ballast.

                         ACOSTA
          Technically, isn't it the same thing as increas-
          ing the lift when you diminish the load to lift
          ratio?

                         ALBERTO (miffed)
          Very well. Let's do a dry run. You will respond
          to the situations I give you by telling me what
          you are going to do and, at the same time, doing it.

                         ACOSTA
          Yes.

                         ALBERTO
          Good. Imagine that you are aloft at two hundred
          feet over the city. You are approaching a hill
          with a tail wind and those hot chimneys are
          coming up fast. What do you do?

ACOSTA
I pull in the front attitude ballast to climb.
(does so)

ALBERTO
Fine. Now the nose of the balloon is pointing
up and the engine stalls. What do you do?

ACOSTA
I should land, shouldn't I?

ALBERTO
I'm not there to advise you! Do something
quick, those chimneys are coming up fast!

ACOSTA
I drop the front attitude ballast to level the
balloon and turn the rudder to avoid the hill.
(does so)

ALBERTO
There is no steering! You are not in a powered ship anymore! You are at the mercy
of the tail wind!

ACOSTA (rattled)
Stop shouting at me!

ALBERTO
Do something quick!

ACOSTA (does so)
I dump ballast as fast as I can!

ALBERTO
Too late! Boom! You hit a hot chimney and
the explosion wakes up most of the neighborhood. Now my balloon is all over the place
and you are a smoldering debutant. (walking
away from her) Perhaps Mademoiselle
should take up safer pastimes. I think croquet
is in vogue.

ACOSTA
Wait! You come back here!

In her haste to get out of the basket she tips it over (dress over her head) and scrambles to
her feet to chase him down

That wasn't fair!

ALBERTO

And neither are the vagaries of the air but
they are there nonetheless. I have seen men
burned alive in their balloons or fallen
from great heights. I have tried to impress
you with the urgency of a pilot's decision
making. I have failed. Let's leave it at that.

ALBERTO walks away from her. A beat

ACOSTA (approaching him)

Oh, now I understand; that you are trying to
frighten me away from my pursuit. I am
used to hearing that I may not do something
because I am a woman. Or maybe that's not
it. Maybe you're just genuinely concerned
about my well-being. That's fine. But I
assure you, Messier, I am determined to fly.
All of my life I have dreamt of flying. Why
shouldn't I? I am as courageous as any man.
Let me try. Please.

ALBERTO (finally)

Shall we say, tomorrow at dawn?

ACOSTA

Thank you.

ALBERTO watches her walk to her carriage for a time and walks into the shed

LACHOMBRE (working)

How did class go today? I heard some yelling.

ALBERTO

Class went well. I'm learning a lot. Were you
able to straighten out the propeller?

LACHOMBRE

No. And I won't have time to make another
for at least a week.

ALBERTO

No, we talked about it; all new silk which will
make the work easier. We were going to put in
another rib and use piano wire throughout,
remember?

LACHOMBRE

You're not listening to me. I have other clients
who need equipment. If I don't service them,
they'll go somewhere else.

232

                         ALBERTO
Why do you think you're getting all this work?
It's because of me!

                         LACHOMBRE
Thank you. These are well paying jobs, too.

A beat

                         ALBERTO
Did you know the Deutsch prize was 100,000f?

                         LACHOMBRE
No, 100,000f?

                         ALBERTO
If I ... when I win that prize, I should give half
of it to you and Alexis.

                         LACHOMBRE
Should or would?

                         ALBERTO
Will.

                         LACHOMBRE
50,000f?

                         ALBERTO
50,000f.

                         LACHOMBRE
All new silk?

                         ALBERTO
And piano wire throughout.

INT. ALBERTO'S TOWNHOUSE, PARIS - DAY

ALBERTO, EIFFEL, COMTESSE, Aida d' ACOSTA are seated at the table in the
dining room for the noon meal. EIFFEL is preoccupied with his desert. ALBERTO is
opening a small gift from the COMTESSE

                         ALBERTO
Oh, it's beautiful. It's a ... very shiny.

                         COMTESSE
It is the medal of St Benedict that protects
against accidents. Wear it next to your
heart for your dear mother's sake.

ALBERTO
Yes, of course. Thank you.

ALBERTO pulls a red scarf with writing on it from the bottom of the box

And what is this?

COMTESSE
A scarf for the young and gallant aeronaut.
"Por mares nunca d'antes navegados!"
"O'er seas heretofore unsailed!" It is poetry.
It is the salute to explorers venturing in
unknown lands. What think you, Gustav?

EIFFEL
I think this fruit pudding and this baked crust
is absolutely delicious. What's your man's
name?

ALBERTO
Charles.

EIFFEL
I should hire him away from you. My wife
is a delightful woman but a dreadful cook
and has fired every cook I've engaged.

ALBERTO
If I have to bid for Charles' loyalty, you
have the advantage of me, Messier.

COMTESSE
Gustav, your wife is a delightful woman who
knows all she needs to know; (to ACOSTA)
where all the finest restaurants in Paris are.

The ladies chuckle

EIFFEL
Never mind, I couldn't steal a domestic from
the most famous man in Europe anyway.

ALBERTO (chuckling)
I hardly think that I'm the most famous man
in Europe.

EIFFEL
Is that so? Name someone more famous or
I shall accuse you of false modesty.

ALBERTO

The Pope.

EIFFEL

Ah, yes. And he's entertaining as well.

COMTESSE

Do not speak glibly about His Holiness,
Gustav.

EIFFEL

Forgive me, Comtesse.

COMTESSE

He has a point, Alberto. I think you know
that your evolutions in the air are reported
world-wide. What think you, Mademoiselle?

ACOSTA

I think modesty becomes a man of accomplish-
ment, be it false or sincere.

COMTESSE

Well spoken. I like you, Madame. May I call
you Aida?

ACOSTA

I would be honored.

COMTESSE

Tell me once again, Alberto, why are we
perched up here like pigeons?

We draw back to reveal the fact that they are seated on seven foot high chairs.

ALBERTO

It is an effort to capture a sensation of flight.

EIFFEL

I know what flight is. It's what will happen
to me if I absentmindedly stand out of my
chair without the aid of your step ladder.

ALBERTO

We can adjourn to lower chairs if you prefer.

EIFFEL

No, we'll stay up here. Let it not be said
that the man who created a thousand
foot tower gets queasy at about ten feet.

COMTESSE

"A tower?" Just the other day it was a miracle of modern science. Make up your mind. In some distant future, will they speak of your tower in the same breath as the pyramids? Or is it just a good view?

EIFFEL (chuckling)

Thank you, Comtesse, for that perspective. But aren't the pyramids relics of an extinct culture? Surely you don't suggest that Paris will go the way of the dinosaurs?

COMTESSE

Certainly not. Paris will survive, albeit as a cultural and moral desert, but it will stand. And right in the middle of it will be your tower. I understand that it is too expensive to consider taking it down.

EIFFEL

I read that as well. Thank God that it will probably just blow over someday and save us all the money.

All chuckle

ALBERTO

I understand that you keep an apartment in the tower?

EIFFEL

I maintain an office on the observation deck. Some operations still need fine tuning. Why just the other day we caught a fellow trying to jump off. At least he had a parachute. Some of them do not. We anticipated this kind of thing, of course, but not in large numbers.

ACOSTA

Oh, dear…

EIFFEL

Forgive me, Mademoiselle. Perhaps this is not an appropriate luncheon topic.

COMTESSE

It is never inappropriate to speak plainly about real danger. What say you, Alberto?

ALBERTO
I agree with you, Comtesse.

COMTESSE
Then tell me, do you not fear that your flying
inventions will be subverted to destroy as in
our wars?

ALBERTO
I have considered it. The idea haunts me.
But I have also thought that if we were free
to travel at great speed and distances, men
would be closer to one another. We may
find that we have more in common with
our neighbors than differences. I saw it as
an instrument of peace.

EIFFEL
Aeronautical science may provide an instrument of peace yet but in an unexpected way.
A terrible weapon that could strike at great
speed and distances could target anyone.
No one, including Kings, Queens, Presi-
dents or Generals, would be safe. Why, the
catastrophe created by such a weapon would
make wars obsolete.

ACOSTA
I think you both give people too much credit.
What say you, Madame?

COMTESSE
I say it's time for aperitifs.

EXT. ROTHSCHILD ESTATE DAY

Aida d' ACOSTA and the COMTESSE are strolling through a grassy grove of trees.
ALBERTO, ROTHSCHILD and EIFFEL are walking well behind the women.
ALBERTO looks like he is dominating the conversation

ACOSTA
We are friends. But, I confess, I don't think
I know him very well. He can be very entertaining with boundless energy and, at
times, be shy and socially clumsy.

COMTESSE
You find him attractive?

ACOSTA
I admire him.

COMTESSE
Nothing more?

ACOSTA
I think not at the present time.

COMTESSE
Then you allow for the possibility?

ACOSTAS
Perhaps. He seems aloof. I thought it was a
"Brazilian" characteristic.

COMTESSE
When it comes to women, there is nothing
aloof about Brazilian men.

ACOSTA
Alberto is a very private individual. I respect his privacy. Perhaps that is the reason he prefers to escort me.

COMTESSE
Will you allow an old woman to secretly
hope for a romantic relationship between
two people that she likes?

ACOSTA
Of course, Madame.

COMTESSE
Good. It's settled then. Your mother and I
shall get along famously and we shall throw
fabulous parties.

The ladies chuckle

INT. SHED, PARC D' AEROSTATION, VAUGIRARD - DAY

Early morning. LACHOMBRE and MACHURON watch ALBERTO pace

ALBERTO
Are you sure the gas is up to pressure?

LACHOMBRE
I'm sure.

ALBERTO
And that the weight…

MACHURON
It's good.

Aida d' ACOSTA enters from the side door

ACOSTA
Well, despite the early hour, it appears that
you have a full house. And a few commis-
sioners out there as well.

ALBERTO
I would never have summoned them had I
known about this damned easterly. I'll be
battling that wind all the way home.

MACHURON
Call it off.

ALBERTO
I can't now!

Emmanuel AIME enters through the side door

AIME
Good morning, Alberto. Are you ready?

ALBERTO
Do you have a quorum?

AIME
Yes, including Messier Deutsch himself.

ALBERTO
Very well, let's do this.

MACHURON opens the large load doors. ALBERTO (smiling now) and his small
entourage exit the shed to the enthusiastic applause of the waiting crowd. ALBERTO
approaches the formally dressed members of the commission

ALBERTO
Good morning, gentlemen. Thank you for your
attendance.

DEUTSCH
Good morning, Messier. Before you depart,
a clarification will be in order. The flight
from Vaugirard to the tower and back within the thirty minute time limit remains the
condition of the contest. But I feel that the
term "and back" is vague in its' meaning.
And so to be more specific, I will tell you

that we will time you from the moment
you let go your lines to the moment
your balloon is brought to the ground.
Any questions?

ALBERTO is speechless

                    LACHOMBRE
No, Messier.

LACHOMBRE ushers ALBERTO off to the waiting balloon, followed by Aida d'
ACOSTA and MACHURON

                    ALBERTO
He just reduced the thirty minute time limit
by five minutes at least.

                    LACHOMBRE
It's his money. He can part with it any way
he wants to.

                    ALBERTO
But it's not fair! Is the horse race timed from
the starting pistol to the finish line or do we
wait until the horse comes to a stop?

                    LACHOMBRE
When we get into the horse racing business
that will become a relevant question.

                    ALBERTO
The task is difficult enough without making
unreasonable demands!

                    LACHOMBRE
Why are you yelling? Do you want to protest
or do you want to fly?

ALBERTO climbs into the basket and starts the engine

                    ACOSTA
Good luck!

                    MACHURON
Good luck.

                    ALBERTO
Let go all lines!

The crowd cheers as he ascends, levels off at about six hundred feet and points the air ship directly at the Eiffel Tower. He's making good time with his tail wind. There are many crowds gathered on roofs and he can hear their faint cheers under his motor

INT. A BAR - DAY

                    DRUNK
          What's all the commotion? What's everybody
          staring at out there?

                    BARTENDER
          It's Le Petite Santos.

                    DRUNK
          Who?

                    BARTENDER
          The balloonist.

                    DRUNK
          I don't want any balloons.

                    BARTENDER
          He's not selling them.

                    DRUNK
          Good. I wouldn't take a balloon if he gave
          me one. Unless he wanted to buy me a drink.
          Does he want to buy me a drink?

                    BARTENDER
          I doubt it.

                    DRUNK
          Damn.

EXT. BASKET OF THE BALLOON - DAY

ALBERTO throttles back as he approaches the tower. The engine sputters and coughs as crowds cheer him from the observation deck of the tower. He straightens out the rudder after the turn is complete, opens up the throttle to full speed and the engine stalls. He works feverously to start it and cannot. Once again he dumps ballast to keep from being blown into the tower. He is blown back to the river and just over the Tracadero Hotel he vents gas in an effort to land in the river, minimizing damage to the balloon. Suddenly a gust of wind blows him sideways and a piece of rigging catches the lightning rod on the Tracadero roof. The crowd below gasps. He ties a rope around his waist to secure himself to the basket. The air ship drops on to the edge of the roof and, with a loud report, the envelope bursts open, throwing the air ship over the edge. ALBERTO remains in the basket but is dangling about forty feet above the street. Someone on the roof shouts down to him about a rope being lowered. While he is waiting patiently, curtains open inside of the window he is hanging next to. A lovely YOUNG WOMAN in a dressing gown is staring at him. Polite as always, ALBERTO doffs his hat to her. A rope drops down to him and he ties it under his arms. The YOUNG WOMAN drops a corner of her dressing gown to reveal a lovely breast under her slip. ALBERTO is transfixed. She then drops the dressing gown off of the other shoulder

INT. THE YOUNG WOMAN'S HOTEL SUITE - DAY

An OLDER MAN calls to the YOUNG WOMAN from the bedroom of the suite

> OLDER MAN
> What are you doing?

> YOUNG WOMAN (shuts curtains)
> Nothing.

The YOUNG WOMAN closes her dressing gown and the OLDER MAN crosses to the window and opens the curtains. He sees nothing but a view of the river

EXT. ROOF OF THE TRACADERO HOTEL - DAY

ALBERTO is hoisted to the roof of the hotel and into the arms of the cheering crowd

EXT. PARC D' AEROSTATION, VAUGIRARD - DAY

ALBERTO is sitting on the ground working on the engine of a dirigible. Aida d' ACOSTA is sitting on a stool near him

> ACOSTA
> Gas pressure. It varies dependent upon the load.
> Generally you're looking for sagging of envelope
> material. It's a good time to make sure the emer-
> gency pressure valve is operational.

> ALBERTO
> How do you do that?

> ACOSTA
> By manually opening them.

> ALBERTO
> Hand me that twelve millimeter wrench, please.

She does so

> Then what?

> ACOSTA
> While I'm checking the valves, I check the
> overhead venting valve.

                         ALBERTO
Good.

                         ACOSTA
Then rigging. Look at the knots and fraying
of cords. The terminal clasps and kinking of
wires. Check that the control cables and ballast
lines are threaded properly. Operate the rudder.

                         ALBERTO (looking at her)
Impressive.

She smiles

Anything else before we weigh the balloon?

                         ACOSTA
Check the engine, of course. Check the propeller for cracks. Make sure the gas and oil
levels are up. Operate at low RPMs for five
minutes. Make sure you're securely fastened
to the ground before you start releasing ballast.
That's all I can think of.

                         ALBERTO
Me, too. That's all I can think of. Are you
ready to fly?

                         ACOSTA (startled)
Now?

                         ALBERTO
Soon.

                         ACOSTA
I think so.

                         ALBERTO (stops working)
If you only think so, you leave room for doubt.
Doubt equals hesitation. Hesitation equals…

                         ACOSTA
I know. Does your equation allow for a little
apprehension? You keep telling me how dangerous it is. Isn't fear a natural re-action to danger?

                         ALBERTO
Yes it is. But fear is not your enemy, indecision
is. Fear is that thing that can overtake your
judgment. You understand that, don't you?

She nods 'yes'

> ALBERTO
> I believe you are ready to fly. Do you believe
> that too?

> ACOSTA
> You're damned right I do.

A beat

> ALBERTO (smiling)
> I like you, Mademoiselle. Perhaps that's why
> I've been too demanding at times. We are alike,
> you and I. You'll not be denied. I've never
> met a woman who flies in her dreams, reason
> enough for wanting to fly. It's time for the
> fledgling to leave the nest.

> ACOSTA
> I've had a good teacher.

INT. A HOSPITAL - NIGHT

ALBERTO and DOCTOR are walking in the hall

> ALBERTO
> But he's only twenty-nine. He's the strongest
> man I've ever known.

> DOCTOR
> It is a very aggressive cancer.

ALBERTO comes to a door, knocks gently. LACHOMBRE opens, hat in hand.
MACHURON is lying in bed, eyes closed with a cold compress on his head. His young,
pregnant wife (teary), with young boy, is seated on a chair on the far side of the bed

> MACHURON (opens eyes)
> Messier, you're not flying today?

> ALBERTO
> No, I need you to look at that engine for me.
> I'm afraid I've made a terrible mess of it. We
> are making a trial run at the tower in a few
> days. You have to get well, we need you.

> MACHURON
> Yes, I'm sorry. The doctor says that I may be
> laid up for weeks.

                              ALBERTO
              Yes, well, the main thing is to gain your health,
              no matter how long it takes.

                              MACHURON
              Here, I want you to have something. Take this.

MACHURON opens his hand. It is his exposition medallion

                              ALBERTO
              No, Alexis, I cannot.

                              MACHURON
              Please, you are the master now. Wear it for
              good luck.

                              ALBERTO
              I will only keep it for you. I am the apprentice.
              You will always be Master of the Balloon.

                              MACHURON
              Thank you, my friend. Wear the medallion
              when you let go your lines and I go up with you.

A teary ALBERTO takes MACHURON's hand

INT. SHED, PARC D' AEROSTATION, VAUGIRARD - DAY

Early morning. ALBERTO, LACHOMBRE, ACOSTA and a new man are quietly
finishing chores in preparation for the flight. AIME enters through the side door

                              AIME
              Good morning.

                              LACHOMBRE
              Good morning.

                              AIME
              I know I speak for the Aero Club when I
              offer my condolences. Messier Machuron
              was a great balloonist and a fine gentleman.

                              LACHOMBRE
              Thank you.

                              AIME
              A tragedy to leave a young family like that.

                              ALBERTO (abruptly)
              Yes. Is there a quorum today?

                              AIME
              Uh, the entire commission is present.

                            ALBERTO
              That's fine. Let's proceed, shall we?

The new man opens the load doors. ALBERTO and his small entourage exit the shed to
the extended ovation of the waiting crowd. ALBERTO walks past the commission
without acknowledging them. LACHOMBRE and ACOSTA follow ALBERTO to the
tethered balloon in the middle of the field. Alberto starts the engine and climbs into the
basket

                            ACOSTA
              Good luck.

                            ALBERTO
              Thank you

                          LACHOMBRE
              Good luck.

ALBERTO kisses MACHURON's medallion that hangs from his neck

                            ALBERTO
              Let go all lines!

The crowd cheers. ALBERTO climbs, levels off at about six hundred feet and points the
air ship at the Eiffel Tower

EXT. PARC D' AEROSTATION, VAUGIRARD - DAY

Below, DEUTSCH, AIME and other members of the commission are on the field

                            DEUTSCH
              Emmanuel, I'm concerned that I've seen
              several stop watches in this crowd.

                              AIME
              I wouldn't be alarmed, Messier. Surely every-
              one is aware that the official time is kept by
              members of the commission only.

                            DEUTSCH
              Yes, except we are but a small body. And
              judging from this crowd's reaction to Santos-
              Dumont, they are largely sympathetic to him.

                              AIME
              True, but it must be clear to all that our judg-
              ment is final.

DEUTSCH
It is clear to me. I only hope there isn't an
incident that seems to question our veracity.
That would be unfortunate for everyone.

EXT. IN THE BASKET OF THE BALLOON - DAY

ALBERTO has made his turn around the tower to cheers of the crowds and is headed
back to the park. Despite a head wind he is making good time but then the engine begins
to sputter. He climbs out of the basket on to the aluminum struts to attempt a repair. He
inspects the engine but, once again, is losing momentum to the head wind that is blowing
him back to the tower. He must drop ballast to avoid being blown into the tower.
He works his way back to the basket and dumps ballast but, refusing to give up on the
engine, he attempts to make his way back to it. Hot oil from the sputtering engine has
made the struts slick and his foot slips off (crowds gasp below). He tries to pull himself
up but loses his grip. He falls to the lowest strut, catching himself with one hand (women
fainting, men praying, ACOSTA crying). Finally he gets both hands on the strut and
swings a leg up. He pulls himself up and is able to stand. He pulls the fuel line off, the
engine stops. He blows out the line, reattaches it and starts the engine. He works his way
back to the basket and opens the throttle to full speed. He is making good speed as
suddenly the head wind diminishes. He is able to point the air ship directly at the park.
Battered and disheveled, ALBERTO rides in the basket like a jockey to the finish line
and home. LACHOMBRE grabs ALBERTO'S guide rope and hangs on despite injuring
himself. Others quickly grab the rope and bring the air ship to the ground.

ALBERTO
Have I won?

ALL
Yes!

SOMEONE IN THE CROWD
I have twenty-nine minutes!

SOMEONE IN THE CROWD
I have twenty-eight!

SEVERAL IN THE CROWD
You have won!

The crowd continues to cheer him as the commission gathers near the shed

DEUTSCH
I was afraid of this. What time did you record?

AIME
I have thirty-one minutes, twenty-five seconds.

DEUTSCH
I have slightly more than that.

                              AIME
We must announce our findings at once.

                            DEUTSCH
No. Look around you. Such an announcement
would make us nothing but quibbling villains
and I would be crucified in the press. It would
hurt business.

                              AIME
What do we do?

                            DEUTSCH
Congratulate him. I'm leaving.

DEUTSCH exits, AIME approaches the balloon

                       AIME (in a loud voice)
Ladies and gentlemen, the commission of the
Aero Club is pleased to congratulate the win-
ner of the Deutsch Prize, Alberto Santos-Dumont!

The cheering crowd hoists ALBERTO on their shoulders

EXT. PARC D'AEROSTATION, VAUGIRARD - DAY

Days later, ACOSTA is standing in the basket of the dirigible, engine idling. She is
wearing goggles but we can still see the fear in her eyes

                            ALBERTO
Stay within the perimeter of the park and no
higher than three hundred and fifty feet or
so. Your guide rope is out now and I'll
be following you on the bicycle. If you get
into any trouble at all, get to the center of
the park and vent gas. I'll be there for you.
Any questions?

                            ACOSTA
What?

                            ALBERTO
Any questions?

                            ACOSTA
No.

ALBERTO ties the red "salute" scarf around her neck

                            ALBERTO
For good luck.

ACOSTA

Thank you.

ALBERTO

Ready?

ACOSTA

Yes.

ALBERTO

I won't release these lines until you say so.

ACOSTA

Oh, of course. Let go all lines!

ALBERTO pulls the slip knots loose and she climbs, tentatively at first. ALBERTO gets on the bicycle and immediately hits a gopher hole. He sprawls on the ground, ripping his coat and scratching his hand. ACOSTA is gaining confidence quickly, climbs again and increases the throttle. ALBERTO is peddling on the dirt road in the park. Looking up at the balloon, he does not see a low tree limb and gets knocked off of the bike, suffering a cut on his forehead. ACOSTA is having the time of her life now. She climbs to about five hundred feet and opens up the throttle to full speed. Her bonnet starts to slip off. She unties and tosses it and heads for the river. ALBERTO is no longer in the park but on a public, graveled road. Looking up, he does not see the horse manure, skids and falls face down, getting manure all over his suit. ACOSTA is banking hard and playing with air currents. ALBERTO has lost sight of the air ship. He sees her bonnet flutter into the top of a tree. Panicking now, he is asking people if they have seen the air ship. He is riding the bike erratically and startling horses. ACOSTA makes a big sweeping turn, taking in the sky line of Paris, points the nose of the ship down to the park and begins to vent gas. ALBERTO peddles into the park and accidentally gets drenched by a groundskeeper watering. ACOSTA levels the air ship, throttles back, vents more gas and shuts off the engine. LACHOMBRE (one arm in a sling) hears her return and steps out of the shed to ground the balloon. ALBERTO drops the bicycle, grabs the guide rope, is pulled off his feet and drug until LACHOMBRE can assist him. The air ship comes down gently as if ACOSTA had flown a hundred times

LACHOMBRE (helps ALBERTO up)
What happened to you, you're a mess?

ALBERTO (dazed)
It's dangerous down here.

LACHOMBRE (tying guide rope)
Well, be more careful.

LACHOMBRE walks back to shed. ACOSTA gets out of the basket and runs to ALBERTO

ACOSTA (hugging him)
Oh, Alberto, it was beautiful! It was thrilling!
I was free! It was everything I hoped it would

be!…What happened to you, you're a mess?

                    ALBERTO (still dazed)
          Flying balloons can be risky. Bicycles are a
          death sentence.

                    ACOSTA (ushering him)
          Let's get to the shed and look at that head
          wound.

INT. SHED, PARC D' AEROSTATION, VAUGIRARD - DAY

Same late afternoon. LACHOMBRE is finishing up some paperwork. ACOSTA is
tending to ALBERTO'S head wound

                    ACOSTA
          I'm sorry but the smell of the manure is
          distracting.

                    ALBERTO
          Yes, it's on my breeches. Let me get out of
          these.

ALBERTO exits into the bathroom

                    LACHOMBRE (standing)
          Well, that's all for me today. I trust the patient
          is in good hands.

                    ACOSTA
          Unless he breaks his nose tripping over a door
          jam.

LACHOMBRE smiles and exits. ALBERTO comes out of the bathroom without a shirt
wearing MACHURON'S very large overalls tied at the waist

                    ALBERTO
          Machuron was a big fellow. But he had the
          good sense to stay out of horse manure.

ACOSTA laughs. ALBERTO sits next to her on the bench, facing her. She resumes
cleaning the wound

                    ACOSTA
          I think the bleeding has stopped but this
          wound should be stitched closed by a surgeon
          or it will leave a scar.

                    ALBERTO
          Let's just bandage it.

ACOSTA
Are you saying that you prefer the scar?

ALBERTO
I don't mind it.

ACOSTA
What?

ALBERTO
I don't like needles.

ACOSTA
Am I to understand that the daredevil of the
skies is afraid of a needle?

ALBERTO
I didn't say that I was afraid. I said I didn't
like them.

ACOSTA
Oh, that's different then. It's a matter of
personal preference. Well, what reputable
daredevil doesn't sport a scar or two…

ALBERTO kisses her, impetuously but deliberately and romantically. He draws away.
She kisses him back and soon they are enthusiastically kissing one another

EXT. ON THE BANK OF THE RIVER SEINE - NIGHT

Chanteuse's love song under couples strolling arm in arm at dusk

INT. SHED, PARC D' AEROSTATION, VAUGIRARD - NIGHT

ACOSTA is fastening the top button of her chemise, ALBERTO is behind her

ALBERTO
I'm not sure what to say.

ACOSTA
Nothing need be said.

ALBERTO
Should…

ACOSTA (facing him)
Whatever you do, don't apologize. I'm not
sorry. Are you?

ALBERTO
No. God, no.

> ACOSTA (putting jacket on)
> I suppose I've always wanted to kiss you.
> But I must go now.

> ALBERTO
> Shall I see you tomorrow?

> ACOSTA
> Perhaps. It's time for me to go. Thank you,
> Alberto, I'll never forget today.

She crosses to the door

> Would you kiss me goodbye?

He crosses to her. They kiss passionately, tenderly. ALBERTO is speechless, she exits

INT. OFFICE OF THE PARIS HERALD NEWSPAPER - DAY

> FIRST REPORTER
> It wasn't even reported in a newspaper at
> the time. Months or so later, someone wrote
> in a magazine that a pair of bicycle mechanics
> had catapulted themselves in a fixed winged
> craft and glided for a few hundred yards on
> a North Carolina beach with hardly anyone
> watching. Hell, I could throw you off of the
> roof and say that you glided for a few yards.

> SECOND REPORTER
> Who knows what happened. At least when
> Santos flies, all of Paris sees him.

> FIRST REPORTER
> Fliers or liars? Which is it with those Ameri-
> cans?

General laughter in the office

INT. ACOSTA'S APARTMENT, PARIS - DAY

ACOSTA is packed to sail for home. The rooms are cleared of all personal items except for a toy Santos-Dumont tin balloon. The red "salute" scarf ALBERTO gave to her is hanging on the balloon. ACOSTA is reading a letter she has just written

> MAID (entering)
> The hotel porter is holding a carriage for
> you, Madame.

ACOSTA puts the letter in an envelope, crosses to the toy, takes the scarf off and puts it in her bag

ACOSTA

I'll post this downstairs. I'm ready to go.

INT. MAXIM'S CAFÉ - NIGHT

Late night celebration. Large crowd on hand. ALBERTO is drunk and reading
ACOSTA's letter at the bar

ACOSTA (V.O.)

My Dear Alberto- Forgive me for quitting Paris
so abruptly but I fear that I might not be able
to leave you otherwise and I must. I cannot
marry you, Alberto. Your first love will always be flying and that is as it should be. I
was wrong to call you a daredevil. You are
a visionary and as such you will belong to
all people in all times. My first love is my
home, my family, and my life there. We
must, both of us, follow our hearts. I pray
that you will think of me with kindness. I
shall never forget you. With love, Aida

He crumples the letter and throws it into the spittoon.

GOURSAT (standing)

Waite, there's more! Come here and sit
down, Alberto!

ALBERTO crosses to the table and sits between a good looking young couple,
GENEVIEVE and VALINTINE.

GOURSAT (reads)

"The Parisian populace must always have a
hero, an idol of some sort, and tonight the
young aeronaut occupies the pedestal."
(GENEVIEVE squeezes the inside of AL-
BERTO'S thigh under the table) "One
knows not what to admire the more- the
splendid courage of this daring youth from
beyond the seas or the inventive genius
that made such a feat possible. He was
popular enough before, but his gift to his
faithful assistants and the poor has raised
Santos-Dumont to the pinnacle of adoration by the people of Paris."(more cheers)

DEUTSCH (at bar with AIME)

This is intolerable. (hands a note to BAR-
TENDER) Give Santos this with the next
round of drinks.

                              AIME
          What is it?

                              DEUTSCH
          A little humility.

DEUTSCH leaves the café

                              GOURSAT
          What's next on the intrepid aeronaut's agenda?

                              A DRUNK
          What's intrepid?

                              ALBERTO
          I plan to drown myself in wine, women and
          whatever. (cheers) No, actually we have been
          invited to the United States to fly at an expo-
          sition and go to New York City where we
          will meet President Roosevelt and Professor
          Langley at the smithssonium…smithsomium…
          that institute.

Laughter and cheers

                              GOURSAT
          At last, official recognition by our allies
          abroad! Ernst, more champagne! (cheers)

Champagne bottles are passed. ALBERTO reads the note from DEUTSCH

                              ALBERTO
          What is this?

ALBERTO staggers to the bar to confront AIME

          What is this, Emmanuel?

                              AIME (intoxicated)
          How should I know.

                              ALBERTO
          It says thirty-one minutes. And it's signed
          by Deutsch de la Meurthe. What does it
          mean?

                              AIME
          Why don't you ask him?

                              ALBERTO (shouting)
          He was standing right here a moment ago!

                        AIME
So what!

                      ALBERTO
Does he imply that I have not won fairly?
The very implication is an affront. I will
not accept the charity of his prize!

                      GOURSAT
Why are you making trouble?

                      ALBERTO
Because I will not suffer these implications!

AIME jumps off his stool

                        AIME
You dishonor yourself! Thirty-one minutes
was the average recorded time of the com-
mittee. You were awarded the prize nevertheless. Do what you want with the money,
I don't care!

AIME exits, ALBERTO is staggering, hyperventilating

                      ALBERTO
I don't want it! If I didn't win it, I don't
want it!

ALBERTO faints off his feet, several come to help him

                      GOURSAT
All right, get him on a table! Make sure he's
breathing.

                     A DRUNK
What got into him?

                      GOURSAT
Ernst, maybe some coffee, he's coming
around.

                    GENEVIEVE
We'll see that he gets home, we're old friends.

                      GOURSAT
Did you hear that, Alberto? Your old friends
here are going to take you home. Is that OK
with you?

                              ALBERTO
          What? Oh, yes.

                              GOURSAT (loud voice)
          Your attention, Madams y Messieurs, our hero
          is leaving. (boos) Farewell, my friend. And
          for God's sake, learn to drink, you're part French!

Cheers, ALBERTO, GENEVIEVE and VALENTINE exit

INT. ALBERTO'S BEDROOM - DAY

Close up of ALBERTO waking in the early morning. He is very troubled right away.
Very slowly, we draw away to see that he has the nude bodies of GENEVIEVE and
VALENTINE sleeping next to him, one on each side

                              OLD MAN VOICE OVER
          Alberto never married. Some biographers
          infer that he was homosexual. A confusion
          about sexual preference would have been
          a trifling matter compared to what was
          evidently the case. There is no indication
          of Alberto ever having a lasting, intimate
          relationship with anyone, male or female.
          It's not uncommon for famous people,
          who share their work, their successes, their
          failures with the world, to be unable to
           maintain personal relationships. They
          have many friends and acquaintances but
          are lonely people. Perhaps their yearning
          for recognition is an attempt to fill the vacuum.
          Perhaps this was Alberto Santos-Dumont.

EXT. MACHURON'S APARTMENT - DAY

Early morning. ALBERTO knocks on the door. MADAME MACHURON answers

                              MADAME MACHURON
          Messier Santos! Won't you come in?

                              ALBERTO
          I may not. My driver is waiting. I've come
          to give you this.(retrieving envelope) It
          belongs to Alexis. It is his share of the prize,
          25,000f.

                              MADAME MACHURON
          I'm overwhelmed! Thank you.

ALBERTO sees the young boy across the room

                              ALBERTO
What is your son's name?

                        MADAME MACHURON
Alexis.

                              ALBERTO
I have something to give to you, Alexis. It
was your father's.

                        MADAME MACHURON
Come, Alexis.

The boy crosses to them. ALBERTO finds MACHURON'S medallion in his pocket. He
crouches down and hands it to the boy

                              ALBERTO
Soon you'll be able to read what it says there.
It says that your father was a very great man.

Suddenly overcome with emotion, he stands and doffs his bowler to MADAME
MACHURON

          Good day, Madame.

EXT. NEW YORK HARBOR - DAY

Ocean liner is entering the harbor. Ship's band is playing the "Star Spangled Banner".
Crowds of people are pressed along the port side of the bow to view the Statue of Liberty.
Among them, Antonio PRADO, ALBERTO, LACHOMBRE and public relations and
newspaper people

                              PRADO
          Alberto!

                              ALBERTO
          Yes, Antonio?

                              PRADO
          They want you to turn to the cameras
          so they can get a picture of you with the
          Statue of Liberty in the background.

ALBERTO and LACHOMBRE turn back to flashbulbs popping. A minute or so of this
goes on

                    (to reporters) Excuse me fellows, give us
                    a moment, would you?

PRADO takes ALBERTO and LACHOMBRE aside

(confidentially) Gentlemen, it wouldn't
hurt to smile a little in these photos.

                    ALBERTO
I don't understand, was I frowning?

                    PRADO
Not exactly. But you didn't seem very happy either.

                    LACHOMBRE
This is silly.

                    PRADO
I know but my job is to attend to your visit
in the United States. You may have to trust
me about things related to public relations.

                    ALBERTO
You're the liaison to the Brazilian Consulate,
I trust you implicitly. Can you cheer up a little,
Henri?

                    LACHOMBRE
Yes, but it's silly.

They go back to the rail of the ship and more flashbulbs while they are grinning like
idiots

INT. THE WALDORF-ASTORIA HOTEL, NEW YORK - DAY

ALBERTO and Professor LANGLEY walk into the lobby and then into the dining hall,
flashbulbs pop and there are a few reporters there

                    LANGLEY
So much for the quiet lunch.

                    REPORTER #1
Professor Langley, does Mr. Santos-Dumont's
visit signal any kind of collaboration between France
and the United States in the field of aviation?

                    LANGLEY
There is always collaboration between men of
science. But there is no specific project that we
are engaged in.

                    REPORTER #2
Mr. Santos –Dumont, is it true that you will be
a featured competitor at the St Louis Exposition's
balloon race?

ALBERTO

I have been invited to participate in events spon-
sored by the St Louis Exposition. I am very happy
to race in a new dirigible made expressly for this
exposition. I hope to set speed records in these
exhibitions.

REPORTER #1

Professor, your work has been mostly with gliders
and Mr. Santos-Dumont's experiments have been
with dirigibles. The two means of flight seem so
dissimilar. Do you gentlemen intend to share your
work with one another and to what end?

ALBERTO receives a note from the bellboy

LANGLEY

Yes indeed. We intend to talk "shop". But I
must correct your misapprehension. The
two means of flight are not so dissimilar.
Both systems address the same inherent
problems of flight; lift, propulsion, and
control and aerodynamics...

ALBERTO

Excuse me, gentlemen, I must take an
urgent call.

LANGLEY

Certainly.

ALBERTO walks out of the hall

As I was saying, lift is a common problem
for both systems; the balloon solves it by
capturing a gas that is lighter than the pre-
vailing atmosphere...

In the lobby, ALBERTO picks up the telephone receiver on the main desk as directed

SPLIT SCREEN TELEPHONE CONVERSATION

ALBERTO

Yes?

LACHOMBRE

Messier, this is Henri. I am still at the U.S.
Customs Office. There has been a problem
retrieving our crates.

ALBERTO
Where is Antonio?

LACHOMBRE
He had some business at the embassy.

ALBERTO
Well, there should be no problem. The crates
are clearly marked "exhibits". According to
U.S. Customs law, I qualify both as an artist
and a scientist. We even pre-paid our tariffs.

LACHOMBRE
Nevertheless, they opened a few of the crates.
They found the engine, the basket, and didn't
know what to make of the silk. They are
charging us the maximum tariff for a "gasoline
powered conveyance" and "fine furniture".
Nine hundred U.S. dollars are needed to clear
our gear for shipment to St. Louis.

ALBERTO
What?

LACHOMBRE
That's what I said. Actually I said other things
that might have gotten me in trouble. Fortun-
ately, no one here speaks French.

ALBERTO
I'll be there as fast as I can.

ALBERTO hangs up, walks back into the hall where LANGLEY continues to "hold
court"

LANGLEY
Alberto, is everything all right?

ALBERTO
Apparently there has been a problem at U.S.
Customs clearing our dirigible and equipment.
I must go back to see if I can help.

LANGLEY
That will be all for today, gentlemen.

LANGLEY ushers ALBERTO into the lobby

What have you been told?

260

                              ALBERTO
I guess they've never seen an air ship before
and didn't know what to make of it. Lachombre
said they are charging us the maximum tariff
for a "gasoline powered conveyance" and "fine
furniture".

                              LANGLEY
What?

                              ALBERTO
That's what I said.

                              LANGLY
Come, we'll go together. If I can't convince
a few bureaucrats that they are inconvenienc-
ing the most distinguished aeronaut in the
world and an invited guest of this country,
then I may sail back to France with you.

They exit out the front doors of the hotel

                              REPORTER #2
Did you get any of that?

                              REPORTER #1
I got all of it. Come on, we can just make our
deadlines.

INT. DOWNTOWN ATHLETIC CLUB, NEW YORK - NIGHT

LANGLEY, ALBERTO, LACHOMBRE and PRADO are having an after dinner port
wine

                              LANGLEY
"If God meant for man to fly, He would
have given him wings" She was thumping
me in the chest with one finger and holding
a Bible in the other hand.

Chuckles around the table

                      Then I said, 'If it was not natural for man
                      to travel faster than his legs or a horse
                      could carry him, why would God allow
                      the invention of the wheel? If we were not
                      meant to see other than by natural light-
                      the sun, moon and stars, why would God
                      allow Mr. Edison to invent the electric light?'
                      Well, this infuriated her even more. She
                      switched hands and started to thump me

with the Bible. "The Lord will deal with
you God-less scientists in His own way!"
Well, I can assure you that the pen is
mightier than the sword and that the power of the Good Book should not be under-
estimated. I have the bruises to prove it.

Chuckles around the table

ALBERTO
Superstition reigns in the back-water villages
of most countries. Where was it, Henri, that
Machuron landed and was almost killed by
the locals?

LACHOMBRE
Yes, yes. A friend of ours' and two others
ascended in a free balloon from a south-
eastern province in Germany. They were
caught in a storm and were blown well
east to Austria. They landed on an isolated
plateau where the local people had never
seen a balloon and wanted to burn the
three of them as witches. The captain of
a military outpost saved their lives.

LANGLEY
The unknown is always frightening. Yet, if
the same villagers saw a balloon a second
time, they would be less fearful. And by the
fifth time, their kids are begging for a ride.
This is the scientist's job - to make known
what is unknown, to take fear out of the future.

PRADO (standing)
Forgive me, gentlemen, but I must depart.
My ten year old son is trying very hard to
stay awake until his father comes home.

ALBERTO
Then by all means do not keep him waiting.

PRADO
Professor Langley, thank you again for your
help at the Customs Office.

LANGLEY
You overestimate me, Sir. It was your
father, the Ambassador, who was influential. I was only pleased to assist in
any way I could.

PRADO

Alberto, you have your tickets?

ALBERTO

Yes.

PRADO (exiting)

Then I'll see you in the morning at the station. Good night, gentlemen.

INT. A DESK - NIGHT

We see a MAN's hands on a telephone that rings. He answers it. We never see his face

MAN

No, it's too difficult in New York. Wait until St. Louis… that's right…a couple of men that you trust. I don't want to know the specifics. Just make sure our French-Brazilian dandy feels welcome.

He hangs up

INT. DOWNTOWN ATHLETIC CUB, NEW YORK - NIGHT

ALBERTO and LANGLEY are now at the bar. LANGLEY is drinking heavily

LANGLEY

When money was appropriated through Congress with the mandate of demonstrating powered flight in a fixed wing craft, I celebrated. Then the other shoe dropped. A payload requirement was stipulated- twenty-five hundred pounds in addition to the craft, engine and pilot. As you can imagine, the additional weight put an exponential amount of stress on the wings and fuselage. More wing surface and/or more horsepower only served to de-stabilize the design and problems continued to compound themselves.

ALBERTO

So, what did you do?

LANGLEY

I went back to my study of aerodynamic theory. We think we solved some problems of the additional weight by putting it as low on the belly of the fuselage as we could. But at the launch, the catapult failed and she took a nose dive into the Potomac. The

263

pilot was able to swim to safety, thank God.
Bartender?

                    ALBERTO
            I have read some of what is available on
            the topic of aerodynamics. I confess I found
            very little practical help in addressing the
            issues of flight control. Trial and error has
            been my method. And sometimes error
            proves to be very painful.

                    LANGLEY
            I admire you, Sir. (toasting) To your success.
            Oh, you don't have cocktail.

                    ALBERTO
            Perhaps just one more.

                    LANGLEY
    Bartender?

The clock on the wall "dissolves" from reading ten thirty to just after midnight. The bar is
almost empty and LANGLEY is pretty drunk

                    LANGLEY
            When we have powerful engines and com-
            posite materials that are strong, flexible and
            light weight, we will solve the problem.
            Speed, of course, will always be the advan-
            tage of fixed wing verses the powered balloon.

                    ALBERTO
            That is true. However, every time my engine
            fails, I am grateful for the advantage of some
            thing other than my engine keeping me aloft.

                    LANGLEY
            Well, I defer to your experience in the matter
            of actually flying. However, I have built
            gliders that have flown hundreds of yards.
            If your craft was light enough and you were
            high enough when the engine failed, you
            could glide to a safe landing. Unfortunately,
            my federally funded design is now so
            heavy that it will glide like a hand full of
            mortar. (he accidentally knocks over his
            glass) I'm afraid, Alberto. If I fail again I'll
            not be given a second chance.

                    ALBERTO
            We only learn by our failures.

LANGLEY
You're right. The catapult problem has been
solved. We will fly. But promise me that you
will experiment with a very light aero plane.
But just in case something...please.

ALBERTO
I will, Samuel. But now it is late.

LANGLEY
Yes, it is.

INT. TRAIN, ST.LOUIS DEPOT - DAY

The train pulls into the depot. ALBERTO, LACHOMBRE and PRADO stand

PRADO
I'll check with Mr. Freeman about our
transportation.

ALBERTO
We'll check on the gear.

ALBERTO and LACHOMBRE walk through a few passenger cars, to a luggage and
freight car. The door is locked. ALBERTO opens an exit door and looks around to the
side of the car

The loading door is open. Let's go see.

They step down off of the train and climb in to the freight car. ALBERTO sees a man
hunched over one of their opened crates. ALBERTO rushes to the man

What are you doing?

The man turns and slashes ALBERTO on the hand. LACHOMBRE takes a couple of
steps toward the man and is clubbed on the back of the head by a second man

INT. A HOSPITAL ROOM - DAY

LACHOMBRE is lying unconscious. ALBERTO has his hand bandaged and in an arm
sling. He is seated next to the bed, staring blankly at the bandaged head of
LACHOMBRE. PRADO is pacing at the foot of the bed

PRADO
It is preposterous that their security is
so poor as to allow this to happen! I'll be
back.

PRADO exits, LACHOMBRE opens his eyes

                    ALBERTO
Henri?

                    LACHOMBRE
Alberto, are you all right?

                    ALBERTO
Yes, how are you feeling?

                    LACHOMBRE
I have a hell of a headache. And the balloon?

                    ALBERTO
Destroyed.

                LACHOMBRE (teary)
Destroyed?

                    ALBERTO
Utterly. He slashed through every layer of silk.

                    LACHOMBRE
What are we going to do?

                    ALBERTO
Go back to New York.

                    LACHOMBRE
What are we going to do in New York?

                    ALBERTO
Sail for France.

EXT. PARC D'AEROSTATION, VAUGIRARD - DAY

ALBERTO (wearing goggles) is sitting in the pilot's seat of a very small aero plane. A large crowd is on hand to cheer him on or see him crash. The idling engine is mounted above the silk covered, eighteen foot wing. ALBERTO is checking cables with LACHOMBRE. When they feel that everything is operational, LACHOMBRE walks to the other end of the grass clearing, getting people out of the way as he goes to make way for ALBERTO'S take-off. LACHOMBRE signals ALBERTO. The crowd cheers as ALBERTO throttles up and takes off. We watch LACHOMBRE as we hear the engine cough. We hear a crunching noise as the crowd gasps. We see LACHOMBRE wince. People are running to the aero plane that is now standing on its' head. ALBERTO is extricated from the wreckage. A young woman gives ALBERTO a handkerchief for his bleeding nose. LACHOMBRE helps a limping ALBERTO back to the shed

                    ALBERTO
What's it look like?

LACHOMBRE
It looks like you broke your nose.

ALBERTO
No, I mean...

LACHOMBRE
It looks top heavy. Tomorrow I'll drop the
 engine below the wing.

ALBERTO
Good thinking.

EXT. PARC D'AEROSTATION, VAUGIRARD - DAY

A few days later. Another crowd on hand to watch the trial. ALBERTO (black eyes, bandaged nose and goggles) and LACHOMBRE are going through their pre-flight routine. This time the engine is mounted below the wing, right between ALBERTO'S legs. Once again, LACHOMBRE walks to the other side of the clearing and signals ALBERTO. He throttles up, rolls down the make-shift runway and lifts off. He clears the trees, then dives down and we hear the crunch. LACHOMBRE and all run to ALBERTO who is still in the craft that is hanging in a tree nose down

ALBERTO
I think I know what the problem is.

LACHOMBRE
What?

Now we stay on LACHOMBRE and only listen to ALBERTO

ALBERTO
It's still nose heavy. Put the engine behind
me and it will balance the fuselage.

LACHOMBRE
Good thinking. How are we going to get
you down from there?

We hear a limb break and watch LACHOMBRE follow the craft to the ground. He winces as we hear the crunch

Well, that's one way.

EXT. PARC D'AEROSTATION, VAUGIRARD - DAY

A few days later. Another crowd on hand. ALBERTO (bandaged nose, bandaged head and goggles) and LACHOMBRE are going through their pre-flight routine. This time the engine is mounted behind ALBERTO, long shaft for the propeller mount. Once again, LACHOMBRE walks to the other side of the clearing and signals ALBERTO. He throttles up, rolls down the runway and lifts off. He clears the trees. This time he makes a big, graceful turn back to the park and, just over LACHOMBRE'S head, ALBERTO gives him a "thumbs up" and a big smile. LACHOMBRE returns the gesture and joins the cheering crowd

EXT. A DIRT ROAD ADJACENT TO THE PARK - DAY

The handsome teenage BOY is taking vegetables to market in a horse drawn wagon. Next to him sits his GRANDPA

                              BOY
              Look, Grandpa, there goes Santos-Dumont
              in his new aero plane. The mathematics teacher
              says that it is by science that men fly.

                              GRANDPA
              Oh?

                              BOY
              Yes. Someday I will fly. In one of those
              machines, I shall defend France against
              her enemies.

                              GRANDPA
              It is by science that men fly?

                              BOY
              Yes.

                              GRANDPA
              Then science is a very bad magic that would
              have young men kill each other with such
              weapons.

                              BOY (happily)
              It will be bad for the enemies of France.

GRANDPA looks at the BOY and sighs

EXT. ALBERTO FLYING AEROPLANE - DAY

A chanteuse's ballad underscores ALBERTO'S flight. He is in complete command of the craft and flying as if in a dream. He flies over the French country side in a manner that is evocative of the ten year old ALBERTO'S daydream of flying. End underscoring. ALBERTO is approaching the park and preparing to land when suddenly he has double vision. He is alarmed by the double vision but it passes quickly. Then just as he touches down, the double vision comes back. He is disoriented enough that he crash lands

INT. A SMALL HOUSE, BENERVILLE, FRANCE - NIGHT

From a height and distance, we slowly draw down to see ALBERTO working in the study at his desk. His telescope is set up in the room

Alberto never flew again. His double vision
was not due to injury but a symptom of a serious
medical condition. He moved to the seaside
town of Benerville near Deauville. He kept his
illness a secret because he could not abide
sympathy. Those that knew he was seeing
doctors suspected a nervous breakdown. Out
of the public eye now, Alberto read about
many young aviators conquering the skies.
Their feats were overshadowing his own
accomplishments. A recluse in his last
years of residence in France, Alberto's
friends numbered fewer and fewer until one
or more of them turned against him.

A knock on the door. ALBERTO opens it to Agent ANDRE and several agents in suits

ANDRE (holding warrant)
Good evening, Messier. I am Agent Andre
from the Ministry of War with a warrant to
search the house.

ALBERTO
I don't understand. There has been no crime
here. Why would the police...

ANDRE (entering)
We are not the police, Messier. Here is the
warrant. The sooner we proceed, the sooner
we will leave you in peace.

The men walk in and start to inspect books on the shelf and other rooms

ALBERTO
What are you looking for?

ANDRE (to an agent)
Search this desk thoroughly. What are these
papers here?

ALBERTO
They are drawings and notes dating back
years. I am Alberto Santos-Dumont. Surely
you've heard of me.

ANDRE
Yes, what is this telescope for?

ALBERTO
I have taken up astronomy as a hobby.

ANDRE
So, you look at stars?

ALBERTO
Yes. Who are you people? What are you
doing here? I demand to know!

ANDRE
I told you, we are from the Ministry of
War. We are here on a matter of national
security. You are aware that war in Europe
is imminent?

ALBERTO
Yes, I read the papers. So what?

ANDRE
Then you might also realize that information
about the comings and goings of ships just
off this coast could be valuable to a power
with ill will against France.

AN AGENT (quietly to ANDRE)
So far we have found nothing.

ALBERTO
This is preposterous! Who accuses me of
being a spy?

ANDRE
You might also concede that a telescope
would be just the instrument used to confirm
such information.

ALBERTO
This accusation is insane and so are you!

ANDRE
You are a foreigner, aren't you, Messier?

ALBERTO
That does it! Do you propose that Brazil is
about to attack France?

ANDRE
No. But perhaps a power allied to Brazil…

ALBERTO
Get out of here! Get out of here now or I'll
call the real police!

                            ANDRE
                I think we're finished for now. If these
                accusations prove to be unfounded, I'm
                sure you'll be receiving a letter of apology
                from the Minister.

                            ALBERTO
                I'll refuse your apology! My allegiance to
                France ended tonight! Get out!

The men leave. ALBERTO paces furiously and weeps

                How dare they? How dare they? I have of-
                fered my service to the French government...
                to be treated like this... the ingratitude of
                those who heaped praise on me...how many
                times have I risked my life for the glory of
                France? Enough! I'll burn it all before this
                damned country benefits from my work again!

ALBERTO strikes a match, lights several papers and stuffs them into a metal trashcan.
He stuffs more papers into the can. Soon the desk catches fire and he cannot extinguish
the flame. The studio explodes into fire. ALBERTO runs outside, his weeping face
illuminated by the inferno

EXT. A BEACH, GUARUJA, BRAZIL, 1932 - DAY

From a distance we see the old and sick ALBERTO absent-mindedly gathering shells on
the beach. He is distracted by the sounds of bombs in the distance

                        OLD MAN VOICE OVER
                The last dozen or so years of Alberto's life
                was spent with his brother, Henrique, or in
                private sanitariums. There were rumors that
                he had several stokes. He made no public
                appearances. But he wrote to several govern-
                ments begging them to take aero planes out
                of their war arsenals. He begged them to
                "de-militarize the skies".

NEWSREEL CLIP

Compilation of black and white still photos and footage of ALBERTO SANTOS-
DUMONT flying and saluting crowds

                            VOICE OVER
                Aviation hero Alberto Santos-Dumont has died
                on July 23 in his native Brazil, after a long and
                courageous battle with multiple sclerosis.
                Santos-Dumont was the popular pioneer of flight
                and credited with many innovations in aeronauti-

cal science. Within only a few years of the Wright brother's accomplishments, he designed and flew his own fixed wing craft and was celebrated internationally as the master pilot of the dirigible. Santos-Dumont was idolized in France where most of his experiments took place but will be mourned by millions in Brazil and the world over. Alberto Santos-Dumont, dead at 59.

INT. RECORDING STUDIO, 1935 - DAY

OLD MAN

My respect for the man isn't diminished because he took his own life. He was pretty sick at the time. Slow and agonizing would not be the way for Alberto to go. He was too dramatic and, perhaps, too much in pain. Civil war was raging in Brazil. He wrote that he could hear bombs drop and with each explosion his 'heart broke'.

A beat

'Who was Alberto Santos-Dumont?' At the turn of the century in France, it isn't enough to say that he was our hero. He was our hope. He demonstrated his courage time and again. He made us all want to be brave. You don't have to fly an airplane to need bravery. Anyone can be afraid.(getting reading glasses) Alberto's friend, Antonio Prado asked Alberto if he was afraid sometimes. I happened to be there. Alberto said he was. "What do you do then?", asked Prado. Alberto replied, (reading) "I grow pale and try to gain control of myself by thinking of other things. If I do not succeed, I feign courage before those watching me, and face the danger. But even so I am still afraid."

The OLD MAN puts his glasses away

When word of his death reached his fellow countrymen, they called a three day truce in the war. Combatants on both sides lined up together for miles to file past his opened casket in Sao Paulo. At the very moment that pallbearers lowered his body into the grave, thousands of pilots around the world tipped the wings of their planes in a final

gesture of respect. On this, the third anniversary of his death, I will mourn my friend,
Alberto Santos-Dumont.

The OLD MAN masks his emotion by taking oxygen

EXT. A BEACH, GUARUJA, BRAZIL, 1932 - DAY

The old and sick ALBERTO absent-mindedly gathers shells on the beach. He is
distracted by the sounds of bombs in the distance. A very young girl, ELIZABETH, is on
the beach with her baby brother who is digging in the sand. ELIZABETH approaches
ALBERTO politely

                    ELIZABETH
          I'll help you gather shells, Señor?

                    ALBERTO
          You're very kind but I'm really just enjoy-
          ing the water. Is that your brother?

                    ELIZABETH
          That is my baby brother, Paulo.

                    ALBERTO
          He looks very determined.

                    ELIZABETH
          He digs like our Labrador. My name is
          Elizabeth. I'm seven years old. That's my
          mommy sitting over there.

The MOTHER watches ELIZABETH over her sunglasses for a moment

                    ELIZABETH
          Who are you?

                    ALBERTO
          I am Alberto.

                    MOTHER (from a distance)
          Elizabeth, don't make a pest of yourself now.

                    ELIZABETH
          I'm sorry if I bothered you, Senor.

                    ALBERTO
          No, no, you have not bothered me. And you
          are not a pest. You are a delightful young child.
          I am pleased to have met you, Elizabeth. Run
          along to your mother now.

ELIZABETH grabs her brother by the hand and happily runs to her mother. Shortly, behind him he hears the whine of a bi-plane in a dive. He climbs a grassy slope and then hears the explosion. People are running toward the burning wreckage of the aero plane. ALBERTO is walking to the fiery scene as his brother HENRIQUE approaches him

> HENRIQUE
> Come away, Alberto! Let's go back to the hotel.

> ALBERTO
> No, I must see.

> HENRIQUE
> Please, brother, go no further. We can be injured.

> ALBERTO
> No, I must!

Close to the carnage now, ALBERTO sees the beautiful young pilot lying dead in the cockpit, going up in flames with his craft

> ALBERTO (visibly shaken)
> What have I done? What have I done?

> HENRIQUE
> You have done nothing!

> ALBERTO
> Oh, my God! Look what I have done!

> HENRIQUE
> Please, Alberto, come back to the hotel with me.

INT. HOTEL - DAY

ALBERTO and HENRIQUE step out of the elevator

> HENRIQUE (walking)
> Are you sure?

> ALBERTO (walking)
> I'm fine. I'm just tired. I need to sleep.

> HENRIQUE (opening door)
> I'll stay with you for a while.

> ALBERTO
> There's no need. Wake me when it is time
> and we'll take supper in my room.

                        HENRIQUE
        Very well. I'll call.

HENRIQUE leaves. ALBERTO quietly locks the door. As he turns, a chanteuse's ballad
will underscore the rest of the scene. A close up of the despondent ALBERTO draws
back just enough for us to see his necktie/noose. He looks up through the window to see a
large sea bird soaring high against a bright, blue sky. Slowly a small smile crosses his lips
as he watches. We go back to the soaring bird

                        ALBERTO (quietly)
        Let go all lines.

The ballad swells

THE ARTIFACT

EXT. PYRAMIDS ON THE GIZA PLATEAU OF EGYPT - DAY

EXT. SITE OF THE ARCHEOLOGICAL EXCAVATION - DAY

Heavy earth moving equipment is off to the side and forty to fifty laborers are carrying baskets of soil out when the shout of discovery is heard. Dr. ANIN and four or five other scientists descend upon the top of the artifact. Excited shouts and excavation continues as Colonel NAJAR (Egyptian military) descends to the artifact

>   CONNOR (V.O.)
>   A month ago U.S. Geological Survey equipment
>   got an unusual reading while in orbit above
>   Egypt. A few miles due east of the Sphinx and
>   almost sixty feet down, the artifact was unearthed.

>   NAJAR
>   What is this?

>   ANIN
>   We don't know.

>   NAJAR
>   What is this writing?

>   ANIN
>   We don't know.

>   NAJAR (to Sergeant)
>   Get all of these civilians out of here!

Close up of the excited but frightened Dr. ANIN

>   CONNOR (V.O.)
>   What if evidence of an extra-terrestrial visita-
>   tion was discovered? And genetic exper-
>   imentations on humans were implied by this
>   evidence? A month ago the world was a
>   simpler place.

INT. LEIGH CONNOR'S UNIVERSITY OFFICE - DAY

Close up of a framed photograph of ANIN shaking hands with CONNOR. Drawing away from the photograph, CONNOR is out of view behind his desk looking for something. A knock on the door, he peers over his desk. Samantha Reynolds (SAM), a twenty-four year old doctorial assistant, unlocks the door

>   SAM
>   Leigh?

                    CONNOR
Yes, Sam, come in. Have you seen my Luxor
disk?

                    SAM
It's already loaded on the computer in the
lecture hall.

                    CONNOR
And the midterms?

                    SAM
Finished.

                    CONNOR
Thank you. You're the best, Sam.

                    SAM
Yes, I know.

She hands him a note with a small stack of mail

I found this in your box. Doc 'Oli' wants to
see you after your morning lecture.

                    CONNOR (looking at note)
What else is here?

                    SAM
I don't read all of your mail, just the juicy
stuff. There's a card from your daughter.
Note that the envelope remains intact.

                    CONNOR (reading)
Thank you.

                    SAM
She misses you. She wants her Father in
her life before she moves on to college.
I didn't read it but I can tell.

                    CONNOR (reading)
I miss her too. I get her for Easter break.
How can you spend two hundred dollars on
a pair of jeans?

                    SAM (exiting)
Easily, you need shoes, of course, and a new
top or two.

                            CONNOR
What was I thinking?

                            SAM
Move it or you'll be late.

                            CONNOR
Sam?

SAM stops at the door

Thank you.

INT. DIMLY LIT CONFERENCE ROOM - DAY

A satellite photograph projected on a screen

                            COMMANDER
This is our first look at the site of the dig. It
appears to be quite a bit deeper in this next
pass. And finally we get a look at the top of
the object. We were able to get several
dozen photographs over the next few days.
As you can see, there are flurries of activity
around the site. And this is our last photo of
the pyramid-shaped object before they cover
it. Six days later they excavate the entire site and
erect a metal building over it. In the meantime
our instruments continue to get a consistent spike.
So, whatever it is, it's still there. We're continuing
to gather Intel but there isn't much.

Back to the 'last photo of it'. Lights up on the conference room, COMMANDER Young, Mr.
HENNESSEY, the Lieutenant working the projector and Dr. BREWSTER

                            HENNESSEY
Any conclusions, Commander?

                            COMMANDER
Damn few, Mr. Hennessey. The Egyptians
have been very tight-lipped about it. We've
had to start making some assumptions.

                            HENNESSEY
And.

                            COMMANDER
Our instruments will detect magnesium-rich
materials or materials with magnetic properties. But this reading looks like a graviti-
tional anomaly.

HENNESSEY

Looks?

COMMANDER

An inordinately dense object might read like
a gravitational anomaly. In order to study
this very heavy object, they may have found it
expedient to erect a building over it. The
Pentagon sees no eminent threat but we're
curious.

HENNESSEY

Dr. Brewster, we're taking guesses. Care to
join us?

BREWSTER

I'm not sure how.

HENNESSEY

Lieutenant, would you dim these overhead
lights?

HENNESSEY refers to the projected photograph

What could this thing be?

BREWSTER

I believe that the USGA's instrument also
reacts to rich deposits of obsidian and other
glassy minerals, even petrified wood. So,
too many possibilities right now to make
guesses. We'll know what it is when we
know what it's made of. I suppose it could
be the work of pre-World War Two Germans
or much earlier French but it's not likely. I
don't know, Mr. Hennessey, I guess it could
be a hoax of some kind. We can only assume
that the pyramid is recently made or it is not.

HENNESSEY

What if this is even older, much older?

BREWSTER

If this is an ancient relic, it is a most important find.

INT. UNIVERSITY LECTURE HALL - DAY

CONNOR is pointing to a section of a projected drawing of the temple at Luxor

CONNOR

We assumed that these columns were an offering by one of the later Ramessids but then someone on Dr. Anin's team found this inscription
on the inside base of an entry pillar. It was
remarkably similar to a Ramsey Two invocation
to Ra, a short prayer that was shortened even
more to, essentially, a cheer, "hooray, Ra", if
you will. The wear and decay of the rock was
comparable to this whole section so we had
to re-access and amend our logs. This was another example of expectation working against us.
Were it not for the meticulous work of Dr. Anin,
the director of this particular investigation, we
might have missed it or not recognized it. I think
I've said in this class that expectation can work
for or against translators. And I believe I used
the example of our investigation of a granary
near Aswan. We expected to find records indicating volumes and weight and because of our
expectations we were prepared to put large
sections of text together in a short time. But
expectation can also lead you astray. Translators
can over-look or misinterpret material
that does not conform to their expectations and,
perhaps, miss valuable information.

JASON, a student, raises his hand

CONNOR

Yes?

JASON

What about when there are no expectations?

CONNOR

There are always expectations.

JASON

There is an English newspaper on your desk
there that reports the find of an artifact in
Egypt with symbols that may be extra-
terrestrial in origin.

Stifled student giggles, CONNOR finds the paper

What would your expectations be in the case
of this translation?

CONNOR

Who reported the find?

                           JASON
An anonymous source.

                          CONNOR
There, you see, that's the thing about some of
those British rags. They have the credibility of
our Global Inquirer.

Small laugh from class

                           JASON
Nevertheless, how would you proceed?

                          CONNOR
Well, first I would determine the nature of
the artifact. Is it a communication left for our
benefit, 'take me to your leader' kind of thing
or is it a domestic item. For instance, a vacuum
cleaner that fell out of the space ship.

Bigger laugh from class

                           JASON
And your expectations?

Suddenly seeing that the student is serious, CONNOR is serious as well

                          CONNOR
There would be few or no expectations other
than the most basic. We would expect symbols
to relate to one another in some way.

Moment of awkward silence as students begin to leave

                            SAM
A reminder: Robinson, chapters eleven through
fourteen for next week!

As students leave CONNOR opens the newspaper on his desk to find the grainy photograph of a
pyramid

INT. THE BUILDING HOUSING THE ARTIFACT - DAY

The artifact under lights. It is a metallic pyramid almost twenty-four feet high, proportionally
identical to the Great Pyramid. There is the flashing light of a welder, someone on a lift taking
overhead photographs and the sound of drills. Egyptian military, scientists, and important
civilians are seated in a glass-enclosed office next to the pyramid, among them is Minister ATEF
and his AID.

                   HARASHIN (referring to notes)
Our tests indicate a solid object. We think it is

stable and not leaching anything into the soil.
Despite the rock-like texture on all five sides,
this is a metallic object composed of iron and
a unique alloy of gold, magnesium and copper.
It is unique because it is not a mixture of mol-
ten metal. It appears to be a molecularly fused
amalgam. Under the microscope it resembles
some gems produced under great pressure and
heat. A block of iron this size might weigh 100
tons. This is over 130. We think the inscriptions were made at the time of the smelting and
pour of this material because we can hardly
make a dent in it at room temperature. And our
welders have only begun to blacken the surface.

                    ATEF
And your chemical tests?

                  HARASHIN
They confirm a clean iron ore and this amalgam.
The incredible temperatures needed to create
this material have made it impossible to be
more specific. In fact, I don't know a foundry
in the world that could... Well, all I can say is
we'll keep testing. Perhaps there is a catalyst
involved.

ANIN enters the office, he is exhausted

                    ATEF
Ah, Dr Anin, we were speaking of the inscriptions. Any luck?

                    ANIN
We think we may have identified mathematical
symbols in all six groups of narrow bands.
We've identified 347 symbols in their various
attitudes, upside down or flipped over. Some
of these symbols are similar to other kinds of
script. But if this is complicated with some
kind of coding, the task of translating could
take a very long time. We are woefully un-
derstaffed to attempt a study of this magnitude.
And I fear that we may fail for lack of resources.

                    ATEF
What do you need, Doctor?

                    ANIN
Help. We have experienced colleagues all over
the world.

                          ATEF
        Make your recommendations. I'll take them to
        Council and advise you of their decision. Is
        there anything else this afternoon?

                       ATEF's AID
        No, that will be all.

The room starts to empty

                          ATEF
        Just a minute, Doctor. Please sit down, Dr.
        Anin. We won't be long. I need to confirm
        one of my observations with you.

                          ANIN
        Certainly, Minister.

                          ATEF
        Metal that we've never seen? Writing that
        we've never seen? And in the shape of the
        great monuments of our country. This just
        didn't fall out of the sky. Or did it? Shall
        we tell the Council that it is a gift from
        little green men from outer space?

They chuckle awkwardly, uncomfortable silence

        There are those who will say that this is too
        great a prize to share with foreigners.

                          ANIN
        Or too great a prize not to share.

ATEF gathers his briefcase

                          ATEF
        How will you proceed?

                          ANIN
        We'll concentrate on the mathematics and
        hope we can continue making progress.
        We'll work around the clock as best we can.

                          ATEF
        And I'll do the best I can to get the help you
        need, Doctor. Good luck.

ATEF leaves, ANIN sits looking at the artifact. YOUNG LAB ASSISTANT enters the office
with clipboard

                    YOUNG LAB ASSISTANT
I'm sorry, Doctor, I'm not sure how to apply
these values in the statistical analysis. Do
all of the characters get…

                         ANIN
No, here, let me show you.

INT. DOOR TO DR. SHAW'S OFFICE, UNIVERSITY- DAY

CONNOR knocks and tentatively enters. The attractive Leslie NICHOLS, early thirties, business suit (jacket and skirt), approaches him

                        NICHOLS
Dr. Connor?

                        CONNOR
Yes.

                    NICHOLS (shaking his hand)
Leslie Nichols from the State Department. Dr.
Shaw was kind enough to let me have this ap-
pointment. Please forgive the ambush. I just
need a few minutes, if you don't mind.

                        CONNOR
Well, I guess I'm intrigued if I'm not in trouble
of some kind.

                        NICHOLS
Not at all. I have something interesting to show
you. Please…

She indicates a seat next to her on the sofa. As he sits she pulls a manila folder out of her briefcase

                        NICHOLS
You probably don't remember me but I'm a
former student of yours. It's been years. I
read your book, "Translations in Time" - The
role of intuition in science- fascinating stuff.

                        CONNOR
Thank you. What can I do for you, Ms. Nichols?

                        NICHOLS
Actually, I'm here to advise you, Dr. Connor.
You're about to receive an invitation by way
of the State Department to go to Egypt and
consult on the translation of texts. I'm here
to confirm your interest and prepare you a

little for the briefing you'll be getting with
the Department.

               CONNOR (dryly)
This is generally not how expeditionary pro-
jects are proposed.

               NICHOLS
I know, apparently this is an unusual situation.
Dr. Anin from Egyptian Antiquities has author-
ized an invitation to you, to the Iraqis and a
French team as well.

               CONNOR
Dr. Anin is a friend of mine. Why hasn't he
contacted me personally?

               NICHOLS
I can only speculate.

               CONNOR
Where did you say you worked?

               NICHOLS
The U.S. State Department.

               CONNOR (quietly)
Damn.

               NICHOLS
Excuse me?

               CONNOR
Our work can be tough enough without involve-
ing government agencies. When did ancient
writings become a matter of national security?

               NICHOLS
They aren't. No, we have no intentions of
interfering with your work, Doctor. The project involves the study of an artifact, recently
found.

NICHOLS removes the satellite photograph of the artifact from the envelope and gives it to him

               NICHOLS
Aside from the shape, we don't know what
to make of it. Computer enhancements tell
us there may be script on all four sides…
What's the matter?

CONNOR
There was a student today who had a photograph… nothing.

NICHOLS
There have been photo leaks to the European
press but the stories have been dismissed.

CONNOR
You mean, the ones about Martians?

NICHOLS (a smile)
The invitation is extended to yourself and a
small staff with stipulations. All materials
and information resulting from this study
will remain in country and property of Egypt.

CONNOR
I don't understand. This doesn't sound like
Philippe Anin. I'll need to speak with him.

NICHOLS
Well, you can try. Or you can talk to him in
person in about ten days.

CONNOR
Ten days? It's not much lead-time.

NICHOLS
It is short notice. However, the department is
prepared to expedite passports and travel, and
help you through departure. Are you interested?

CONNOR
Of course.

NICHOLS (gathers her things)
Fine. I'll call in the morning to arrange the
briefing. I know this is a lot to digest, Dr.
Connor. We'll answer as many of your
questions as we can.

CONNOR
Is Dr. Anin all right?

NICHOLS
He's fine. And we expect that you and your
people will be treated with the usual respect
and courtesy. Otherwise, we would advise
against you going.

CONNOR

Thank you, I guess.

NICHOLS moves to the door, CONNOR follows her

Miss Nichols, what's going on here?

NICHOLS

No one is sure, Doctor, I'll talk to you
tomorrow.

NICHOLS exits, worried expression on CONNOR's face

INT. CONNOR'S APARTMENT - NIGHT

Blinking light on telephone answering machine. We hear CONNOR entering, ice into glass. He
pours whiskey, turns desk lamp on and plays answering machine.

KATHERINE (on machine)

Leigh, this is Katherine. Just a reminder
that Michele's school break starts this Fri-
day. She will be with you for the week.
Give me a call if there is any problem
with you picking her up on Saturday
morning as I plan to be busy this weekend.
Hope you are well, bye.

CONNOR realizes that he will be unable to take his daughter for the whole week, takes a big gulp
and big sigh

INT. CONNOR'S DREAM - DAY

CONNOR is ushered by government officials down the stairs of an older Cairo hotel. He meets
ANIN at the front door.

ANIN

Have you got it?

CONNOR

Got what? What am I supposed to have?

ANIN

Never mind. Follow me.

INT. INSIDE OF OLDER TAXICAB IN CAIRO - DAY
ANIN gets in front with DRIVER and CONNOR gets in the back seat where SAM is in her
bathrobe. A crowd gathers

ANIN

Don't say anything to them.

287

CONNOR
What? About what?

Suddenly the crowd starts to rock the cab and yell. They open the front passenger door and drag ANIN out of the cab

ANIN
We found it, Leigh! We found it!

CONNOR
Where are they taking him?

DRIVER (leering at Sam)
I don't know.

SAM
Come on, Leigh, let's go.

CONNOR
But Philippe…

SAM

Let's go!

SAM strattles him in the back seat, kissing him and they begin to make love. Katherine appears in the front passenger seat. The driver is taking photographs of SAM and CONNOR

KATHERINE
What is legalese for caught in the act?

DRIVER
In flagrance. Your lawyer will love these.

SHAW and MICHELE (CONNOR'S eighteen year old daughter) walk by the cab, clearly in disapproval of CONNOR

CONNOR
No!

CONNOR is kissing SAM. As she draws away from him, she has become the young and beautiful KATHERINE. They begin to make love and CONNOR notices that people are laughing and jeering at them. This causes him anxiety, laughter becomes rhythmic and loud

INT. CONNOR'S BEDROOM – NIGHT

CONNOR wakes from his dream. He turns off the alarm (which was beeping in the cadence of the laughter in the dream), rolls to his back and experiences the anxiety of the dream again

INT. CONNOR'S OFFICE - DAY

CONNOR is blearily going over notes as SHAW walks in with an extra cup of coffee

SHAW
Good morning, Dr. Connor, you look like hell.
How are you?

CONNOR (taking coffee)
Thank you, I'm fine. I didn't sleep well last
night.

SHAW
So, are you being stolen from us? I got a little
preview from the lovely Ms. Nichols. She kept
pulling her skirt down over her knee and
saying things like "political currency" and
"international cooperation in the fields of
science". She works in government somewhere, I'm not sure, I couldn't think of
anything but her knees. Where are you going
this time?

CONNOR
Egypt- a new artifact.

SHAW
Yes, well, I guess the old ones are getting
old. When, next Fall?

CONNOR
Ten days.

SHAW (after a beat)
What a glamorous life you must lead and
what a living hell it makes of mine.

CONNOR
I know, I feel terrible.

SHAW
Let me help you feel that way. Replacing
you through the term is going to be a pain
in the ass.

Door knock, in walks SAM

SAM
Leigh, you need to… Oh, I'm sorry, Dr. Connor,
I didn't know you were busy. I'll just leave these
for your signature and pick them up later.

SHAW (crossing to her)
Wait just a minute, Miss Reynolds. Samantha,
how close are you to your Doctorate?

                        SAM
Well, I hope to get my thesis reviewed in about
five months.

                        SHAW
Excellent. I may have an opportunity for you.
Dr. Connor here will be in the field for weeks
at a time starting, oh, next week.

                    SAM (to CONNOR)
Really, what's up?

                        CONNOR
Anin has an artifact.

SAM produces newspaper photograph of the pyramid

                        SAM
Anything like this?

                   SHAW (referring to photo)
Haven't they already found those?

                        CONNOR
Where did this come from?

                        SAM
A New York daily. It says that the discovery
is over a month old. Why hasn't anything
appeared in any of the journals?

                        CONNOR
I'm guessing the Egyptian government is
screening out-going information.

                        SAM
What's going on?

                        CONNOR
I don't know.

                        SHAW
Anyway, my point is, Samantha, if you could
consider substituting for Dr. Connor as lecturer
for the remainder of the term, you would be
doing the college a huge favor. We would
shorten the course a bit and everyone in the
department would be at your disposal. Not a
bad resume item either, substituting for the
distinguished Dr. Leigh.

                    SAM (hoping to go)
Well, unless Dr. Connor would like me to
go to Egypt with him?

                    CONNOR (difficult for him)
I think in this situation, I need to be as sup-
portive of Dr. Shaw as I can and allow him
to make the call.

                    SHAW
Thank you. Well, how about it, Ms. Reynolds?
I'll pay you a lecturer's salary.

                    SAM (hopes dashed)
I'd be honored to substitute teach, Dr. Shaw.

                    SHAW
Excellent. Come by this afternoon and we'll
get the paperwork started.

SAM exits, a beat

That went well.

                    CONNOR (crossing to door)
No, it didn't, it went really badly. In fact, you
can't have her.

                    SHAW
What?

                    CONNOR (moving into hall)
I need her. Sam!

CONNOR crosses down the hall to her, has a brief exchange. SAM issues a squeal of joy and
leaps into CONNOR's arms to hug him. SAM composes herself, has a quick exchange with
CONNOR and walks down the hall as CONNOR walks back to his office. SHAW sees all this
from CONNOR's door

                    SHAW
So it's going to be that way, is it?

                    CONNOR
I couldn't do it to her.

                    SHAW
Yes, well, I'll be on a mission to torture
you over the next day or so. Drop by after
classes today and we'll start making a list
of instructors we know.

                              CONNOR
                    I really am sorry about this, Oliver.

                              SHAW (crossing to door)
                    You don't have to explain. You're a talented
                     man, Leigh. Go do something miraculous
                    and make us all famous. And rich would be
                    especially nice.

SHAW exits. CONNOR dials a long distant call

                              CONNOR (on phone)
                    Good morning. Dr. Leigh Connor for Michael
                    Whych, please? I'll wait.

INT. ENCLOSED SHOPPING MALL - DAY

CONNOR and MICHELE are walking near the indoor fountain. He has a coffee, she has a soft
pretzel

                              MICHELE
                    How long will you be gone?

                              CONNOR
                    Depends on how it goes. It'll probably take
                    us days to load and interface data. I guess
                    we'll take our first break and reassess the
                    project in a week and a half or so. After that,
                    I don't know.

                              MICHELE
                    You'll miss my birthday.

                              CONNOR
                    I'll have no choice.

                              MICHELE (handing him pretzel)
                    Here, hold this. They won't let you take
                    food in here.

MICHELE ducks into boutique. CONNOR sips coffee, eats pretzel and enjoys his daughter as she
shops. A young, well-dressed man is in the shop and slowly begins to notice, and then flirt with
MICHELE. CONNOR's cell phone rings

                              CONNOR
                    Yes, Sam?

                              SAM (on phone)
                    Where are you?

MICHELE has enjoyed the young man's attention but eventually tells him that she is with her father today

>   CONNOR
> We're at a place called "Hot Topics". It's
> got screaming neon, you can't miss it.

>   SAM
> I know it, yes.

>   CONNOR
> We're here on the lame pretext that she is
> shopping for her mother.

>   SAM
> You're learning fast.

As MICHELE gestures toward the door, the young man flashes a big smile at CONNOR who then, embarrassed for some reason, walks away from the door

>   CONNOR
> You won't believe what I just saw. My daughter
> just spurned the advances of some good-looking,
> young stud in preference to the company of her
> father. Can you imagine? How did Katherine and
> I do it? How beautiful she is!

>   SAM
> You are learning fast. See you guys in a minute.

Phone off, CONNOR walks to another store front. His attention is captured by a golden pyramid atop a display of lady's shoes. The low, whirring sound of a jet engine is heard as CONNOR'S focus on the pyramid gets tighter and tighter. The pyramid seems to be vibrating

INT. BACK TO SHOPPING MALL - DAY

>   SAM (approaching CONNOR)
> So, are you looking for something in an opened
> toe?

>   MICHELE
> There you are. I thought you were trying to ditch
> me. Hi, Sam.

SAM smiles

> What's the matter, Dad, you look tired?

>   CONNOR
> No, I'm fine. Where do we go next?

MICHELE
I thought we'd try the big stores first.

CONNOR
Lead on, my Captain.

MICHELE (turning to walk)
This way troops.

SAM (taking CONNOR's arm)
You're not getting narcoleptic on me, are you?

CONNOR
Does that mean senile?

They follow MICHELE

INT. OFFICES IN THE ARTIFACT BUILDING - NIGHT

HARASHIN
Can't this wait until tomorrow?

ANIN
No, Dr. Sali is ready. We need good news. I'm
calling them in.

ANIN steps out of the office into the big room and they begin to gather slowly

Please, my friends, let us convene and hear an
important report. I know we are tired but we
must share this news before we rest. Please, bear
with me. We are close to a breakthrough. Dr. Sali,
will you bring us up to date on your work?

SALI
When we started running our models for a twelve-
digit system we got high probabilities that we were
identifying simple addition/subtraction functions
and their indicators. (murmurs of approval) We
think that our models, with some modifications,
may yield higher functions..

Small spontaneous applause

ANIN
Outstanding! It's an important beginning. Uda
and Hakara, let's apply our geometric models
using this twelve digit system and see if we can
get a match. We have done excellent work today.
Soon our neighbors and colleagues abroad will
be joining us. Congratulations, Dr. Sali. Good

work everyone. Enjoy your evening meal, my
friends.

Various mutters of well-wishing as they depart. ANIN crosses to the pyramid and puts a hand on
an edge, then both hands as if trying to understand by osmosis. SALI (with printout) and Dr.
HARASHIN approach him

                         ANIN
I know this is unscientific of me but I believe
that I feel something here. Perhaps it is nothing.

                    SALI (handing ANIN paper)
We think these are the integers, twelve of them.

                         ANIN
How elegant in the economy and precision of
design.

                    SALI (in awe)
…as if written by the hand of God.

A beat

                    HARASHIN
Or by someone who could get this metal hot
enough to stamp or etch.

                    ANIN (laughing)
Good point, Doctor.

                    HARASHIN
If we can melt this alloy, then we will prove
that men created this.

                         ANIN
"written by the hand of God" is rather hard
to prove- scientifically.

                    SALI (exiting in a huff)
Oh, good night you two quacking old hens.

                         ANIN
Good night, my friend.

HARASHIN crosses to pyramid and slowly puts both hands on it.

                         ANIN
You don't believe that for a second, do
you.

HARASHIN
What?

ANIN
That this isn't some kind of miracle.

HARASHIN
This could be five or twenty-five thousand years old,
we don't know. If it is very old, then it is a miracle
and it's creators would have been like Gods. And
so today we are still trying to solve the riddles of
the Gods. I am a scientist and will work toward
discovery. But I am also a man who is afraid of
God's secrets. May it not be dangerous to know?
…Ah, I must be getting tired to talk like this. I'll
leave you now, get some rest.

ANIN
Yes.

HARASHIN exits. ANIN touches the pyramid prayerfully

INT. BACK TO THE SHOPPING MALL- DAY

CONNOR and SAM enjoy watching MICHELE try on cloths, SAM encouraging, CONNOR
discouraging sexy cloths

CONNOR (reading a message)
The Iraqis are sending Yassari, good. And I told
you about Dr. Whych and his student, a program-
mer. Four of us; enough to start our own journal
and lend a hand. I have yet to talk to him but I'm
sure Dr. Anin is busy mapping out a strategy for
the weeks of the study.

INT. OFFICES IN THE ARTIFACT BUILDING - DAY

ANIN is standing over the table on which are four or five charts and maps of the artifact with
transparencies, computer, and a hand-held keyboard that is connected to the computer. He enters
precise locations of symbols for ten full seconds and then checks the screen. It's all wrong. His
worst fears come true as he pages up and realizes that he has just wasted forty-five minutes of
work. As if in a spell, he disconnects the keyboard, wraps the cord around it and walks into the
big room to throw it. About the time he has made up his mind to shatter it on the pyramid, Dr.
HARASHIN walks up beside him.

HARASHIN
How are you, Doctor?

ANIN
I'm fine.

ANIN follows HARASHIN into the office to enter the data again

INT. BACK TO THE SHOPPING MALL- DAY

SAM and MICHELE are trying on outrageous clothes, modeling for CONNOR. He is talking on his cell phone

> CONNOR (on phone)
> There's a possibility that their readings have nothing to do with the pyramid... Yes, well that's the government for you, what's classified this week shows up in the Washington Post the next...That's right. Fine, Michael, thanks for the call... No you haven't met her, Samantha Reynolds, Sam, she was with me on the Mexico dig... Good... Excellent, I'll see you then. Give my best to Pat.

INT. OFFICES IN THE ARTIFACT BUILDING - DAY

Two excited, young students rush into the office.

> FIRST YOUNG STUDENT
> Dr. Anin! Dr. Anin, we were taking photographs from on top and I touched the cap. It seemed warmer than the rest of it so we took measurements. There is a temperature difference of almost five degrees from the top to the bottom.

> HARASHIN
> Impossible.

> FIRST YOUNG STUDENT
> We took ambient temperatures from the height of the pyramid to the bottom and the difference wasn't that much. We took soil sample temperatures from all four corners and close to the pyramid. They were consistently cooler than the bottom. So, we thought something else might be affecting the temperature. We got filters for our camera enhancing the red end of the spectrum. And I got very slow film. And this is what we got.

Shares a photograph of the pyramid with a glow coming from the top. Gasps of amazement

> FIRST YOUNG STUDENT
> I would say that our pyramid has an aura. At the very least, it is radiating heat somehow.

> HARASHIN
> Impossible! We have recorded no energy emission at all.

ANIN
Then how do you explain?

HARASHIN (finally)
I can't.

ANIN
Good work, gentlemen. Let's see if we can create a thermal map of our artifact. Congratulations!

INT. INSIDE CONNOR'S CAR - DAY

CONNOR driving, MICHELE in front passenger seat

CONNOR
It's not that I don't think about it sometimes but it just feels so contrived and awkward. The prospect of dating fills me with dread. I think I've forgotten how.

MICHELE
Nonsense. What about Sam, Samantha?

CONNOR
What about her?

MICHELE
You seem comfortable enough around her.

CONNOR (defensively)
We're friends, yes. She's also my student. I'm the chairman of her thesis review, for Christsakes. I'm twice her age. I think there is a rule about not dating your students.

MICHELE
So, you don't find her attractive?

CONNOR (flustered)
No, I mean, she's an attractive young woman…

CONNOR pulls over to the curb next to a hedge in front of MICHELE and KATHERINE's house

All right, Missy, you're home.

MICHELE
It's just that I worry about you, Dad. You seem lonely.

> CONNOR
> I'm fine, honey. Sometimes I miss you and this
> house...

EXT. A DARK JAGUAR PULLS INTO THE DRIVEWAY - DAY

> Did your mother get a new car?

> MICHELE
> Uh, no, that belongs to a friend of hers.

Unaware that they are being watched, RICHARD, a well-dressed man, gets out of the driver's side and crosses to the passenger side to open the door for KATHERINE. He gives her a warm kiss on the cheek

INT. CONNOR'S CAR - DAY

Close up of Connor watching KATHERINE

> MICHELE
> I'm home a little earlier than I was expected.

> CONNOR
> Have you met him?

> MICHELE
> Briefly. He seems nice enough. He's a real estate
> agent, works in the city.

Still on CONNOR as he watches KATHERINE cross to the front door and go inside. We hear the Jag door close, start and drive off

> He's rich and he's handsome. I hate his guts.

> CONNOR (smiles)
> Thank you, honey.

We draw back in the car to include MICHELE

> MICHELE
> You miss her, don't you?

> CONNOR
> I love your mother but sometimes I don't like
> her very much. I think the feeling is mutual.

> MICHELE
> Can't you talk to her? It's been over a year
> and a half.

                    CONNOR
It's not that simple.

                    MICHELE
I wish there was something I could do. Are
you sure you won't come in and fly into a
jealous rage?

                    CONNOR
No, thanks. And don't tell her that I saw her
today. There's no point.

                    MICHELE
You're a prince.

                    CONNOR
Not really, I'm going to catch up with the big
city boyfriend and beat the crap out of him.

                    MICHELE (hugging him)
I love you, Dad.

                    CONNOR
I love you, honey.

MICHELE gets out of the car and gathers her overnight bag and new clothes, and walks to the
front door. CONNOR watches for a moment and starts the car

INT. OFFICE OF CHANCELLOR CARDINAL ROSELLE- DAY

ROSELLE is looking at the newspaper photograph of the artifact. CARRARA (fifties, middle-
eastern, well dressed) is playing a taped interview. CARRARA is translating Arabic to English on
the tape. The interviewed man is barely audible

                    CARARRA (on tape)
He says that it was covered with symbols of
different kinds. They were cut into the rock.

CARRARA asks a question in Arabic

                    CARRARA (on tape)
He says that he has never seen these symbols
before. They were not hieroglyphs but some
of it seemed familiar. He doesn't know why.
He thinks they were drunk with excitement.

CARRARA asks a question in Arabic

                    CARRARA (on tape)
He says they were replaced by soldiers but
that soldiers were also amazed. The place

300

made them feel holy. Some were crying and
did not want to leave but were forced...

CARRARA turns off tape.

> ROSELLE
> We need more eyes and ears in Egypt.

> CARRARA
> I'm pursuing that now, Your Eminence.

> ROSELLE
> Who is this eyewitness?

> CARRARA
> An itinerate worker, easy enough to find,
> questionable credibility.

> ROSELLE
> I believed him. That's all right, for now. Let's
> keep an eye on it and see what develops. Holy
> Mother Church has withstood attacks from
> the dark armies of daemons and men. And now,
> Heaven help us, the media may test our reso-
> lution. We'll be ready. Let us make our own
> discovery of this artifact. Let's do it now.

> CARRARA
> Yes, Your Eminence.

INT. HEATHROW INTERNATIONAL AIRPORT - DAY

CONNOR and Dr. Michael WHYCH are walking ahead of SAM and MANUEL (WHYCH's
student) in the deplaning apparatus

> WHYCH
> It should take about eight hours to set up the
> carbon spectrum tests.

> CONNOR
> That's fine. I don't know what Anin has yet
> but I'm sure his mineralogist has the material
> thoroughly analyzed by now.

> WHYCH
> This process will confirm his results and, per-
> haps, give us additional information. Once the
> tests are set up, they only need monitoring. In
> the meantime our students can be writing pro-
> grams and loading data.

                         CONNOR
Very well. Thanks, Michael.

                         NICHOLS
Dr. Connor.

Leslie NICHOLS is standing off to the side of the entrance into the terminal from the deplaning apparatus

                         CONNOR
Miss Nichols?

                         NICHOLS
And you must be Dr. Whych?

                         WHYCH
Yes.

                         NICHOLS (shaking WHYCH's hand)
Leslie Nichols of the U.S. State Department.

                         CONNOR
I didn't expect to see you on this side of the
pond, Ms. Nichols.

                         NICHOLS
Neither did I. I guess the Department thinks I'm
indispensable.

                         CONNOR
I see. Well, these are our colleagues, Samantha
and Manuel.

                         NICHOLS (shaking hands)
Pleased to meet you and welcome. We have about
three hours before the connecting flight so I've
reserved a suite for us. Right this way.

                         WHYCH
Why don't you go ahead, Leigh. I'm going to grab
a cup of coffee and see to the equipment.

                         NICHOLS
Your luggage and gear are being taken care of and
 there is coffee and snacks in the suite.

                         WHYCH
Great.

                         NICHOLS (turning to walk)
So, if you'll just follow me…

CONNOR (walking)
This is certainly first class treatment by the
State Department. What's up?

NICHOLS
It seems the artifact is generating international
interest. Soon, the regular press and broadcast media
will be all over it. This expedition is sure to be a
prominent feature of the story. That kind of notoriety
can make travel difficult. I'm here to help.

CONNOR
Our concierge?

NICHOLS casts a glance at CONNOR

NICHOLS
The French government says that they only
requested preliminary data. The Egyptian
government refused. The French were haughty.
The Egyptians were angry and almost pulled
the plug on the whole study. While you're on
a plane to Cairo, I'll be meeting an Egyptian
official at our embassy in London smoothing
ruffled feathers. As I said, I'm here to help.

CONNOR
Amazing, the oil and water mixture of politics
and science. Is there anything else you're not
telling me?

NICHOLS
No. Nothing that you need to know.

CONNOR
You're charming, Ms. Nichols, in an infuriating
kind of way.

NICHOLS (stops at a door)
One of the perks of working for the government.
Speaking of perks…

NICHOLS knocks on the door. A large, professional-looking young man answers and then opens
to reveal a luxurious suite reserved for traveling dignitaries

INT. A LARGE FRATERNITY PARTY - NIGHT

Loud music, lots of booze and college-aged people. MICHELE is dancing with an odd young
man who is trying to be "sexy" with her. She excuses herself to go to the kitchen. Working her
way to the refrigerator, she sees the image of a grainy photograph of the artifact on a small
counter-top television. She quickly moves to turn up the volume of the TV

INT. TELEVISION IMAGE FILLS SCREEN

                    ANNOUNCER V.O.
Secretary of the Air Force, Brigadier General
Randle Pierce confirms the development of or-
bital scanning equipment that detects variations
in the earth's electro-magnetic and gravitational
fields. And it was this scanning equipment that
first located the pyramid deep underground. Is
that right, Mitchell?

                    MICHELL (on telephone)
That's correct, Robert. Since then the Egyptian
government has been very secretive about the
finding.

TV image changes to ANNOUNCER at news desk

                    ANNOUNCER
Let me interrupt you for a minute, Mitchell. We
have photos of two members of the American
delegation to Egypt...

TV image changes to photograph of CONNOR and WHYCH

Yes, on your left, Dr. Leigh Connor and next to
him, Dr. Michael Whych. These distinguished
American archeologists and other scientists will
get a first-hand look at the object. Mitchell, when
might we expect to hear more?

A YOUNG WOMAN at the party runs into the kitchen

                    YOUNG WOMAM
Michele, your dad's on TV! He's on TV!

JASON has followed the YOUNG WOMAN into the kitchen to see who is CONNOR's daughter.
There is other unassigned, ambient party dialogue (e.g. "What did she say?" and "I guess her
father's a big shot.") over the remainder of the audio of the TV broadcast

                    MICHELL (on telephone)
It could be just a matter of days, Robert. There
is an interesting side story. Actually several ac-
counts by Egyptians claiming "euphoria" experienced at the site of the discovery. So, as you
can imagine, we have been busy sorting fact
from what may be colorful rumor.

                    ANNOUNCER (snickering)
Thank you, Mitchell. We'll look forward to
your next report. Mitchell Ali Said, our co-

304

respondent in Egypt. We'll take a break and
be back with some national stories, among
them- a look at our sagging Wall Street, profit
taking on a corporate level…

Suddenly self-conscious, MICHELE walks outside onto the porch. JASON follows her

                    JASON (offering)
Cigarette?

                    MICHELE
No, thank you.

                    JASON
I was in your father's class before he got
called away.

                    MICHELE (quietly)
He chose to go.

                    JASON
What?

                    MICHELE
It wasn't a mandatory thing.

                    JASON
Oh. I told him it was aliens from outer space.

                    MICHELE
What?

                    JASON
Aliens from outer space.

                    MICHELE
Where did you hear that?

                    JASON
It was just a story in a London paper. Probably
nothing.

                    MICHELE
Oh.

                    JASON
And now it's a big deal. I mean, I guess it is.

                    MICHELE
Yes, I guess so.

                    JASON
Are you OK?

                    MICHELE
Yes.

A beat

                    JASON
Your Father's a smart guy. He knows what
he's doing.

                    MICHELE
Thank you. I'm Michele.

                    JASON (shaking her hand)
Jason. Can I get you a beer?

                    MICHELE
No, thank you... But you can have one.

                    JASON
No, that's all right.

                    MICHELE
So, are you named after Jason, the explorer?

                    JASON
That's me, the explorer.

                    MICHELE
Yes, that's my dad too. His translations are like
ordeals...

                    JASON
Are you worried?

                    MICHELE
I don't know, he said he wasn't sleeping well.
I'm afraid.

                    JASON
Afraid of what?

                    MICHELE (breaks into tears)
I'm just afraid for my Dad.

She quietly sobs in JASON's arms for a moment then composes herself

Oh my God, you must think I'm a total
basket case crying on a stranger's shoulder.

                              JASON
I think you're a brave woman. Are you sure
I can't get you that beer?

                              MICHELE
Thank you but I really must be going.

                              JASON
May I walk you to your car?

She smiles and they walk

                    I'm fascinated by archeology because
                    carvings in stone were meant to survive
                    the authors by thousands of years. For in-
                    stance, the builders of the pyramids must
                    have imagined that their monuments would
                    be an everlasting testimony of themselves.
                    What balls. I mean, it's interesting, that's all.
                    Listen, do you think that maybe we could,
                    uh… do you think that maybe we could go out,
                    or something?

                              MICHELE (enjoying his nervousness)
Maybe.

She pulls a short pencil from a pocket and writes a telephone number on a scrap of paper, hands it
to him

                    For coffee or a glass of wine?

                              JASON
Sure. Thanks.

EXT. INTERNATIONAL AIRPORT IN CAIRO - DAY

CONNOR and party are exiting the airliner to go to an awaiting military personnel transport
helicopter. ANIN, HARASHIN, and Colonel NAJAR are waiting at the foot of the deplaning
staircase. All are speaking up to be heard over the roar of helicopter and jet engines.

                              CONNOR
Philippe!

                              ANIN
Leigh! God bless you for coming! You look well.

                              CONNOR
And you, I didn't know what to think.

                              ANIN
              No need to worry, my friend. What a discovery
              we have made.

                              CONNOR
              I'm anxious to see.

At a distance we see quick introductions before they all move to the waiting troop transport helicopter

INT THE HELICOPTER EN ROUTE - DAY

Again, all are specking up to be heard. NAJAR is paying close attention to the Americans

                         WHYCH (with clipboard)
              And your character position grids yielded nothing?

ANIN shaking head 'no'

                              CONNOR
              Philippe! We brought random dispersion models,
              refined models that might be of help.

                              ANIN
              I don't think so. Wait until you see it.

                              CONNOR
              We have a puzzle, then?

                              ANIN
              And you are welcome to it.

                          CONNOR (laughs)
              You look tired, Philippe. How is your sleep?

                              ANIN
              Not good. I am a crazy man sometime!

                              CONNOR
              No. You are a crazy man all of the time.

Big laugh as helicopter banks east

INT. INSIDE THE ARTIFACT BUILDING - DAY

The door slowly rolls up to reveal the blinding light of day. The Americans are approaching the artifact as if in church

                              ANIN
              Well, this is the treasure, my obsession and
              our puzzle. Beautiful is it not?

CONNOR
My God…

ANIN
See these shorter lines of text? We're calling
them the mathematic bands. Using a twelve
digit system, we were able to identify integers
and we think we are close to identifying some
functions. We've begun to apply models involving rudimentary physics problems. Relative
value relationships should emerge and, perhaps
we can start understanding some math concepts.
See this sideways 'H' in the bottom band here?
We think it is a symbol indicating gravity or
mass. In the bands there are few curved characters and the angles are very precise. We think
the two wavy parallel lines here are a symbol
for velocity but we're not sure yet.

CONNOR
I'm sorry, I've lost you.

ANIN
Where?

CONNOR
From the beginning.

ANIN (chuckling)
Ah, yes, I forget. It is awe inspiring. Never mind
what I said. We have scheduled a meeting before
the evening meal when we will bring you up to date
on our work. Why don't you settle into your trailers
for now and rest? I'll see you in a couple of hours.

CONNOR
I don't think anyone is in the mood to rest.

WHYCH and HARASHIN emerge from the other side of the pyramid

WHYCH
Leigh, listen to this.

HARASHIN
It is hypothetical at this point, but I was saying
that, the fused gold, copper, and magnesium
amalgam is almost identical, ounce for ounce,
to the atomic weight of the iron which might
explain why it bonds so tightly. It also helps to
explain why this material stores energy so
efficiently, except…

WHYCH

Show him.

HARASHIN shows CONNOR 'the aura' photograph

CONNOR

This is just an infrared photo of heat loss, right?

HARASHIN

The rate of energy loss follows no law of physics
I have ever seen. It is almost a flat line graft and
has been for two weeks.

CONNOR

That's...

WHYCH

Impossible.

From above the pyramid in a cantilevered lift, Dr. YASSARI shouts down to the gathering

YASSARI

Is that Leigh Connor and Michael Whych?

CONNOR

Dr. Yassari, what are you doing up there?

YASSARI (coming down)

Last minute touches on the anchor for a robot
I got from a hospital.

WHYCH

Was this robot a patient?

YASSARI

Yes, yes, always with the joke. How are you, Michael?

WHYCH

Well. And yourself?

YASSARI (shakes WHYCH's hand)

Yesterday I gave up all of my vices and today
I am so miserable that I am going to steal
some liquor and drown my sorrows in my
mistress's arms. (grins) I apologize to the
lady for my crassness. (crossing to SAM) I am
Dr. Yassari, unmarried physicist, and you are?

SAM

Samantha.

YASSARI kisses SAM's hand and crosses to CONNOR

> **YASSARI**
> Thank you for bringing the beautiful woman, Leigh, always trying to cheer me up. And how are you, my friend?

> **CONNOR**
> Amazed.

> **YASSARI**
> Yes, that was my reaction, still is. It is like a big present waiting to be opened. It makes me so happy.

> **WHYCH**
> What does your robot do?

> **YASSARI**
> Harashin has had a devil of a time heating this to a molten state. I was going to see if I could penetrate it with a laser, or high intensity beam, especially at the top where it is smooth as glass like these edges. The robot will move the beam and cameras millimeters at a time and map the entire object.

> **WHYCH**
> Good thinking.

> **YASSARI**
> Want to see the robot?

> **CONNOR**
> Go ahead, Michael, I'll be along.

YASSARI and WHYCH exit, SAM crosses to CONNOR

> **CONNOR**
> What is the nature of the artifact?

> **SAM**
> To communicate.

> **CONNOR**
> Like we are communicating?

> **SAM**
> No. How about, to commemorate? It is rather monumental…

CONNOR has put his hands on the pyramid

INT. CONNOR'S VISION - DAY

Close up of the little golden pyramid at the shoe store. The sound of the whirring jet engine and the golden pyramid is vibrating

INT. THE ARTIFACT BUILDING - DAY

                  SAM
         … or a gift from an Atlantian king to the
         queen of Sheba. I don't know. Leigh?

                CONNOR
         What?

                  SAM
         What's the matter?

                CONNOR
         I don't know, I feel nauseous. I'm going to
         sit down.

INT. OFFICES IN THE ARTIFACT BUILDING - NIGHT

The meeting ANIN mentioned. The conference table

                ANIN
         We are not surprised to have found no historical
         reference to this object. That is, it does not appear
         in any literature we have reviewed thus far. But,
         in the interest of being thorough, Leigh, I won-
         der if one of your young colleagues might help
         us in our review of more material?

                MANUEL
         I'd be happy to help.

                ANIN
         Thank you. Why don't you proceed, Doctor.

         HARASHIN (with clipboard)
         We have discovered shocked quartz fused to
         the iron on the bottom and have carbon dated
         the quartz at about seven to eight thousand
         years. The bedrock has carbine dated at over
         eighty thousand years. As for the site itself,
         this area was undoubtedly part of the flood
         plain, which means that tons of material would
         regularly migrate to the river and back. This
         kind of soil movement would serve to level

an area, not bury objects as deep as this. We infer that it was purposely buried.

                    WHYCH
You mean constructed on site and then buried.

                    HARASHIN
We assumed that was the case. But the bedrock is not cut or even scarred and there is no slag debris of any kind. As impossible as it sounds, we now think that it was made and placed here.

                    WHYCH
When?

                    HARASHIN
Ah, that is at the very heart of our mystery. The technology required to move an object like this has been developed only in the past two hundred years or so. But the local people swear that this place has remained undisturbed for decades, generations. There was nothing out here. Indeed, were it not for an American satellite, we would not be here. So, when did it happen?

All stare at the artifact

                    ANIN
Yes, well, as we are all now assembled, we hope to make that determination. We are eager to get to work and address the many questions that the artifact poses. I will ask all of you to ignore the sensation that it has created. The satellite photography by the Americans and stories of alien creatures already abound in the world press. This is not a secure facility. Soldiers come in and go out regularly and it is impossible to sensor rumor. Just the technology involved in the making of this pyramid has some of you convinced that it is the work of extra-terrestrials. Please do not put your conjecture ahead of the science. Our job remains to collect evidence. Let's go to work. Dr. Yassari, is your robot ready?

                    YASSARI (exiting)
Yes. Give me twenty minutes to run cables and start the generator. I'm going to see if an electric charge on the dome of the pyramid has any effect as well.

ANIN

Excellent!

SAM crosses to HAKARA, the only other woman in the gathering

SAM (To HAKARA)
This is fascinating but I really must use a ladies room.

HAKARA
I wouldn't use the washroom in this building. Your trailer would be the closest.

Sam smiles and exits

EXT. SAM'S TRAILER IN COMPOUND - NIGHT

SAM starts to climb the stairs to her door when NAJAR steps out of the trailer on to the landing, startling her

NAJAR
Forgive the intrusion, Madame. I was testing the key to your trailer.

NAJAR offers her the key. SAM composes herself and takes the key

SAM
Yes, thank you, Colonel.

NAJAR
If there's nothing else...?

SAM
No, thank you.

NAJAR
Have a pleasant evening.

SAM enters the trailer, closes the door and listens as NAJAR leaves.

CONNOR (V.O.)
The military was watching us and monitoring our personal computers for Internet activity. Najar had orders and was prepared to interrupt this multi-national study if technologies be-gan to emerge that warranted guarding.

INT. OFFICES IN ARTIFACT BUILDING - NIGHT

ANIN, WHYCH and CONNOR are looking at a large illustration of the inscriptions

                              WHYCH
You said that these non-math characters repeat
regularly?

                              ANIN
Some repeat as many as twenty times but there
is no pattern to the arrangement that I can find.
And some symbols that are found regularly in
the math bands are found all over. We have not
detected a pattern.

                              WHYCH
No pattern and yet there is such precision in the
whole design.

                    HARASHIN (entering office)
We think our test on the inscriptions is con-
clusive- the artifact was inscribed by machine.
I scanned detailed photographs of the cuts and
the variances were negligible. But the edges
of the cuts aren't sharp. Perhaps the pyramid
was still hot at the time of the inscription.

                              CONNOR
Yes, it was.

They all look at him

I meant to say that it makes sense.

                    LAB ASSISTANT (entering)
Dr. Yassari is ready.

                              ANIN
Let's go see.

They go in to the big room

                              YASSARI
Lower me on my signal. All right, go… and
stop. And power the beams.

YASSARI is using welding glasses to look directly over the two beams; a bright white light that
is focused on the top of the pyramid. He is moving the beams

                              YASSARI
No, I'm getting some penetration but not
much and it is murky.

Suddenly a shimmering light passes under the surface of the pyramid and dimly lights some
inscriptions

                    CONNOR
Wait! Did anyone else…?

                    SAM
Yes, what was that?

                    CONNOR
Go back, Yassari!

                    YASSARI
What is it?

                    ANIN
There was a light.

                    CONNOR
Take the beam back to where it was a moment ago.

                    YASSARI
I just saw a reflection or some-thing up here.
There it is again. Let's record this… Contin-
uing the scan.

As before, a shimmering wave of light passes under two surfaces of the pyramid. Next three lines
are simultaneous

                    SAM
There!

                    WHYCH
Yes!

                    CONNOR
There it is! Can we turn off these overhead lights?

                    ANIN
Yes, turn off many of the lights. Can you see
enough to work, Doctor?

                    ASSARI
Yes. Continuing on.

                    CONNOR
Philippe, how many cameras do you have?

                    ANIN
This one and four more. Why?

                    CONNOR
We should be recording all four sides with
chronometers on the cameras.

                            ANIN
Good idea. Uda, Hakara, let's set up our other
video recorders.

As before, waves of light pulse under the surface of the pyramid.

                            WHYCH
Yes!

                            CONNOR
There! Beautiful!

                            ASSARI
Is the generator grounded to the bottom of the
pyramid?

                    YOUNG LAB ASSISTANT
Yes.

                            ANIN
Be very careful, gentlemen!

                            YASSARI
All right, give me the hot end. And don't touch
any metal on the basket or we'll fry a physicist.

YASSARI touches the cable to the dome of the pyramid and, as before, light scurries across one
face over to the other

                            CONNOR
Can I playback what I just saw?

                            ANIN
Yes, surely. Dr. Sali, can we have the disk?

SALI rushes to pull the CD out of the camera

                            YASSARI
Should I continue?

                            ANIN
Give us a minute. What are you thinking, Leigh?

                            CONNOR
It's just a hunch but I think if we can slow the
movement of the cable or beam down or slow
the recorders, we might see more detail.

SALI enters with the disk and loads it into a computer

Let's look. Yes, at regular speed, it looks like a
wave of light under the surface. But if we slow the
playback down...There!

All view the monitor and see individual symbols light up from the top down and connect in an
uneven way. Every one reacts with astonishment

> YASSARI
> What's going on? I'm coming down! Did you hear
> me? I'm coming down.

INT. RICHARD'S BEDROOM - DAY

RICHARD is in his bathrobe serving KATHERINE breakfast in bed. He is balancing an elegant
tray with a rose on it

> RICHARD
> Here I come. I'm coming in for a landing. There you
> go.

> KATHERINE
> It's beautiful.

> RICHARD
> Not as beautiful as the lady. What do you say to break-
> fast in bed for the rest of your life?

They kiss. A beat

> KATHERINE
> I wish Michele wasn't so angry.

> RICHARD
> In three months you are going to be a single woman.
> Officially, a single, desirable woman. Is the daughter
> going to continue giving the mother a curfew? Or are
> we all going to move on with our lives?

> KATHERINE
> Richard, you've been very patient. We just need a little
> more time.

RICHARD takes one of the two cups of coffee off of the tray and walks to the door

> RICHARD
> You need to make a decision as to whether or not
> you're still In love with the man you are about to
> divorce.

RICHARD walks out the door. Close up of KATHERINE. The whirring engine noise fades in as
the close up of KATHERINE gets closer and closer until it features only her face. She is

searching her feelings for CONNOR. When she admits to herself that she may still love him, she looks directly into the camera

EXT. 'CREATION OF THE ARTIFACT' - DAY

Deafening jet engine noise as the pyramid, hovering just under a huge space ship, is shot into the ground with a crashing thud waking CONNOR

INT. CONNOR'S TRAILER - DAY

Close up of CONNOR. He is confused and frightened

EXT. THE OFFICE IN THE ARTIFACT BUILDING - DAY

CONNOR crosses to a table with coffee and granola bars on it and helps himself to breakfast

> CONNOR (V.O.)
> Harashin eventually found that there was a decom-
> position occurring. The minerals were oxidizing
> now that it was above ground and sloughing off
> minute traces of a gaseous chemical that builds up
> in the blood stream and acts on the glandular
> systems. We were very emotional. Hakara and
> her husband, Uda, had to leave. The two working
> so close together and living in a camp full of men
> put too much stress on their marriage. Everyone
> was affected in some way. Sam took up smoking
> and crying a lot. I was the worst. I thought I was
> in the first stages of epilepsy or suffering little
> strokes during the day. And at night I was having
> a reoccurring dream about a pyramid.

SAM and MANUEL approach the table with lit cigarettes and they pour themselves coffee

> CONNOR
> Any luck with your carbon spectrum tests?

> MANUEL
> We've abandoned it to help Harashin. They're
> making progress with the math.

> CONNOR (to SAM)
> You don't smoke.

> SAM
> I'll quit when we go home.

> CONNOR
> That's what they all say.

                          SAM
            What happened to you? You look terrible.

                        CONNOR
            I couldn't sleep. I dreamt about a pyramid.

                          SAM
            Go figure.

                      ANIN (outside)
            Let's gather, every one!

INT. STUDENT UNION BUILDING - NIGHT

Beer and sandwiches bar, lots of posted materials and big comfortable chairs. MICHELE is
reading in a chair. The ODD YOUNG MAN who tried to dance with her at the frat party is at the
bar getting a little drunk with his FRIEND

                      ODD YOUNG MAN
            Hey, there's the daughter of what's his name. You
            know the space invaders guy.

                        FRIEND
            What?

                      ODD YOUNG MAN
            You know, the 'Day the Earth Stood Still' guy.

                        FRIEND
            Michael Renee?

                  ODD YOUNG MAN (crosses to her)
            Let's go ask her... Hi, remember me? Say, could you
            settle something for us? I was trying to remember
            your father's name. He thinks it's Michael Renee.
            Is that right?

MICHELE is trying to ignore him when JASON walks up behind her.

                        JASON
            What's up?

Relieved, MICHELE is gathering her things to leave with JASON

                      ODD YOUNG MAN
            Well, it's possible that I got my space movies mixed up.

                    JASON (taking her hand)
            I don't think we can help you.

> ODD YOUNG MAN
>
> Well, how do you know until you try, you rude son
> of a bitch?

JASON stops

> MICHELE (pulls JASON away)
>
> Please don't, Jason.

> ODD YOUNG MAN
>
> Please don't what, Jason?

A very large and WELL-BUILT MAN with an apron on steps in between them

> WELL-BUILT MAN
>
> Hey, what's going on here? No trouble, I hope be-
> cause they would pull our license if there was a lot
> of trouble.

> MICHELE (exiting with Jason)
>
> Thank you.

> WELL-BUILT MAN
>
> No problem. You folks have a nice night now.
> (to the ODDYOUNG MAN) Here, let me take
> that mug from you and explain how upset I would
> be if there was a lot of trouble and they pulled our
> license to operate here on campus.

INT. THE OFFICE IN THE ARTIFACT BUILDING - NIGHT

It is late. Teams that were moving cables on the top of the pyramid and others taking photographs are putting equipment away. ANIN approaches several of his staff at the dry erase board

> ANIN
>
> How are you doing?

> HARASHIN
>
> This is definitely a calculation involving gravity
> and mass but we're just not following it.

> ANIN
>
> I've asked the others to quit for the night. Let's
> get some rest. Tomorrow Dr. Yassari returns.
> His fresh eyes will help.

They start to gather their personal possessions. WHYCH, SAM and MANUEL are huddled around a computer in the office. CONNOR is off to the side looking in a box

> Don't work too late, Leigh.

No answer. ANIN is exiting

                    WHYCH
          Good night, Philippe.

                    CONNOR (to SAM)
          Where are my Mayan disks?

                    SAM
          They should be with the others.

                    CONNOR (testy)
          They're not here. None of the Mexican catalogues
          are here.

                    SAM (defensively)
          Well, I'm sorry. I'll ask Dr. Shaw to send them.

A beat. CONNOR crosses to glass to look at artifact

                    CONNOR
          No, I'm sorry, Sam. They were my responsibility.
          I'm frustrated because I have nothing but bits and
          pieces. And I don't know what the hell this is!

                    MANUEL (after a beat)
          A big piece of metal?

Finally all chuckle

                    WHYCH
          And on that succinct observation, I think that
          we've all been working pretty hard and could
          use a break. Don't tell the locals but I've got
          some pretty good scotch in the trailer.

                    CONNOR
          Sold, brother.

INT. WHYCH AND MANUEL'S TRAILER - NIGHT

Very late at night. CONNOR, WHYCH, SAM and MANUEL sit sipping their whiskey.
CONNOR sips

                    CONNOR
          So, I've become overly dependent on Sam, I'll
          admit. Not only does she do the lesson planning
          and assigns grades but she gives me the topics of
          my lectures. I wonder if I'm as boring as I feel.

322

                            SAM
You under-estimate yourself, Professor. You are
the show. I just keep the records.

                          CONNOR
Some show. Symbols light up, one after the other
and still I'm stumped. Maybe I should go home
and back to "sort of" teaching.

                            SAM
Boo-hoo.

                          MANUEL
Don't give up, Dr. Connor. Those rotten Martians
are trying to make it tough on you.

                          CONNOR
Tough is fine. As long as they're not bad spellers.

WHYCH gets up to pour himself another drink

                          WHYCH
Please, no more Martians.

                          MANUEL
Hey, I haven't said a word, it's the locals.

                      SAM (standing)
I've had all the fun I can take. I've got to sleep.

                  MANUEL (standing)
I'll walk you to your trailer.

They exit. A beat

                          WHYCH
We'll crack this, Leigh. If one approach doesn't
work, we'll try looking at it another way.

CONNOR slowly gets an idea

                          CONNOR
Yes, like Yassari's approach-from the top. Dr.
Whych, would you care to join me in one more
test this evening?

                          WHYCH
Can I bring the whiskey?

                          CONNOR
Doctor, this is largely an Islamic country.

WHYCH
Good point. I'll hide it.

INT. OFFICE IN THE ARTIFACT BUIDING - DAY

Morning. All are gathering at the coffee and granola table. CONNOR and WHYCH have the dry erase board set up in the corner with symbols drawn on transparency sheets. SAM enters, crosses to CONNOR

SAM
You've been up all night, haven't you.

CONNOR
Yes, we hope lots of scotch and caffeine will make for an entertaining fifteen minutes or so.

SAM
What have you got?

CONNOR sees ANIN walk in

CONNOR
We're not sure. That's why we're doing the show and tell.

SAM
Well keep it down. My head's splitting.

CONNOR crosses to ANIN and has a quick chat. Then he crosses to MANUEL and WHYCH to finish preparations

ANIN
Well, if we are all gathered, Dr.Connor tells me that he and Dr. Whych have a small presentation for us this morning. They look excited about something and that makes me very happy. Please begin, gentlemen.

CONNOR
Thank you. Dr. Yassari's experiments using direct current and various light beams have shown us how we might associate symbols. We were looking at them sequentially, in the order in which they lit up. And then it occurred to us to stack the symbols in sequence and look down on them, through them and combining them when it was appropriate. Manuel, tell us about your work this morning.

MANUEL
Dr. Harashin's measurements of the inscriptions indicate a precision which made the probability

very high that they were cut by machine. He noted that they were cut in varying depths ranging from one eighth to one half inch deep. This morning, in a sample of almost four hundred symbols, I measured six precise cuts in depth.

CONNOR

Thank you, Manuel. We've been grouping, or more accurately, stacking symbols according to their cut in depth. The samples of script that we are testing are the very short pieces that appeared when a light beam was directed at the exact center of the dome of the pyramid. All four phrases or short statements start and end with this symbol. (WHYCH points to the "arms") Michael observed that it was reminiscent of a glyph I'm sure you'll recognize. (WHYCH shows the enlarged glyph of the priest praying)

SALI

It is the hieroglyph meaning 'adoration'.

CONNOR

Or in the verb form?

SALI

To adore or worship.

CONNOR

If you focus on just the arms of the priest and compare them to our symbol, you'll see similarities. In both drawings, the palms are up. And the angle of the bend in the elbows are almost identical. The essential element of this ideogram is in the gesture of the arms. If our guess is correct, then our symbol is a simplification, a short-hand or distillation of the hieroglyph we know. As I said, this symbol appears at the top and bottom of all four pieces. Perhaps as indicative - 'This is a prayer' and as determinative - 'This has been a prayer' These next three symbols appear in this sequence and are cut to the exact depth. So, let's stack them.

The scientist audience reacts with astonishment as the picture of the eye emerges

Yes, this is a glyph we are all know. It can mean several things, depending on the context. Uh, 'to see', uh,...

YOUNG LAB ASSISTANT

'Knowledge'?

CONNOR

Yes. But in this context I'm going to go with a
meaning as it appears in Pharonic cartouches.
It was how they referred to themselves.

ANIN

'We.'

CONNOR

Thank you, Doctor. We un-stack these symbols
again, as each symbol probably has its own meaning or purpose. But before we do that, please look
at the following text. (WHYCH puts two lines of
hieroglyphs on the board) Anyone care to read
this first line?

SALI

Uh, for or 'an appropriate gift or offering to one
of true voice'.

CONNOR

Well, Doctor, as they say in my country, you are
on a roll. Would you take the next line as well?

SALI

Yes. 'lasting in this life and through the next,
for all time'.

CONNOR

Good. If you take out modifiers and the phonograms and determinatives, you leave only
essential figures and representations. This arm,
although only a line, clearly has the palm up.
And this line above with the sun setting in the
center is clearly the ancient Egyptian ideogram
for land- essential figures meaning 'offering'.
And this feminine bowl and serpent, yes, we
think this wavy line with the dot for a head is
a close representation of a snake- essential in
a glyph meaning 'everlasting'. Moving on,
we have no idea what the 'c' means, possibly
a syntax or grammatical notation. And finally,
we get an easy one. It is this symbol here, it
looks like an 'A' on its side like the bow of a
boat. I've never seen this sign mean anything
but 'love'. Translation? "we offer everlasting
love" And if we stack symbols again, there is
your sign for 'Re', the sun god. I have a feeling
that we are going to be finding phonograms
and grammar signs which are unknown to us but
I think we may be on to cracking this.

A spontaneous applause erupts from the small audience and Dr. ANIN shakes CONNOR's and WHYCH'S hand

INT. OFFICE IN THE ARTIFACT BUILDING - DAY

All scientists are seated at the conference table.

> WHYCH (passing photographs)
> And look at these lit groupings in band number five.
> Note that the chronometers on these two cameras
> are identical throughout this sequence.

> ANIN
> What do you think, Dr. Yassari?

> YASSARI
> I am beginning to think that my beams and power
> cables are crude instruments. Rather like opening
> a jewelry box with a crow bar. I'll try pinpointing
> the beams and higher amperages.

> WHYCH
> Nevertheless, the results are consistent.

> YASSARI
> The mapping has indicated four sets of rows of
> something just under the surface, extending
> from the very top down to the edges. I'm guessing
> they are crystals or something that bends light and
> acts like circuits.
> ANIN
> Dr. Harashin?

> HARASHIN
> We believe that some of these new lit groups are
> mathematical descriptions of three-dimensional
> objects. We have identified several in the past
> few days. We found numbers that are incredibly
> accurate figures describing the density of the
> planet relative to the sun, as well as earth to sun
> orbital distance numbers, even orbital and den-
> sity numbers describing our moon. We are not
> fully understanding the calculations involved
> but we have not made errors identifying these
> numbers. The Egyptians of several thousand
> years ago were as advanced scientifically as any
> pre-Renaissance culture, but they could not
> have come up with these numbers.

Whispers from those at the table

ANIN
Anything else, gentlemen?

HARASHIN
There are calculations involving gravity that we
may not grasp for some time. There is a rather
lengthy and confusing listing of text and numbers.
We are guessing that it is an account of minerals
or gases. As we start to cross reference, we'll
know more. Finally we came across figures
that Dr. Whych recognized. Michael, you have
a better organic chemistry background than I.
Would you care to share our next observation.

WHYCH
Sure. There is an unmistakable mathematical
description of an animal's living cell and of the
chromosome. I say unmistakable because the
DNA detail is too specific to be anything else.
I understand that we are not sharing conjecture
but the implication is pretty clear. The creators
of the artifact may have been capable of genetic manipulation.

Looks shoot around the table.

INT. COMMUNICATION SHACK IN THE COMPOUND - DAY

NAJAR takes off his head set and considers what he has heard

INT. THE VATICAN- DAY

A large, vaulted room, marble fireplace, leather couches and chairs. The eighty-year old POPE, in
a gray cassock, is seated in a large straight-backed chair. He is attended by a young priest. The
POPE's SECRETARY, middle-aged man in a formal business suit, escorts ROSELLE in.
ROSELLE kisses the POPE's ring, ROSELLE receives a benediction from the POPE and sits on
the couch. The SECRETARY hands the POPE a manila folder

POPE
Yes, I have read this and I have seen these
photographs. Tell me, Cardinal Roselle, what
is the latest information?

ROSELLE
Your Holiness, the builders of this unique object,
this pyramid, have not been discovered. But it
is speculated that it was created thousands of
years ago by space travelers.

POPE (smiling)
Truly?

                    ROSELLE
Yes, Your Holiness. The scientists charged to
study the artifact claim that these space travelers
were able to perform medical experiments, and
influence or accelerate the evolution of mankind.
I find these allegations troublesome and unsettling.

The POPE reviews the photographs

                    POPE
When was this intervention by space travelers
supposed to have happened?

                    ROSELLE
They say in the distant past.

                    POPE
Ten or twenty thousand years ago?

                    ROSELLE
I suppose.

                    POPE
Eight or eighteen thousand years before the
birth of Christ.

                    ROSELLE
It seems that the interpreters of this artifact
threaten to rewrite our history.

A beat. The Pope gives the folder back to his SECRETARY

                    POPE
They threaten to rewrite the natural, scientific
history of man. Do not be troubled, Cardinal
Roselle. The souls of the faithful remain the
purview of The Church.

                    ROSELLE
I fear that this will test the faith of many.

                    POPE
Science seeks to explore and explain life. That
is the role of science. But understanding life
does not diminish the miracle of living or of
Our Lord and Savior, Jesus Christ. The scientist
and the saint are touched by the hand of God in
equal measure. Let faith be tested and, perhaps,
strengthened. Is that not the trial of faith?

Yes, Your Holiness.

ROSELLE looks up and into the surveillance camera in the corner of the room.

INT. MICHELE/KATHERINE'S HOUSE - NIGHT

KATHERINE is in the kitchen sipping wine in the evening and watching a talk show on a counter top television

INT. TELEVISION IMAGE FILLS THE SCREEN

Split screen, Dr. BREWSER on the left and Assemblyman TALBOT on the right

TALBOT
The investigating scientists readily admit that
they really don't know what they are dealing
with and yet a few sideline Galileo's would
have us believe that we are the result of medical
tampering by a race of space men. Forgive me
if I don't jump on the band wagon just yet.

HOST (chuckling)
Well, thank you for your straight forward and
concise comment, as always, Assemblyman…
or is it appropriate to call you the Right Rev-
erend James Talbot?

TALBOT
Both are legal and appropriate.

HOST
Thank you, Assemblyman. Well, chime in here,
Dr. Brewster. You have been a consultant to
NASA and two Administrations in the fields
of applied physics and related technologies.
What do you make of these developments?

BREWSTER
Well, first of all let me say that many of us in
the scientific community are very excited to
hear anything about the artifact. The deafening
silence that was the posture of the Egyptian
government has caused quite a stir politically
and quite a bit of conjecture scientifically.

HOST
Can you share any of those conjectures?

BREWSTER
I think it would be imprudent of me to be

specific in this forum. By the time it is re-
peated two or three times, it takes on the
look of fact instead of rumor.

                    HOST
But let me press you a bit, Dr. Brewster. Is
there any foundation for this notion that,
as the Assemblyman said, we are the pro-
duct of genetic experimentation?

                    BREWSTER
I would say no, we do not have the facts and the
report that would support such an idea.

                    TALBOT
Thank you. Now there's a scientist with common sense.

                    BREWSTER
Let me add that we probably will not have a
report until these men and women have completed their job; run all of their tests and addressed
the entire translation. It's how they work. Their
goal is to collect evidence, independent of their
prejudices and beliefs. And without bias, they
must deal with fact. That also means they must
allow for any reasonable possibility, including
extra-terrestrial visitation.

                    TALBOT
Oh, boy. Maybe I spoke too soon.

                    BREWSTER
The odds of the existence of other civilizations
in our galaxy are very good. An advanced civilization capable of star travel is a possibility.

INT. KATHERINE IN KITCHEN - NIGHT

The rest of the TV show becomes background noise as KATHERINE hears a key in the side
door. MICHELE walks into the kitchen followed by JASON

                    TALBOT
Here we go again. We have been hearing about
space men for a good many years now. They are
a part of our popular culture and make for a great
Saturday morning cartoon. But where are they?
There is not one shred of evidence…

KATHERINE turns off the TV

                    MICHELE
Hi, Mom. This is Jason. He wanted to see some of
Dad's journals. Is the library locked?

                    KATHERINE
Shouldn't you ask your father?

                    MICHELE
Why? Most of them have been published.

                    JASON
Listen, if this is a bad time, uh…

                    MICHELE
Not at all. The den is just down the hall on
the right. I'll be with you in just a minute.

JASON exits toward the den

        What's the matter?

                    KATHERINE
Michele, you could at least tell me if you are
going to start bringing boys home.

                    MICHELE
This is not boys! Jason is one of Dad's students
and a friend. And he wanted to look at Dad's
journals. And, by the way, I'm not the one who
is staying out weekends.

                    KATHERINE
How dare you! That's not fair. Did your father
tell you that he has signed and returned the
divorce papers?

MICHELE was not aware

        Of course not, of course he would leave it to me.

                    JASON (appearing in hall)
The library cabinet was locked. It's just as well,
it's getting late. I should be going. It was nice to
have met you, Mrs. Connor.

                    KATHERINE
Yes.

                    MICHELE
I'm sorry, Jason.

> JASON (moving to door)
> No, don't be. I'm sure you both must have a
> lot on your mind with Dr. Connor out of the
> country and all. I'll see you some other time.

> MICHELE
> Let me walk you out.

MICHELE shoots KATHERINE a scathing look and follows JASON outside.

EXT. DRIVEWAY OUTSIDE OF THE HOUSE - NIGHT

They walk quietly to the sidewalk

> MICHELE
> Are your parents still married?

> JASON
> They were. My father died three years ago.

> MICHELE
> I'm sorry.

> JASON
> It's OK.

> MICHELE
> Were you close?

> JASON
> Yes.

> MICHELE
> My father is my best friend. I don't think I can
> be strong without him.

> JASON
> I don't think we know how strong we can be until
> we have to be.

> MICHELE (smiling)
> Have I told you how much I like you?

He takes her in his arms. They kiss tenderly

> JASON
> You have now.

They continue to walk down the sidewalk arm in arm.

EXT. A DESERT CAMPSITE - NIGHT

CARRARA and an OLDER ARAB MAN are speaking. We see the faces of two young Arab men dressed as soldiers seated by the fire. CARRARA hands a satchel full of cash and C-4 explosive to the OLDER ARAB MAN

                    CARRARA
        The detonator is set at two minutes. This is
        enough explosive to take down a large building
        so they must be well away when it goes.

                    OLDER ARAB MAN
        They will understand.

                    CARRERA
        The ensuing confusion after the blast may afford
        them the opportunity to bring back a sample of
        the artifact. Contact me through my associate in
        Cairo in three days after the mission is complete.

The OLDER ARAB MAN nods in agreement

INT. THE OFFICE IN THE ARTIFACT BUILDING - DAY

Early evening. WHYCH is at the dry erase board. CONNOR, SAM and MANUEL are huddled around a computer. ANIN joins them

                    ANIN
        What do you have here?

                    WHYCH
        We've been testing the non-math symbols asso-
        ciated with the mathematic descriptions of the liv-
        ing cell. It's incomplete but we're piecing to-
        gether something. Thus far it goes, 'The Devoted...

                    ANIN
        The what?

                    CONNOR
        I'm sorry, Philippe, that was my little conceit.
        The eye symbol meaning 'We' never appears
        without the adoration arms. 'The Devoted' won
        out over 'The worshipping we'.

                    ANIN
        I see. Go on, Michael.

                    WHYCH
        Yes. 'The Devoted reject, ignore or discard',
        we're not sure yet, ' by right or responsibility
        of those living before 'The Devoted.'

                              CONNOR
The next six inscriptions do not stack and we're
guessing they are a series of multi-syllabic
phonograms. I've sent home for more dispersion
models which may help.

                              WHYCH
Well, this line finishes, 'will help those living
before and they will be called Brothers of
The Devoted, Children of Re'

                              ANIN
What do you make of it?

                              WHYCH
It's too early to tell, there is a lot of un-trans-
lated text.

                              MANUEL
Yes, but…

                              ANIN
Yes?

                              MANUEL
Well, it seems The Devoted rejected this place
because… people were already living here.

All look at MANUEL in silence. Suddenly YASSARI appears in the office doorway holding a
crate

                              YASSARI
Am I late for supper? Anything happen while I
was gone?

Several chuckle

                              ANIN (standing)
I was just about to call the evening meal break.

                              YASSARI
Let me help you. (shouting) All right everyone,
it's time to eat. Put down your equipment. Put
down your cameras. Put down your calculators.
Everyone, I insist. It's time for our evening meal.
Come, get those photographs off of the table.
(opening crate) Everyone gather around. I have
special treats. Here, Michael, open this wine and
pour. I wish to make a toast. I have kippered
herring for our leader, Dr. Anin.

                    ANIN
Oh, this is a special treat.

                    YASSARI
And Havarti cheese for my beautiful American.
Someday she will fall madly in love with me.

Laughter

                    SAM (smelling cheese)
The way to a woman's heart.

                    YASSARI
And baloney and bread, olives, humus, more
cheese and good mustard for the not so beautiful
rest of you.

Spontaneous cheers, he raises his glass to toast

                    In celebration of this ninth or tenth wonder of the
                    world, who's counting, and to you, my brilliant
                    friends. To the first leg of our study and to success!

Spontaneous cheers and handshaking all around

INT. THE ARTIFACT BUIDING - NIGHT

SAM and MANUEL are seated together at the base of the pyramid sipping wine, their backs
against the pyramid

                    MANUEL
You know, like a navigational buoy. We were
here. We did this and that. Mr. Spock, chart a
course to the next star system with a class "M"
planet. What do you think?

                    SAM
Do you have a cigarette?

                    MANUEL
Yes.

                    SAM
Let's go.

INT. OFFICE IN THE ARTIFACT BUILDING - NIGHT

ANIN, CONNOR, WHYCH, HARASHIN and YASSARI are sipping wine at the conference
table

336

WHYCH
When do you make your preliminary report to
Minister Atef?

ANIN
A week from this coming Monday. He has seen
the results of most of our tests. And he will ask
the same question, "What is it?" The answer will
be the same- I don't really know.

YASSARI
You will need to invent a science-based civilization
predating written history, perhaps more technically
advanced than we are or you will propose the only
theory that remains viable- that this is an object
made by extra-terrestrial beings.

ANIN
That's easy for you to say. You don't have to stand
before the Egyptian Supreme Council and say the
words "extra-terrestrial" Oddly enough, we joked
about that possibility a few of weeks ago. This time
it's not so funny. Half of the council will be fitting
me for a strait jacket.

HARASHIN
This is seven to eight thousand years old. What
other explanation is there?

WHYCH
So, what is it, a marker? A time capsule?

ANIN
I promise you, "alien time capsule" will not be
words featured prominently in my report. What
am I saying? I don't know anymore, Leigh, I am
only an archeologist. I dig for our past, but this…
I am more comfortable with pieces of pottery.

CONNOR (chuckles)
You will gather your evidence and tell the truth
as you always do. People will understand it or
not, come to their own conclusions and believe
what they choose to believe.

ANIN
Thank you, my friend. I have one more toast.
To my colleagues, thank you for coming.

EXT. AROUND THE TRAILERS IN THE COMPOUND - DAY

SAM is in her dressing robe behind her trailer; crying, smoking and drinking a cup of coffee. Unable to sleep, CONNOR is out in his bathrobe and sees her.

CONNOR

Are you crying?

SAM

No. It's just my parents' anniversary and I can't tell them how much I love them.

CONNOR

You can e-mail them today.

SAM

I know, I can't tell them in person. And don't laugh at me!

CONNOR

You nut.

CONNOR walks her back to her trailer, arm around her shoulder.

EXT. COMPOUND GATE - DAY

The two young Arab men dressed as soldiers pull up in a military jeep, PASSENGER shows a paper to the guard who waves them through, they pull up in front of the artifact building. PASSENGER gets out carrying satchel with explosive and hands the same paper to the guard at the door. (some of this can be sub-titled)

PASSENGER (in Arabic)

I have papers for Dr. Anin that I am to deliver personally.

GUARD (in Arabic)

He is in the office. I will alert the Colonel.
(operates a radio)

PASSENGER steps over to the side door next to the rolling door and then steps in.

INT. SAM'S TRAILER - DAY

CONNOR is seated at a table drinking a cup of coffee, SAM is standing.

SAM

Only three more days and then a real shower and my own bed.

CONNOR

You'll miss camping?

SAM

Like a toothache. When do we come back?

CONNOR

No more than a couple of weeks, Philippe still
has to clear it.

SAM starts to sniffle again

CONNOR

Why are you crying now?

SAM

I don't know.

CONNOR stands to hold her for a minute. The comforting turns to delicate kissing

INT. THE ARTIFACT BUILDING - DAY

PASSENGER is walking around the pyramid in awe of it, satchel on his shoulder. The GUARD walks into the office and the PASSENGER hides behind the pyramid

GUARD

There was a soldier here with papers for you.

ANIN (with SALI)

We have not seen anyone.

GUARD starts his search of the building with one other soldier, PASSENGER makes a break for the door.

GUARD

Stop!

PASSENGER jumps into the jeep and the jeep speeds toward the gate.

GUARD

Stop them!

The GUARD pulls the radio from his belt, another soldier fires two rifle shots at the fleeing jeep.

INT. SAM'S TRAILER - DAY

SAM and CONNOR are still in their robes but they are in a passionate embrace and kissing deeply. They hear the two rifle shots. A quick look at one another, SAM runs to the big window and pulls open the blinds

EXT. THE COMPOUND GATE - DAY

The jeep crashes through the gate, automatic weapons fire and the jeep and the two young Arab men are disintegrated in a huge explosion.

INT. SAM'S TRAILER - DAY

SAM is looking through the window, we hear the automatic weapons fire and the explosion blows glass into SAM and rocks the trailer. CONNOR struggles to his feet and crosses to SAM. She is on her back, unconscious and cut badly.

                    CONNOR
          Oh, my God, Sam! Sam!

INT. HOSPITAL - DAY

CONNOR is at SAM's bedside holding her hand. She slowly opens her eyes.

                    SAM
          Are…are you OK?

                    CONNOR
          Yes. Shhh, don't talk. Rest.

SAM slowly touches her head bandages and silently cries.

                    SAM (softly)
          I hope you don't mind an assistant who looks
          like Frankenstein.

                    CONNOR
          Shhh…you're beautiful.

                    SAM
          Where is your hand?

                    CONNOR
          Here.

Holding hands, they cry. A male NURSE and his young female assistant appear

                    NURSE
          Excuse us. Oh, good, you're awake. We need
          to take some x-rays.

They transfer SAM onto a gurney. CONNOR watches as they roll her down the hall

                    CONNOR (V.O.)
          She had a bad concussion and had lost a lot of
          blood but she was going to be all right. I wanted
          to stay with her until she was discharged but,
          under the circumstances, the Egyptian gov-
          ernment did not want to be responsible for
          our safety. We were on a plane bound for home
          the next night. SAM would be a few days behind.

INT. THE CHAMBER OF THE EGYPTIAN HIGH COUNCIL - DAY

ANIN and ATEF sit at a small table waiting to be addressed by the Council

CHAIRMAN (report in hand)
Dr. Anin, your work, as usual, is commendable.
However, the implications of your findings are
quite incredible. If fact, they are completely un-
substantiated.

ANIN
Mr. Chairman, it is true that much of our work
is conjecture that implies but does not prove
anything. The torturous task of translating could
take years. This is the only sample of this script.
There is no Rosetta Stone. I understand that, for
political reasons, the Council is entertaining
the decision to exclude foreign scientists from
this study. Please reconsider. Experienced
colleagues are our greatest resource. Surely,
pursuing this study is in our national interest. I
will argue that it might have profound international interest, paling any political concern.

COUNCILMAN
Mr. Chairman, I must object to Dr. Anin's tone
about our paling political concerns. Our dili-
gence in guarding our political concerns has
insured our sovereignty and the protection of
Egyptians around the world.

ANIN
Forgive me. I do not mean to criticize Egypt
or Egyptians. I am proud of my heritage. We
are a strong people. I believe we are strong
enough to open our borders to foreign scientists
and open our minds to the opportunities that
continued study of the artifact may afford.

CHAIRMAN
Dr. Anin, many of us in this chamber are very
interested in this artifact and believe, as you
do, that wondrous things may be learned. The
value of scientific discovery is not in question
here. Our decision is to limit access to the artifact for the time being. When the perpetrators
of this attack are identified, we may amend our
decision. It is unfortunate that scientific pursuit
must be sullied by political concerns but that
is the case and the Council's directive.

ATEF (gathering briefcase)
Thank you, Mr. Chairman, ladies and gentlemen.

341

ANIN

May I speak once more?

ATEF remains seated but gives ANIN a look of warning

>Mr. Chairman, Council, thank you for your de-
>cision today. Certainly, I do not mean to imply
>that the goals of science outweigh all other
>concerns. The social and political stability of
>Egypt provide the fertile ground in which the
>scientist may toil. But, I am forced to ask, what
>drives the attacker of scientists and science. I'm
>not sure. I only know that they are afraid. Are
>they afraid of a new weapon or new technologies?
>Possibly. Are they afraid that the artifact will
>become evidence of an extra-terrestrial visita-
>tion? Such evidence would be the discovery of
>the century but also shake us to our foundations.
>There may be much to fear. The path of explor-
>ation can be treacherous. But there is also much
>to hope for. That is the nature of science. We
>can feed and cure millions or we can destroy
>them with a bomb. There is risk and reward,
>hope and fear in all of scientific endeavor. My
>colleagues and I choose to be hopeful and,
>with this Council's permission and protection,
>we will continue with our work. Thank you.

INT. CONNOR'S UNIVERSITY OFFICE - DAY

CONNOR is gathering papers and putting them in his briefcase. SHAW is standing just inside the door

SHAW

My point is, you don't have to say a damn
thing. Anin's preliminary report should be out
in a little while and we can let the Egyptians
take the heat.

CONNOR

Heat?

SHAW

Damn it, Leigh, I asked you to make us famous,
not infamous.

CONNOR

I'm not trying to make us anything.

SHAW

Let me put it another way, as soon as you say

the words 'extra-terrestrial', we might as well
board this place up and call it Roswell High.

CONNOR
Oliver, aren't you at all interested in the truth?

SHAW
What does that matter? All I'm saying is, let
Anin be the fall guy.

CONNOR's cell phone rings, he answers

CONNOR
Hi, honey. Did you pick up Sam?

MICHELE (on telephone)
Yes, we got her.

CONNOR
We?

MICHELE (on telephone)
Yes, there's someone that I want you to meet.
Actually you already know him.

CONNOR
Oh?

MICHELE (on telephone)
So, can we come over?

CONNOR
I'd rather meet you somewhere else. I have to
make a fool of myself in front of television
cameras for the next half hour or so.

MICHELE (on telephone)
Come on, Dad, let us come over now.

CONNOR
No, honey, I'm sure to bore everyone and
embarrass myself.

MICHELE hangs up, CONNOR picks up his briefcase and walks toward the door

CONNOR
After you, Doctor. Don't worry, I'll keep my
mouth shut.

SHAW (walking with him)
Actually what I had in mind was a generous

and self-effacing ambassador without a lot of information but polite as hell. And mention the university's name about nine times. Do you think you can pull that off?

                    CONNOR
I don't know, I just had lunch.

SHAW'S SECRETARY meets them about halfway down the hall.

                    SHAW'S SECRETARY
Oliver, there are more television people in your office.

                    SHAW
More? How much more?

                    SHAW'S SECRETARY
Two more crews.

                    SHAW
They're breeding like rabbits.

                    CONNOR
Can't we just give them a written statement?

                    SHAW
That's not good public relations.

                    CONNOR
You are in public relations, I am a teacher.

                    SHAW
Don't be droll. When in doubt smile, I'll be there to save you. And watch your facial expressions, TV people don't need much, innuendo will do. Be nice to them, they can hurt us. A fluffy, 'I don't know what's going on but isn't it exciting' will do.

SHAW stops just before he opens his office door and turns to look at CONNOR

                    CONNOR
What?

                    SHAW
Smile.

CONNOR puts this sad, sick smile on his face, SHAW opens the door to a crowd of reporters, cameras and operators.

SHAW
Thank you for coming today and welcome to
Brannion University. Before he answers your
questions, let me say that we at Brannion are
very proud of Dr. Leigh Connor, one of our featured educators and certainly world class in his
expertise. As you know, at the request of the
Egyptian government, he has participated in
a study of an artifact. The findings of the first
phase of this study will be available at the dis-
cretion of the Egyptian government and so it
may be inappropriate of Dr. Connor to provide
too much detail of that study. However, he is
available today to answer any questions that he
can. Is there anything else you'd like to add?

CONNOR
No, let's just go ahead.

FIRST REPORTER
Dr. Connor, is it true that someone tried to
destroy the artifact?

CONNOR
There was an incident, an explosion, a very
powerful explosion at the compound gate. The
artifact was not damaged. They don't know
who the culprits were, they were almost vapo-
rized in the explosion.

SECOND REPORTER
What is this artifact?

CONNOR
It is a metallic pyramid, almost twenty-four
feet high with inscriptions on four sides.

FIRST REPORTER
Does this artifact prove that the earth was
visited by beings from another world?

CONNOR
That is not conclusive.

FIRST REPORTER
But is there evidence?

CONNOR
That is a question pertinent to the translation
of the artifact and it would be inappropriate of
me to...

SAM walks into SHAW's office, followed by MICHELE and JASON. SAM is wearing a scarf hiding some bandages. They stand behind the cameras.

> inappropriate of me to talk about... What was
> your question?

> FIRST REPORTER
> Is there evidence of a visitation by beings from
> another world?

> CONNOR
> The translation is incomplete and so there has
> been no conclusions. However, in my thirty years
> in the field, I can tell you that this was unlike
> anything I have ever seen. Soon after we
> arrived the Iraqis stumbled upon a translating
> tool when they directed a high intensity beam
> at the top of the pyramid. It highlighted charac-
> ters into new associative groups and break-
> throughs were made. The Egyptians had iden-
> tified mathematical symbols well before our
> arrival. In the two weeks that we were there
> they had interpreted calculations and formulas
> suggesting that the creators of the artifact were
> very scientifically advanced.

Several reporters raise their voices vying to get their question asked. SHAW has moved behind CONNOR on his way out of the room.

> SHAW (softly to Connor)
> I'll be in the bathroom cutting my wrists.

> SECOND REPORTER
> Advanced scientifically in what way, Dr.
> Connor?

> CONNOR
> There was evidence demonstrating a molec-
> ular, perhaps genetic, understanding of liv-
> ing tissue. There was also evidence suggesting
> a profound understanding of gravity and mass.

Again reporters vie to get their question asked

> SECOND REPORTER
> Where is this evidence? May we see it?

> CONNOR
> Unfortunately, all materials remain in Egypt.
> It was a condition of the invitation to par-
> ticipate in the study. Hopefully, when we go

back in two weeks, we will be allowed to bring
home the report.

> FIRST REPORTER
> Dr. Connor, what do you say to the millions of
> Americans and millions more around the world
> who do not believe and who are, frankly, uncom-
> fortable with the notion of this tampering with
> our genetic design?

> CONNOR
> I do not jump to that conclusion. Nor do I strive
> to shape beliefs. The scientist's job is to present
> evidence. Several decades ago many people
> were uncomfortable with Darwin's evidence
> that man may have evolved from an earlier pri-
> mate. We all got over it and, fundamentally,
> it is accepted scientific fact. Ultimately, if the
> evidence supports some kind of imposition in
> our evolutionary history and that makes people
> uncomfortable, I would say to them, get over it.
> The truth about people may be that they will
> believe what they chose to believe, regardless
> of evidence.

Tumultuous simultaneous talking by reporters, CONNOR looks to the back of the room to see a
smiling SAM

INT. CONNOR'S OFFICE - DAY

SAM has walked in ahead of CONNOR, he closes the door and goes to hug her

> SAM (pulling away)
> Be careful. I have to be very careful with these
> tapes.

> CONNOR (holding her hands)
> What do they say about your recovery?

> SAM
> They say I should be gorgeous. Probably better
> than before.

> CONNOR
> Excellent.

> SAM (crossing away)
> Leigh, I was flat on my back for days in the hos-
> pital with nothing else to do but ask myself
> what's important to me and what do I want. I
> can't love you. I mean I do love you...

                    CONNOR
It's OK, Sam.

                    SAM
But I can't love you like that.

                    CONNOR
It's all right, Sam. I'd like to we go back to
the way we were.

                    SAM
What? Yes. When did you come to this reali-
zation?

                    CONNOR
Since I've been back. You're not the only one
who can figure out what's important and what
they want.

A beat, SAM crosses to take his hands

                    SAM
I'm not sorry, Doc. I'm not sorry for any of it.

                    CONNOR
Thank you. Let's go find my daughter.

INT. INSIDE OF CONNOR'S CAR IN ROUTE - DAY

CONNOR is in the back, MICHELE is driving with JASON next to her.

                    MICHELE
And it will give me a little more time. It sure
wouldn't hurt to put off the expense of moving
right now especially if you're not going to be at
Brannion anymore.

                    CONNOR
Don't worry about me, honey. In the fall my
classes will be packed. We'll have to provide
"e-classes" and on line feeds of my lectures. If
there is one thing Oliver Shaw understands,
it's income.

                    MICHELE
So, what do you think?

                    CONNOR
I think it's a great decision but for an entirely
selfish reason. I'll have my daughter around
for at least another year.

MICHELE pulls up at the curb behind the hedge in front of her house

                         MICHELE
          Well, here we are.

CONNOR exits the car on the driver's side with a bouquet of red roses. MICHELE rolls her window down

                         CONNOR
          Wish me luck.

CONNOR bends down to give her a kiss on the cheek and stays down to address JASON

                         CONNOR
          I do remember you, Jason. I think I owe you
          an apology.

                         JASON
          You don't owe me a thing, Dr. Connor.

                         CONNOR
          Yes, I do.

                         JASON
          Good luck.

CONNOR crosses the sidewalk and into the front yard, stopping to check his appearance and the flowers

                         MICHELE
          What was that all about?

                         JASON
          Owning up to mistakes. And starting over again.

EXT. CONNOR WALKS TO THE FRONT DOOR - DAY

                         CONNOR (V.O.)
          Our study of the artifact was postponed indefinitely.
          Anin was apologetic and pledged to try to get
          us back but he was battling the cautious majority.
          Caution is a survival instinct. But curiosity is an
          instinct too and serves us as well. Whatever the
          artifact is, it is both immutable and screaming to
          communicate. It brings both of our instincts to
          bear. It's up to us to make the decision. When
          Sam walked into Oliver's office and stood in the
          back in her bandages, in her courage, I remem-
          bered what I said to Philippe. 'You will tell the
          truth, I said, as you always do'. Could I do less?

Today I figure to error on the side of bravery. All she can do is tell me to get the hell off her porch.

CONNOR pushes the doorbell. First fear, then bravery crosses his face

CPSIA information can be obtained at www.ICGtesting.com
Printed in the USA
BVOW052334220513

321440BV00006B/33/P